MORE PRAISE F

AFTER THE DAM

"Told with heartbreaking clarity about what it means to be a mother—a complex and vulnerable human being with responsibilities to the past and the future, *After the Dam* is a story about discovering the difference between knowledge and wisdom. Amy Hassinger's lyrical prose is a joy to read."

—KAREN SHOEMAKER
author of *The Meaning of Names* and *Night Sounds and Other Stories*

"This book does what my favorite books always do: grab the reader with tautness and fierce intelligence, so that even the quiet drama of it gets pulled into the page-turning qualities of the narrative. I could say, Read this book. Instead I'll say, Start this book. You won't stop reading until its terrific ending."

—LEIGH ALLISON WILSON
author of *Wind* and *From the Bottom Up*

"Forces of nature—big water and big love—come together in this unforgettable literary page-turner. Amy Hassinger has woven a tale out of the very earth where the Ojibwe live. Her protagonist—Rachel—is a lover, mother, and activist, a woman of our time on a hero's journey toward wholeness."

—PATRICIA HENLEY
author of *Hummingbird House* and *Other Heartbreaks*

"Amy Hassinger's elegiac novel about the shifting, elusive nature of family and love made me feel, while reading, as if my heart were pumping inside the author's fist. By the end, I was reminded by *After the Dam* and its characters that, to borrow a metaphor from the novel, we humans make our lives from sand, and sand will always slip."

—SUSANNA DANIEL
author of *Sea Creatures* and *Stiltsville*

"*After the Dam* weaves threads of connection between several generations of two families split by history's implacable seasons of growth, death, and renewal, as one generation passes onto the next the unresolved moral legacy left by the one before. Lush with description, *After the Dam* draws us beneath the surface of its characters' lives into an undertow of emotional conflict that makes you feel you are immersed in the minds and hearts of people you know. It's a compelling read that's hard to put down once you have been drawn into its tide."

—RICHARD DUGGIN
author of *Why Won't You Talk to Me?* and *The Music Box Treaty*

"A dam built of dirt may give way to the force of water, and a marriage built on convenience may give way to the force of desire. In this compelling novel, the heroine's disruptive desire is not only for sex, that staple of human stories, but also for a home place and a purposeful life. The place she chooses has been loved and cared for by several generations of her own family, and for many more generations by the native people who call themselves Anishinaabe. How to reconcile rival claims to the same homeland? How to reconcile the needs of her infant daughter and her dutiful husband with her own need for self-fulfillment? Amy Hassinger poses the questions vividly, without pretending there are easy answers."

—SCOTT RUSSELL SANDERS
author of *Earth Works: Selected Essays*

"The women of two families, one Native, one White, and the piece of earth both feel they own are at the center of this lyrical and compassionate novel. A moving story about the consequences of historical amnesia and the healing power of mother love."

—CAROL SPINDEL
author of *Dancing at Halftime: Sports and the Controversy Over American Indian Mascots*

"*After the Dam* begins with a phone call's unexpected news, a young mother's drive through the night with her infant in tow, and then the arrival at a family farm that offers multiple hidden pasts and more than one future. With an impressive empathetic skill, Amy Hassinger guides her conflicted characters through a complex path where personal regret and longing confront and echo the moral dilemmas of our country's troubled history. This is a brave and beautifully written novel, one that offers quiet wisdom and no easy answers."

—PHILIP GRAHAM
author of *The Moon, Come to Earth*

AFTER THE DAM

a novel

Amy Hassinger

Red Hen Press | *Pasadena, CA*

Book layout by Mark E. Cull
Cover image by Ilse Moore, www.ilsemoore.com

Library of Congress Cataloging-in-Publication Data
Names: Hassinger, Amy, 1972– author.
Title: After the dam / Amy Hassinger.
Description: First edition. | Pasadena, CA : Red Hen Press, [2016]
Identifiers: LCCN 2016023197 (print) | LCCN 2016029630 (ebook) |
    ISBN 9781597097536 (softcover) | ISBN 9781597095013
Subjects: LCSH: Self-actualization (Psychology) in women—Fiction. |
    Self-realization in women—Fiction. | Life change events—Fiction. |
    Motherhood—Fiction. | BISAC: FICTION / General.
Classification: LCC PS3608.A86 A69 2016 (print) | LCC PS3608.A86 (ebook)
    | DDC 813/.6—dc23
LC record available at https://lccn.loc.gov/2016023197

The National Endowment for the Arts, the Los Angeles County Arts Commission, the Los Angeles Department of Cultural Affairs, the Dwight Stuart Youth Fund, the Pasadena Arts & Culture Commission and the City of Pasadena Cultural Affairs Division, Sony Pictures Entertainment, and the Ahmanson Foundation partially support Red Hen Press.

First Edition
Published by Red Hen Press
www.redhen.org

For Scoop and Teddy Vincent, founders of a beautiful dream

and

for Adam, my deep, wild river

... and Lois –

Lovely to meet you! Good luck
with your writing!

All my best,

Amy Hassing 2018

AFTER THE DAM

This is the most beautiful place on earth. There are many such places.

—Edward Abbey,
Desert Solitaire

Justice is what love looks like in public.

—Cornel West

BOOK ONE

THE RETURN

June 2003

1

The phone in the Clayborne-German household was ringing.

"My hands are dirty!" Michael shouted from the kitchen.

"Our daughter is attached to my breast!" Rachel returned from the study.

The phone stopped ringing. Michael appeared at the study door, the cordless in one hand, a dishtowel draped over his shoulder.

"It's your Dad." He handed Rachel the phone, following her gaze to the TV news. Just that morning, a hunter had discovered a baby left in a cabin in West Virginia, badly dehydrated, but alive. The mother was nowhere to be found.

"They drag the river yet?"

"I just turned it on."

They waited, but the network was leading with a story about the number of American soldiers dead in Iraq since the start of the war two months earlier. Michael muted the sound and set the remote on top of the TV. "Dinner's soon," he said, on his way out of the room. Rachel put the phone to her ear.

"Hey, honey," her father said at the other end. "How's my girl? You getting any sleep yet?"

"Ha ha, very funny."

"How's Deirdre?"

"She's fine. Doing what she does best."

A shot of the West Virginia cabin appeared on the TV—a one-room rustic thing, walls of rough-hewn logs and a roof of bark. Rachel glanced longingly at the remote. Then came the image of an old photo—a teenager with big hair and long, fringy earrings, her eyes thickly lined in black. The missing mother.

"She's a star, already. And her mama's holding up, I gather?"

Rachel sighed. "What's up, Dad?"

"Well, I'm calling with a thought, Rachel. Just a thought. I spoke with Grand this morning, and she said something disturbing. Something about how Diane would be living on the Farm after she dies. As if this were common knowledge."

"Diane Bishop? Joe's mom?"

"Yes, Diane Bishop. Grand's nurse."

"Right. What did she say, exactly?"

"I can't remember her exact words. We were talking about Linda's upcoming visit, and how Diane is arranging it, and she said something about how Diane's life will be so much easier when she, Grand, is finally gone, that she'll be free to just enjoy the Farm in peace."

"She's probably just confused, Dad. I mean, it's a brain tumor, right? She's probably not thinking clearly."

"That's what your mother said. But Grand goes in and out of clarity these days, and she'd been fairly coherent otherwise, during the rest of the conversation."

"Did you talk to Diane about it?"

"Diane? No, no. I'm not sure she'd tell me the truth anyway."

Rachel disagreed—if there was anyone you could trust to tell the painful truth, it was Diane Bishop.

"Anyway, Rachel, this was my thought. What if you were to go up there for a little while? Introduce Deirdre to Grand? Grand would love it—she was nearly salivating at the pictures we showed her. She couldn't remember the last time she'd seen you."

"Christmas. I just saw her last Christmas. At Aunt Linda's."

"She didn't remember that. Anyway, while you're there, you could scope things out a bit. See if everything seems all right."

"You want me to spy for you."

"Not spy, exactly. Just kind of check things out."

"Dad."

"All right, spy. I'm concerned is all, Rachel. I don't want Grand taken advantage of."

"Dad, I've got a baby to take care of, remember? It's a six hour drive up there."

"Your mother and I used to drive all over creation with you. I'd be working on a brief and she'd drive, feeding you with one hand while she steered with the other."

"Okay, well, this is the twenty-first century, Dad, if you hadn't heard. We believe in trying to keep our children alive in these modern times."

Her father chuckled.

"Anyway, Deirdre still eats on demand. And Michael's teaching summer session, which means I'd be stopping every half hour to feed or change her. Why don't you go?"

"Your mother and I were just there last week. I've got to be in court in two days."

"Well, what about Derek, then?"

"Derek's a plane ride away, just like us, and besides, he's not exactly the right candidate for the job at hand. Subtlety is not his strong suit, you know that."

"And Linda?"

"Linda's coming in a few weeks, like I said, and she's already been there twice this month."

"And I'm the crappy granddaughter who hasn't been at all."

"Honey, I didn't say that."

"But you implied it."

"No one's expected you to be there, Rachel. You just had a baby. But Deirdre's a few months old, now . . . All I'm asking is for you to think about it." He paused then added, "It might be the last chance you get to see Grand."

Rachel swallowed. The news had gone to a commercial—a glossy-haired woman with sparkling teeth was holding up a package of squeezable yogurt, her apple-cheeked kids smiling at the kitchen table. Rachel looked down at Deirdre, nose smashed into boob. Flakes of yellow skin still clung to her scalp. The doctors told her it was cradle cap, a normal infant condition, that she'd grow out of it eventually. They just needed to keep her head clean and scrub it with a special plastic brush. But Rachel couldn't bring herself to use the hard bristles on Deirdre's scalp, so the flaky yellow stuff had stuck around. Every time Rachel looked at it, her insides clenched. She worried she'd screwed everything up already, given her baby a lifelong skin disorder.

"I'll think about it, Dad. But I'll warn you, that's not saying much. My thoughts are not terribly cogent these days. Thinking looks a lot like dozing, or drooling, actually, staring into space like a catatonic—"

"You'll get through this stage, honey. You're paying your dues now. Later you'll reap the rewards."

"That's what they tell me."

"Give Michael my best. And kiss that little girl on both cheeks for me. Tell her not to forget her Grandpa Chris."

They hung up. Rachel set the phone on the desk beside her and picked up her water glass, beaded with condensation. She sipped, watching Deirdre's eyes flutter beneath closed lids. The moving images on the television cast a pattern of changing light on Deirdre's skin like sunlight dappling a lake. The Farm. Rachel hadn't been to the Farm since the wedding. God, eight years ago. Was it really that long? She smelled again the pine needles drying in the sun, saw the blue lake wink between the trees, heard the eagles chirp their fire-alarm chirp from the nest above the house. She felt the evening wind blow off the lake through the screen porch, where they'd gather for cocktails—or tonic on the rocks when she was young. And Grand, too— her tanned skin and smart, laugh-lined eyes, her silky gray hair. She'd curl on Grand's lap in that evening wind as the sunlight dropped through the trees. She'd listen to the murmur of the grown-ups and trace finger lines in the condensation on Grand's glass. Grand always smelled of the lake.

"Rachel?" Michael stuck his head in the study. "Dinner's ready."

Dinner was a piece of broiled salmon, some rice, a couple of spears of broccoli. Deirdre slept in the vibrating chair by Rachel's feet. They ate in silence, utensils clinking against the ceramic plates. Finally, Rachel spoke. "Dad wants me to drive up to the Farm and spy on Grand."

Michael looked up, his mouth full of salmon. He swallowed, sipped his water. "Spy?"

"Apparently Grand said something about leaving Diane the Farm, and he wants me to go check it out."

Michael picked up his fork. "Remind me who Diane is?"

"Diane Bishop. Joe's Mom." Rachel studied her plate; it had been thirteen years, and she still had a hard time saying Joe's name in front of Michael. "She's been Grand's live-in nurse since she got sick."

"Oh. That Diane." They chewed in silence a moment longer.

"That would be kind of a radical move, wouldn't it?" he said. "Restoring the land to Native ownership? I mean, even for your ultra-progressive grandmother." This last comment was tongue-in-cheek; they were all, in Rachel's family, ultra-progressives, and Michael topped the list.

"It would."

"Does he think Diane pushed Grand into it or something?"

"Maybe. I don't know. Anyway, it's insane. I can't go to the Farm."

"Of course not. Summer session starts tomorrow. I've got to teach."

"Well, he thinks I could go by myself."

"That doesn't seem like a good idea. You'd have to stop every two hours to feed Deirdre. It's bad for the baby's development to keep her strapped in an infant seat for more than three hours at a time, particularly when she's awake. She needs to make eye contact with you, feel you holding her."

"I *know*, Michael. I've read all the same books as you."

"If Grand wants to leave the Farm to Diane, let her. I mean, that's what should be done with that place. Give it back to the rightful owners."

Rachel grabbed the salt and sprinkled her soggy spear of broccoli. Michael had left it too long in the steamer.

"You know how I feel about it," he added.

"I do indeed."

"What's that supposed to mean?" He squinted at her from behind his Lennon-style glasses.

"Only what I said. I know how you feel about the Farm. We all—the whole family—know how you feel about the Farm." She tossed her fork on the table and put her forehead in her hands.

"Whoa, Rachel. What's going on?"

"I'm just exhausted, as usual. Anyway, I'm not going. So please don't start haranguing me about the Farm, because I'm just not in the mood."

He cut another piece from his salmon. "No one's haranguing anyone."

"Good." She took a mouthful of rice and chewed it distastefully before dousing the pile with soy sauce. She could feel Michael's eyes on her, on the amount of soy sauce she was squirting from the bottle, could feel his brain tallying up the milligrams of sodium that would pass into her breast milk and soon salt the tender cells of Deirdre's esophagus, stomach, intestines. She set the bottle down, hard, on the table.

They chewed.

"Have you spoken with Susan yet?" Michael asked.

"No, for Christ's sake. I haven't spoken with Susan." Susan was the therapist she'd seen when they'd first moved to Illinois and Rachel had been struck with a series of panic attacks.

"I just think it might not be a bad idea, Rach. Just to get a baseline for what's normal."

"I know you think that, Michael. You've only told me that about five hundred times."

"Ok. Well . . ."

"Michael, the fact is that people, when they are tired and not sleeping, tend to get cranky. Also, it so happens that when people feel sad, they cry. And when they are sleep-deprived *and* sad, they cry a lot. Crying and exhaustion are not evidence of postpartum depression, they're evidence of being a human being. And as I haven't gotten a full night's sleep in close to four months, it's pretty natural that I might be a little touchier than usual."

"Rachel, please don't take it personally."

"How can I not take it personally? You're telling me I'm crazy."

"I have never once said that. I'm just concerned. It's the tears, yes. And this sudden obsession with the news, with every grisly catastrophe out there."

"I'm just worried about that poor teenage mom. She's probably scared to death."

"Rachel. Honey. All I'm saying is that you've been unhappy for a while now, and that it couldn't hurt to just talk with someone about how you're feeling. Susan helped you before. You liked her. Maybe she would help you now."

Rachel glared at him. "What would help me is a good night's sleep." She forked another sodium-soaked mound of rice into her mouth, watching for his wince.

"Listen." He set his fork down on his plate. "Why don't you go lie down? See if you can rest. When Dee wakes up, I'll give her a bottle from the freezer."

She rubbed her eyes. "Actually, that sounds perfect."

"In fact, I'll take all the feedings tonight, if you want. You can sleep all the way through."

"God, that would be so amazing, if it were possible."

"It's completely possible. Give it a try."

She pushed her chair back and went to kiss Michael on the top of the head. His scalp smelled of dried sweat. "Thanks. Sorry for being such a bitch."

"You're not a bitch." He squeezed her hand. "Go on, before she wakes up."

Rachel dragged herself up the stairs. She brushed her teeth, then stared in the bathroom mirror. Her face looked unfamiliar to her still—fatter than usual, and strangely discolored. Pregnancy had made her freckles flare into patches of brown around her mouth that looked as if she hadn't bothered to wash in a few days, which was probably true, actually. She washed now, scrubbing at the spots to no avail. The same hormones had also made her normally slight mustache grow thicker and more non-fictional. That, plus the bags under her eyes, and she was a perfect candidate for those "before" shots in the women's magazines, the ones where they deliberately poured a bottle of grease in the woman's hair and told her to look as if her best friend had just killed herself. Welcome to motherhood! Baggy eyes, sore tits, and a brand new bitchy attitude to enchant your husband with!

Rachel trailed her fingers along the wall on the way to the bedroom. She couldn't believe it had actually been eight years since she'd been to the Farm. The Farm had been her favorite place in the world when she was a kid. She'd spent every summer, all summer there, tramping through the woods, swimming in the lake, running barefoot over the open lawn, all with Joe. Even now, every time spring hit and the chance scent of pine needles warmed by the sun graced her nose, she would yearn to go back there, feel that old hunger of the heart.

And now Grand was up there, dying, and Rachel was down here, scorched to her soul by motherhood. And why couldn't she go, really? It would be a trial, the drive, but it was only one day of her life. She could manage it. And would it really be such a bad, morally corrupt thing, after all, to visit her grandmother on that land? To walk those old woods? Dip her body in that lake?

She tossed her clothes on the floor, pulled on her nursing nightgown, and fell on the bed in a sudden swoon of longing, tears fresh on her cheeks. A moment later, she was asleep.

In her dream, Rachel rocked in a cane-backed rocker like the one at the Farm. The carpet at her feet grew damp, then soggy, then submerged. The water rose, inch by inch, up the legs of the pine coffee table and the wicker couch, covering the brass piano pedals. Soon it reached the coffee tabletop; the cork coasters bobbed away like driftwood. Sheet music floated from the upright, big white lily pads. Rachel continued to rock, watching, until it became clear that she held a baby in her lap, a baby who patted the water as it pooled around her thighs and belly. The water rose and Rachel rocked, and when she next looked down at the baby, now submerged up to her neck, she saw that it was not Deirdre but a miniature Grand, with Grand's soft tanned skin and adult eyes, staring back at Rachel with resignation, as if this were the fate she'd always envisioned for herself.

Rachel woke with a start, her heart racing. Next to her, Michael snored in his steady, unruffled way. The house was silent. Everything was fine.

She turned on her side and felt the ropy rigidity of her breast as it pressed into the mattress. Her breasts were engorged. Michael must have fed Deirdre a bottle before he went to bed, which meant that Deirdre wouldn't need to eat for a while yet. Mastitis could set in if you let the milk build up. She should probably get up and pump, replace that used bottle of freezer milk. But then, what if Deirdre woke up just after she'd pumped? Rachel would be empty. They'd have to use another bottle of freezer milk, and their supply would start running low . . .

She slipped out of bed and padded to Deirdre's room. The fancy nightlight—a gift from Rachel's parents—cast a slowly-rotating simulacrum of the starry sky across the ceiling. Deirdre was slumbering in Zen-baby mode, arms and legs splayed, face slack. Rachel marveled at the delicate precision of Deirdre's features: the tiny perfection of her upper lip, as if its heart-shaped rise had been painted on with a fine-hair brush, the moon-like fullness of her cheeks, the single black curl at her forehead. (The dark room hid the flaking yellow skin.) She was beautiful, her baby, this madly growing thing Rachel had nourished for nine months, and was still nourishing now, day by day, feeding by feeding. She was absurdly proud of this achievement—of feeding her child—prouder than she was of almost any other accomplishment in her life thus far. It was ridiculous, really, because it was only biology. All she had to do was eat and drink and stick her boob in the kid's face every couple of hours. Still, breastfeeding made her feel magical, like Wonder Woman. It certainly beat the pants off slaving over a master's thesis on the environmental impact of small-scale embankment dams, her most recent so-called accomplishment.

Deirdre's face flickered like a flame, from total slackness to a fleeting smile, a fluttering of the eyelids, and then her tongue began working, making that involuntary sucking motion. And Rachel knew, all of a sudden, that she had to go. She had to go north to the Farm. She had to see Grand, to introduce Grand to this child—her *child!*—before it was too late.

She watched the play of expressions across Deirdre's face as she might watch a fire and thought it through. She could leave in the morning. It wouldn't take long to pack—the diaper bag, the Pack 'n Play, an extra bag of diapers. The baby front pack. Throw some clothes in a bag for herself. Well, and she'd want the vibrating chair, too, since Deirdre slept in that so well. And the nursing pillow. Oh, Christ, it was already getting ridiculous, all the gear she depended on. Women had been doing this for millennia, before Target's infant department ever existed. How did mothers in Mongolia do it? They fucking strapped their babies to their backs while they forked in the hay. What did she need a vibrating chair for?

She turned back to her own bedroom, where she stood in the doorframe. Michael, as always, was sleeping the sleep of the dead, his body as erect lying down as it was standing up. Michael always kept himself utterly straight. It was partly his years of yoga practice and partly his skinniness that made him look so stick-like, but it was also just him—his total rectitude. Michael was as straight as they came. It was funny and sweet, sometimes, and at other times maddening, but right now, it made her panic. He would not allow her to go. He wouldn't forbid her—he would never presume to do that—but he would insist, in his calm, reasonable way, that it simply wasn't a good idea. If she was so set on going, then why not wait until summer session finished, three weeks out, and then he'd go with her, just this once, just so Grand could meet Deirdre, and Rachel could say goodbye. And this would make so much sense that she would feel like an unreasonable whiny bitch if she complained. But the fact was that Rachel wanted—*needed*, all of a sudden—to go, and to go now. Three weeks might be too late. Grand was losing ground every day. A week ago, Grand had barely recognized Rachel's mother. She wondered if she would even recognize her. She couldn't wait three weeks. It had to be now.

Flushing with adrenaline, Rachel tiptoed to the closet, where she found their big duffle, and began stuffing clothes into it—handfuls of underwear, balls of socks, a grab of shirts and pants. The baby front pack. No time to dress—she'd change later. Quietly, she stepped into Deirdre's room, where she crammed a full bag of diapers, some onesies and little infant pants and hats into the duffle. She lugged the bag downstairs, filled a water bottle, grabbed a package of sunflower seeds, her purse and her cell phone, then shushed out the back door to the car. Michael would be fine without the car; he biked everywhere anyway. She stowed everything in the trunk, then unlatched the car seat from its base.

Back inside, she tiptoed up the stairs, giggling silently. She couldn't believe she was doing this, she was actually doing it. She set the seat on the floor of Deirdre's room, and then, as noiselessly as possible, lowered the side of the crib. Clasping Deirdre to her chest, she knelt before the car seat, and gently, ever-so-gently, laid Deirdre in its curve. Deirdre's tongue fluttered, but she slept on. One at a time, Rachel slid Deirdre's arms beneath the straps, then held her breath and snapped the latch closed. The click resounded in the silent room. She froze, listening for Michael. All was quiet.

Once again, she padded down the stairs, hefting the car seat with two hands. At the back door she slid on her clogs, gave one last look around the dark kitchen, and then escaped into the night.

2

A deep orange glow crept into the sky just above the tree line over the dark lake. Joe Bishop watched from his stump on the shore, a mug of coffee steaming in his hand. His dog Sal lay on the ground beside him. The deep orange spread through the sky like a blush, then brightened to a yellow that gilded the undersides of the few wispy clouds above. It was the first good sunrise all week. All week, dawn had been dark and wet, the sky lightening grudgingly late into the morning. It had been hard to get out of bed, harder still to don the heavy, clammy raincoat and rain pants, the tall rubber boots, and tramp down the puddled trail to check the levels, make his morning report. Sal always gave him a doleful look from her curl by the wood stove on those mornings, a look that perfectly reflected the way he felt. But today she'd run out ahead of him to the water's edge, as glad as he was to see a dry, clear dawn. Might even make a good day for a dive.

The first jay screeched, and soon the air was thick with birdsong and the general scuttling and coming alive of the woods. A woodpecker drilled into a nearby trunk and the woods echoed with its *ratatatatat*; a couple of squirrels scrambled up one side of a tree and down the other. Sal perked her ears at the distant breaking of sticks deep in the woods behind them, then laid her head between her forepaws, not alarmed enough to investigate. The sky changed from pale yellow to a near-white blue, deepening into azure overhead, patterned with drifting clouds. Joe took the last sip of his coffee, rehearsing the coming day. He'd promised his mother he'd finally get out to the Clayborne place and help move some of the furniture out of the downstairs office, so she could convert it to a bedroom for old Mrs. Clayborne. It was a chore he'd put off for a few weeks, until yesterday his mother had put it to him plainly. *I could lose my job, Joe. If Madeline were to fall on the stairs on my watch—God forbid—I'd never work in hospice again.*

He hadn't bothered to ask why she didn't just ask someone from the hospice agency to come. Not every hospice nurse had a big burly son living nearby who could be called on day or night for any little job that might need doing; they had to have provisions for this sort of thing, people who could be called upon to help. But he knew his mother well, and he knew she had a second agenda. She wanted to set eyes on him, to see that he was all right, that he had gone another day, another week, another month sober, even after seven years of unfailing sobriety. She wanted to check up.

A new red glow edged a cloud at the tree line, turning its neighbors varying shades of lavender and pink. Joe watched until the riotous display calmed to a simple blue and white when the sun finally breached the horizon. Then he stood and stretched; Sal followed suit. He trudged up the muddy bank, stopping to set his empty mug on the small deck he'd built off his yurt, then headed up the trail toward the dam, Sal at his heels. He gauged the height of the lake as they walked; it looked like it'd held more or less steady since last night. They passed the put-in spot where he kept his dinged up aluminum canoe, upended to keep out the rain. The lake was high this spring, higher than it had been in the six years he'd been working here. A banner year for rain it was, and no end in sight—they were predicting more to come later in the week. But at least it had stopped for today. He'd probably recommend a slight draw-down this morning to alleviate some of the pressure on the gates, and then wait and see if the dry day brought the level down further by evening. Definitely a good day for a dive.

An eagle soared into view, its gleaming white head aimed in the direction of the dam. The eagles liked to fish the dam, or just beyond it, where the lake became a river again. Unlucky fish got spat out the other side, freshly dead or dazed, easy pickings. Joe watched for the eagle's sudden plunge.

But this eagle evidently had other plans; it kept flying, riding a thermal high over the dam to the hilltop. A flash of white there caught Joe's attention: a figure stood at the overlook. A little early for a tourist. You didn't usually see many gawkers at dawn. He squinted. This one looked like she was wearing a long white dress—kind of gothic, kind of ghostly. Maybe a religious nut conducting some weird ritual. The dam attracted all kinds.

Joe reached the causeway and plodded over to the small shed of an office, where a long-handled net hung from a hook. He grabbed it, then strolled the length of the concrete pier that jutted into the lake. Sal had run back down to the shore and was sniffing at the reeds. Joe leaned over the water with the net, trying to catch a soggy Leinenkugel's case. The cardboard bobbed away once, twice, three times before he snagged it. He dumped the dripping case onto the pier, where it fell with a splat.

Next he went for a couple of green plastic bottles that were bobbing near the penstocks. The amount of garbage that people tossed into the lake never failed to piss him off. He knew who the culprits were, too. Those jackasses in their snazzy speedboats with their turbo-powered engines, whipping around the reservoir like it was their own personal oversized swimming pool, pounding beers and tossing the empties over the side. Every year it was the same. 'Round about Memorial Day, the crap that drifted down-lake and ended up at the dam tripled. That's how he knew tourist season had begun.

He snagged the bottles, too, and dumped them on the pier, then hung the net back on its hook. Carrying the dripping haul, he walked over to the trash bin by the parking lot. Sally ran up to meet him, leaving muddy paw prints on the asphalt. She'd been sniffing around the water's edge like crazy these last few weeks, sometimes digging in the silt, as if she was looking for that old shoreline, the one she was used to, the one that was disappearing bit by bit under the rising water.

Garbage disposed of, Joe stepped into the office-shed, pressed the button to boot up the ancient IBM desktop, and grabbed the log—a black three-ring binder, one piece of notebook paper for each day since January 1 of this year—then stepped back out again, his keys jingling in his pocket. He strode down the causeway toward the control house, where he checked the gauges on the back wall. The levels were holding steady enough. Only a minor rise since last night, when he'd raised the gates two inches. He wrote the date, the time, and the numbers in the log.

Outside again, he glanced up at the overlook. The woman in the white dress was gone.

3

Just at dawn, Rachel squatted in the woods by the road, and lifted her night-gown. The pee whished out in a steady stream, forging a channel in the duff.

She'd parked the Prius on the shoulder. Finished, Rachel peeked in at Deirdre, her black shock of hair, her perfect sleeping pout. Still as a carving. Rachel considered lifting out the car seat and carrying it with her, but the disturbance might wake Dee up, and besides, the goddamn seat was so heavy and awkward. The car was in the shade and the windows were cracked, allowing for plenty of airflow. There was no one around. Rachel would be gone all of five minutes. Deirdre would be fine.

Rachel walked briskly along the overgrown trail to the lookout. She was startled to see how small it seemed, smaller than she remembered. She stood well back from the edge, her eyes on a young white pine that jutted almost horizontally into empty air, its roots grasping at the earth. One good shove and that pine would careen down to the river below. It was a good thing she hadn't brought Dee—what if she'd tripped? In the distance was the flowage, still and blue, and at its foot, the Old Bend Dam. It looked just as it had when she was a kid: a long hill, topped by a road, three gates in the middle, the water rushing beneath. Very fast, it seemed. And loud, even from this distance. The rains must have been heavy here, too.

The last time she'd been here was with Michael that summer they were married. She'd made him stop to look at the dam, just as her father had always done with them, and she'd told him the story: how her great-grandfather, Benjamin Turner, hydraulic engineer for Wisconsin Power and Light, had designed it and built it back in the twenties, bringing power to the hinterlands. But she added her own spin: how before the dam went in, the Name River (pronounced *nah-may*, Ojibwe for sturgeon) had been a great place for freshwater sturgeon, how after it went in, hundreds of acres of reservation land were flooded, including thousands of ancient graves and the tribe's traditional ricing grounds. They'd stood together, holding hands, steaming in tandem indignation at the societal and ecological horrors dams were: the gorgeous canyons and prairies and wetlands, forever submerged; the once-wild rivers, turned into bathtubs and trickling streambeds; the fish, dying en masse, unable to reach their spawning grounds. Traditional ways of life destroyed. A dam, any dam, they felt, was a bad, bad thing. And this dam, the Old Bend Dam, seemed to her especially bad, since it belonged, in a sense, to her family. She remembered making a bitter joke about wiring it with explosives. "Just like in *The Monkey Wrench Gang*," she'd said. "We could sneak out here in the dead of night and blow the thing to smithereens."

"Your father would love that," Michael replied.

"He'd never know. We'd run off before anyone could catch us."

"Rachel," he chided, in that voice, the one that condoned rational action and restraint, the one that always seemed to remind her of his five-year edge in age. And she'd dropped the subject.

A movement in her peripheral vision alerted her to an eagle soaring in her direction, its wings spanning the air. It passed overhead and out of sight.

Down below on the causeway, two tiny figures appeared—a man and a dog. Rachel watched them until they disappeared into one of the buildings. She couldn't remember ever having seen a person on the dam before, in all the times they'd stopped at the lookout, and the sight struck her somehow as ominous. She thought, suddenly, of Deirdre, and spun around, tripping up the path toward the car.

A tribal police cruiser, its engine still running, was parked behind her Prius, and peering in the back window at Deirdre was a cop in a brown uniform.

"Oh!" she sputtered.

He swiveled around. His face was rough and jowly, cheeks hanging like coin purses. "This your car?" he asked.

"Yes. I was just—I only stopped for a minute. I had to pee. I didn't want to wake her up."

The cop flinched at the word "pee," as if Rachel had swung at him. "Not a good idea to leave your kid in the car."

"I was literally gone for five minutes, tops."

"Woman left her kid in the car not too far from here just the other week. Went in to a store to get a pop. Came back out, the car was gone. We're still looking for the kid."

"Really? That's terrible." Rachel's pulse raced. She put a hand out to steady herself on the nearest tree. The cop eyed her suspiciously, and she realized how she must look, emerging from the woods in a nightgown, hair loose, like some escaped madwoman. Her boobs were probably poking out of their nursing slits. She pulled at the front of her gown.

"Happens all the time. That's why you don't leave your kid in the car. Ever. Even for a second. There are a lot of nutcases out there. They're out there, and they're looking for your kid."

"Okay, officer," she breathed. "I understand." She snuck a glance at her chest—no skin visible.

The cop squinted doubtfully at her. "Where you headed?"

"My grandmother's place, just up the flowage a ways. We'll be there in twenty minutes. Really, I was just stopping to pee."

"Well."

"I swear I won't do it again."

He nodded curtly. "All right. Drive safe now."

"Thank you. Thank you. I will."

He touched his hat, then got in the cruiser. Rachel, her hands shaking, slid into the driver's seat. She pressed her palms against her thighs, trying to stop the shaking. In the rearview mirror, she could see the cop writing something in a log. Deirdre's head had tipped forward, her neck stretched uncomfortably long. Rachel knelt on her seat and reached into the back, gingerly pushing Deirdre's head to upright. Immediately, it fell forward again, the neck muscles pulled tight beneath the tender skin. She tried again: no luck. She gave up. If Michael were here, he'd rig up a fail-proof support with his pocket handkerchief, no doubt. If Michael were here, Deirdre would never have been left alone in the car.

When she turned back around, the cop was gone. Still trembling, Rachel pulled back onto the road and followed it out to the state highway. A pickup passed, the driver saluting her with a raised index finger. Behind it, an eighteen-wheeler pushed its luck along the narrow curves. A herd of Holsteins munched the grass over the peak of a rolling hill. What an idiot she was. What a basket case. She should have turned back when she'd had the chance, hours ago. A few miles over the Wisconsin border, she'd realized she hadn't even left a note for Michael, and immediately the insanity of what she was doing hit her full-bore. At that point, she'd only been driving an hour or so—she could have turned around and gone home, even snuck back into the house without waking Michael. But she'd kept driving, bullishly. Turning tail would be admitting to wrongdoing, a thing she didn't want to do. Plus, there was Grand. She'd kept going. And after that one panicked moment of doubt, driving six hours north in the middle of the night had felt like the right decision. Deirdre slept peacefully in her seat, lulled by the hum of the tires against the road, and Rachel sped up the empty interstate, her ribs lifting with a new sense of freedom. She'd stopped only once, just north of Madison, when Deirdre started to fuss. Rachel fed her (relief! her breasts had grown hard with milk) and changed her (once before eating and then again after, the first diaper already heavy with mustard-colored poop), and then set out again, and Deirdre had fallen back to sleep almost immediately. Rachel had even congratulated herself on what a good choice she'd made—the roads were clear, no traffic to speak of, and Deirdre had never slept so well through the night in her whole three-and-three-quarters months of life.

And then had come the episode with the cop.

She could hear Michael's voice chewing her out, could hear his carefully measured anger: *You need to be more careful, Rachel. Deirdre's life is in your hands.* She began to cry. Oh, fuck, she thought, wiping at the tears with the back of her hand. Not now, not when she was almost at Grand's. Fuck that cop. Fuck that cop, fuck the dam, fuck her own stupid nostalgia that had made her want to stop in the first place, and fuck Michael. She didn't need him. She had Deirdre, and soon she would have Grand and the Farm, and that would be all she'd need.

She passed the old bait shop where her father used to trade tales of the muskies and northern pikes that got away, the cranberry bog, and the little bridge over the stream where the heron fished and the turtles deposited their eggs. The stream was high, higher than she remembered, rushing close to the road. There, to the left, was the meadow spotted with Indian paintbrushes, and there the rusted-out pickup, an enterprising birch now growing through the window. Ahead a quarter mile, she saw the big green and blue welcome sign that marked the boundary of the Name River Ojibwe Indian reservation. And here, on her left, the field where her great-grandfather used to pasture his cattle, spotted now with puddles, and there—there!—

through the trees at the far edge of the field, the same blue flash of lake that used to make her bounce up and down in the backseat when she was a kid, her thighs peeling off the vinyl.

She made a left onto the lane, slowing to savor the familiar sights: the caved-in chicken shack, the ancient ice house, the cheerful red barn, now a garage. Turning onto the dirt drive that led to the house, she felt the old swelling of her heart in her chest. Grand, she would get to see Grand! Grand: who used to take her berry picking, taught her how to swing a tennis racquet, read to her in the early mornings by the old stone fireplace, and made her lunches of grilled cheese and tomato soup. Grand, who once lanced her pus-filled poison ivy blisters with a sterilized sewing needle, and who then fed her lunch when her hands were too stiff with the same blisters to pick up a fork. Grand, who gave great backrubs and laughed at any joke anyone had the courage to tell; Grand, whose favorite lunch was a bottle of beer and a chocolate bar; Grand, who had been, for as long as she could remember, her one shining example of how a person should live a life.

Stray sticks cracked under the tires as she pulled up to the house, steering the car beneath the tunnel of overarching pines and birches until the vision of the place opened up before her: the clay tennis court, the guest cabin, the open lawn—puddled like the field—and the house itself: stone foundation, peeling white paint, red roof. Everything as it had been, and everything as it should be. The yellow morning light winked off the puddles. Rachel eased the car around the grassy circle that rounded the flagpole and parked next to the house. She killed the engine and sat reveling in the silence.

Then a woman who was not Grand appeared at the kitchen window: a stranger with cropped black hair and dramatic cheekbones, a woman who inspired the word *pert*. Of course: Diane. Diane Bishop, Joe's mother—her hair shorn, a little heavier, the skin a little baggier around her eyes, but still the same woman who used to clean the house and cook the big family dinners when Rachel was a girl. Somehow, Rachel had forgotten all about Diane. She hadn't seen her for thirteen years. Not since that summer, the summer before Joe had gone to war. And here the woman was, looking relatively unchanged, peering quizzically out at her.

Rachel unfolded herself from the car and stretched. The screen door slammed, and Diane marched toward her. Her face held the polite but distant expression of someone approaching a stranger. Rachel was aware once again of her own unkempt hair, old-fashioned Ophelia nightgown, a watery smile on her face.

"Can I—?" Diane stopped in mid-sentence.

"Diane. Hi. It's Rachel."

"Rachel?" she breathed. "Rachel! Oh, my Lord. But—but I had no idea you were coming!"

"I wanted to surprise Grand."

Diane gaped at her. "You must have left in the middle of the night!"

"I couldn't sleep anyway. Might as well drive. And it worked out great, actually. Deirdre slept all the way through." Rachel gestured to the car.

Diane went to the window and gasped. Dee was just blinking awake. "Maddy showed me pictures, but she's even more beautiful in person. Congratulations."

"Thanks."

"Well." She gave Rachel a feathery, insubstantial hug. "Your grandmother will certainly be surprised. Though honestly, Rachel, you could have let me know. I can keep a secret, you know." She stared at Rachel with an unreadable, vaguely hostile look. "I'm afraid she's still asleep at the moment," she went on, "but when she wakes up—"

"Oh, that's fine. No big deal. I might need to take a little nap myself." Her rush of adrenaline after the encounter with the cop had subsided, and now she felt only exhaustion. "You look great, Diane," she added. And it was true: the short haircut made Diane's angular cheekbones stand out, and though she must have been at least in her fifties by now, there wasn't a gray hair on her head. Next to her, Rachel felt haggard and elderly.

"That's nice of you to say."

From the backseat, Deirdre began to cry. Instantly, Rachel's breasts pulsed, the milk buzzing at her nipples.

"Uh-oh," Diane said. "Poor thing."

Rachel opened the car door and unbuckled the straps at Deirdre's chest, then lifted her out and began to sway back and forth. The screaming ceased. "Deirdre, this is Diane Bishop." To herself she added, *The mother of Mommy's first love.*

Diane offered a finger to Deirdre, who grabbed it. "Hi, little doll. What a good grip you have." Deirdre dropped the finger and turned back toward Rachel, grabbing a fistful of her hair.

"And your husband? He didn't come?"

"He couldn't make it this time." She backed away, looking toward the tallest of the white pines that towered behind the house. The Eliza tree, they used to call it, after her great-grandmother. "Are the eagles nesting this year?"

"Oh, yes. Noisy as ever. You just missed feeding time, actually—they were screeching a little while ago."

"I'm glad. And how's Grand holding up? I mean, I know she's not . . ." Rachel hesitated, unsure how to put it, ". . . her usual self."

"She's hanging in there. Some days are better than others. You'll pep her up, though. She'll be thrilled to see you. And your little one, especially." Deirdre was gnawing thirstily on her fist, slurping at the knuckles. "That girl looks hungry," Diane said.

"Yeah. Feeding time for baby, too." Rachel opened the trunk for the duffle, but Diane reached in first.

"I can get it," Rachel protested.

"You've got the baby, don't be silly."

"All right. Thank you."

Rachel held the screen door as Diane sidled through, the duffle on one shoulder and the diaper bag on the other. "We'll put you in the corner room, near the bathroom. It's far enough away from your grandma's room so her nightly wakings shouldn't disturb you."

"Is she getting up at night?"

"Oh, Lord, yes. Every few hours. Wakes up with some dream and needs to be coaxed back to sleep. Kind of like having a baby again, come to think of it. You and I will probably meet in the hallway at 3:00 a.m."

They made their way through the kitchen and Rachel took in the cheerful sights: the wooden cabinets with the white knobs, the blue- and yellow-tiled backsplash, detailed with the figures of frolicking children, the hanging ring overloaded with pots and pans—the cast iron skillet, the hand-cranked food mill—and the cracked old butcher block counter, where for years they'd sliced bread and made sandwiches and mixed up bowls of chocolate chip cookie dough. The fraying braided rug underfoot. Rachel pushed open the swinging door that led into the dining room and held it for Diane. Immediately she was ten again, holding the door in the very same position (*sans* baby) as Diane carried in the trays full of food for the family gathered at the table. She'd been wary of Diane back then. There was a hardness under her polite exterior that had made Rachel want to keep her distance.

"It's been quite a while since you've been here, hasn't it?"

"Eight years."

"Eight years! Goodness."

"Not since my wedding." She felt afresh the guilt she'd felt back then when they'd decided not to invite the Bishops. Michael had been too threatened. Joe had understood—at least that's what Grand had told her. But she hadn't fully considered until now how Diane might have felt about being left out.

They made their way through the dining room—the mounted musky, the birch bark paneling, now curling at the corners, the scarred mahogany dining table, with its curvaceous legs and moth-eaten gold-upholstered chairs, and the corner fireplace with its chain mesh curtains and its stone chimney rising up the wall like a castle turret. They passed the shag carpet in the living room, the upright Steinway in the corner, piled high with stacks of moldering songbooks that Rachel used to try to fake her way through. Tears pricked at her eyes, and she cast about for something to say, something to distract herself from the sight of all the old, neglected objects.

"How's Joe doing these days?"

Diane dropped the duffle at the foot of the staircase. "He's just fine. Works over at the Old Bend Dam, managing the facilities there. Lives over there, too, as a matter of fact. Nice to have him close by."

"Oh!" She thought of the man and the dog she'd seen earlier that morning. "I didn't realize he was around."

"Well, sure he is. He's always been kind of a homebody, my Joe." The *my* fell between them like a warning.

Diane re-shouldered Rachel's duffle and they climbed the stairs in silence to the corner room, which smelled as it always had, of mothballs and wool. Diane set the bags by the blond wood dresser. "Take your time getting settled. Take your nap, if you like. I'm sure Maddy will be awake when you get up." She closed the door behind her.

Rachel sat on the edge of the bed with the nubbled white spread and cradled Deirdre while parting the slit in her nursing nightgown. Deirdre opened her mouth wide as a baby bird and aimed it at the target. The smell of the house, the sight of all the old elements, like images rising up from a dream, the strange presence of Diane and the absence of Grand—all of this, combined with the fact that she was now sitting here in this pink-striped room, the one she'd slept in so often as a child, but now with her own child sucking at her fat breast, overwhelmed Rachel to the point of disorientation.

She thought back to the last time she'd spoken with Diane. It had been on the day she'd agreed to marry Michael. Alone that night, she'd called to talk to Joe, half-wanting him to talk her out of it, to tell her he forgave her, to tell her he still loved her and wanted to be with her. But, as always, she'd gotten Diane instead. *He's not here now, hon, but I'll be sure to give him the message.* The usual empty promise.

A flood of tears swelled once again behind Rachel's eyes and she squeezed them tight. Oh, hell. That was all ages ago. She was married now, a supposed master of Environmental Studies, on her way to a doctorate (the purpose of which she still wasn't clear on), and a mother—or trying to be. Joe had his own life, Diane hers. It was all water over the dam. And if she longed for the past at all, it was only nostalgia. Pure, sentimental nostalgia. Michael would say she was just tired. What she needed was rest.

Michael. He'd be waking up soon, wondering where they were. She should call him right away.

She leaned her head against the wall behind her. Deirdre hummed with each swallow, lulling Rachel toward a doze. She'd call in a few minutes. And then, once Grand woke up, they'd sit together and talk like old times. Grand would help steady her, help her get back on her feet. Grand and the Farm.

4

Diane stood musing at the top of the stairs, one hand on the newel post. The sight of Rachel Clayborne as an adult, Rachel Clayborne with a baby in her arms, was almost dizzying. She'd seen pictures, of course, over the years. Just last month, Maddy had asked her to get out the photo albums, and they'd lingered at each shot, Maddy cooing a litany of Rachel's achievements: Rachel in cap and gown, receiving her college diploma, Rachel in a simple white cotton wedding dress and sandaled feet, her long hair tied back in a braid, Rachel and Michael (a skinny white kid, prematurely balding, with an intellectual's dark-framed glasses and goatee) sitting on the concrete steps of their first house, their arms resting on one another's shoulders. Every photo evidence of Rachel's success—she'd grown up, studied hard, married well, made herself a good, respectable life. This was the story Maddy saw, anyway.

Still, despite the photos, Diane was stunned, completely bowled over by the sight of the actual, in-person adult Rachel. It wasn't just the nightgown, though that was eccentric, to put it mildly. But new mothers often did eccentric, slightly loopy things; she saw it all the time in the maternity ward. What struck her was the fact of Rachel's adulthood, her grown-up self, here in person. It was as if Diane hadn't really believed those photos and stories, as if they were only images of the possible Rachel, the Rachel that might yet be, as if the real Rachel were still out wandering in the woods, still that long-limbed girl Joe used to disappear with first thing after breakfast and then return with hours later, their arms full of treasures—polished lake stones, iridescent duck feathers, partial fish skeletons. The girl—half tomboy, half forest nymph—who used to look at you with a fierce scrutiny one moment and a delighted light in her eyes the next. A part of Diane believed—or wanted to believe—that *that* Rachel was still around.

But of course she wasn't. The war had happened, Joe's accident had happened. And that had changed everything.

Rachel, too, had changed. She looked the same, or mostly the same, anyway—same chiseled face, same figure (chestier now, and a bit of a paunch, but that would be the baby), same flashing eyes. A tracery of first wrinkles at the eyes and around the mouth, a gather of flesh at the hips—these Diane might have expected. But there was something else, too, something resigned in her manner, something beaten or quashed. That was different, unexpected.

In a daze, Diane floated down the stairs to the kitchen. She dialed Joe's cell, and stared out the window as it rang. The morning sun cast its angled light through the pine boughs and onto the lawn. He'd be out on the dam by now, and probably didn't have his phone on him. She tried the dam office next, with no luck. After the beep, she left her message: "Joe, hon, something's come up, and I don't need you today after all. Call me back when you get this please." She hung up, praying that he'd check his messages before setting out. Or, that he'd forget his promise, forget her entirely for today.

She returned to the half-empty dishwasher, picked up the dishtowel she'd left on the counter, and lifted a wet glass from the top rack. She had not anticipated this, Rachel Clayborne springing a surprise visit. And after such a long boycott of the Farm. But maybe it wasn't such a bad thing. It might be their chance—*Maddy's* chance—to finally air her decision about the Farm. Diane had been trying for weeks, ever since Maddy had finalized the papers with her lawyer, to help her find a way to tell the family. But Maddy didn't like to make waves. And now she was failing, quickly. Day by day she lost more ground. Still, Diane knew that if Maddy didn't tell the family herself, if she didn't make it absolutely clear that the decision was her own, that she was giving the land freely, without any undue influence from Diane—well, the shit would hit the fan after she died.

In fact, she thought, as she rubbed the next glass more vigorously, despite her *feelings* about Rachel, she really was the best person to break the news to, the best liaison. She was the only Clayborne who would understand, even applaud the decision. And then Rachel could help tell the rest of the family. So maybe it was a good thing she had come. And maybe it would be a good thing, too, or at least a harmless thing, if Joe showed up and saw her again, after all these years. Joe was on his feet now, doing his best, and

Rachel was married, a new mother, with no room for him. They were all grown up. All that heartache, all that drama—it was all long ago.

"Diane?" A small voice spoke from the monitor on the kitchen windowsill. Diane hung the dishtowel on the rack and headed for the back staircase that led to Maddy's room.

Maddy was sitting up in bed, her white hair a cone of cotton candy spun wildly about her scalp. Her eyes were open, but she appeared to be only half awake, staring straight ahead at the silhouette of a dancing pine bough on the window shade.

"Good morning, sunshine!" Diane sang. She went to the shade and snapped it up, revealing the bough itself, swaying against the window glass in the morning light.

Maddy blinked. "I heard something."

"You did indeed. And you'll never guess. Rachel's here."

"Rachel? Rachel who?"

"Rachel your granddaughter. With her new baby. She's got your eyes, I can see."

Maddy gasped. "What are they doing here?"

"They came up to surprise you, hon. To visit you. Isn't that sweet? Rachel wants you to see the new baby. Her name is Deirdre."

"Well, where are they?" Maddy moved as if to stand, but Diane stepped forward fast.

"Whoa, now. Don't hurt yourself. They're resting now. Rachel drove all night by herself. Looked about ready to drop dead."

"*Dead?*"

"That's just an expression, Madeline. Rachel's all right."

"I thought you said she was dead."

"No, hon. Rachel's not dead. She is alive and resting in her room with the baby. I'm sure that when the baby is fed and Rachel has caught her breath, she'll come right out to see you. Now, how about getting you dressed to receive your visitors?" And with that, Diane whisked off Maddy's covers to reveal the old woman: the white cotton nightgown, bunched at the knees, the two shins, bruised in several places, veined with purple, the skin as crazed and flaking as weathered paint. Maddy protested as usual and tried to draw the covers back up, but they were out of her reach. "Come on now," Diane coaxed, "legs over the side. Sit up. Lean on me. That's right." She helped Maddy sit, her legs dangling over the edge of the bed, and held her there a while, one hand on her back, letting her blood pressure stabilize. Then she strapped the pink canvas belt around Maddy's waist, just as she did every day. "Lift your arms, please, hon."

"What is this?"

"Your belt. We use it to help you stand."

"I don't need a belt. I'm in my nightgown!"

"It's not for fashion, hon. It's to help you stand. Come on." And Maddy complied, as she always did, letting Diane lace the strap through the clasp and cinch it closed. The walker stood within reach, but that alone was not enough to give Maddy her balance, so Diane held the pink belt with one hand and circled Maddy's waist with her other arm, and then with a cue to Maddy—"Ready now? One, two, three"—pulled on the belt, lifted Maddy at the waist, and held her steady while Maddy grabbed at the walker. Each time it was a trial, and each time Maddy gasped with the terror of standing, but each time, they managed the extraordinary task of getting her on her feet and down the hall to the bathroom.

Today, though, Maddy seemed particularly confused. It took an extra effort to get her up the three shallow steps that led from her room to the upstairs hallway, and Diane thought again about how foolish it was to have Maddy upstairs at all, and hoped that Joe *would* come, for Maddy's sake, and finally install her in the first-floor office so she didn't have to bother with stairs.

As usual, they stopped at the portraits of Maddy's parents, hanging side by side in the hall. Maddy's mother Eliza, her dark red hair swept into a bun, gazed out from the photograph with a thinly disguised bitterness. And her father, the infamous Mr. Benjamin Turner, pictured here in his sixties: the thinning white hair, the wire spectacles, the face a drapery of skin.

"My father was an engineer," Maddy said. "He built dams."

Diane nodded, feeling uneasy. This was new, this explaining. Usually, Maddy said something like "Terrible picture" or "Mother hated that tie," something that acknowledged Diane's long-time involvement with the family. But this offering of information, information Diane had known all her life—this was a change. "He was a handsome man," she said.

"He was."

Diane waited to see if Maddy had more to say. "Three more steps," she urged finally, tugging on the pink strap. Forward they went until they reached the bathroom, where Diane lifted the walker over the threshold.

They plodded to the toilet. Diane helped lower Maddy onto the seat, and then stepped into the hall, to give the old woman some privacy.

The corner door opened and Rachel emerged, her eyes slitted against the light. Deirdre was on her shoulder, her black hair sticking up like the spines of a porcupine.

"Diane, could I ask you a huge favor? Would you mind watching Deirdre, just for a bit, while I have a snooze? She's fed and has a new diaper and everything."

"Would I mind? Come here, baby." She took Deirdre and kissed her baby cheek.

"Thank you," Rachel said. "I'm just so beat."

"No problem, hon. Your grandma's up, but it'll be a while before she's done with her toilet. She'll be so excited to see you, little peach!" she cooed to Deirdre. "She'll just about squeal in delight."

"I'll be out soon."

"Take your time."

Rachel stumbled back into the room and closed the door behind her. Deirdre burped up a splotch of curdled milk onto Diane's shoulder. "Well, aren't you a generous thing, christening me so fast," Diane wiped at the cheesy spot with the cloth Rachel had stuck in her hand.

"Diane?" croaked Maddy from the bathroom.

Diane pushed the bathroom door open with her elbow. "Guess who I've got?"

"Is that Rachel? Oh, my goodness, look at her." Maddy gazed up from the toilet.

"No, hon. This is Deirdre. Your great-granddaughter. Rachel's baby. Remember?"

"Oh, oh! Such a tiny thing! Let me see her face." She went to stand up.

"Wait now, Maddy," Diane warned. "You trying to break your other hip? Sit down."

Maddy obeyed, her eyes fixed on Deirdre. "She's got a big head, just like her grandfather. Just like a jack-o'-lantern, Chris's head always was. Poor boy got teased for it in school."

Diane laid Deirdre on the soft bathroom rug, away from Maddy's feet.

"Don't put her on the floor!"

"I need to help you get dressed, don't I? She's fine. Up now." Diane hoisted Maddy to upright again and lifted the nightgown over her head. With a wet cloth, she washed Maddy's armpits, neck, belly, and mole-spotted back, and up the inside of the thighs, just in case Maddy had missed some urine with the toilet paper. And Maddy, while Diane washed her, watched the baby, who lay peacefully on the rug, staring at Maddy.

"You know what I'd like to do?" Maddy said.

"What's that?"

"Bring the baby out to the porch, where she can watch the sunlight through the pines."

"Oh, Lord, Madeline. You want to climb down all those stairs?"

"Why? You think I can't make it?"

"I didn't say that. Just that it will be an effort. Right foot first, please." Diane pulled a pair of pink satin underpants over Maddy's buttocks.

"I think the baby would like it out there, don't you? Babies like to watch patterns of light."

"All right, hon. You're the queen. Give me your arm, please."

"Oh, hush."

"Actually," Diane said as she laced Maddy's arm through a sleeve, "that sounds lovely. Once Rachel's well rested she'll come down, and you can chat with each other a while, out where you can hear the lake and the eagles. Maybe you can even tell her about your decision." Diane paused in her buttoning to give Maddy a meaningful look. "About the Farm."

"My decision?"

"What you've decided about the Farm. What you've put in your will."

"Oh! About leaving it to you, you mean."

"About restoring it to its original ownership, yes."

"Right. Of course! Though I must admit, I'd really rather not bring all that up. Rachel might not like it."

"Maddy. Rachel will think it's a wonderful idea."

"You think so?"

"I know so."

"Rachel's always loved the Farm."

Diane sighed. They'd been over this a million times, and it never seemed to stick. "It's not that she doesn't love it, hon. But she and Michael—" Maddy's face looked blank. "Rachel's husband, Michael? They believe that since it fell within the original boundaries of the reservation, that it should have remained Indian land. They don't believe it's right that this land should be owned by a white family. You told me that yourself, years ago. Remember?"

Maddy nodded slowly. "That's right," she said. "I'd forgotten. Well, then, that's good, isn't it? Rachel will be happy to hear that the land is going back to its original owners."

"I think she will, Maddy. I think she'll think it's a very good idea."

"But look, Diane." Maddy gestured to Deirdre, who was waving her hand at a dust mote. "Rachel's too young to understand."

5

In her dream, Rachel sat behind the wheel, turning a faulty ignition. The motor revved, but didn't catch. She was younger—big hair, eye makeup—the missing mother, the one on the news, ineffectually pumping the gas while in the rearview mirror a cop strode toward her. The revving engine began to ring. Rachel sat straight up, her pulse pounding, the bed covers damp with sweat. She blinked at the striped pink walls, the nubbled bedspread. Oh yes: the Farm. Deirdre was with Diane. Her cell phone rang on the night table. She checked the caller ID. Michael.

"I'm here," she said into the phone, her voice still gravelly with sleep. "I'm okay. I'm sorry I didn't call."

"Where are you?"

"It's okay. We're at the Farm. Deirdre's fine. I'm fine."

"You're at the *Farm*?"

"I couldn't sleep. Again. And in the middle of the night, I just felt it was important that I go. I figured I might as well drive while Dee was sleeping at least. She didn't make a peep the whole drive." She picked at the bedspread. One of the white nubbles came off in her fingers and she tried uselessly to stick it back on.

"I can't believe it. You decided out of the blue to take our daughter on a six-hour road trip in the middle of the night without even *consulting* me?"

It did sound bad, when he put it like that. "I didn't want to wake you."

"Do you know how worried I was when I woke up and you were nowhere? I mean, the crib was empty, the car was gone—"

"I'm sorry. I should have left a note. I just—I was kind of frantic to leave while she was still asleep. And, well, to be honest, I guess I thought you might try to talk me out of it."

"Well, you're right. I would have. I mean, it's insane! Who decides to take a six-hour road trip in the middle of the night? With their three-month-old?"

"Actually, a lot of people do it that way with little kids. Derek did it all the time. They sleep. You don't have to stop every two hours for this and that."

"Yeah, they sleep and *you* sleep. Do you know how easy it is to fall asleep at the wheel? Accidents happen all the time that way."

"Michael, calm down. Please. We made it. Deirdre is fine. I'm fine. All is well."

He let out a long breath. She could picture him perfectly at the other end of the phone, one hand spanning his eyes, the fingers pressed into the sockets, as if staving off a bad headache. "Well, I'm glad you're both okay, anyway," he said finally. The pulley cord outside dinged against the flagpole—once, twice, three times.

"I really am sorry I worried you. I realize it was an impulsive decision."

"That's one way to put it."

"But it's the *right* decision, I'm convinced."

"It's the right decision, to spy on your grandmother? Last night you didn't think it was such a good idea."

"That's not why I came. Grand is *dying*, Michael. One of the most important people in my life is dying. I want her to meet Deirdre while she's still alert enough to understand who she is. I can't let her die without meeting my daughter." Her voice wobbled, and she caught herself. She didn't want to use tears to win the argument.

"*Our* daughter."

"Our daughter."

Michael exhaled again. "How's Grand doing, anyway? Was she glad to see you?"

"I haven't seen her yet. She was asleep when I got here."

"How long are you going to stay?"

"I don't know. Maybe a week? Depends on Grand, I guess. I'm going to play it by ear."

"Because it's awfully quiet here."

"Well, you'll be busy teaching, anyway. No distractions this way." She knew he was making an effort, trying to salvage some civility, some affection. She tried for a kinder tone. "Just think of it as a retreat, okay? We're here, we're fine, you're there, you're fine. I want to spend some time with Grand and I don't want to feel like I have to rush back home."

"Okay. I don't mean to rush you. I'll miss you, that's all."

A loud avian gibbering sounded through the open window.

"What was that?"

"The eagle, I think." She peered up toward the treetops, but the eaves blocked her view. "The nest is active this year."

Again, that heavy silence. He was waiting, she could tell, waiting for her to offer him something, to say she'd miss him, too. "I should probably go check on Deirdre. Diane's got her."

"Okay. Give my best to Grand. I love you."

"Love you, too. I'll call you later." And she turned off the phone.

She opened the window wide, feeling the breeze coming off the lake. The pine boughs swayed, alternately revealing and concealing glimpses of blue. Rachel pressed her face to the screen and took a deep draught of air. Below, the empty rope hammock swung between two trees. The sun shone on the red roof beneath the window, baking a scattering of dried pine needles. Rachel inhaled deeply once more. God, but it was good to be here, to smell this piney air again. To feel this wind on her skin. The eagle—or eaglet, probably—gibbered again, very close. Then came a great winged fluttering and then quiet. Mama eagle back with her catch.

As if in sympathy, Deirdre's squeal rose up from downstairs—a pleased squeal for now, but the kind that could quickly go south. Rachel caught a glimpse of herself in the mirror: hair clumpy and lifeless, face puffy from the interrupted sleep. She looked longingly over at the bed, the shape of her body an indentation on the bedspread. Oh, well. She'd try to nap again when Deirdre next went down.

Rachel lifted the duffle onto the bed, and quickly unpacked, tucking clothes into the dresser drawer. A ghost of the scent of mothballs rose to her nostrils, and she was again a child, tucking her clothes into these same drawers. This had been her room, the one she'd always stayed in. The pink room, it was called, because of the pink and white striped wallpaper, and the dark pink, wobbly-legged night table, with the lamp whose shade always tipped to one side. There, across the room, was the marble-topped washstand, with the old-fashioned washbasin and pitcher set on top. And in the corner, the wooden doll's cradle, the two porcelain-faced dolls lying haphazardly on top of each other. Rachel rearranged them, sitting each doll up against the side of the cradle, smoothing out their dresses. She'd always hated those dolls. The baby, with its thick black eyelashes and hard, uncuddly head, and the older girl, with the painted-on eyes and the fake, tangled curls.

Rachel unpacked Deirdre's clothes next, folding the onesies next to the few pairs of infant pants she'd brought, the little button-up jacket and hand-knitted baby sweater (a gift from her aunt Linda) next to each other in a single drawer, wondering if her own lack of interest in dolls as a child was some kind of reflection on her instinctual nurturing abilities, whether it said something about her as a mother. She knew women who went nuts for infant clothes, who actually spent good money on booties, which never, ever stayed on a baby's foot, who shopped at The Children's Place and Gap Kids, spending absurd sums on stylish outfits that their kid would wear maybe twice, if they were lucky. These mothers had probably played with dolls. Deirdre's baby clothes were either hand-me-downs from Derek's kids, sales rack items at Target, or grabbed pieces from the kids' consignment shop right next to the grocery store, when all the onesies were in the wash.

Rachel hung the empty duffle in the closet, knocking a hanger to the floor. The other hangers danced on the rod, just as they used to when she hung up the one dress she'd bring every summer at her mother's insistence. There it would hang undisturbed all summer. She used to like unpacking—choosing how to arrange her clothes in the drawers, her hairbrush and hair ties on top of the dresser, everything neat to begin with, though it all became a scattered jumble within a few days. It was a kind of meditation, that ritual, a laying out of her summer self. Each year, when she returned, she felt the jump in her age and understanding since she'd been there last, and so the unpacking of her stuff and arranging it in the room was a way of dreaming this older Farm-self into being. What would she do this summer? Perfect her tennis serve, finally? Learn those impossible piano pieces from Linda's old book of Mozart Sonatas? Get Grand to teach her how to make perfect fudge? Any and all of these were possible, and while she unpacked, she'd dream of them, plan who to be, make promises to herself, a set of resolutions that she rarely carried out. The whole time she was making them, she knew in the back of her mind that she'd spend this summer in some variation of the same old way: running around with Joe, tramping through the woods, splashing in the lake, dreaming up futures. Sooner or later, he would appear at the door of the house, and she'd run out and they'd stare at each other, examining how the other had grown in the past year, and that's how the summer would begin.

Rachel set the box of nursing pads on the dresser, next to the diaper wipes, the digital ear thermometer, and the extra pacifiers. She put the single toiletry item she'd remembered to bring for herself—a cherry-flavored ChapStick—upright on the corner of the dresser. She dressed in a pair of loose-fitting jeans and a T-shirt. In the bathroom, she washed her face and squirted a seed of toothpaste on her finger. She discovered an abandoned hairbrush in a drawer, which she dragged through her hair before gathering it all into a ponytail. Deirdre's squeals had turned to fitful cries; Rachel hurried downstairs, following the sound of them out to the wrap-around porch.

There she found Diane sitting in a wicker chair, bouncing a crying Deirdre on her lap. In the corner, on the chaise longue, lay Grand, or rather, a pale, skeletal impression of Grand, her legs covered by the old tartan blanket they used to snuggle under in the cool summer mornings when Rachel was a girl.

"Grand." Rachel went to take Grand's hands in her own; they were as light as birchbark. "Oh, Grand." She looked centuries older than when Rachel had seen her last—which had been when? Last year's Christmas at Aunt Linda's? Or had it been the year before? Oh, she'd been a bad granddaughter. Neglectful, self-absorbed. That would end now.

Grand pulled her hands away, holding them to her chest as if Rachel might steal them.

Rachel looked to Diane, alarmed. Diane nodded reassuringly at Grand. "It's all right, hon," she chirped over Deirdre's wails. "It's Rachel, remember? Your granddaughter. She's woken up. After a very short nap, I must say. I thought you'd at least give us a couple hours to enjoy this little one."

Rachel went to Diane and took Deirdre in her arms, jiggling her in the motion that had, in a few short months, become involuntary. Immediately, the crying stopped.

"Rachel, Rachel, honey," said Grand, suddenly sure of herself. "Here, come give me a kiss."

Her arms felt like branches on Rachel's shoulders, her lips dry berries on her cheek. Rachel perched on the edge of the chaise, beside Grand's sticks of legs.

"Don't look so shocked, dear!" Grand chuckled, patting Rachel's hand. "Do I look that bad?"

"No, no. I'm sorry. I didn't mean—"

"I may be a little thinner, but I'm still your grandmother."

"Even more so, now that she's had her coffee. Right, Maddy? Coffee helps her clarity of mind."

"Lord knows I can use all the help I can get these days."

Rachel cleared the huskiness from her throat. "It's good to see you, Grand."

"And you, darlin'. Diane and I were just going over how long it's been. She was saying eight years? Can that really be true?"

"No!" Rachel barked. "No, Grand. That's how long it's been since I've been up *here*, at the Farm. But we've seen each other many times in the last eight years. Last Christmas at Linda's, for one. And regular Thanksgivings at Mom and Dad's place in Maine. Family gatherings. We've seen each other at all of those. Diane probably wasn't aware of those."

"Oh, of course! I'd forgotten all that. Well, then I must have seen the baby before."

"Well, no. Not the baby, Grand. Deirdre's only three months old. Last time we saw each other, I was still pregnant." As she uttered this, she realized that it was a lie: it had to have been the Christmas before last. Michael hadn't wanted her to travel this past Christmas, even though the doctor had said it would be fine.

"Anyway, she is *some*thing." Grand reached to touch Deirdre's leg, which was clamped around Rachel's waist. "Fattest thighs I've ever seen. And that head! Too many brains for her own good. Just like her mother." She coughed into a Kleenex.

"She's ninety-fifth percentile for her head size. Michael says her head's from his Uncle Max, but I think it's Granddaddy."

"Oh, yes. Your Granddad had to have hats made specially."

"Here we go again with the heads!" Diane interjected. "Whenever heredity and the Clayborne family comes up, we always have to talk about the heads."

Grand snickered, but Rachel bristled. "Well, I guess it's just a fact about the family. Every family has their common traits."

"That's for sure."

Rachel eyed Diane, feeling as if there were some insult lurking beneath her words, but her expression was unreadable, as usual. She turned back to Grand. "So how are you feeling? You doing all right? I mean, I know you're not . . ."

"Oh, I'm still here. That's the best I can say. But what about you, dear? How do you like being a mother?"

"Honestly, Grand, I think I'm too sleep-deprived to be able to answer that fairly. I'm going to have to say the jury's still out on that one."

Diane piped in. "Motherhood will throw you, that's for sure. It's a whole new universe."

"Well, in my defense, I was never really around many babies until now. And no one told me how bad it could get, the sleep thing. Or lack thereof."

"I wasn't attacking you," Diane said.

Rachel flinched. "What?"

"You said, 'in my defense.' But there was nothing to defend yourself from."

"I was simply terrified when your father was born," Grand said, unfazed.

"Were you, Grand?"

"Oh, my, yes. Of course in those days, there were more people around to help. My mother stayed with us for weeks, doing the housework, showing me how to bathe him, to clip his little fingernails. And then other women in the neighborhood were home with their little ones, too. We'd help each other, take the babies to the park together."

"It sounds nice."

"None of us mothers worked then, of course. I don't know how you all do it these days. Everyone so busy."

"People sending their babies off to day care at three weeks," Diane said.

"I'm not working," Rachel rushed to add. "Not right now, anyway. I took a semester off from my coursework. I'll be going back in the fall, of course. But Michael's schedule is fairly flexible, and so with some babysitters here and there . . ." She couldn't help but feel that Diane was judging her every word. It made her skittish.

"Of course you will, darlin'. It's not complicated, you know. All you have to do is love them." Grand tickled the bottom of Dee's foot, and she cooed in response. "How is Michael, anyway? Working hard, I expect?"

"Oh, yes. Always. But he's good. He loves being a daddy. Unequivocally, actually. He would have answered your question with "unqualified enthusiasm.""

"My question?"

"I have to admit," Diane cut in. "I'm surprised to see you up here, Rachel. I mean, beyond you arriving out of the blue. I thought you and Michael had declared you wouldn't be returning to the Farm."

Rachel gaped at Diane. Why bring up such an unpleasant subject, if not to prove something to Grand? If not to underscore some kind of agenda? Maybe her father was right. Coolly, she replied, "That was a long time ago. We did have certain—" the word *reservations* popped into her mind, and she searched for a less loaded term, "—*views*, I guess you could say. But that's in the past. And anyway, I really wanted Grand to see Deirdre." She turned back to Grand. "Would you like to hold the baby, Grand?"

"Oh! Would I! But what if I drop her?" She looked to Diane.

"You'll do no such thing." Diane was on her feet. "Rachel and I will be right next to you. We'll spot you."

"I can spot her on my own," Rachel said, but Diane tucked herself between the chaise arm and Grand, as if she hadn't heard.

"Well, if you're sure," Grand said.

"Hold out your arms, Grand."

Grand's hands trembled in the air.

"She's hefty for a three-month-old."

"All right. I'm ready."

Rachel laid Deirdre face-up in the crook of Grand's arms, gradually releasing her weight. When she finally let go, Grand tipped forward. "Oh!" she said. Immediately, Rachel's arms were beneath Grand's, and Diane's body blocked the route to the floor. Grand righted herself, then leaned back against the chaise, Deirdre's weight against her chest. Baby and great-grandmother gazed at each other.

"There, now," Diane cooed. Rachel relaxed.

"She is hefty, isn't she?" Grand said.

Deirdre's face spread into a big, goofy grin. They all laughed.

"She likes you, Grand!"

"Who doesn't like Maddy?"

"She's absolutely precious."

But Deirdre's smile flickered into discontent. She began nuzzling the inside of Grand's elbow.

"Oh! Oh! She's kissing me!"

"She's probably hungry. Again. That's all she does, really, is eat. Her favorite activity."

"Well, of course," Grand replied. "She's got to grow, doesn't she?"

Deirdre slurped at Grand's arm, as if aiming for a hickey. She began to fuss.

"Oh, she's unhappy. Poor Deirdre," Grand purred. "Your momma's right here."

"Sorry, Grand." Rachel lifted Deirdre out of Grand's arms. "You can hold her again, later."

"See now?" Diane said. "You didn't drop her."

"It's been a long time since I've held a baby," Grand said dreamily. "I'd forgotten that sweet smell."

"Yeah, that's pretty great, isn't it?" Rachel took a seat on the wicker loveseat across from Grand.

"I'm so glad you came, darlin'! What a gift!"

"Me, too, Grand. Seeing you hold Deirdre was worth a night's sleep any day."

Diane jumped to her feet, as if she'd been pricked. "Well, I'll let you two catch up. I've got to get the blueberry muffins from the oven." And she whisked her way out of the room.

Rachel shifted Deirdre to a nursing hold, puzzling over Diane's suspiciously sudden exit.

"You're breastfeeding!" Grand exclaimed.

"Yes. Didn't you, Grand?"

"Oh, no dear. I was too vain. Thought I'd lose my shape. Course back then we thought that baby formula was more nutritious. What we didn't know!"

Rachel smiled at Grand's familiar self-deprecating patter. "You knew plenty, Grand."

They listened for a moment to Deirdre's humming swallows, to the pines rustling above the house. "You and Diane have known each other a long time, haven't you?"

"Oh, my, yes. A very long time."

"How long?" Then, worrying that her question sounded too pointed, she added, "Just out of curiosity."

"Well, now. Diane was Mary's granddaughter. I knew her father when we were children."

"Mary. Who's Mary?"

"Mary was our cook back then. She made all the meals for us, every summer."

"Like Diane did when I was a girl."

"I suppose so. But Mary was a hard one. Not like Diane. Never a smile on her face. She and her husband lived in the old caretaker's cabin out by the chicken shed. And we children were terrible to them. I remember one summer we snuck into the henhouse with a stove iron and cracked every egg we found. That was the only time Father ever spanked us. We deserved it, of course."

"Wow, Grand. I never knew you were such a terror."

"Oh, we ran wild up here. Which was part of the reason Mother hated it so. She didn't like Indians, and Mary was Indian. Or—Native American, I suppose I should say. From the reservation down the road. Now, her husband, the caretaker, he was no Indian. He had the yellowest hair I'd ever seen on a grown man. They had two children, two boys. One of them was my age, and I loved him from afar. A handsomer boy you never saw. That was Diane's father, Robert. But Mother wouldn't let us near those boys. Thought they'd be the undoing of us. Still, we girls used to sneak around, spying on them. We must have galled them no end . . ." she trailed off into silence, her eyes distant.

"So, then, you've known Diane since she was born?"

"Diane? Oh, no. No, we lost touch with the family when we sold the Farm. No, it wasn't until much later that Diane and I met. She'd just had her baby, her little boy."

"Joe."

"That's right. Joe was his name."

A loud screeching, like the repetitive creaking of a rusty hinge, came from the trees above. Grand craned her neck; Rachel, carrying Deirdre, strode to the screen door, pushed it open with an elbow, and stepped down onto the pine-needled ground. Just then, the adult eagle soared in off the lake, a fresh catch in its talons. It dropped the food in the nest, and sat on a branch a few feet off while the juvenile ate, cheeping throatily. Rachel stepped back inside, letting the door slam shut behind her. "Sunfish for breakfast," she said. "Yum."

"Sunfish? I thought we were having blueberry muffins."

"I meant for the eagle."

"Oh! Of course. Do you remember, darlin', how you used to go out on the lawn with the binoculars and just watch the eagles for hours at a time? You always loved them so."

"I still do. And I love how they keep coming to this nest year after year. You know, eagles are usually very touchy when they're nesting. That's what all the literature says. People are supposed to keep their distance. But these ones don't seem to mind us. They're used to us, I guess."

"Yes. Mutual respect, that is. We let each other be."

Rachel sat back down on the edge of Grand's chaise. She unlatched a drowsy Deirdre and switched her to the other breast. She would be asleep in a couple of minutes. What she *should* do right now was take Deirdre upstairs and finish feeding her in bed, where they could both fall asleep. Rachel was aching for sleep, and she knew she'd be an anxious wreck later on if she didn't get a nap.

But there was Grand, her cloud of white hair, her kind, leathery face, her wide open eyes, staring lovingly at Deirdre. She hadn't talked like this with Grand since . . . since she didn't know when. And the chance might not come again.

"So, Grand, I'm still curious about something. You said you'd lost touch with Diane's family when you sold the Farm. What did you mean by that?"

"I haven't sold the Farm."

"No, I mean earlier. When you were young."

"Oh! Father sold it. He'd fallen on hard times, and one summer we were simply told that we would no longer be going north, that the Farm no longer belonged to us. Oh, how I wept! I don't think I stopped crying for three straight days."

"So then how'd you end up owning the Farm as an adult if your father sold it when you were a kid?"

"He bought it back and gave it to Jacob and me on our wedding day."

"*Really?*"

"He'd never wanted to sell, and when I got engaged to your grandfather, the timing just happened to work out. Father knew how much I loved this place, how I'd held it inside me all those years. It was the best gift anyone ever gave me."

"I bet it was." Grand's words rang in Rachel's ears: *how I'd held it inside me all those years.* That's how it felt; those were the words for it. Rachel had held the Farm inside her all these years, like a dormant seed. Being here once more with Grand, it felt like sunlight flooding in. The seed was trembling, a new sprout breaking through its shell into the light. "That's just how I feel," she admitted, in a low voice. "That I've been holding this place inside me. I never meant to stay away so long."

"Didn't you though, dear?" Grand's voice was gentle, but the question still stung.

"No! Honestly, Grand. I know it must seem that way. But, really, Michael's the one with the strong feelings about this place. He's such a—" she caught herself, began again, "He's such a stickler when it comes to matters of principle."

"A good quality."

"He can't stand hypocrisy. And, you know, he's supposed to be—he *is*—an expert on modern Indian land tenure issues, so ever since he finished his dissertation, he's felt it would be a betrayal of his entire belief system to even set foot on this land again. And I guess I just went along with it. Not wanting to rock the boat."

"I see."

"But the fact is, Grand, that he doesn't really understand this place, what it's meant to me, to our family." Rachel spoke quickly, letting herself gush because she knew Grand would listen and sympathize, and because it felt good—it felt really, really good—just to let the words run. "I mean, this place has been a gift to me, too, my whole life. Coming up here again, it feels like coming home. We've moved around so much, and Mom and Dad have moved—nowhere else really feels like home. Except here."

She stopped. Grand looked worried.

"Sorry, Grand. Am I talking too much?"

"No, no, dear." With obvious effort, Grand leaned forward and grasped Rachel's knee. "It's good to hear you talk."

Rachel covered Grand's hand with her own. "I think I've just been working so hard," she went on, "at being the person I thought I should be—good student, teacher, wife, mother—trying to fit perfectly into all these molds. But none of them *feel* right. It's like I've been forcing myself into tighter and tighter clothes until I just can't even breathe anymore!"

Grand released Rachel's knee and slumped against the chaise seat. She closed her eyes, and the crease between her brows made it look like she was in pain.

"God, listen to me. I came here to be a comfort to you, and the first thing I do is lay all this crap on you. I mean junk. All this junk."

"Don't be silly, dear," Grand said. "I just tire a little more quickly than I used to. Sometimes I need to rest my eyes a bit." She opened them once more and smiled weakly. "But I can't tell you how glad I am to see you. How glad that you thought to come and be with me."

"Well, of course! I want to spend as much time as possible with you, Grand. We can play cards, I can read to you, tell you stories, whatever you like."

Grand lay still against the chaise, her breath coming slow and long.

"Should I let you rest, Grand?"

"I am resting, darlin'. Just listening is resting."

"Okay." She paused, watching Grand's bony sternum rise and fall beneath her satin pajama blouse. Grand was dying. Grand, her favorite person in the world. She was leaving this earth; she was half gone already. And Rachel had virtually neglected her for eight years. Her eyes filled and she sniffed, trying to stanch the flow. "I guess I don't have much more to say. I just want you to know that I love this place and I have always loved it. I've missed it and you. And I don't want you to think that I disapprove of it or you in any way because—" she choked on the words, and grabbed a tissue from the box on a nearby table. "Just because, Grand. That's all."

Grand remained quiet, and looked like she'd fallen asleep. Deirdre, too, was sleeping in Rachel's arms. Gently, Rachel stood up from the chaise. Maybe it was nap time after all. She began to tiptoe out of the room, toward the door, when Grand spoke. "This concerns me. I find all of this very disconcerting."

"You do? Why?"

"Well, now. That's a good question, dear. I'm trying to think just why." She trailed off into another long silence while Rachel waited, feeling chagrined. She shouldn't have let herself go on like that. It had obviously upset Grand. She rocked the sleeping Deirdre in her arms. The woven rug pressed into her bare feet, a sensation she knew well from childhood, and she savored it as she rocked, back and forth, soothing the baby, soothing herself.

"It's the strangest thing, though," Grand said, finally. She sat up in a fit of strength. Her eyes were fixed on the opposite wall. "Look, Rachel. Do you see that?"

Rachel followed Grand's pointing finger to the gray clapboard wall. "What, Grand?"

"That house there. Those people." Her finger shook. "Right there. Can't you see them? Right there!" Grand's voice was full of impatience.

Rachel looked closely again at the wall, pretending to scour it for a sign of Grand's vision. Then she stopped. What was she going to do, lie? She went and stood close to Grand, taking care not to get in the way of her trembling finger, not to block her view. "I'm afraid I can't see anything, Grand. Can you tell me about them? What do you see?"

But the moment had passed. Grand slumped once more against the chaise and sighed deeply, shaking her head. "They were right there, poor things. Just sitting on the porch. While all around them the water rose and rose."

6

In the kitchen, Diane tried to calm herself by scrubbing a set of dirty muffin tins with a Brillo pad while a dozen muffins in pastel papers steamed on the counter beside her. Seeing Maddy with Rachel and the baby, it was clear that Maddy wasn't going to say a word about the Farm. And really, how could she? With the baby in her arms, Rachel fairly shimmered with elemental motherhood. How could any woman be expected to disrupt the transcendent moment of greeting a new great-grandchild with something as heavy and earth-bound as the dispensation of property? Certainly not Maddy; Diane knew her too well. No, she'd have to find another way to break the news to Rachel. And from the way she was talking out there, Diane had the feeling that it wasn't going to be easy. Rachel clearly was not as anti-Farm as Diane had thought.

There came the sound of tires on gravel, and she went to the kitchen door to see Joe's red pickup navigating the long drive. He parked beside the tennis court and loped across the lawn, his baseball cap pulled low over his eyes. Even after thirteen years, Diane still shivered when she saw his face: the strange stretched skin around his mouth, the unfamiliar jawline. The docs had done their best, God knows, but there were scars. They ran like two mismatched railroad tracks, from his lips across the plain of his cheek to his ear and down again to his lower jaw. It wasn't the face he'd been born with, the face she'd watched lengthen and sharpen as Joe grew into a man. She still missed that face.

The screen door wheezed open. "Who's driving the fancy Prius?" Joe pushed past her into the kitchen, where he grabbed a muffin from the cooling rack.

"You didn't get my message, I gather."

"Nope."

Diane sighed and took a dishtowel to one of the muffin tins, rubbing it with enough elbow grease to strip off decades' worth of burnt-on butter. "Rachel's here. Rachel Clayborne. I tried to call and warn you, but as usual, you were impossible to reach . . ."

Joe stopped in mid-chew, his eyes flashing to the kitchen door. "No kidding."

"She's out on the porch with Mrs. Clayborne. If you turn around right now, she won't be the wiser."

"Whoa, Ma. Slow down."

"I just thought it might be easier if—"

"She here with her husband?"

"No. But she's got a baby now. A baby girl."

He stuffed the rest of the muffin in his mouth, then looked out at his truck, as if measuring the distance. "You still need that furniture moved, right?"

"It can wait."

"I'm here today."

Diane sighed once more and dried her hands on the dishtowel. "I'll show you what needs moving."

She led him through the living room toward the office, but Joe stopped near the porch door. "Hang on. I'll say hello first. Be polite, like my mother raised me to be."

Rachel appeared in the doorway, Deirdre at her breast, her T-shirt draping over the baby's body. "Oh!" she sputtered. "Oh my God. Joe! Your face. It looks so—so different."

Joe snorted. "Different's a nice word for it."

"No! No—I didn't mean . . . it looks good, Joe. It looks fine. It's just . . ."

"After eighteen surgeries, you bet your life it looks good," Diane interjected, her voice shaking. "His jaw was completely shattered."

"Take it easy, Ma," Joe said. Then, to Rachel, "You look different, too."

"More wrinkly, right? Bags under the eyes? A little like the walking dead?"

"Actually, I was thinking of that baby you've got attached to your middle there. You didn't used to have one of those."

Rachel looked down at Dee, as if she'd forgotten she was there, then blushed and tugged her T-shirt down. When she looked up, Joe was grinning, a big, brazen, lopsided smile. It caught. They stood grinning at each other like idiots, both of them oblivious to Diane, who was looking on with the horrified expression of someone watching a traffic accident.

"Quit that, would you?" Joe said finally.

She broke away, laughing. "Sorry. It's just good to see you." She glanced at the stairs. "Hey—you going to be here a while? Because I was just about to put Deirdre down for a nap. But once she's down . . ."

"Sure. Lots of furniture to move, right Ma?"

Diane glared at him. "Only a sofa and a desk, really. Shouldn't take but a few minutes."

"I'll help you!" Rachel replied. "Just let me put her down, and then I'll be right back." She glided up the staircase, taking care not to jostle Deirdre. Joe watched until she was out of sight, then turned back to Diane.

"Chill out, Ma. We're just moving the furniture."

"I didn't say a word."

"You don't have to say anything. You're bubbling like a geyser over there."

"That's not fair, Joe."

"Truth isn't always fair."

Rachel appeared on the landing once more, the baby still attached. "Sorry, but I got to my room and realized I haven't set up the crib yet. I can't really leave her on the bed—she might roll off."

"It's really not a big job," Diane said.

"Why don't I help you with the crib first?"

"Are you sure? I don't want to take up your time."

"I'm a rich man when it comes to time."

"Well, that'd be great. It's probably in the storage room up here." She gestured up the stairs.

Joe climbed the stairs two at a time, leaving his mother fuming on the living room rug.

Upstairs, Rachel pushed open the door to a musty, unfinished room, packed full of tossed-off odds and ends: a tall wardrobe, one door hanging half open, behind which a few suit jackets hung in plastic dry cleaner bags. A cardboard box jumbled with used tennis shoes sat beneath a filmy window; on a nail hung a few wooden tennis racquets old enough to have been strung with actual catgut. One of them had warped into a curve. A dusty painting of a sailboat tilting on a green lake was propped against the wall next to a plastic shelving unit packed full with stacks of folded beach towels, bed sheets, pillow cases, and mattress pads. The room smelled like a mouse nest. Against another wall, behind a stack of cardboard boxes, leaned the crib parts and a cracked mattress.

Rachel pointed at it with her foot, her hands still holding Deirdre. "That's it."

Joe moved the boxes aside, then lifted the mattress. "Where am I going with this?"

"My old bedroom."

"Right."

She followed him—he remembered the way—around the corner into the pink room, where he set the mattress on the floor, near the dresser. He took a moment to look around.

"You remember how we used to hang upside down off the bed, pretending we were bats?" she said.

He smiled. "I do now."

"Bursting thousands of blood vessels, probably, all that blood going to our brains."

"That would explain a lot." He stood a moment longer, as if on the verge of saying something else, then turned on a heel and went back for the crib.

Rachel knelt beside the mattress, lifted her T-shirt, and unlatched Deirdre. Her mouth worked for a moment, seeking, but she fell back into her doze. Rachel laid her on the crib mattress, then snapped her bra back into place, just as Joe came in with two crib sides, one in each arm.

"She'll be all right on the crib mattress," she spoke fast to cover her embarrassment, "since it's on the floor. The truth is she hasn't rolled over yet, but you never know. She might decide today's the day. I figure it's better to be safe, right? I'd hate for her first experience rolling over to be a bad fall, you know? And plus, she could really hit her head."

Joe raised an eyebrow.

"Am I babbling?"

"Kind of. You want the crib by the window?"

"Sure. Yeah. Wherever it fits."

Together, they brought the rest of the pieces in: three more sides, two metal rails, and four mysterious curved metal rods, as well as a little baggie of hardware. They covered the two twin beds and the empty areas of floor with all the stuff, then stood back and stared at it.

"I should know how to do this," Rachel said. Michael had put their crib together at home. "Maybe Grand has a manual somewhere."

"Real men don't use manuals." Joe picked up one of the metal rails and examined its end.

"Oh ho. Pardon me, *muchísimo macho*."

Grinning that lopsided grin, Joe slid the end of the metal rail over two screws on one side of the headboard. He did the same with the rail's other end and the footboard. Suddenly, the skeletal suggestion of a crib appeared: head and foot, connected.

"Not bad," Rachel said.

"This is what comes on the Y chromosome. Putting things together. That and a passion for explosions."

Rachel laughed. "You sound just like yourself."

"Who else would I sound like?"

"No one. It's just—it's been such a long time."

A loaded silence followed. Joe attached the other side rail, then lifted one of the crib sides and held it in place. "Hand me one of those rods, will you?" He pointed to the bed.

Rachel took one by its curved top and handed it over. "Thirteen years, I guess."

Joe carefully threaded the rod, curve side up, through a hole at the top of the crib side, down through another hole at the base of it, and finally, through a hole in the metal side rail at the bottom, which gave onto a spring. "I guess."

"1991. The year of the perfect little war. It seems almost quaint now, next to all the shit that's gone down over there since."

"We're gonna need a screwdriver." Joe was still holding the crib side in place with one hand, the metal rod in the other. "I've got one in my truck."

"There's probably one around here somewhere."

"I know exactly where mine is. Can you hold this a minute?"

Rachel stepped next to Joe and placed her hands just behind his: one on the crib side, the other holding the metal rod. For an instant, her face was almost touching his shoulder; she smelled wood smoke and sweat, and breathed in, deep.

"Be right back," he said, and left.

Rachel held the rod, savoring his scent. It reminded her of the day he'd pressed her against the workbench in the darkened woodshop. She remembered how his mouth had felt, hot against her collarbone as the workbench jutted into her back. He'd only just found her nipple with his thumb when Diane had appeared, a small shadow vibrating in the doorframe. Rachel had pushed him off; he'd stumbled back, frozen like a trapped animal under the full power of his mother's gaze.

The sound of a motor came through the open window. She craned her neck to look, and was amazed to see Joe's pickup speeding away down the drive.

7

An hour later, Joe stood calf-deep in the lake off Old Bend Island, hunched over his headgear, his body sheathed in a black exposure suit and a buoyancy control device, a nitrox tank on his back. Sal leaped in and out of the canoe that rested on the sloping bank. The water lapped at his flippered feet as he slipped on the mask, then adjusted it so that it fit snugly against his cheeks.

Something had happened to him on his way to get the screwdriver. The farther he'd gotten from Rachel, the farther he wanted to get. As soon as he opened the door of his truck and saw the comforting sight of his crumpled paper coffee cup, the newspaper he'd stuffed into the side pocket of the passenger door, the tear in the seat with the stuffing beginning to poke out around the duct tape he'd used to fix it, he came to his senses. What was he doing, putting together a crib for the girl who'd pissed all over his heart and then pitched it in the nearest dumpster? What the hell did he think he was doing? He'd sat in the driver's seat for a long moment and then he'd driven off, feeling as if he'd just escaped the closing jaws of a trap.

But now, as he waded out into deeper water, readying himself to submerge, he wasn't so sure he'd done the right thing. Rachel had been perfectly nice to him, overly nice, really. Ready to help with the furniture, glad to see him. She'd looked so . . . hopeful, as if he had something to give that she wanted to receive. And he'd left her there, holding the crib together with her hands. He'd messed up, again. He was angry, guilty, and confused, a toxic brew. What he needed, the very thing he needed, was a good dive in the lake.

He swam along the surface for several minutes, out toward the deeper water, counting his kick cycles—about thirty kick cycles took him out far enough—breathing through his snorkel, trying to blow his anger out the tube into the air. Kicking and gliding, he passed over the shallow lake bottom. A walleye darted away into the deeper water ahead, where the lake floor began to slope downward into the sepia-lit underwater world. Twenty-eight, twenty-nine, thirty. Letting his BCD keep him afloat, Joe removed his snorkel and bit on the mouthpiece of his regulator, and then, holding his nose to equalize the pressure in his ears, he dumped the air from his BCD and descended.

Visibility was piss-poor, as usual, but still, it felt good to be in the water, looking around. Diving in the flowage was frowned upon by the tribe. Divers—*white* divers—had been guilty of ripping stuff off from the flooded village and even messing with the graves. But Joe didn't care. He never took or even touched anything from the site. He was a member of the tribe, his family had lived here for generations, he'd lost his jaw to protect this land, and he felt he had a right to time travel a little, to pay homage if he felt like it. He wasn't going to let any top-down tribal edict tell him he couldn't.

Diving calmed him, and diving in the water above Old Bend calmed him in a particular way. When he dove here, he dreamt of the past, of how things once were, years ago, when the people of Bend still riced and sugared and beaded and prayed in their native *Anishinaabemowin*, when the woods were old and tall. He thought of that time as the time before. In his mind, the dam rose up out of the earth like a wedge in space-time, thunked down by a trickster god. There was the time before the dam, and the time after it. Before the dam, the basic proportions of the universe were aligned; before the dam, his great-grandmother Mary had grown up among her siblings, raised by her father and mother and aunts and uncles, moving about through the lost village as easily and naturally as an eagle through the air: provided for, loved, at home. Now, in the time after, Joe spent his days taking care of the very thing that had destroyed his great-grandparents' way of life. The irony was not lost on him.

Nor was he unaware that his vision of the past was romanticized, only partially true. When his great-grandmother was a child, the forests all around the reservation were already being felled, swath by swath; the missionaries had been preaching their barren promises for centuries—promises that had convinced Joe's ancestors, who were regular attendees at the Presbyterian mission near their home; the trading post in the center of town had been established by a French fur trapper, who, from the moment he arrived, doled out liquor and metal goods in exchange for a sustained holocaust on beavers. For years, the men had traveled to work in the lumber camps during the winters, and for years, many of them returned empty-handed, having wasted their money on booze and women on their days off. For generations, the steady lethal encroachment of European-descended society had been unfolding, day by day. Joe knew this. But he preferred to imagine that his great-grandmother had grown up in a world of purity, of stability, of beautiful, choreographed movement—a world that, in his imagination, was like an underwater dream. This was why he dove here, and why he would not be deterred. He felt that somewhere under the flood, the movements of her day were still going on, and if he could only find the right entry point, the right portal, he would find her again.

So far, he'd had little luck. When he'd first begun his underwater excursions here, he'd thought he might discover the actual house his great-grandparents had lived in. He'd studied maps of the old village, and the single picture his mother had of the house—a simple A-frame, painted white, a boulder by the front steps, a small open-air porch—imagining that with enough planning and the help of his compass, he might locate what remained of it. But he'd long since given up that hope. The flowage was not deep—sixty feet, max—nor was it terribly cold, not like Lake Michigan, where centuries-old shipwrecks were preserved in the frigid anaerobic water. Here, the water was warm, hosting legions of encroaching algae and marauding wood-worms that colonized and digested most of the submerged wood. It appeared, in fact, that there were no structures left at all. All that remained of the village, as far as Joe could tell, were remnants of metal objects—old plowshares, sections of stovepipe, fallen window sashes, all covered with a thick layer of concretions. And gravestones. Several gravestones. Joe had run across what he suspected was a drowned churchyard, the ten or twelve remaining gravestones lying flat against the lake bottom, the names long ago washed away. Still, even though the search for his great-grandparents' house was a lost cause, he still tried to get close to where the house might have been, if only for something to focus on, if only to allow the off chance that some small thing—a tin kettle, an iron axe blade—might have survived.

The sunlight dimmed, and Joe switched on his light. Immediately the murky water in front of him revealed itself to be thick with floating algae, particulate seaweed, stray mosquito larvae, darting minnows. A long green-scaled fish passed at the far end of his field of vision, and then another. Joe kicked deeper, the water growing colder, until an old beam, pitted and scarred and covered with a blanket of algae, materialized out of the murk. This was his first landmark, one of the few identifiable remnants of Old Bend. Joe thought it might be a beam from the school, the one his great-grandmother went to as a kid. A few cement blocks were scattered across the bottom here, probably remnants of the foundation. Several yards on, his lamplight played across the narrow cylinder of an old stovepipe, its surface also algae-furred. Just beside it hung the long body of a big fish—a lurking musky, waiting for its lunch. Joe stayed out of view, just in case.

He'd seen a picture of the schoolhouse taken about the time his great-grandmother would have been there, when the building was still new, the logs hewn clean and straight, the cedar-shingled roof fragrant, even in black and white. All the children and their teachers had gathered in front of the building, staring doubtfully into the camera. No one knew whether his great-grandma was even there, but he'd picked out a girl he thought might be her, based on nothing but his own desire. The girl stood off at the edge of the gathered group, a bit older than most, dressed in a handmade shift buttoned up to the throat, her dark hair pulled back from her face. Around her neck was tied a gingham scarf, an apron at her waist, and in one hand she held a slim book while the other gripped the tow-rope of a little toy wagon, in which a chubby little boy sat. The two of them squinted at the camera reluctantly, as if they'd rather return to whatever they'd been doing.

Joe hovered over the spot now, trying, as was his habit, to invoke that picture, that building, filled with life, to imagine that little girl inside the schoolhouse, seated at a rude wooden desk, kicking her legs with fidgety energy. The place would be toasty—a fire burning in the corner stove—and on the wall a set of slates would hang, wiped clean and ready to be marked. The picture appeared momentarily in his mind—the rows of tables and chairs, filled with barely-contained childish exuberance, the stack of primers on the teacher's desk at the front of the room—or maybe there were no primers, maybe they were too poor to have primers, maybe all they had was the harried young teacher, pacing the aisles. The images appeared in a flash and then were gone, and before him lay the lake once again, the negative space of what had once been.

He pointed himself due east and began his kick cycles again, gliding along the bottom in the direction of where his great-grandparents' house would have been, letting his light play across the sand. A circle of stones materialized, and with them a gathering of ghosts—a group of men, poking at a fire; in another spot, a flatiron appeared, half-buried; in a third, a doorknob sprouted from the sand like a mushroom. As he swam, the lake bottom dropped deeper, the penetrating sunlight grew fainter, and the lake weeds that had been brushing his belly gave way to smooth sand. The water felt a few degrees colder. He was suddenly in unfamiliar territory.

He checked his compass and saw that rather than follow his usual course due east, he had somehow drifted into more of an east-southeasterly direction. He moved more slowly now, shining his light all around him, illuminating mostly emptiness, the murky particulate-full lake. He had lost count of his kick cycles, and so wasn't sure how far he'd swum. And then his light played across an enormous round of tree stump, its diameter twice the size of his torso, the interior concentric rings rippling out from the center of the sliced wood. Another—not quite as big, but close—lay a few yards away from the first, and a third not far from the second. He swam on, kicking and gliding, kicking and gliding, shining his torch on stump after stump, each of them cut close to the ground, most of them wider than any stump he'd seen on land. This was a drowned clearcut, a stump field—preserved here because of the colder water—stretching on for as far as his torch would illuminate.

Joe knew about the clearcuts, the way the timber had been harvested en masse from the land that was to be flooded—for why waste good timber? But the width of these stumps and the apparent expanse of the field struck him with awe, and filled his mind with images of what might have been. The men, descending upon the forests like ants on a dropped crumb, armed with crosscut saws and skids. The sounds of cracking branches and the mortal thud of the fallen trees. The rafts of logs floating down the undammed river, collecting by the banks, jamming at the bends. The men leaping across the rolling logs as if they were climbing on the back of some great, cylindrical beast, their peaveys poised like spears. The rivers and the air thick with sawdust, sawdust foaming over the shallows, sawdust lining the lungs, sawdust hanging in the air like the particulate matter hanging in the water in which he now swam. He wondered if his great-grandfather himself had been here, in this spot, sawing through the trunks of these great old trees. And his great-grandmother—would she have watched these woods come down? Would the people have stood on the outskirts of the work grounds, counting the trees as they crashed through the understory? He glided over the drowned clearcut, squinting at the remains of the once-great forest that had grown here.

But it was no use. Rachel was here, too, in the ghost-forest, in the lake. The days they'd spent together as kids tramping through the woods, trying to sustain themselves solely on what they found there: berries, nuts, fiddle-heads in the spring, clover leaves. (The bag lunches his mother packed for them didn't count.) The afternoons splashing in the shallow water, and then, later, when they were teenagers, swimming across the lake to the opposite shore, or paddling for hours in the canoe, looking for otter slides or turtle eggs, surprising the occasional great blue heron that would take silently to the air, its legs stretched in arabesque. That one delicious summer, the summer they'd spent bleary-eyed and sleep-starved, their skin smelling of the lake and of each other. That summer goodbye had been different than all the others: Joe had left for boot camp with the impression that he had himself a girlfriend, and not just any girlfriend, but the romantic affection of his *best* friend, a girl he'd loved as long as he could remember, a girl he'd grown up around like a vine around a tree.

The last time they'd seen each other had been during his ten-day leave late that September, before shipping out to Saudi. He'd bought a ticket to Maine, where Rachel was at school, not Wisconsin (his mother was pissed at him for months), and had used the bulk of his paycheck on a room at the Waterville Holiday Inn. He fantasized all day, every day about the week they'd have together, and, being nineteen at the time, his fantasies tended to hover around the king-sized bed in the hotel room, where he imagined they'd spend most of their time. As it turned out, Rachel was only partly willing to go along with his plans. She agreed to stay with him in the room, but she wouldn't skip her classes or blow off her homework, so rather than the orgiastic week he'd imagined, it turned into eight days of sweating through seven-mile runs, working out in the hotel fitness room, and jacking off in front of the TV, waiting for Rachel.

She was always worth the wait, though. She'd come in, drop her bag on the floor, kick off her shoes and fall into bed with him. He could still get a boner, thinking of those nights lying naked beside her, on top of her, beneath her, all mixed up in her hair, her arms, her legs. They'd fuck fast as rabbits right when she returned, then order some pizza or Chinese and watch the news while they ate, and then fuck again, longer and sweeter, taking their time. Rachel would always insist then that she had to study, and she'd make an honest attempt, but he couldn't keep his hands off her: he'd play with her hair, nuzzle her hip with his eye socket, kiss her appendectomy scar that led like a trail down her belly, or just travel his fingers lightly beneath her shirt, until he reached her bra, which he'd unclasp—because what else do you do with a bra strap when you're nineteen?—and then they'd be at it again, long into the wee hours.

That was late September of 1990. Things were heating up at that point in the Gulf—Saddam had invaded Kuwait, declaring it Iraq's nineteenth Province. He'd shipped international hostages to targets throughout the country to act as human shields; hundreds of thousands of Iraqi Republican Guard were digging in at the Saudi border. When he and Rachel weren't joyously fucking, they would cling to each other, naked, in front of CNN, watching Joe's fate unfold. One night, Saddam trotted out a seven-year-old British kid, one of his hostages, and tousled his hair in front of the camera, asked him if he was getting his cornflakes. The kid's face was as pale as a mushroom cloud. Rachel whispered, "What a bastard," under her breath, and Joe declared that Saddam deserved whatever hell he was unleashing upon himself. Then they turned the TV off and fucked themselves into forgetfulness.

Generally, they were silent about Iraq. Joe knew Rachel didn't want war, that Bush's willingness to risk American lives—Joe's life—to defend the country's oil interests disgusted her. And Joe didn't want war either, at least in theory. But he wanted to prove himself, to wield the power that his newfound incarnation—Marine, warrior, strong and capable man—seemed to demand of him, and if it came to war, he wanted to fight. Two days after he returned to base, he'd be on his way to Saudi, where he would be deployed for the next six months. And the drumbeat was steady and growing.

On their last day together, Rachel came home early, having blown off her bio lab. She carried a bouquet of roses and a box of condoms, which they'd torn open right away. After their first I-missed-you-all-day fuck, Rachel suggested they eat out. "Somewhere special," she said. Joe would have preferred to stay in and make the night special in the usual way, but he acquiesced. Rachel insisted they dress up—she went into the bathroom to change. Joe donned his dress blues: sky blue pants, midnight blue jacket with red trim and brass buttons, white web belt, and white barracks cover, emblazoned with a gilt Eagle, Globe and Anchor. In the full-length mirror on the back of the hotel door, he thought he looked pretty damn good.

When Rachel appeared in a little black dress with a devastating neckline, Joe whistled low. "That dress doesn't exactly help your cause of going out," he said. "It makes me want to tear it right off."

But Rachel looked wounded. "Why are you wearing *that*?"

"You wanted to dress up. Not too shabby, right?" He struck a pose and saluted.

"You look great," she said sadly.

He dropped his hand. "You don't like the uniform."

"No! No, it's not that. I just wasn't expecting it."

They drove to the restaurant—a vegetarian place on a hill a few miles outside of town. They were the youngest people there by far, and Joe couldn't help but notice that they'd steered clear of campus town, where Rachel might have been likely to run into one of her friends. Still, it was a nice place, and they had a delicious meal, and were treated respectfully by the wait staff. The owner quizzed Joe about his service, and Joe replied proudly, playing the role of the disciplined young Marine. Rachel brooded, and only spoke to him in single syllables the whole rest of the meal. He pretended it was because the black bean burger with chipotle cream sauce was so mouth-watering.

On the way home, she gave him to understand otherwise. "It's not some game, you know, Joe," she said, staring straight ahead, her knuckles white against the black steering wheel.

"I'm not playing games, Rach. I'm only trying to keep everyone's spirits up."

They were headed north, back toward town and their by-now-claustrophobic little hotel room, but Rachel wrenched the wheel to the right and made a U-ey, throwing Joe against the passenger door. He stared at her, but she ignored him, her eyes dangerous.

She navigated the night roads several miles to a darkened parking lot by a woods. She pulled into the lot, the headlights playing briefly on a sign that read "Closed After Sundown." She parked the car and turned off the engine.

"Come on," she said.

He followed her along a narrow path into the dark woods. The moon was high and full that night and it cast some light on the path. Rachel walked barefoot before him, dress shoes in her hand, the nape of her neck glowing in the moonlight. She walked at the cusp of a run, dancing over roots and stones. Joe kept pace with her, though his pants were stiff and his smooth-soled shoes unequipped for rough terrain. As they ran, he became aware of the significance of the moment: it seemed that they were running down the knife edge of time, both surrounded by and creating the pulsing, tremulous unfolding of it, striving to touch it, hold it, taste it even as it passed into memory.

The path opened onto a secluded strip of beach curving around the narrow bay, the sand fine-grained and smooth. The night was calm, and the water licked the shore lazily. To their right, a peninsula rose out of the water, and on its modest cliff perched a small house with two lighted windows. Wood-smoke rose from the chimney, even though the night was warm, and the scent of the smoke drifted their way. To their left a few small sailboats moored in a little marina, their masts shipped. The night waves knocked rhythmically against their hulls.

Rachel stood in the sand, looking out over the dark ocean, her back to Joe. She wore a fuzzy shawl around her shoulders and her hair was pinned up. The breeze blew a few tendrils against her neck. Joe lifted the stray hair and pressed his lips into the cool of her skin, smelling her heady combination of flower, spice, and salt. He felt dizzy with desire—he wanted to dive inside her mouth, to crawl beneath her skin, to pour himself out into a tonic for her to drink. He nibbled her neck, kissed the hollow between her collarbone and throat. His hands traveled her hips, pressed against her belly, climbed the ladder of her ribs—

But she turned, abruptly, and spoke sharply to him. "I'm not kidding, Joe. This isn't a game. I don't want you to go. You don't have to go."

He stepped back, startled. "I do, actually, Rach. I mean, it's against the law for me to desert."

"So break the law. You wouldn't be the first person in history. We're not so far from Canada, here. We could just drive north, over the border, and we'd be in Quebec. Six hours away. We could do it tonight."

"Rachel."

"Why are you doing this? I don't get it. Why did you go off and become a Marine? Why do you want to fight for a country that has treated your family and all your ancestors like shit for generations? It doesn't make any sense! It's stupid, Joe! It's stupid of you!" She was crying now, yelling at him through her tears. He tried to wipe them away, but she swatted his hand off her face. "Don't patronize me, Joe! I'm asking a serious question. Answer me!"

He backed away. A lighted window in the house on the ledge went dark, leaving one lit, its yellow glow leaping and flickering. He imagined the people inside: a man, squatting by the fire, stoking it with a poker, a woman, curled on a sofa, reading. Rachel stood before him, glowering over her wet cheeks, the light in her eyes like the flickering window. "I can't explain it to you, Rachel," he said, finally. "Every time I try, you don't believe me."

"Because everything you tell me is bullshit! You say you want to defend the *land*, not the country. That it's 'an Indian thing,' I wouldn't understand. As if just because other Indians think it's cool and, I don't know, somehow *Indian* to be a warrior, it means you should go ahead and do it."

"See, that's what I mean—you act like my reasons are stupid. What do you want me to say? They may be stupid to you, Rachel, but they're not to me. They're real reasons to me."

"They're rationalizations, Joe. I think the only real reason you want to fight is because you want to be a big, tough man, and the only way to show that you're a big, tough man is to go out and squash a bunch of weaklings."

"Saddam Hussein is not exactly a weakling, Rachel. He's just invaded Kuwait. He's appropriated their oil wells. He's threatening to take out Israel. He's boasting about nuclear warheads. He's gassed thousands of his own citizens. The man's an insane criminal, Rachel. Are we all supposed to just stand back and let him have his way with the entire Middle East? Because we don't want to get hurt?"

"So big Joe Bishop, big Marine Joe Bishop is going to go over there and whup some Hussein ass. Show that bully who's boss."

"Rachel, for Christ's sake."

"Don't you see what a crock it all is, Joe? How they're pumping you up, giving you this ultra-dapper uniform, making you feel like the big man, piling guns and ammo on you, just so they can send you over there and get you killed? Just so we can be sure we have enough petroleum to power our minivans and speedboats and big fat 747s over here? Don't you *see* that, Joe?" She was crying again, furiously. The moon shone on a taut tendon at her neck.

"Who else is going to fight the wars, Rach?" he asked quietly. "Who else but the young warriors? It's always been that way."

"Always doesn't mean right."

"Maybe not. But right isn't always the way things go."

She glared at him, then dropped abruptly to her knees. He thought she'd been hurt somehow, or maybe so weakened by her own anger that she'd lost her balance, and he went to her, arms outstretched. But she dug her hand into the sand, and threw a fistful of it at his chest. Some of it sprayed into his mouth. He spat. "What the fuck?"

"I hate that stupid uniform." She threw another fistful of sand at his belly this time, and he saw she was aiming for the clothes, not his face. "Those fucking shiny buttons, and the fancy red stripes down your jacket. That stupid hat. You look like you should be playing in a fucking marching band, Joe." Fizz, fizz—the sand hit his chest, his side. He began to dance for her, turning to supply her with clean targets of cloth, feeling the soft sandy explosions against his belly, ribs, and back.

"Take it off," she demanded finally, sitting back on her heels. "Take the fucking thing off, Joe."

He looked up at the one lighted window of the house on the cliff.

"No one's around. No one's looking. Just take it off." Her voice was low and serious.

He started with his barracks cover, which he set gently in the sand, the Eagle, Globe, and Anchor winking in the moonlight, and then unclasped the white belt before unbuttoning each of the buttons on his jacket. He slipped his arms from the sleeves, then folded it carefully, creasing it as he'd been taught. Beneath his jacket, he wore a plain white shirt, which he also unbuttoned, then folded and creased it, too, and laid it on top of the jacket and cover. He unbuttoned his pants and stepped out of them. He knew he would be excoriated by one of his officers if they saw him putting his dress blues in a pile on the sand—creased or not—but there were no supervising officers here. Only Rachel, kneeling before him, her shawl splayed across the sand, her shoulders gleaming in the moonlight. He stepped out of his briefs and dropped them on his folded uniform, and then stood naked before her, his dick pointing to the stars.

"That's better," she said. Then she stood, and in a single motion, lifted her dress over her head and tossed it on the ground near her shawl. She shook off her bra and panties, then went to him and wiped the stray grains of sand from his chin and cheeks. He lifted her in his arms, she wrapped her legs around him, and like this, he carried her step by step out into the water, where they stood and fucked and wept, and then swam together into the glassy bay, their moonlit skin like phosphorescent schools of fish, diving and surfacing.

When Rachel's teeth began to chatter, they came ashore, and Joe wrapped her in his arms and breathed hot air onto her breasts and belly and thighs to warm her. "Please, Joe," she murmured sleepily. "Let's just escape to Canada. Tomorrow morning we can pack up and go. We could be there by tomorrow night, start our lives up there, together."

"And what will we do there, Rach?" he whispered.

"I don't know. Wait tables. Bartend. Man tollbooths. Raise goats. Who cares?"

"And if they come looking for me?"

"They won't. We'll just lay low for a while. A long while. They'll forget about you eventually. They're too busy fighting their stupid wars."

"We could build a little cabin in the woods."

"Yeah, like pioneers."

"Like Indians."

She pinched him, he laughed. "Okay, like Indians. You could make me into your Indian princess."

"I could go hunting, bring home the meat."

"And I'd tend the garden and gather the berries."

Their voices grew quiet and barely audible, a low hum of sound over the knocking of the waves against the hulls and the gentle lapping of water on the shore.

Eventually, when they both got too tired to talk, they pulled their clothes on and made their way back to the car. Joe was not half as tired as Rachel, who had stayed up late the previous night studying, so he drove while she dozed on his shoulder. When he pulled into the hotel parking lot, it was close to 2:00 a.m., and by the time they'd found the room, and Rachel had fallen into bed, still wearing her dress, it was 2:13. Joe took off his dress blues, brushed each piece briskly with the back of his hand and shook it out several times, trying to knock off any clinging grains of sand, and then creased it once more and put it in his suitcase. Quietly, he packed the rest of the clothes he'd brought, put on his desert camo and boots, and kissed Rachel on the top of the head. He checked his watch. 2:42. It was seven miles to the bus station, and the first bus to the airport left at 4:00 a.m. He'd better start walking.

That was the last time they'd seen each other.

What would she think of his life now, was the question? He'd built a good, honest life for himself out here by the dam. He lived in a yurt, not a cabin, but still, it was the same idea—something like the dream they'd shared together, that night. The days spent checking the levels, picking up trash, adjusting the gates, swimming, diving, hiking. Maintaining, most-ly. Your garden-variety maintenance man. Would she approve? Would she judge him, like his mother did? And why did he care, anyway? She'd dumped him thirteen years ago, when he needed her most. Why was he hung up still? He liked his life. Why should he give a fuck what anyone thought of it, especially Rachel Clayborne?

Well, apparently he did. Rachel was back, and her presence, the sight of her newly lined face, her tense mouth, her baby—already it was changing everything. He felt as if he was looking out at his own life through a scuba mask, seeing it through dimly-lit waters. All its colors were washed out, its edges softened and furred in algae. What had he been doing all these years, anyway? It seemed to him that he had only been coasting along, managing largely by pushing Rachel out of his mind.

Joe took a deep breath of the nitrox mix through his regulator and checked his air gauge: the nitrox was getting low. Time to resurface. The usual magic wasn't working this morning anyway. The week of rain had made the already-bad visibility even worse. His heart wasn't in it. He switched off his torch and kicked upward, toward the light.

When he reached the surface, he popped his head out like a seal and, treading water, removed his mouthpiece to breathe some fresh, uncannis-tered air. It took him a moment to reconnoiter—he looked around at the surrounding land, trying to establish where he'd ended up. He identified Old Bend Island—he could see the canoe on the bank—but Sal was gone.

He refastened the snorkel in his mouth, then swam a strong crawl to-ward the island, where he stepped onto the beach. He shed the heavy tank from his back and took off his mask and snorkel. Dog footprints led up the beach to the woods.

"Sal!" he called.

A moment later, Sal emerged, wagging her entire body. The smell reached him before she did.

"Uch, Sal! What did you find?"

She rubbed up against him, but he pushed her away: her fur was streaked with a slime that smelled like animal carcass.

"You earned yourself a bath, girl." Grabbing a stick from the edge of the woods, he waded into the water again, calling her to him. He used the stick to scrub away the smears of death, then tossed the stick aside and pushed the canoe into the water.

Sal tried to follow him into the boat, but he put a hand on her chest. "No, girl. You stink. You can swim." And he pushed off shore, pulling stroke by stroke through the water, while Sal doggie-paddled alongside.

8

Once Rachel realized that Joe was not coming back, she found their screwdriver and tightened the screws herself. Having watched Joe slide one of the metal rods into place, she managed to do the same with the other three, smarting all the while at his abrupt exit.

When she'd finished assembling the crib, Rachel stretched out on the twin bed and sank immediately into a deep slumber, which lasted for a good fourteen minutes before Deirdre squeaked awake. Drowsily, Rachel lifted Dee from the crib mattress and fed her while she dozed a while longer. Eventually, Dee began squirming to be upright, so Rachel dragged herself out of bed, hooked Deirdre into her front pack, and shuffled downstairs to the kitchen, where she descended upon the blueberry muffins cooling on the rack. Diane caught her peeling the paper off a third muffin while she was still chewing the second.

"These are delicious," Rachel said, spitting crumbs.

"There you are. I thought maybe you'd gone off somewhere with Joe."

"Oh, no. No. I was napping. Joe left. I guess he must have forgotten about something he had to do."

Diane pursed her lips. Rachel held the last bite of muffin out of the reach of Deirdre, who was trying to grab it. She stuffed it in her mouth.

"I meant to ask you, Diane. The weirdest thing happened earlier," Rachel went on, after she'd properly swallowed. "Grand seemed to be having some kind of hallucination. She pointed to the wall and said something about people on a porch, and water rising around them . . ."

"Hmm," Diane said. "That's new."

"Is that from her medication or something?"

"Possibly. It could be the meds."

"You don't sound convinced."

"Well, it's hard to say exactly what it is. But—" she hesitated.

"Go on."

"Often when people get closer to death, they start having visions like the one you're describing. It's a recognized stage of passing."

Rachel's eyes welled. She stepped onto the back porch. Diane followed.

"Listen," Diane continued. "I'm just trying to be straightforward. I figured since you're here, you'd want to know the nitty-gritty."

"It's okay. I do. I just have this crying problem lately. It's like a reflex." She wiped her eyes.

"She was actually quite alert for some time this morning, though. While you were napping. She played with the baby. We chatted a while. I think your presence helped her focus."

"How much does she know about what's going on? I mean, do you think she's anticipating her own death?"

"Well, of course. When she's alert, I think she's completely aware of what's happening. She's refused to set foot in another hospital, remember. I don't think she has a sense of how long exactly it will be, but sure, she thinks about it."

"Do the doctors know? How long, I mean?"

"Didn't your father talk with you about all this?"

"He might have. I haven't been operating at a hundred percent brain power lately."

"The neurosurgeon who met with them said we were looking at probably three to six months, if we didn't operate. The operation could have extended that period by a year or more. But the risk of complication was very high—it always is in an older person."

"Three months? And he said this how long ago?"

"About a month."

"And no one's told Grand this?"

"Hey, don't look at me. It's not my decision."

"It just seems like something she might like to know."

"Well, take it up with your father," Diane snapped.

Rachel looked out at the over-long lawn and the old red barn, its roof covered with a thick layer of fallen pine needles. "I guess I wasn't thinking it was going to be that soon."

Diane softened. "No one's ever really ready. No matter how prepared you think you are. It's always a shock at the end."

Rachel sat on to the sagging sofa swing with Deirdre. The springs squeaked with their weight. "Dad warned me she'd been getting confused, but I wasn't really expecting her to seem so—so old." She laughed sadly. "I guess that sounds pretty stupid. I mean she is almost ninety years old, for God's sake. It's amazing she made it this long in such good shape."

"She's an amazing woman."

"She certainly seems to think highly of you."

Diane looked up sharply, as if Rachel had accused her of something. "Why do you say that?"

Rachel, who had been trying for kindness, shrugged. "I can tell."

"Well, she's a good friend."

Rachel stood up. "I think I'll go sit with her a while. Is she still on the other porch?"

"Right where you left her. She's having lunch."

She found Grand sitting upright, a fold-out tray of food perched on her lap. A can of Diet Coke sweated next to her plate while she shakily brought her sandwich up to her lips.

"Hi, Grand!" Rachel kissed the top of her head.

Grand dropped her sandwich onto the plate, spilling out half the tuna. "Look what you made me do!" she spat, in a tone Rachel had never before heard her use.

"Sorry," Rachel murmured, half in shock. She helped shovel as much of the tuna as possible back into the sandwich with one hand, while Deirdre pulled at her hair.

The sandwich mostly salvaged, Rachel sat on the wicker sofa across from Grand, letting Deirdre's legs dangle between her own. Deirdre kicked and cooed, watching Grand, who was making a valiant effort with the sandwich: the shaky hand, the mouth, working, half-open as she chewed. A flake of tuna fell back onto the plate, another onto her chest, where Diane had tied a napkin. A few crumbs of bread clung to her bottom lip, then fell after the tuna.

"Did I hear a man's voice here this morning?" Grand asked after chewing. "I thought I heard a man."

"You did, Grand. Joe was here."

"Who?"

"Diane's son, Joe. You know Joe, Grand."

Grand looked confused. "I suppose. What did he want?"

"He was helping me put together the crib for Deirdre. You remember that old crib? We found it in the storage room upstairs."

"I thought it might have been Father."

"Father? You mean, *your* father?"

"He's been around quite a lot lately. Of course, he loves it up here. Comes every chance he can."

"Does he, Grand?"

"Oh, heavens, yes. Haven't you seen him? Out walking early in the mornings. He always used to get up before anyone else and walk the grounds, just looking at everything. Sometimes he'd bring me back a flower or some berries he'd found. I'm surprised you haven't seen him."

Grand turned her attention to her dish of applesauce, scooping a spoonful to her mouth, her hand trembling dangerously. She nabbed at the spoon like a praying mantis striking, and succeeded: a clean bite, no spill. She beamed.

"You loved him a lot, didn't you, Grand?"

Grand looked surprised. "Of course. And you know, I've given it a lot of thought. I'm sure that if he'd known about Mary's father's feelings, he never would have agreed to the deal. He wasn't the sort of person who would go behind someone else's back, just to get something he wanted. That wasn't him at all."

Gently, Rachel asked, "Mary, Grand? You mean Diane's Grandmother Mary? The one who—"

"Mary! Our cook! She was just here a little while ago." Grand gestured indignantly toward the house.

Rachel inhaled sharply. "Of course. Silly me."

"Anyway, I'm sure Father agrees with my decision, knowing what he knows now. It's the right thing to do."

"Your decision, Grand?"

"I think what he's doing now is simply saying his goodbyes, making peace with it. If I were in better shape, I'd do it with him."

"Why does he need to say his goodbyes, Grand? Can't he always come back?"

"Oh, no, dear. No. I wish it worked that way. But no, you can never go back."

Rachel waited to see if Grand might say anything further, but she had grown interested in the chocolate chip cookie on her plate. Feeling on the verge of another cry, Rachel stood and moved toward the porch door. She didn't want to burden Grand with her incessant weepiness, especially not twice in one day. "You know, Grand," she said, in an artificially bright voice. "I haven't been down to the lake yet. I think I'll go for a little stroll down there."

Grand, who was now blissfully masticating the cookie, her eyes closed in pleasure, did not say a word.

Rachel left by the porch door, stepping on the soft needled ground with her bare feet. She picked her way over fallen branches, feeling some of the pine needles stick to the soles of her feet with the pitch they'd brought down with them. A little ways from the house, she squatted awkwardly— Deirdre tipping forward in the front pack—to examine a sunfish that had dropped from the eagles' nest. It was almost completely whole, except for a chunk that had been taken out of its head. Why had they dropped it? she wondered. Clumsiness? Petulance? Was the eaglet a picky eater? Poor eagle mother, who'd flown and hunted and dove for that fish, only to have them hurl it out of the nest in disgust.

She continued to the edge of the woods, wincing now and then at the sharp pricks she felt from pebbles and sticks in her path, keeping her eyes trained on the edges of the path, where poison ivy liked to grow. At the edge of the woods, she stopped and breathed deeply, filling her lungs with the fresh air. A breeze came up from the lake, blowing Deirdre's hair into a spike. Deirdre kicked and whistled a gasp.

"You like that air, baby? It's good air. Like a tonic, Dee. That's what Grand always used to say. Good for what ails you."

Rachel walked through the woods, ignoring the pain in her feet as she picked her way over the overgrown path to the water. The dropped fish had reminded her of a time that she and Joe had discovered a fish skeleton beneath the eagle's nest one summer, when they were young. It must have been only a partial skeleton, or just the head that had fallen, but in her memory, it was a perfect whole, the bones picked clean and gleaming, their points as sharp as pins. They had held a fish séance there under the pines, sitting cross-legged under the nest, at serious risk of being doused in eagle shit, the gleaming skeleton on the ground between them. "Rise," they had chanted, their eyes closed, knees touching. "Rise, and live again." Or something like that.

Rachel had broken her own sternly-stated rule and peeked, and when she saw the skeleton sitting just where they'd placed it, as bony and unfleshed as ever, she couldn't bear it: she picked it up between her forefinger and thumb, and hurled it into the woods. Then she closed her own eyes again and joined in the chanting: twenty times, as they'd planned. When they were finished, she watched Joe stare in surprise at the empty space between them.

"It's gone," he whispered.

She nodded, her eyes gleaming like the bones. "In order for it to come back to life, it has to be in the water. So the bones disappeared, but the fish is alive again, swimming down there in the lake."

Joe gaped at her, in obvious admiration of her magical knowledge and power. And for the moment, she believed it, too: that she'd somehow conjured life back into the poor dead fish.

"I have an idea," he said. "Let's bring a *person* back."

Rachel's stomach dropped. "Who?"

"There's a grave in the woods here. My Grandpa's little sister. She died when she was a baby. I bet we can find it if we look hard enough." And he'd gone on to tell her about the grave, about the little house built over it—a spirit house, they called it, with sides and a roof and everything, even a little window. And inside the house his great-grandparents put the baby's moccasins and a special beaded vest, for her to take with her to the other world. "My Grandpa used to visit it all the time," he added. "He said he could always feel her spirit whenever he went there, like she was still living in that little house. I bet she still is."

They'd looked and looked, tramping through the woods for hours that day, even digging beneath fallen trees that might have squashed the little house beneath their weight, but hadn't found a trace of it. Disappointed, they'd finally decided to hold the séance without the grave. Once again, they sat cross-legged on the forest floor, knees touching, just as they'd done with the fish, and imagined the dead baby, her feet clothed in tiny beaded moccasins, and they'd chanted their chant twenty times, then thirty, then a hundred, pressing their eyes tighter together, twitching at every breeze that lifted the hairs off their skin, at every crack of a stick in the woods. In the silence, they waited for some kind of sign, some kind of demonstration that their will had effected an actual resurrection. By that time, the sun was winking low through the woods, casting long shadows over open ground, appearing and disappearing between the tree trunks. "It's her," Rachel breathed, pointing. "She's winking at us, there. It worked, Joe. She's alive."

She'd been making it up of course, but at the time, she'd half felt she was speaking the truth. Just imagining that little girl's spirit flashing through the woods seemed to carry a certain power, to somehow make it so.

Maybe this was what Grand was feeling now, thinking of her father.

A path forked off to the left, and Rachel, moved by her thoughts, took it. It led down a little slope into the Memorial Garden, a small clearing in between the birches and pines where a wild forest garden grew, punctuated by two wooden benches and a big boulder, put there by Grandpa Jacob, after Granddaddy—Grand's father—died. On the boulder, they'd affixed a metal plaque that read: "For those who loved and nurtured the Farm." And here, over the years, they'd buried the ashes of Rachel's ancestors: first Granddaddy Turner, the man who built the dam and bought the land that started it all and her great-grandmother Eliza, then Rachel's great-aunts Jennie and Dorothea, and, eventually, Grandpa Jacob, several years after he'd hefted the boulder into place. Rachel remembered that memorial well: a year after his big Chicago funeral, the whole family had gathered up here, and held a small service beneath the pines, singing a few hymns and reading some of his favorite passages, and then they'd marched down to the garden, where Rachel's father had already dug a hole. In silence, Grand had lifted the lid from the urn, and knelt—even in her cream-colored linen skirt, she'd knelt in the dirt—and shook the ashes into the hole. Rachel remembered watching her stand, with help from Linda (though Grand was still agile then; this was over ten years ago), looking at the black spots on her knees, the empty urn in her hands, and feeling so overcome by love for Grand and for her whole goddamn family, who insisted on conducting rituals with this kind of integrity.

An integrity that she then proceeded to totally squash. They had walked from the garden to the lake, led by Grand, who had saved some of the ashes to sprinkle into the water. One by one, they took turns shaking ash from the urn into the water below. When her brother Derek tipped the urn, a breeze kicked up and blew some of the ash sideways, so that it caught in the branches of one of the birches leaning over the lake. As he handed her the urn, he whispered, "Fuck, Walter," in her ear. (This was a quote from the ashes scene in *The Big Lebowski*, a Coen brothers movie that they'd watched together at least eight times, always collapsing in hysterical laughter when

Walter Sobchak commits Donnie's ashes to the Pacific Ocean, and the wind blows them back in the Dude's face.) Rachel had gotten such a bad case of the giggles she had to skip her turn. She'd stood there, even after they'd finished, even after her father declared it was time for lunch, even after the rest of the family had hiked back up the path to the house. Rachel stood by her grandfather's ashes hanging in the tree, feeling like an insensitive jerk.

But Grand had come up behind her and put a hand on her waist. They watched the wind touch the water, making ripples on its surface, listening to the waves gently plash against the pebbled shore beneath their feet and the distant hum of a lawnmower from somewhere across the lake. "I can't think of a better place to spend eternity," she had said.

Rachel, feeling forgiven, rested her head on Grand's shoulder. "Me neither, Grand," she'd said. And they'd walked up the path arm in arm.

A powerboat went by, interrupting Rachel's reverie, and she watched its wake ruffle the glassy water, then roll closer in rhythmic ridges, until they finally washed against the bank beneath her feet. The water seemed high, higher than she remembered it being. Yet another change. Joe's face, Grand, the lake—all these changes, all of them so terribly sad.

Her phone rang in her pocket, startling Deirdre, who jumped inside the front pack, then began a half-hearted cry. Rachel looked at the screen: it was her father.

"Yes, boss," she answered. "Reporting for duty." She swayed and Deirdre quieted.

"Honey. I didn't mean you should leave in the middle of the night, for God's sake."

"You talked to Michael."

"He's worried about you, Rachel, and frankly, I am, too. Are you all right?"

"I'm fine, Dad. Everything's fine. I don't know why everyone is freaking out so much. I decided I wanted to come—not to spy for you, by the way, but because I wanted Grand to meet Deirdre. It was a good time to go. Deirdre slept the whole way. I can sleep when I'm dead."

"Ha. Very funny."

"And I'm glad I came. It's really good to be here."

"Well! I never thought I'd hear you say that."

Rachel sighed. "Michael's the one with the issues about this place, Dad. I've always loved it. I just hadn't realized how much I'd been missing it."

"Well, good, then. Sounds like I don't need to worry."

"Not about me. About Grand, maybe. She really is failing, Dad. This morning she was trying to get me to see something that wasn't there. It was like she was having a vision—her eyes looked like she was staring at something solid, something I just couldn't see. And just now she was telling me how Granddaddy has been around a lot lately, as if she could see him as well."

"Yes, she mentioned him last week."

"She said she thinks he's here to say his goodbyes to the Farm."

"See, that's what I'm concerned about. Did she say anything else?"

Rachel sighed again. It appeared she was succumbing to her father's wishes, as usual. "There's definitely something up, Dad. Diane was acting strange earlier this morning when I mentioned I wanted to come back next year, and then Grand just now was talking about her 'decision,' and how she thought Granddaddy would be pleased with it, 'knowing what he knows now.' She hasn't said anything outright, and she is fairly confused, so it's hard to know for sure. But it does seem like she's made some decision about the Farm that has to do with Diane."

"Unbelievable. She's been brainwashed."

"Looks that way."

"Have you talked to Diane about it?"

"Not yet, boss. I'll get right on that."

"Sorry, honey. I don't mean to push you. I'm just concerned is all. Grand is in a very vulnerable state right now. Christ, I thought Diane was someone we could trust."

"I don't know why."

"Grand thinks the world of her. She put her through nursing school, did you know that?"

"No," Rachel replied, surprised. "I didn't know that."

"I mean, Jesus. That's an expensive piece of property to just be handing off to somebody else."

"Well, that's not really part of the equation."

"What do you mean? Of course it is. I'm not ready to just kiss a valuable property goodbye because of some sentimental idea about restoration."

"Whoa, Dad. Hang on. First of all, aren't you a lawyer? Doesn't that profession have something to do with justice?"

"Don't tell me you're on Diane's side. Rachel, can't you see how this whole thing stinks? Grand is not right in her mind, and this woman comes along and feeds her some sob story and basically milks her out of her money. It's a classic case of undue influence."

"Why do you care so much about the money? I mean, it's not like you would see any of it, even if Grand left the Farm to you."

"Me and Linda. And why wouldn't we? We'd split in half whatever we made from the sale."

"*What?!*"

"You didn't think we were going to keep that place, did you?"

"Actually, yes, the idea had crossed my mind."

"Rachel, no one goes up there anymore. You and Michael certainly don't use it, and Derek and Traci go to the Hamptons in the summer these days. Linda and Richard go to see Grand, just like your mother and I, but once she's gone . . . Honestly, I'm looking forward to vacationing elsewhere for a change. Plus, it's expensive. Do you know how much it costs just to keep that place afloat?"

"No."

"At least several thousand a year just for taxes, utilities, the bare-bones maintenance. That's not counting all the work the place desperately needs. There's a new roof due, the front porch is infested with termites, there's a colony of bats in the attic . . . It's never-ending."

"How does Grand pay for it?"

"She can't. That's why the place is going to seed. It's completely impractical. But you know Grand. Always the romantic. I think she's been hoping one of us would step in at the very end and see things her way." He paused a moment, and Rachel could almost see him at the other end of the line, knocking against the edge of his desk with his knuckles, the absent-minded gesture he made whenever he was thinking. "Poor Grand," he added.

"But Dad," Rachel tried. "If you sell it, it'll be gone. Forever."

"No one's going to sell your memories, Rachel," he joked. When she didn't laugh, he added, "It just doesn't make sense to hold onto it, honey."

"Why didn't anyone ask my opinion?"

"Well, Rachel, I'm sorry, but to be honest, I'm a little surprised. I mean, you and Michael have made your perspective on the Farm abundantly clear. The word 'boycott' was used at one point, if I recall correctly. I thought you'd be glad we were divesting ourselves."

Rachel colored. "I've got to go, Dad. Deirdre just pooped." Deirdre, in fact, was cooing happily, captivated by the leaves rustling above her head and the breeze coming off the lake.

"You're not angry, are you?"

"No, Dad," she said, steaming. "I'm fine."

"All right." She could hear him thinking again. "Well, listen. Let me know if you hear anything else about Grand's plans for the Farm. I guess the bright side of this whole thing is that we'll have an open and shut case, if Diane has actually convinced Grand to leave her the Farm. It would be a hassle and an expense to sue, of course. Not to mention unpleasant."

"Dad."

"Right. Sorry to keep you. Give that baby a kiss from her Grandpa Chris! I'll call again soon."

They hung up. Rachel tucked the phone back in her pocket and nuzzled Deirdre's scalp for comfort, mouthing some of her stray hairs. She felt light-headed. She wiped the sweat from her palms, then held them up: she was shaking. Quickly, she sat on the bench by the picnic table and breathed deeply a few times, keeping a grip on the edge of the table. Fainting while carrying her baby would not be good; fainting down here, without anyone to find her for hours, would be very bad. Breathe in. Breathe out. Breathe in: Diane. Breathe out: Michael. Breathe in: Grand. Breathe out: Joe. Breathe in: her childhood, her whole body of dreams. Breathe out: Deirdre.

"I'm not giving it up that easily, Dee," she said, speaking into Deirdre's sweet-smelling scalp. "Not when I've only just found it again. You watch and see, baby. You just watch Mama work."

BOOK TWO

A Dam Is an Evil Thing

May 1994

1

Twenty-one, a newly-minted B.S. in wildlife biology, Rachel stood on a dock in the Kennebec River a mile or so down-current from the Campbell Dam, watching the water for leaping sturgeon. Beside her stood her fish biology professor *cum* boss, Dr. Brian Speckel—with blowing sandy hair and a tightly trimmed beard—and Margaret Richards, his graduate student. It was early morning, the first day of Rachel's summer internship. The boat awaited them, lashed to the dock, equipped with outboard motor, gillnet, holding pen, fish box, and a tower of five-gallon buckets.

"There's one!" Brian shouted, pointing out over the dark surface of the water. The long body tipped, fins like a set of atrophied feet splaying out from beneath the tail, then smacked the water and submerged, droplets shooting away.

"Wow," Rachel murmured.

"That looked like a four-footer," said Margaret. She was twenty-seven, an exotic age. Brian was thirty-three.

"At least," said Brian. "Maybe five. Immature Atlantic sturgeon."

It was prime spawning season for most sea-run fish in the Kennebec— shad, alewives, and the sturgeon they would spend the summer catching, measuring, tagging, and releasing back into the river. Brian—he asked all his students to call him Brian—had told Rachel's class all about this seasonal migration, how every spring, hundreds of fish from multiple species traveled untold miles, forgoing food and rest, up-current from the ocean, back to the place of their birth to mate and lay their eggs. *Homeland* was the word he'd used; Rachel remembered the way he'd hummed a little when he pronounced the *m*. Historically, he told them, the rivers used to be so clogged this time of year that boats could barely navigate. Some old-timers (Native Americans mostly, Brian said) used to say you could almost hop the river fish to fish, like stepping stones. But the dams changed all that. As soon as people started building dams, the fish were shit out of luck. Their passage blocked, they couldn't return to their homelands (*mm*), so they languished and exhausted themselves in frustration, and basically came to the brink of dying out, which is where they were now. Atlantic salmon were barely hanging on; shortnose sturgeon were endangered; Atlantic sturgeon were on a watch list. Still, he'd said, even now, you could catch a few of them breaching during mating season near the Campbell Dam, trying to find a way upstream. This was the first time Rachel had ever seen it in person.

"Another!" she cried, pointing at a smaller silver body that barely broke the surface.

Margaret fixed a cold blue stare at her from underneath the brim of her Red Sox hat. "That's shad."

Brian put a hand on her shoulder. "You'll get the hang of it. There're a lot of fish out there right now." He had a way of looking at Rachel that made her feel as though all the energy of the universe was contained in the space between them, and that as long as she stood there, maintaining that connection, she was at the center of something great, something vital. She smiled gratefully up at him.

"Anyway!" Margaret chirped. She marched down the dock to the boat, stiff-legged in her heavy-duty bib pants, her thick braid bouncing between her shoulder blades.

"Margaret's an extremely disciplined worker," he apologized *sotto voce*, his hand pressing Rachel's shoulder. "She's always anxious to get out on the water."

They boarded the boat. Brian sat behind the wheel and Margaret at starboard, checking one of the gillnet buoys. Rachel shipped the lashing rope and pushed them off the dock, then stood warily near Margaret, unsure what to do next. Margaret bent over the buoy, knotting a line to it, her brow notched.

"Can I help?" Rachel asked.

"It's really a one person job," she said, "and anyway, it's done." She tugged the knot, checking its hold.

"Why don't you show her how we set up the holding pen?" Brian called.

With a sigh, Margaret led Rachel to starboard, where she showed her how to lower another smaller net into the water, where any fish they caught would be held until they could be brought aboard for tagging. Rachel had a million questions about how the process was going to work, and what she should be doing, exactly, at every moment, but she sensed that Margaret was not in the mood to answer. So she tried to learn by observation.

Despite Margaret's pissyness, Rachel was thrilled to have the internship, to be out on the water with Professor Speckel (Brian!) all day, to get to help him with the work he loved (and which she just *knew* she would love, already she loved it), to see in person the fish he had dedicated his life to saving. Rachel was, she would admit, a little bit in love with Dr. Brian Speckel. All the women in her fish biology class were, as well as a few of the guys. He was ruggedly devastating, yes, and that was enough for most people—but for Rachel, it wasn't only his cleaned-up hippie look and his intense eyes that got her; it was his passion. On the first day of class, he'd told them he had three great loves in his life: his wife Sara, his baby boy River, and sturgeon. But really it seemed that sturgeon was his greatest love. When he talked about sturgeon, his face took on a faraway expression, as if he were speaking from across a great distance, as if he'd crossed over into ancient times, when sturgeon would mass at the estuaries in the thousands, waiting for the river to warm. More than once, he asked them to imagine that time—to imagine themselves as Abenaki Indians, waiting on the bank, spear in hand, for the long bone-plated flesh of the fish to appear within striking distance. "Or hell," he said, "imagine being a sturgeon! Scouring the ocean bottom for dropped goodies, and then, once a year, feeling the call back to your natal river, and swimming, rushing home, with the hundreds of slick bodies, fighting the current, all the way to the Great Spawning Grounds." (They were in college, yes, but still, a few girls giggled when Brian Speckel said "slick bodies" and "Great Spawning Grounds.")

"Except, of course," he continued, "they can't get there. They can't do the thing that every cell of their evolutionary history compels them to do, because there's a huge, motherfucking dam in the way." Brian liked to swear in class.

Rachel's friend Josie thought Brian's obsession with sturgeon spawning was weird, but Rachel thought it was breathtaking. She'd never been very interested in fish—birds were her thing, usually, eagles in particular—but he made sturgeon sound so mysterious, so primal, and so much on the brink that Rachel easily transferred her concern to their plight. So when he'd advertised the summer internship in class ("come squeeze some fish with me," he'd said), she'd jumped on it, and brought her résumé to his office the very next day. By the end of the week, she had the job.

Their mission was to catch and tag as many sturgeon as possible. They were tracking the movements of the sturgeon not only for scientific posterity, but because the Campbell Dam was coming up for federal relicensing later that year, and Brian was putting the final touches on his ten-year data collection so the Natural Resources Council of Maine could use his numbers to argue their case. Brian believed—with a faith that Rachel found bracing—that his numbers would impress not only the dam owners (a remnant of the manufacturing company who sold the dam's miniscule 3.5 megawatts of hydropower to Central Maine Power), but, more importantly, the Federal Energy Regulatory Commission. FERC, he instructed Rachel, would likely come back with one of two options: a.) they would renew Campbell's license with no strings attached, despite the overwhelming evidence that the dam severely endangered the river's ecosystem, or b.) they would renew the license with the stipulation that Campbell mitigate the damage in a number of ways, including instigating a spring "spill" over the dam to normalize the hydrograph, manually catching adults below the dam and releasing them above, stocking hatchery-raised fish in the river (which caused a whole host of other problems), and/or building a fish ladder. The never-in-a-million-years dream response that he and the NRCM and Kennebec Anglers United and American Rivers and the Atlantic Salmon Federation and the Confederation of Maine's First Nations—all of the groups that had come together to fight this thing—that all of them were hoping for was c.) that FERC would deny Campbell's relicensing application, tear down the dam, and give the sturgeon the run of the river once more.

Brian had given her this whole speech on the way to the river that morning, with Margaret staring sullenly out the passenger-side window, and Rachel leaning forward from the back seat. "But this is science," he'd said. "And science doesn't know hope. Science knows data. We're just the worker bees, gathering the nectar for the queen. The queen makes all the decisions. But we have to gather good nectar—precise, perfectly calibrated data—so the queen can make the right decision. Got it?"

"Got it," Rachel replied.

"Who, exactly, is the queen, Brian? You've never clarified that."

Brian glanced at Margaret, then back at the road. "Margaret's heard this speech before."

Now they were motoring out to the middle of the river, where they would set their net. The sun was coming up over the eastern bank, winking shards of light through the trees, the wind gusting. It blew the hood of Rachel's slicker off her head. Margaret fiddled with the fish box. Rachel glanced back at Brian, behind the boat's wheel. The sun reflected off his mirrored shades, the wind tossed his hair. He smiled at her. She thought she had never seen such utterly straight teeth.

Finally, Brian downshifted and joined Margaret at the stern, where she was hefting the buoy. He motioned to Rachel. "You should do this. It'll be you helping Margaret, starting tomorrow." She climbed down to stand beside him, her life jacket brushing his.

Margaret tossed the buoy in the water, the net trailing. "Stand there," she ordered Rachel, pointing to the bin that held the net. "You pay it out while I check for tangles."

"What do I—?" Rachel began, but Margaret was signaling to Brian, who gunned the motor and began driving the boat away from the dropped buoy.

"Pay it out!" Margaret yelled, and Rachel began dropping the corks that buoyed the net into the water one by one. The net unspooled, the corks bobbed atop the waves, and Margaret tested the net's tautness while Brian motored them away. When Rachel dropped the final cork, Margaret pushed past her to the grab the flag marking the end buoy, and dropped it in the water. The net was set.

Rachel, confused and exhilarated, looked to Margaret for a sign of approval—or even disapproval, some feedback to let her know how she'd done. But Margaret only moved to the bow, where she began to scribble in a log. *Well, screw you*, Rachel thought. If Margaret wanted to hate her, she could go ahead and hate her. It was none of Rachel's business.

The morning air was cool on her face, but inside her slicker, bib pants, and lifejacket, Rachel was sweating. She unzipped her slicker at the throat and turned into the wind, letting it cool her, when an enormous sturgeon breached, penetrating the air: an iridescent bullet of muscle as long as a man, diving upward, its ridged back thrusting into the air. Rachel froze. Brian was beside her. He grabbed her hand. They stood there together, not breathing, for what must have been only a few seconds, but what to Rachel felt like a caesura of time, the fish hanging in the air, Brian gripping her hand, until finally, the fish dropped back into the water, as cleanly as an Olympic diver. "That's what we do this for, Rachel," Brian purred. "That's why we're here." He squeezed her hand once before dropping it.

Rachel was hooked. She loved everything about the job: slipping out of her parents' house before dawn, sipping from her steaming travel mug of coffee as she hugged the curving roads to the river. She loved the melancholy peals of the gulls' calls as they wheeled down close to the boat and then away, and the occasional eagle sighting—the black body soaring high over the water, plummeting down for the catch and swooping up again, fish glinting in the sun. It put her in mind of the eagles at the Farm, and consoled her for missing her time there. She loved being out on the water—the thunk of the waves against the hull, the fishy tang to the air, the weight of a wet line in her hand. And the suspense! They never knew what they'd find thrashing in their nets: the occasional salmon or striped bass, maybe a rainbow trout, sometimes shad. And non-fish items, too—smooth driftwood logs, a rusty car hood, an old logging spike. Once, they pulled up a blown-out, waterlogged snare drum. They puzzled over that one a long while, she and Margaret, making up stories about how it ended up in the river.

Margaret relaxed once Brian left them alone. He stuck around the first week—several days longer than he'd said he would—making sure Rachel was learning the ropes, and that whole time Margaret said only the minimum necessary to both of them. But as soon as he'd gone back to the office, Margaret warmed up, and actually apologized to Rachel for being so unpleasant. "Brian gets under my skin," she said, and while Rachel couldn't commiserate, she accepted Margaret's apology, and they became friends.

Sometimes they'd snag an outdoor table at the local brew pub at the end of the day and bask in the summer evening with their beers, slapping at the black flies and mosquitoes. Margaret would gripe about Brian—how he was infamous in the department for hiring pretty undergrad hourlies, how he'd taken Margaret on because she was tall and blond like his wife, and had learned too late that she was a dyke, how once he'd learned, he grew distant and weirdly deferential. How she was just hanging on until she finished her masters, and then she was hightailing it out of there to find a *female* biologist to do her PhD with, someone who could see past her looks to her mind. "Men can't do that," she said. "They've got some deficiency in their genome that makes them stroke their dicks and spew bullshit at the sight of a beautiful woman."

Rachel laughed with her, but privately she thought Margaret was making a bit much of herself. She wasn't all that beautiful. She was tall and blond, yes, but her face was chalky and wedge-shaped, and her eyes too squinty most of the time. She wore her resentment too broadly, and it put people off—not just Brian. Her claim of resembling Brian's wife was, well, a stretch.

Now Sara Speckel *was* a beautiful woman. She glowed with a natural luminescence that drew all eyes to her when she entered a room. She wore no make-up, and was even a little bit heavy in her legs and thighs—sturdy, the word was—but her eyes were quick and kind and deeply blue, and her cheeks always appley and hale, as if she'd just come off a good 10K. And she was a Brian-magnet, a thing that fascinated Rachel. Occasionally, Rachel and Margaret would run into Brian and Sara and their nine-month-old baby River at the pub, and they'd all sit together (Margaret, strangely enough, didn't seem to mind, despite all her bitching about Brian. Rachel guessed she was crushing on Sara). Rachel would sneak glances at them while they ate. Brian never stopped touching Sara: he rested his arm against the back of her chair, sniffed her hair, ate with a hand on her knee, gave her sips of his beer and watched the bottle enter her mouth, her head tip back, her throat shine out, as white as a sturgeon's belly. He always drank from the bottle the instant she handed it back to him, as if trying to capture her saliva on his tongue before it evaporated. Sara was quick to laugh, and a generous listener—she leaned in close when anyone spoke, as if the words coming out of the speaker's mouth were the most important words that could be said, the only thing worthy of her attention.

The only exception to this rule was when River needed her. But this, too, seemed easy for Sara. She seemed to know instinctively how to handle each of the baby's grievances. Usually, any fussing was immediately solved by breastfeeding. Sara would whip out a boob at the table like it was no big deal. The merest hint of a whine from River, and she'd apply baby to breast so discreetly that you barely noticed what was going on. Except for Brian; he noticed. He gazed at River with envy whenever Sara fed him. This Rachel found amazing, that a man could be so into his wife that he would actually be jealous of his own kid. Sara, she thought, must be pretty fucking special, to have so thoroughly ensnared a catch like Brian.

One night at the pub, they got to talking about the public hearing that had just been scheduled over the fate of the Campbell Dam. Representatives from FERC were going to be there, as well as state legislators, reps from

Central Maine Power, and all the major players from the Save Our River Coalition—NRCM, American Rivers, the Kennebec Anglers Association, and the tribes. It was to be a chance for the public to ask questions and to voice their own concerns and opinions about the state of the river and the proposition to renew the Campbell Dam's license. "Sara's going to speak," Brian bragged. "She's going to nail Campbell to the wall with her spectacular soils data."

Sara rolled her eyes affectionately at him. "You guys should come," she urged Rachel and Margaret. "The more people there, the better—it'll show FERC the strength of our concern."

"I'll be there," said Rachel. Margaret was squinting at the boxing match on the TV above the bar.

Later, Rachel bumped into Brian on her way back from the bathroom. "Listen," he said, pulling her aside, out of view of their table. "I'd like you to think about making a public comment at the hearing." His breath smelled deliciously of the spicy stout he'd been drinking.

"Me?"

"Yes, you. I see how you watch the fish. You get it, I can tell. Just get up there and speak from the heart. Talk about how you feel about the sturgeon. Coming from someone like you, it'll mean a lot."

Rachel agreed immediately, then spent the rest of the week wondering what he meant by *someone like her.*

As the hearing neared, Rachel worked on her speech late into the night, writing and cutting and writing some more, rehearsing it so it didn't sound too staged, doing her best to get across the right blend of passion, intelligence, and politeness. She knew, as the daughter of a lawyer, that overly-emotional testimony did not help anyone's case; the ideal was to hit all the right arguments, deliver them with just the right amount of measured feeling, with courtesy and respect, and keep it short and to the point. This, it turned out, was a lot harder than it sounded. She brought her drafts to her father, and sat beside him at the kitchen table as he read them over, bouncing her knees while he marked the pages, his reading glasses perched on the end of his long nose.

On the night of the hearing, Rachel sat in the back of her parents' Subaru while they drove, reading her speech over and over, no longer seeing the words. "Set it aside, honey," her father said, meeting her eyes in the rearview mirror. "You know it cold by now. Just trust yourself."

She followed his advice, closing the manila folder and sitting on her hands to stop them from shaking.

When they arrived, the room was dense with people and thick with body heat. Rachel surveyed the crowd, looking for Brian and Sara. She spotted Brian's sandy head toward the front, and jostled and slipped between bodies toward him. His face cracked into a grin when he saw her—she watched for the lines at his eyes—and he grabbed her shoulder. "You made it!" he said. "I was beginning to worry."

She swallowed. "Where's Sara?" She spoke directly into the ear he offered her, noticing its whorls, the light peach fuzz on the skin.

"Home with River. He's sick. She's bummed to miss it."

Rachel filled unaccountably with joy. They turned back toward the speaker, a middle-aged man with a crew cut and a suit, a representative of the dam, who was droning on, pointing to a graph he'd set up on an easel, talking about the electricity generated by the hydroplant, how a renewed license with altered terms (and some minimal construction) could allow them to generate eight more megawatts, how hydropower was renewable, unlike fossil fuels, how the dam had created the reservoir above it, that people used for fishing and boating, how the dam helped control the water flow and prevent flooding—etc., etc., etc. Rachel stood next to Brian, feeling the heat pulsing from his body.

After the power plant speaker, there was a lawyer from NRCM—also suited, middle-aged—who perched his own graphs and pie charts on the easel, and then after him, an octogenarian fisherman from the Kennebec Anglers Association, who spoke in a meandering way about how he used to fish the river with his father, back in the day, when the salmon were plentiful and would bump into their boat like dogs nosing for treats. After him, there was a man—they were all men, Rachel was noticing; not one woman among them—from the Penobscot tribe who introduced himself as a tribal elder and talked about the spiritual significance of salmon, and the sustenance fishing rights of the tribe, "which become meaningless," he said, "if there aren't any fish," and after that, there was someone from American Rivers, who talked about the science of a healthy river, how there are good dams and there are bad dams, and that the Campbell Dam was a bad dam. The speeches went on and on, and Rachel stood close to Brian and listened fervently to each one.

And then, finally, the official presentations were over, and it was time for public comment. Show time. Brian took her hand and led her through the crowd to a line that was forming along the side of the room. Already there were at least ten people ahead of them, and so they leaned against the wall and listened to each person speak. Rachel had anticipated that most people would be on their side, but the reality seemed to be that the group was pretty well split down the middle. The man directly in front of her—an old farmer with cauliflower ears and red suspenders whose land abutted the river, and who liked the dam because it kept the water from flooding his fields—spoke courteously and softly, but his age and his well-reasoned argument shook her, and so when she stepped up to the podium with Brian at her side, her paper danced in her hand. Brian spoke first: he introduced himself, talked about his and Sara's work on the Kennebec, how he'd been training young biologists, and then introduced Rachel as "one of the brightest students he'd seen in a long time.

"I thought I'd just give her the opportunity to speak to you folks briefly about the fish whose habitat is affected by the dam, as I know she'll be more eloquent than I will." Then he nodded to Rachel, and stepped aside.

She set her papers on the podium and looked out at the crowd. The auditorium was packed with people, hundreds of them. Some of held signs in the air—"Save Our River!" or "Power For the People!"—others were gathered in clear factions: middle-aged men in button-downs and good shoes (the moneyed anglers; anti-dam), older couples with stern faces (conservatives, firm supporters of industry; pro-dam), naturalists in T-shirts and Tevas (anti-dam), and younger scientists and intellectuals like Brian (anti-dam). She saw her parents, standing toward the back of the room—her mother, small and birdlike, her long gray hair becoming flyaway in the heat of the room, and her father, his tall, encouraging confidence. She swallowed, then looked again at Brian, who was nodding, and then she looked out at the crowd one more time, seized with a tongue-tying panic.

It helped, she'd learned years ago in a high school public speaking class, to isolate one person in the crowd that you could imagine talking to, and to just block everybody else out. Just one person who seemed civil and kind, willing to listen to what you had to say. Her eyes fell on the Penobscot tribal elder, the man who'd spoken about the spiritual significance of the salmon and of the river. He was stocky and spectacled, with short hair and skin as light as any white man's, but he wore a beaded vest and an eagle feather head-dress, and when he spoke, his voice reminded her of Joe. She found herself wondering what Joe would think of all of this—of Brian and their work on the river, of this whole gathering and the fact that Rachel was speaking at it—and suddenly, she grew calm and centered, and knew that she could speak.

"I'm not really an expert. I'm just someone who's spent a summer on the river, handling and watching and tagging the sturgeon that have happened into our nets. But doing this work this summer has opened up a whole new universe to me. I knew from Brian—uh, Dr. Speckel's—class that sturgeon were amazing animals. They come down to us from the era of the dinosaurs, almost exactly as they were then. Where other fish have scales, they have bony plates, *scutes* we call them, and their bodies are primarily cartilage: so they're like us in that way, bone and cartilage and muscle. They can live as long as us, too—some even as long as a hundred years. They're bottom feeders, which is good, because they clean up our rivers and oceans, like a whole team of living vacuum cleaners. And they're big. Some of them—Atlantic sturgeon especially—as long as eighteen feet. A fish that big in the ocean makes sense to me; but a fish that big swimming up the river, as far inland as they do—or *would* do, if they could—that seems truly amazing.

"So I learned all these things from Br—from Dr. Speckel, but I didn't really understand them until I saw a sturgeon in person, until I actually held one in my arms. They are beautiful. I know that sounds cliché, but I don't know how else to say it. They leap out of the water, high in the air—these huge fish! leaping yards into the air!—and their skin is a kind of color you've never seen before on land, a red-brown color that catches the sunlight, and reflects it back in this swirly way, like an oil slick without the pollution. And to hold one—they're heavy and strong and their heart is beating, and it's like you're holding a part of the earth's history. Like you're going back in time and touching the deep past.

"But they're in trouble. Shortnose sturgeon are endangered, and Atlantic sturgeon are close, and part of the reason for this is because of dams like Campbell. The dam blocks their way; they can't reunite at their spawning grounds, upriver, and many of them die trying, because by the time they reach the dam, they're so worn out from their journey, they haven't eaten, and they simply can't do it. They get pushed back by the heavy current, or, if they manage to get up that far, lacerated by the turbines.

"I know there are other things to consider beyond just the fate of a single species of fish. I know we need power, and that hydroelectric is renewable, which is better than a coal plant, for sure. I'm not here to demonize the power company, or anyone. I'm here to speak for the sturgeon. Call me the sturgeon Lorax. As sturgeon Lorax, the main thing I want to say is that *they need this river.* If we don't give them this river, then we will lose them. And that would be a terrible, terrible thing."

She was finished. Shakily, she gathered her papers, and stepped down from the podium, making a point of not looking at her parents, who, she knew, were clapping far too loudly, or even Brian, because she felt, at the moment, as though she might puke if anyone looked her in the eye. She moved quickly out of the way of a determined older woman with close-cropped gray hair, who was next in line. Her thoughts remained with Joe. The whole time she'd been speaking, she'd kept him in her mind, and now she was feeling almost as if she'd just spent some time with him, as if he might have actually heard her in some way. That stupid sturgeon Lorax joke, that no one had laughed at; Joe would have laughed at that.

She pushed her way through the crowd to the doors at the end of the room. They whooshed shut behind her, muffling the miked voice of the old woman, who was scolding the dam owners and Central Maine Power and just about everyone in the room, it sounded like. The lobby was high-ceilinged and tiled in smooth brick, the air refreshingly cool. Then the doors opened behind her—*unconscionable,* the woman shrilled—and Brian was at her elbow. "Rachel," he stage-whispered, taking her by both shoulders and staring intensely into her eyes. "That was perfect. You were perfect."

"Thanks," she got out, feeling her pulse like a moth in her throat. He was holding her like he was either going to shake her or kiss her, and she both hoped it was the latter and hated and feared it, too, because of Sara and the baby and what a despicable person receiving a kiss from Brian would make her. Still, she didn't want him to let go of her shoulders.

And then the doors whooshed open again—*unconscionable,* the same woman was still somehow saying, only louder—and her parents appeared, and Brian dropped her shoulders. Then her father was hugging her and her mother was wiping tears away, and they were saying how eloquent she was, and how humble and passionate and *true,* the best speaker yet, and how proud of her they were, their voices echoing in the empty lobby. Someone tapped her on the shoulder, and she turned to face the old man with big cauliflower ears and red suspenders who'd spoken before her, whose quiet, sober objection to the removal of the dam had so impressed her. He offered her his hand.

"Young lady," he said, his hand smooth and dry and as big as a dinner plate, "You've made me think. I haven't changed my mind yet. But you've made me think." He dropped her hand, then, nodded graciously to her parents and to Brian, and hobbled on a shaky hip through the lobby to the double doors.

"Thank you, sir," Rachel said belatedly, and he raised a hand in the air without turning around, and then pushed his way out into the night.

"Wow," Brian said.

"That's a case well-argued, Rach," her father added.

"It's because you spoke from your heart," her mother said.

"Well, he's not the one we have to convince."

"Actually, he is," Brian said. "He totally is. FERC is going to look toward public opinion as much as anything." Then, out of the blue, he swept her into a bear hug, lifting her off the floor. "See? I knew you were the person to deliver this. I just knew it!"

She laughed giddily. Her father's eyes narrowed laser-like onto the back of Brian's head.

Then the doors to the inner hall opened once more, and a young man stepped out—skinny, wearing an intellectual's chunky glasses, and carrying a clipboard.

"Hey, Michael!" Brian said, setting Rachel down and going to shake the young man's hand. "How're you doing, man? We were just celebrating out here. Wasn't she terrific?" He gestured at Rachel, who was straightening her rumpled shirt.

"Yes. I think the tides may have turned in there." He stared at Rachel, gripping his clipboard.

"Really?" She was stunned.

"Well, that may be over-stating it. Hard to say yet. But you definitely caused a ripple of some kind."

"Sorry," Brian cut in. "My manners must have dissolved in glee. Rachel, this is Michael German. Except he's Irish. Michael, Rachel Clayborne, my star student. Well, not anymore—she's my star intern."

Rachel blushed fiercely, wishing, for the first time ever, that Brian would shut up. "Uh, hi. These are my parents, Chris and Lilly Clayborne."

"Let me just say that you fashioned a fabulous person here," Brian said. "You'll have to share your secrets with me sometime, so I can try some of them out on my son."

"Just stay out of his way," her Dad said, which, for an instant, she misheard as *stay out of her way,* meaning *stay away from her,* and her blush began to pulse like a heart spread thin across her entire upper body. She wished they could leave, right now.

"Michael works for the NRCM," Brian said. "He's been on this case for years as well."

"Just three," Michael added, pushing his glasses up his nose. "But I'm off to Cambridge in the fall. Grad school." He was still studying Rachel as if she were a specimen. He looked as if he might begin making notes on his clipboard.

"No shit," said Brian. "I didn't know that."

"Yeah. Actually, that's why I came out here. I wanted to talk to Rachel about my job. The NRCM is looking for someone to replace me, and from the way you spoke tonight, it seemed to me you might be a good candidate. Can I buy you a drink and tell you more about it?" He spoke seriously and directly, with no indication that he meant anything beyond exactly what he said.

Brian was staring at Michael with a weird look on his face. The same look, Rachel realized, that he got when he watched River breastfeed.

"I'd love to," she replied quickly. "But I came with my parents, and we're a forty-minute drive away."

"I could take you home," Michael offered.

"I'll take her home," said Brian.

"We'll just wait for you here," her father said. "The hearing's still going on; we'll have plenty of entertainment." He leaned in to Rachel and whispered, "Go get 'em, champ."

The three of them—Rachel, Michael, and Brian—walked together to a nearby pub, where they found a table close to the window. They each ordered a beer. Brian—whose glee had shifted into something darker—stared at the big screen TV over the bar. Michael glanced at Brian, at the TV, at Rachel, and back to Brian again. It was clear he didn't want Brian there, that he hadn't meant for Brian to come along. Rachel saw that Michael's tactical error had inadvertently launched her into the center of a pissing match, which was not a place she'd ever been before, but which, she was discovering, was an uncomfortable place to be. Trying to make the best of things, she smiled at Michael. "So, what are you going to grad school for?"

"Indigenous studies."

"Oh! For some reason, I thought you were going into science."

"No. I'm a humanities partisan."

"Are you Indian?"

He actually flinched, as if she'd taken a swing at him. "You mean *Native*? No. Why does everyone ask me that? No, I'm Irish, remember? The Irish guy with the name German."

Rachel raised her eyebrows. "Sorry," she muttered, and looked away.

The bartender arrived with a tray of three bottles and three frosty glasses; he set them on the table and left. Brian drank directly from the bottle, his eyes still on the TV screen. Michael tipped his glass and poured his beer in a steady stream against the inside of it, coaxing it gradually back to upright as the glass filled with headless beer. When he was finished, he set the empty bottle on the table with a gentle finality.

"I'm sorry," he said. "I get sensitive about that question."

"All the Native people I know call themselves Indian."

"Where are you from?"

"Here. Well, between here and Portland. Sort of. My parents moved here my senior year of high school." She knew Michael was fishing for information about the so-called Native people she knew, but she didn't want to talk about Joe with him, or with Brian, for that matter. "So tell me about the job."

"Right, the job." He explained that it was a full-time position, a kind of jack of all trades kind of role—canvassing, research, some envelope-stuffing, though not much, some answering of phones. "The NRCM's a nonprofit, as you know, so they're strapped for cash. Everyone helps out however they can."

"He's a gofer, is what he's saying," Brian piped in.

"Excuse me? I'm not a gofer."

"Let's be real, Michael. Basically, that's the job. Whatever needs doing around the office, right? Whoever needs their coffee cup refilled. It's only fair you be up front about it with Rachel."

Brian and Michael were now openly glaring at one another.

"My title is *Project Manager*."

"Exactly."

Rachel stood up, her beer untouched. "I think I'd better head back. My parents are waiting for me."

Brian threw a twenty on the table. "I'll walk you back."

Michael half-stood, knocking the table with his thighs. Beer splashed from his carefully-poured mug onto the table, wetting the twenty. He grabbed a napkin and wiped up the beer and the money, then sat back down, looking defeated. "I'm going to finish my beer." He scooted his chair away from the table and aimed it in the direction of the TV screen, his back to them. Rachel glanced at him on their way past the window: he sat erect in his chair, his beer—what was left of it—making the long journey from table to mouth and back again.

Brian had much to say about Michael on the way back to the hearing. "Michael's great and all, don't get me wrong. He's done some really good work for the NRCM. But socially, the guy is a bit clueless. Which can be a liability when you're working with people. He's making the right move, going into academia. That's where he belongs. Holed up in his own mind, with occasional forays into the classroom."

"*You're* in academia."

"True. But science is a much more collaborative field."

Rachel picked up her stride, making Brian, who was more of an ambler, jog to keep up with her.

"I don't want to harsh on Michael. The guy's very smart. But it's just the thing that bugs me about him, the way he handled this whole job offer. I mean, for Christ's sake, *I'm* your current employer. It didn't even occur to him that he might be stepping on my toes by offering you a job right in front of me. Who *does* that?"

"This job is a summer internship."

"Right. But it's possible that I might have more work available after the summer. I mean that sort of thing just doesn't occur to him."

Rachel stopped in her tracks and glared at him. Was *he* offering her a job now?

"Sorry, Rachel. This isn't exactly how I wanted to bring it up with you. Michael kind of forced my hand. But listen!" He touched her arm. "It's exciting news. I've gotten a grant to hire someone full-time for the coming year. Someone to tabulate all my data. It's decent pay—a little more than you're making now. And really great experience, particularly if you think you want to go into biology or the sciences in any way."

They had reached the steps of the auditorium. People were beginning to stream out of the building, shouldering on jackets against the cool breeze that had come up. Rachel saw her parents standing at the top of the steps, her father's arm around her mother's shoulders. They were watching the moon, which was low and huge, a big yellow deflating balloon.

Brian took her hand and squeezed it, bringing her to face him, to fall into his gaze as she had so many times before. "You're the perfect person for the job, Rachel," he said in his oily voice, and suddenly, she got it. She understood Margaret's annoyance with him, finally snapped out of the spell and saw clearly what she hadn't or couldn't or wouldn't before: Dr. Brian Speckel was a player.

"I've got to go," she said, pulling her hand away and running up the steps to her parents, her dear, sweet, uncomplicated parents.

"Think about it, okay?" he yelled after her.

That night, she lay awake in bed under a single sheet, watching the headlights of passing cars travel up one side of the wall and across the ceiling before disappearing into the dark. The hum of the tires on the road outside made a welcome distraction from the silent filmstrip flickering out of sequence across her interior screen: Brian's beaming face after her talk; Michael, spilling his beer at the pub; the old man stiff-legging his way through the cavernous lobby; her parents holding each other under the heavy moon. The many faces at the hearing, all turned toward her, each of them fronting a mind with an opinion about her and the words that had emerged from her mouth. It had overwhelmed her, all of it: the exhilaration at having given the speech, the pride in a job well-done, and then the embarrassment and shame over the pissing match at the pub, and the realization that the man she'd been grooving on for the last six months was a possessive lech.

She thought of Joe. He'd come alive in her mind tonight, in a way he hadn't for months. She missed him. She missed him in the same flu-achy way she'd missed him four years earlier, after he'd left her in the Waterville Holiday Inn, his absence lodged in her gut like something indigestible—a stone, a slug of metal, a fistful of wet heavy sand. She'd spent those next weeks tethered to CNN in the student lounge, watching the images of soldiers training in the desert wearing cammies and gas masks, hands gripping their inky-black weapons. The news sputtered on about the threat of chemical weapons, how Saddam had gassed thousands of Kurds in the past, and how it was very possible he would level the same weapons against the amassing troops at the Kuwaiti/Saudi border. She watched the obsessive discussion of the latest in military technology: the Patriot air-defense missiles, precisely programmed to intercept in midair any Iraqi-launched Scud; the F-117A Stealth fighters, armed with smart bombs and constructed from state-of-the-art radar-eluding composite materials; the Tomahawk Land-Attack cruise missiles, able to fly at sub-sonic speeds and low altitudes, to sneak beneath Iraqi anti-aircraft weapons. She followed the deliberations of the U.N., every address President Bush gave, every grandstanding oration by Saddam and all the analysis afterward.

Joe wrote her regularly from his encampment at the Saudi border, his letters determinedly jocular and upbeat. He rarely complained—mentioning only in passing the brain-bending heat and the inescapable sand—but his letters focused on mundane accounts of days spent on drills and brutal workouts, the comings and goings of patrol copters and Hummer convoys, the nightly runs through the sand, lapping the base, and the Scud alerts that screamed into their sleep, sending them stumbling into their fighting holes, half-filled with slipping sand in the night wind, their gas masks muting every desert sound except the steady drumbeat of their own blood in their ears. He addressed each letter *Dear Indian princess* and signed them *Your young warrior, Joe.*

To each of these letters, she'd responded, addressing him as *Big Man Joe Bishop*, and recounting the latest meeting of Students for Peace, making a point of lingering over her description of the good character and even better looks of the group's leader, Jeremiah Thurber, and how he'd personally asked her to pin up flyers with him all over campus, and then invited her to a party at his off-campus house. *Better come home soon, Big Man*, she wrote. *Lots of competition here in the Maine woods, just hours away from the Canadian border.* She signed her letters *Your Indian princess (for now), Rachel.*

In reality, she thought Jeremiah was a pompous asshole, and didn't even consider going to the party he'd invited her to, but she was angry at Joe, and wanted to prick him with something like the same abandonment she'd felt the morning he left, when she woke to an empty bed, still wearing her little black dress, with not even a goodbye note to assuage the chasm in her gut. Her proposition, for them to run away to Canada together, might have been reckless and naïve, but it was also utterly sincere. She had been ready, that night, to forge a life with him, to beat a path through the wild future together. It was as vulnerable as she'd made herself, ever, in the whole history of Rachel. And Joe had basically laughed it off, treated it as the silly rantings of a girl, a girl who didn't understand the hard edges of war, or the brutality it took to become a man.

The last letter she'd opened from him had arrived a week after Christmas, when she was home for break. In it, he chewed her out for being such a crappy girlfriend, and asked her to write him something nice and comforting and *decent* for once. In this letter, he laid into the complaints he had apparently been holding back in all his others—how the food sucked, the days were mind-numbingly boring and as hot and smelly as the inside of a car engine, how he was averaging four or five hours of sleep a night, interrupted at that, and how the other guys were a bunch of shitheads who called him "Chief," like it was 1964. *A non-sarcastic letter from you would actually really help me feel better, Rachel,* he wrote. *If that's not too much to ask.* She scribbled the following response on a single sheet of paper: *Dear Big Man Joe, You want me to be nice? Come the fuck home. Rachel.*

And then his letters ceased, and the war came.

Back at school, she watched the war on the TV in the student lounge at the end of her dorm hall. The first wartime salvo fell mid-newscast, one bitter cold night in January. Newscasters yammered pruriently, superimposed against a background of the night sky above Baghdad, blazing trails of missiles streaming through the black like a Fourth of July fireworks display. As torpedoes hit their marks, areas of the city lit up in miasmas of illumination before dimming to a low glow—the slow burn of smoldering rubble. Rachel didn't leave the lounge: she dragged the mattress off her twin bed and dozed on the floor in front of the TV, the sound on low all night long. Iraq would retaliate fast, she was convinced, and the troops at the Saudi border were well within Scud range. She watched the war superstitiously, as a sports fan watches a game, believing that her faithful attention would keep Joe out of danger, wherever he was.

The girls on her floor all knew she had a boyfriend in the war, and they gave her plenty of sympathy, but their good intentions weighed on her like a shroud. She knew they whispered about her and avoided the lounge—she saw plenty of them poke their heads in and then leave, quickly, when they saw she was in there. It got so they wouldn't even board an elevator she was on. She ate alone in the cafeteria.

She couldn't blame them, really. Who wanted to sit with a perpetually gloomy, pissy person, whose greeting had become something more akin to a silent glare? Only her good friend Gina kept the faith. Gina sat with Rachel in the lounge, reading her psychology textbook while Rachel glowered at the screen, and brought her corn muffins and Diet Cokes from the late night snack bar. Gina listened to her rant about the war, how the media glorified it as if it was a game, how the names of the weapons—Patriots, Tomahawks, Apaches—siphoned off any scent of their actual purpose, which was to kill real live human beings, and how she thought it was pretty despicable that a government that had been in the business of eradicating Indian lives, language, and culture for generations felt it was totally cool to then turn around and co-opt that same language for their own dastardly purposes. Gina, sweet girl that she was, would always stay until Rachel's theoretical and political rant turned into the personal: how she was so angry at Joe for *choosing* this, for being so stupid as to put himself at the mercy of this merciless government, for drafting himself onto the killing fields—or sands, as it were. And Gina would then hold her hand as Rachel dissolved into incoherent tears, weeping about how she was sure he'd been gassed, that he was probably lying with his face half-eaten away somewhere in the desert, that she hadn't heard from him in two weeks, and she shouldn't have written him that awful letter—that she was a terrible bitch and deserved to be gassed herself, etc., etc. Gina stayed until Rachel was finished, when she would gently suggest that they go for a walk or shoot some pool at the union, or hey, maybe change the channel for ten minutes, just to see if they could find a good movie or something. By that point, subdued by her own tears and grateful for Gina's ear, Rachel usually relented.

What she didn't know then, of course, was that Joe was already back stateside, lying on a hospital cot, the bottom half of his face a mash, doped into unconsciousness.

On the night he called—once he had finally gained enough functionality in his jaw to form discernible words—Rachel was on her way to a peace protest. Students for Peace, in cooperation with various church-based antiwar groups throughout central Maine, were planning to caravan to the state capitol in Augusta, where they'd meet up with hundreds of other protestors. Rachel and Gina, along with the other members of Students for Peace, had worked until 1:00 a.m. the previous night, slipping paper skirts onto hundreds of candles to keep people's fingers from being scorched by dripping wax. When the phone rang, Rachel was hefting a box of these candles onto her hip, and was about to follow Gina out the door to her car, where five more boxes were tucked into the trunk and the backseat. Their plan was to form a human traffic barrier, and to march down the main drag to the state capitol, candles lit, chanting and singing peace songs.

Even four years out, Rachel's gut seized with nausea when she thought of that night, of what she'd said to Joe. The memory would hit her sometimes out of the blue, and normally, she'd push it out of her mind by finding someone to talk with until it went away. But on this night, the night of the hearing, as she lay awake in her childhood bedroom, missing Joe with an ache that reached from her fingertips to the very center of her groin, she let it come, let it flood her thoroughly with shame and grief and regret.

His voice had come low and slurred over the phone, and she thought at first that it was this guy Phil she'd stupidly given her number to the previous weekend at a bar, and so she'd said, "Who is this?" with the same vituperation that her father reserved for telemarketers who called their house during the dinner hour. Joe's response came slow—whether that was the drugs, the injury, or his own nervous hesitance, she didn't know.

"Rachel," he said. "It's Joe."

She'd dropped the box of candles on the bed; they bounced once and fell to the floor. She sat stiffly on the edge of the mattress, feeling the blood coursing from her head to her heart, tunneling somewhere inward, flowing in fear, maybe, from the sudden electrical storm of her own emotions. Gina, who was waiting by the door—well-bundled in wool hat and scarf, two pairs of mittens, and a bulky down jacket as puffy as a marshmallow—looked inquisitively at Rachel, but Rachel couldn't afford to look back: all her attention was going to maintaining a reasonable amount of breath coming and going from the lungs that until this moment had operated just fine without conscious control.

"Rachel? Are you there?"

She cleared her throat. "Where are you?"

"I'm home. I'm back in the States. At Walter Reed Hospital. There was an accident, but I'm all right. I'm alive, anyway." He spoke deliberately, enunciating like someone who'd only just learned the language, with that strange slur.

Rachel's eyes narrowed, and the thought occurred to her that maybe this was some kind of a sick prank by one of the girls on the hall, trying to get her to stop moping around; maybe someone got their boyfriend to call in and pretend to be Joe. "Who is this really? You don't sound anything like Joe."

"A helicopter blade busted my face apart," he slurred. "I lost my jaw. It makes me talk funny."

"How do I know it's you?"

"Big Man Joe saves the world, with his Indian princess at his side? His Indian princess with the beautiful scar like a rainbow trail, all down her belly?"

Rachel flushed. "Jesus."

Gina held up a note that read, "Do you want me to wait?" Rachel shook her head. Gina picked up the box of candles, touched Rachel's shoulder, and left the room, pulling the door shut behind her.

"They're putting me back together down here," Joe continued, "Humpty Dumpty-like. When they're finished, I'll be ready for anything. College, Canada, you name it."

The tips of her toes began to tingle, the precursor to numbness, and she realized she'd been sitting on her heels on the bed, squeezing her knees together so tightly, she'd cut off circulation to her lower legs.

"Are you there?"

"Yeah. Yeah, I'm here."

A long pause. "Well, so, anyway. I guess I just wanted you to know that I came the fuck home, just like you asked."

Her memory of what she said next was fuzzy at best, compromised, she supposed, by the power-surge of emotion coursing through her, obliterating any and all rational response, but it was something like the following: *How could you do this, you bastard, how could you put yourself in this situation, do you know how crazy it's made me, wondering whether you're alive or dead all these weeks, how little I've slept, and how all my friends have written me off as some raving war widow, and now you're home and you just call out of the blue and expect me to what?—cry with relief and joy that you're home and rush down there with chocolate chip cookies and some fucking needlepoint, to hold your head and coo in your ear? Well fuck that, Joe. This is a bad war, an evil war, and you did it to yourself, do you hear me? You didn't have to go. You shattered your own jaw, Joe.*

Something along those lines.

She'd stopped, finally, and sat there, having shocked herself into silence. And just as she found the breath to utter the next necessary words—*Joe, I'm sorry. I didn't mean it*—she heard a click from the other end and the phone went dead. By the time she'd tracked down the number to Walter Reed, and asked to be connected to his room, Diane had picked up and said that Joe was resting and couldn't come to the phone.

And that had been the shitty, shitty end.

She kicked the bedcovers off her feet and rolled over on her side, grabbing the enormous fluffy red pillow she'd kept since grade school and hugging it close. What was up with her? Why was she thinking so much about Joe? It had been four years since that awful night, two years since she'd made her last attempt to get in touch with him—she'd spent the intervening two years calling and writing and leaving messages, with never a word in reply. Finally, she'd given up, acknowledged her own reckless mistake, and tried to move on. And gradually, she'd thought of him less and less, other than the occasional blindsiding memory. But now tonight he was back, as present in his absence as if she'd only just lost him again, the grief that fresh and pure. She wished she could call him up and tell him all about the night she'd had, the whole episode with Michael and Brian. Joe would turn the whole thing into an absurd joke, particularly the whole "Native versus Indian" thing. They could laugh about it together and dispense with the whole evening that way.

But she couldn't call, of course, didn't even have his number, or know where he was living or what he was doing now. Maybe he was finally in school somewhere, studying engineering, like he'd wanted to do. Probably he had a new girlfriend now, someone beautiful and acquiescent, who knew how to be nice when it was required. It did her no good thinking of him; it was like taking a razor blade to a scar.

She threw the covers off, slid on her slippers, and shuffled downstairs to the kitchen, where she poured herself a glass of milk and put it in the microwave. The green numbers glowed 12:42 before she punched in the one-minute cook-time and pressed start. 11:42 central time. Still before midnight. She picked up the cordless and dialed.

"Grand? It's Rachel. I thought maybe you'd still be up."

"You know me well, darlin'. I'm here with my book. Granddad's long gone, but he doesn't hear a thing over his snoring. Is everything OK?"

The microwave beeped, and Rachel took out the mug, the handle hot to the touch. "Everything's fine, Grand. I just miss you. I miss the Farm. I wish I'd gone up there this year."

"Is that all? Well, we miss you here, too, darlin'. No getting around that. But you've had your adventure on the fishing boat this summer! The Farm'll be here next year."

And they continued in this vein, chatting about Rachel's summer, about life on the "fishing boat," and the sturgeon. Rachel told Grand about the hearing, and her speech, and then about how she'd gotten two job offers out of the evening, and even about the weirdness between Michael and Brian, and how it made her feel like she didn't want either job, and basically, like she just wanted to go to the Farm and hide for a while. "I was so excited to get this summer job, I didn't really think about what I'd do when the summer was over. And now it's almost over, and I don't know what to do."

"And these two offers tonight don't appeal because of the way they were offered?"

"Because one guy is a condescending jerk, and the other guy is an egotistical womanizer." Rachel sighed. "Do you think I'm being too picky?"

"I didn't say that, darlin'. It's important that you like the people you work with."

"I was wondering, Grand. Would you happen to have Joe Bishop's number? I was just thinking about him, wondering how he was doing."

"Well, let me see. It's the same as Diane's as far as I know. Hang on, let me find it . . ." Rachel heard the hushing sound of pages turning, and then Grand dictated Diane's number to Rachel, which she jotted down in blue ink on a piece of yellow sticky paper.

"Thanks, Grand. I should let you go to bed. Say hi to the eagles for me."

"Oh, they've flown off by now. Probably gone looking for you, darlin'— they missed you this year."

Rachel smiled at Grand's habitual fiction, said good-bye, and hung up the phone.

She looked at the number on the pad. She could already hear the sound of Diane's thin cheer and the thud of her rejection like a slammed door, the words she'd finally spoken the last time Rachel called: *Joe's not interested, hon. I'm sorry to have to be so blunt, but it's time you heard. Better not waste your time.*

She peeled the sticky note off the pad, tore it in half, then quarters, then eighths, then finally tossed the pieces into the downstairs toilet, watching them darken as they took on water. She flushed, and the yellow flakes swirled in a descending whirlpool.

Rachel spent that weekend at home, helping her mother split hostas in the garden. Lilly showed her how to dig beneath the plants with the trowel, then carefully lift the pile of dirt, roots, and plant and set it all on a tray. They transported each plant halfway around the yard, to a patch of shady soil beneath a big sycamore, where grass did not like to grow. There they dug, placed the hosta clumps in the holes, and then troweled the soil back into place, finishing off with a generous soaking from the watering can. Rachel gratefully followed her mother's meditative movements, her silent care. Even when all the rest of her life was going to hell, she thought, at least there were hostas to split.

The phone rang, and Lilly went inside to answer it, then returned through the sliding door, phone in hand. "It's for you, Rachel."

Rachel tossed her gardening gloves on the built-in bench surrounding the deck and took the phone inside.

"Is this Rachel? This is Michael German. We met the other night?"

"Right."

"Right." She heard him swallow. "Listen, I wanted to apologize for that evening. Things didn't go exactly as I'd intended. I was hoping I might be able to try again. Are you free for coffee tomorrow afternoon?"

Rachel hesitated.

"I really do think you'd be a great candidate for the job. I'd love to have the chance to tell you more about it, without—" he stopped. "Well, without any interruptions."

"All right," Rachel said grudgingly. "Tomorrow afternoon."

They agreed on a place to meet—a café in a little town by the water that Michael knew of—and hung up. Rachel shook her head in disbelief that she'd agreed to meet with a guy who'd made such a poor first showing. But hey, a job was a job.

The café was a beautiful little place with a flagstone patio out front, facing the river, its planters overflowing with bright purple petunias and clematis climbing up its sun-yellow clapboard. Michael sat at a small table under the clematis, his head bent over a stack of papers. He was more attractive than she remembered, at least when he wasn't standing next to Brian: well-dressed, in a blue button-down and chinos, his face intelligent and serious, a thin line of concentration drawn just above the nose-piece of his glasses. He probably smelled good—he had that look about him, like a guy who pays attention to how he smells. He couldn't sit still, evidently: he jiggled his knee under the table, tapped his pencil against the paper, but otherwise, kept his eyes on the paper, immersed in whatever he was reading. It wasn't until she was standing directly over his table, casting a shadow on his page, that he looked up.

"Rachel!" he said, as if he hadn't been expecting her. He stood up quickly, knocking the table with his thighs—apparently a habit of his. "Hi!"

"Am I early?"

"No, no, right on time. Please." He gestured to the chair opposite his. She scooted it away from the table a bit, so she could see the water, and perched on its edge.

He closed the manila folder that held his papers and pushed it aside. "So."

"So," she echoed. Michael was gazing at her purposefully, which made her nervous.

"You know Brian's got a . . . *reputation*, right?"

She raised her eyebrows. A waiter appeared with a tray and set two waters in front of them, as well as a bagel with butter for Michael. She ordered a large coffee with cream and biscotti. Michael continued to gaze at her.

"I just want to make sure you know that. Because a lot of people—a lot of *women*—they kind of fall into his charm and get stuck there. He's like a male Siren, with all these women littered at his feet."

"Except he's the one on the boat."

Michael laughed, or giggled, really, with a startling childlike cuteness. She smiled. "I figured that out, about Brian." *Finally*, she thought. Just last week, she was close to becoming one of those women.

"Good. I'm glad."

"How do you know him, anyway?"

"Oh, he's over at the NRCM office a lot. All the women in the office are gaga for him. I mean, he does good work, don't get me wrong. And we're grateful. But seriously, the man is a sexual harassment case waiting to happen. I'm glad you're smart enough to see that."

Rachel, feeling dumb, took a sip of her water.

"Anyway, enough about Brian. I want to start this whole thing over. I really was impressed with your speech the other night. You hit all the right notes—you were articulate, accurate, and both passionate and rational, which is a really hard balance to strike."

"My father's a lawyer. He taught me some of his tricks."

"Well, he must be a good one." Michael gazed at her again. He had this disarming way of looking at her—like he was both seeing her but also the person she would be in five, ten, fifteen years. Something about his stare gave her the impression that his mind was whizzing ahead, tabulating the possibilities. He did seem to be, as Brian had mentioned, very, very smart.

"Thanks," she replied. "He is."

The waiter arrived with her coffee in a large mug decorated with a sunflower, the biscotti on a small orange plate. She dipped the end of it in the coffee. "Biscotto," she said, trying to provoke that little-boy giggle again. But his face was blank. "Since it's only one."

"Right. Anyway, this job involves a lot of that—having to explain the situation with the Campbell Dam and NRCM's position to people in a clear, rationally argued, convincing way."

"Can I ask you something?"

"Of course."

"Why are *you* recruiting for the position? Isn't that the task of your supervisor or someone like that?"

Michael peeled the paper from a pat of butter. "Good question. The fact is I believe in the work. It's not glamorous in any way, and really, Brian's half-right—there is a lot of grunt work, making phone calls, filing mail, stuff like that. But organizations like the NRCM thrive when everyone in the office believes in the work and the organization, and when everyone's doing their utmost to help. I don't want to leave them in the lurch, I guess. I want to make sure someone good is coming up behind me, so I know things will continue down the right path. The dam's still there, you'll notice. No one's removed it yet."

Rachel sipped her coffee. "So you're taking the time to seek out the right person solely for the benefit of the NRCM. There's nothing you're getting out of it. Other than getting to have coffee with me."

He colored and began fiercely buttering his bagel.

"Just kidding, Michael."

"No one's paying me extra, if that's what you mean. I've invested a lot of time there. And now, finally, the relicensing year has come, which was the year we all were working toward, and the amazing thing is that we have no idea how it's going to turn out. I mean, even last year, I would have told you that our dream—of getting the dam decommissioned and eventually removed—was a serious long shot; that the relicensing was very likely, even extremely likely. But now . . . honestly, I don't know. It could turn out any number of ways. Which is great." He took a big bite of one of his buttered bagel halves. He was so skinny; he looked like one of those people who forgot to eat, a thing that had never, in her whole life, happened to her.

"So why are you leaving now, then?"

He held up a finger, finished chewing, swallowed. "This was what I planned—that I would work there for three years, and then go to grad school. My time ran out."

"How do you know I'm good?" she asked coyly. Something about sitting in this sweet little café by the water, Michael's little-boy laugh and his total transparent sincerity—she couldn't resist teasing him, just a little. He was low-hanging fruit.

Michael smiled. "I just have a hunch."

They sat a while longer, sipping their drinks and chatting. He told her why he'd chosen indigenous studies as his field of interest—that he'd been a history major in college (Tufts) and had taken an Indigenous Americans Literature class that had just blown his mind. Also, working with the Confederation of the First Nations of Maine group over the last few years had opened his eyes to a way of life and a history that was, it seemed to him, largely invisible in mainstream culture. He was fascinated by it. And Rachel told him a little bit about the Farm and its proximity to the Ojibwe reservation, how she used to go for walks over the boundary line as a kid, and that things were different there: houses were smaller and more ramshackle, there were fewer fields and more woodlots, dogs were allowed to run loose. Michael nodded excitedly. "That's what fascinates me. It's like this alternate existence, right under our noses. Only most people don't bother to look."

A flock of seagulls perched on the nearby pier. One by one, the gulls took to the air flying up into the wind that was coming off the water, and then just hanging there, riding the current. They were clearly enjoying themselves—their flight had no other purpose that Rachel could see; they weren't diving for food or even looking for it. They were simply riding the wind, enjoying the feel of it over and beneath their feathers, alternately resisting it and giving over to it, dancing in the air.

Eventually, they ran out of things to chat about. Michael was not a particularly skilled chatter; Rachel could tell he was starting to get antsy, and probably wanted to get back to his work. She left him a copy of her résumé, which she'd brought along, and he said he would personally walk it into his supervisor's office and tell him all about her. She shook his hand when she left, and walked back to her car, feeling pleased with herself and a little bit amazed, as though she'd crossed into some alternate reality, where ultrasmart, serious people like Michael German shared their thoughts and ideas with her in a way that made her feel respected and grown up. No longer just a kid, waiting for something to happen. Who knew? Maybe by this time next week, she'd have a real job.

2

As it turned out, it took a month. There was a phone interview first, and then an in-person interview, and then another. There was the matter of requesting a reference from Brian, which was uncomfortable, to say the least. ("I'll do it," he grumbled. "But honestly, Rachel, I think you're making a mistake. I thought you wanted to be a biologist.") There were the painful final days to get through on the boat and in the lab, during which Brian punished her by lavishing all his sunny attention on another pretty female hourly (which only confirmed Rachel's feeling that she'd made the right choice). And then, finally, she was walking into the NRCM office her first official day on the job. Her boss, Don Kurtz, a wiry suit with a perpetually distracted expression, showed her to her desk—a sprawling industrial-strength thing, which took up most of a wall. She shared the room with Paula Berglund, the Development Director, who wore her gray hair butt-long and smelled of Altoids, and Cleo, Paula's wraith of an assistant, who took frequent smoking breaks and rolled her eyes good-humoredly while she was on the phone.

Immediately, Rachel was swamped. Don handed her two very thick black binders, labeled "Campbell Dam," which he asked her to read through, cover to cover, as soon as possible. Since the hearing, they had been gathering data for a report on the relative success of fish ladders throughout the state; Rachel's immediate task would be to collate that data, organize it into a logical structure, and draft a narrative, due Friday morning. Also, that afternoon, she was to take the minutes at the weekly staff meeting, by hand—this was 1994, and laptops were only available at a premium. She had never in her life taken the minutes of any meeting, and didn't have the first notion of what they were supposed to look like; she spent the whole meeting frantically trying to write down every word anyone uttered, an impossible task. Her first day was only an indicator of things to come. The weeks rolled by, full of deadlines, research, phone calls, meetings. Every so often, she went with Steve Pritchard, the lead attorney on the Campbell project, to meet with a legislator over at the State House, or to take lunch with someone from the Kennebec Anglers Association. She was insanely busy, always behind, but happy.

The upshot of the hearing was that there were more hearings—three of them in different parts of the state planned over the course of the next six months. It fell to Rachel to publicize them, so she wrote and mailed press releases, made more phone calls and followed them up, printed flyers and walked through the city streets, stapling them to telephone poles and community bulletin boards. She stayed up late, tracking the latest legal conundrums that had arisen in the negotiations, catching up on the scientific literature—some of which had been published by Brian—that documented the decline in anadromous fish populations, or the rise in silt levels and heavy-metals content of the flowage. She drank lots of bad office coffee. She worked hard and long, and went out occasionally on Friday nights with Cleo and Paula and a few other people from the office to the Bear Brew Pub, where sometimes they would run into Brian and Sara and River (Margaret was entrenched in her schoolwork). Rachel would chat amiably with Sara and civilly with Brian, and would make all the appropriate sounds about River, even though in general, she felt basically indifferent toward babies. They were cute and all, but nothing that interested her. What interested her was her work, her officemates, and Michael.

At the beginning, Michael would call her in the evenings from time to time, to see how things were going. Always, she had a question for him; always, he answered it thoughtfully and thoroughly; always, his measured, rational perspective made her feel capable and sane. By late September, they were talking on the phone every night. Rachel would tell him about the latest awkward exchange with Don (who could be standoffish), or Cleo's most recent exploit, or the encouraging uptick in fundraising dollars, despite Paula's broodiness. (Paula sometimes fell dark over a perceived slight that no one else noticed.) Or, Rachel would gripe about how long it took people from the Confederation of First Nations to return her phone calls, or how the fishermen at the Kennebec Anglers Association treated her like a little kid. Michael counseled her: let Paula vent, eventually she'd come around;

be patient with the tribal council, they had a lot on their plate; be professional and tough with the fishermen, they respected toughness. Be patient and kind, he would tell her, and do your job well. People are difficult and imperfect, but they're the only allies we have.

At first, Michael seemed reticent to talk about himself, but eventually he began to share details from his own life: the monstrous demands of his coursework, the argument he was trying to frame for a literature review he was writing, the strange population that could be found at a Harvard Square Laundromat at 11:00 p.m. on a Wednesday night. Rachel found herself soothed by his steadiness, and impressed by his astounding intelligence and work ethic. He regularly stayed up studying until two or three in the morning, but never complained—if anything, his work seemed to *give* him energy, rather than sap it. If he needed, he'd take a power nap in the afternoon. He would, as she had accurately guessed, forget to eat; she took to asking him what he'd had for dinner that night, as a way of reminding him. In so many ways he intrigued her: his almost old-fashioned politeness (he *never* consciously said anything that might be construed as sexually provocative, and if somehow an ambiguous statement slipped from his mouth, he would backpedal immediately to clarify; in contrast to Dr. Brian's constant innuendo-bombs, as well as the transparent lasciviousness of most of the guys she'd known in college—and a few of the state legislators she had the displeasure of working with now—Rachel found this charming and sweet), his total absorption in the world of ideas, his unfettered ambition and confidence in his own intellectual power, and his almost complete lack of irony. It was almost as if he'd been dropped into the late twentieth century from somewhere in the middle of the nineteenth—his determination and focus, his earnestness, and his clear faith that the system would reward hard work—all of this fascinated her.

She could tell, too, that she was making her own impression on him. There was always a moment in their conversations, when she'd finished updating him on things at the NRCM, and he'd finished telling her about his life at school, when they both fell silent, and something unspoken sat between them, waiting to be acknowledged. For the longest time, they let it sit. Rachel was always the first one to break the silence—she'd never been good at enduring social awkwardness—and she'd clear her throat, or sigh or yawn, and say she guessed she'd better get to bed, etc., and Michael would politely agree that yes, it was late, and he had however many hundreds of pages left to read, and they'd get off the phone. But Rachel could tell he was waiting for an opportunity to say something more, and she would usually lie on her bed a while after they hung up, staring at the ceiling, wondering whether he was trying to get up the gumption to ask her out on an actual date. And, if he ever did get up the gumption, what she might say.

One afternoon, just after Thanksgiving, Paula hung up the phone in the office and declared, "We did it. FERC issued their decision. They denied Campbell the license."

Cleo let out a raspy whoop, grabbed a handful of paper clips and threw them in the air. Rachel stared dumbfounded at Paula. "What?"

"That was Don—he just got off the phone with Congressman Black. 'This is the first time FERC has denied the relicensing of a hydropower dam based solely on the environmental costs of its operation.' That's what he said. They're going to have to take it down. It's historic. We just made history."

"I can't believe it," Rachel finally uttered. "Paula, that's amazing."

"*You're* amazing, sweetie! Don said they were on the verge of just making Campbell install a fish ladder, but your report convinced them otherwise. He said to congratulate you specifically. So congratulations! You did it!"

"*We* did it!" Rachel clarified.

Cleo flipped on her radio, spun the volume to blasting—Aretha Franklin was wailing away—then ran to the door and shouted down the hall, "Campbell Dam is coming down!" She danced over to Rachel's desk and took her by the hand. "Conga with me, baby." Laughing, Rachel grabbed Cleo's hips and they shook and kicked over to Paula's desk. Paula joined on, and together the three of them snaked through the door into the hallway, where they were met by Franklin and Tiffany from Grants and Membership, and the whole Public Affairs team. They congaed down the hall to the break room, where Paula revealed the bottle of champagne she'd hidden behind the paper towels, for this very occasion, and they broke it open and poured it out into Dixie cups, and toasted each other and the river, and the wild fish swimming in it, with Cleo's radio tinnily blaring from down the hall.

None of them could focus after that, and it was a Friday anyway, so they knocked off early and went to the Bear Brew Pub to continue their celebration. They ordered a round of drinks, and then another, and then it was dinner time, and so they ordered quinoa-tahini burgers and corn-tomato salsa, and yet another round with their food. Brian showed up late into their meal, beaming and slapping hands all around, and they ordered another round with him, and before she knew it, Rachel found herself sitting thigh to thigh with Dr. Brian Speckel, asking to taste his stout. The pub had grown dark and loud, busy with the regular Friday night crowd, and their party had dispersed: Paula had gone home, Cleo was off having an extended smoke with some guy she'd met at the bar, and Don and Franklin had migrated closer to the TV, ostensibly to watch the Celtics game, though Franklin seemed to also be enjoying the increased accessibility of the vodka shots. Rachel and Brian were alone at the far end of the long table, two part-time college interns whispering together at the other end.

"What do you think?" Brian asked, after she'd set the bottle back down.

"Yummy." She watched to see if he would sip from it in the same place she had, just as he always did with Sara, and sure enough, he lifted the bottle and put his mouth directly on the ChapStick mark she'd left on its lip.

"I guess you made the right move, Rachel Clayborne," he spoke into her ear. "The NRCM is clearly rocking it with you on their team. Don's been telling me. You're a dynamo."

"It's all the hearings we've been having. People are finally getting it." She sipped from her own beer again, thinking about how she was going to need a ride home.

"Not that I'm surprised. People like you can excel at just about anything."

There it was again: *people like you*. "What do you mean?"

"You know. You've got a spark. It's unusual. I saw it the first moment you walked into my class. It's some kind of special energy that people notice and respond to—it's intelligence and beauty, for sure, but it's more than that. Some flame or something, inside. It lights you up."

She flushed, feeling woozy. She'd forgotten about his gaze, what it could do to her. "That's how I'd describe you," she heard herself say.

His hand went to her thigh, his mouth at her ear. "People like us usually find each other, one way or another."

Ten minutes later, they were in the front seat of Brian's Nissan in the parking lot, pawing each other through their winter coats. The night was cold, below freezing, and their breath made ephemeral clouds as it left their mouths, dissipating into the dark air in the car. The streetlights on the road pooled circles of wan yellow light on the sidewalk. Brian's mouth tasted beery; his hands were cold when they first slipped up her shirt, but they warmed next to her skin. When he climbed onto her, pulling the lever that reclined the seat, her head bounced against the seatback.

Vaguely, from some inner, buried voice, she heard the word *Sara*. Brian slipped his hand beneath the waistband of her pants, beneath the waistband of her underwear, and inside her. She gasped, then melted.

Sara, she heard again.

"What about Sara?" she heard herself ask, in his ear.

"Sara's one of us, too," he replied. "She gets it. She knows what it is to be a passionate person. Christ, you're so wet." He was wrestling with her pants now, sliding them over her hips.

She sat up, suddenly, making him knock his head against the roof of the car.

"Whoa," he said. "What did I say?"

"This is a mistake." She pulled her bra back on, buttoned her pants. "Get off me, Brian."

"Okay, okay. You don't have to tell me twice." He climbed over the emergency brake, back into the driver's seat. Rachel pulled her parka closed and zipped it firmly, then unlatched the car door.

Brian leaned after her. "Aren't you even going to tell me what went wrong?"

"Try *you're married*," she snapped, slamming the door.

She strode back to the pub, where she called her father from the pay phone by the restrooms, then waited for him outside, her breath making funnels of frost in the night air.

About twenty minutes later, Rachel's father pulled up. After seeing that she was upright and coherent, he congratulated her on calling him for a ride rather than trying to get home herself. They drove the rest of the way in silence, Rachel pretending to be asleep against the window. She was enjoying the quiet of the car, the chill of the glass against her face. At home, she scrubbed her face with a washcloth, brushed her teeth and rinsed with Listerine, put on her flannel nightgown, and crawled into bed with the phone. She dialed Michael's number from under her big red pillow.

"Rachel!"

"The dam's coming down."

"Are you all right? You sound . . ."

"I'm drunk. Did you hear what I said?"

"Where are you?"

"I'm safe at home, Michael. The dam's coming down, though! FERC denied the license."

"I heard. That's amazing."

"We celebrated."

"I get it. Well, congratulations! I knew you'd be great for this team."

"Don's planning a party next weekend, at his house. You have to come. Can you come?"

Michael was quiet.

"Hello?"

He cleared his throat. "Yeah, sure. I mean, I've got exams the following week, but if you want me to be there, I'll be there. I'll take the bus up, study on the bus."

"I want you to be there, Michael. I'll come down and pick you up myself if I have to."

"You don't have to do that. I can take the bus."

"You know what I like about you, Michael? You're a total gentleman. Through and through."

He laughed. "You really are drunk, aren't you?"

"But I mean it. I'm truth-serum-drunk. Not throw-up-my-guts drunk."

"That's good to hear."

"Not that I believe in chivalry or anything. Just that you're a really thoughtful person. Like, you consider everyone's feelings as much as possible, and really try to do the right thing all the time. Am I right? I mean, I don't know your whole life history or anything, but it seems like that's the way you are. Like you would never purposefully hurt another person if you could help it. Am I right?"

"Uh, well . . ."

"See! You're even too nice to say yes. That's so rare, do you know that? It's just really rare to find someone so just totally deeply *considerate*, is what I'm saying."

"Well, thanks, Rachel."

"Just because I'm drunk doesn't mean I don't mean it, okay?"

He laughed again. "We'll see how you feel tomorrow."

"I'm sure I'm going to feel like shit, but I'll still think you're the nicest guy around."

The next morning, Rachel woke up late with a dry mouth and a pounding head, and the lingering sensation of Brian's fingers pumping inside her, which flushed her with shame, which in turn, made her head pound even more. She took a long, hot shower, downed two Tylenol with one full glass of water, then another, and then a third, and then burrowed into long underwear, sweatpants, a turtleneck, and a bulky sweater. Downstairs, her father was reading the paper at the kitchen table, her mother at the sink, washing a mixing bowl. A plate of pancakes sat on the kitchen counter.

"Here she is," her father said, as she slid across the kitchen in her slippered feet.

"Hi."

"You doing all right this morning?"

"No. I mean yes, but no."

"Well, let it be a lesson," her mother said. She poured a hot cup of coffee and set it in front of Rachel. "The pancakes are cold, but I'll toast one for you if you want."

"No thanks, Mom. I think I need to ease into food this morning." She took a sip of the coffee. "FERC announced their decision yesterday. They denied Campbell the license. We got a little excited. Hence the excessive celebration."

"No kidding!" Her father smacked the paper down on the table. "That's great news."

"That's wonderful," her mother conceded.

Rachel sat and drank her coffee, feeling grateful for the morning, for sobriety, for her mother's calming movements at the sink, her smooth wiping down of the kitchen counter. When she was finished cleaning up, she set a damp hand on Rachel's forehead. "Maybe you should spend the day in bed. You feel a little hot."

"I'm all right."

"Well, take it easy, anyway." She sighed, and Rachel knew she was shaking off a night's worth of worry. "I'm off to the store, then." She picked up her purse and went to the closet for her coat.

"Maybe you should pick Rachel up a fifth of Seagram's. A little hair of the dog."

"Very funny, Dad."

A half hour later, as Rachel was taking her first bite of reheated pancake, the phone rang. Her father picked up.

"Sure, she's here. More or less." He handed her the phone. "It's Michael German."

"I'm glad you think my hangover is so hilarious." She put the phone to her ear.

"Are you feeling okay?" Michael asked.

"I'm gradually entering the land of the living. Thanks for asking."

"You were funny last night. On the phone." He paused; she could hear his nerves vibrating over the telephone line. "Do you remember calling?"

"Sure. I wasn't that far gone. I remember what I said, even. And it's still true this morning."

"Okay, then. True to your word."

"You still coming next weekend?"

"Well, I had a better idea. I was thinking, or hoping, really—" he cleared his throat, started again. "Just, well, wondering if maybe you might be able to get down to Portland. Like, later today. There's a great band playing at the Hangout. I thought maybe we could meet up, get some dinner, and you know, go to the show together. If you're feeling up to it, that is. I mean, if you're not, I understand."

Rachel chewed a bite of pancake, her temples aching, then swallowed, the noise of her working throat adding to the ache in her head. She was not, exactly, feeling up to it. But she had some sense of what it was costing Michael to ask, and knew that a rejection, of any kind, would probably table indefinitely any prospect of a repeat invitation. "That sounds great. Sure. Where do you want to meet?"

By mid-afternoon, Rachel was feeling substantially more human. She had to sweet-talk her mother a while to convince her she was fine, and to promise her father she would not be calling him from Portland that night expecting a ride. "Because I'll be damned if I'm driving two hours to come get you, even if you're drunk as a skunk," her father said. Michael had named an Italian restaurant, and mentioned that she might want to dress up, just a touch. "It's not a jeans kind of place," he added, which made her wonder if he thought she was a shabby dresser in general, which in turn made her wonder if maybe he had a point.

She decided on a pair of pressed wool slacks and a form-fitting turtle-neck sweater, accented with a silver fish pin that Grand had given her a few years back. She even went so far as to brush on some mascara, and stuck a tube of "natural" lipstick in her pocket. On the way down, she listened to Ella Fitzgerald and John Coltrane, watched the sun slide down behind the beauty strip of spruce trees along the highway, and wondered if the fluttering in her stomach was residue from her beery night or nerves. She found the restaurant without any problem—it was on the main street in the downtown—then pulled into a public parking lot by the water, a block away. She was early. Flicking on the dome light in the car, she applied her lipstick while looking in the rearview mirror, then locked up, tugged on her wool cap with the earflaps, and went for a stroll.

The air was frigid, burning her cheeks. She shoved her mittened hands deep into the pockets of her thrift-store peacoat, and turned the collar up. She'd foregone the down parka she owned in favor of style, but now wished she had the warmer coat. Still, it was good to feel the winter air on her face, in her throat—it felt cleansing, renewing, somehow. The memory of last night's tryst had risen in her mind again and again throughout the day, and each time, it filled her with a hot rush of shame. She felt in need of an internal scrubbing.

She found a pier that extended into the harbor, and walked the length of it. At the end, she set a foot on one of pilings. The dark water winked and rolled in the chill night wind. It looked like oil, and it made her think of the oily waves lapping the Kuwaiti beach, footage she'd seen during Operation Desert Storm, when bombing and Iraqi sabotage had released all those thousands of gallons of oil into the Gulf. The viscous waves, an unearthly black, sliding down the sands; the land-bound shorebirds, their wings slicked to their bodies; the thick plumes of smoke, billowing out of the water, blots of fire on the ocean's surface. The burning oil wells, she remembered, had raised surrounding air temperatures so much that in some places, the heat had melted sand. An apocalyptic sight for her apocalyptic mind-set at the time: beaches of molten glass, oceans in flame, and Joe, gone from her life. A mad, mad world.

Forty thousand birds had died in that spill. Ten to fifteen percent of the world's petroleum reserves had either burned or been poured into the ocean. Kuwaitis and Saudis were coughing up black mucus for months. Even now, all of them the world over, were probably breathing in some measure of that burnt oil, were drinking, in their morning coffee, some miniscule portion of that spill. Yet the world had not ended; here they were yet, living and dying in natural time. Here were the gulls along the Portland shore, their heads tucked into their wings, not a drop of oil evident on their feathers. Here was a restaurant, at the end of a neighboring pier, strung with white lights, candles glowing inside. There, at the window, a young family sat reading their menus, a basket of bread between them. And here was she, Rachel, standing on two feet, looking out at the churning ocean, the dark horizon, the moonless sky, too early yet for stars. The air smelled like snow.

She stomped her feet on the pier to warm them. She felt deeply alone, and yet somehow comforted by her aloneness, by the purity of the feeling, its stark truth. Out on the water, a single headlight trawled the harbor—a lone lobsterman, maybe, coming in from a day's haul. Fleetingly, she wished she might be on that boat, that that might be her life: shipping out every day into the mysterious void of the sea, spending her days trawling those depths, alone with her own thoughts, with the majestic reach of ocean and sky. People were so entangling, she thought. No matter what, you got entangled. She thought of Sara, her open, freckled face and shy smile. Of sweet little River. And then of Brian, his hand down her pants.

She pulled off her mittens, stuffed them in her pockets, and unbuttoned her coat. The cold air rushed in around her torso, grabbed her fingers and held them. She pulled off her hat and let the cold penetrate her hair, touch her scalp. The thing to do was to stay free. To never get married. Never to invest in that lie, in the societal groupthink that promised life-long happiness with the person you loved. It was a good thing, in the end, that Joe had refused to shirk his military duties, that he'd left her alone in the Waterville Holiday Inn that bad morning years ago. What if they'd gone together, escaped in the night to Canada? Where would they be now? Hating each other, messing around, saddled with children neither of them wanted? Full of regret? Thank God he'd left her there. She'd much rather have that perfect week in memory than a flawed and fragile marriage. No, the thing to do was stay single, to revel in the bracing honesty of solitude.

When she got to the restaurant, her cheeks were fiery with cold, her lips numb and unresponsive. Michael was there, waiting at a small table toward the back. He stood when the host led her to the table, dapper in a black turtleneck and blazer, a pair of polished shoes. He took her hand to greet her, then sandwiched it immediately between his two warm ones. "Good lord, Rachel, you're an ice cube."

He smelled of sandalwood and clean clothes. "I like how you say that."

"What? Ice cube?" He touched her cheeks, then took her chin in his hand, and turned it to one side. "Is that frostbite?"

"Good lord. It's so old-fashioned. It's cute."

He turned her head the other way. "You have two quarter-sized white disks in the center of each cheek, and the rest of your cheeks are fire-engine red. What did you do, walk all the way here, or something?"

She took his two hands and pressed their warmth against her cheeks, holding them there. "You can warm me up."

He stared at her, his face flushing behind his glasses.

A waiter approached, so Michael dropped his hands, and they both sat and listened politely to the specials. When the waiter was finished, Michael asked what they had hot to drink. Rachel ordered a hot chocolate, Michael a lemon tea. They spoke about their respective drives—Michael had gotten stuck in some traffic on the way out of Boston, but then made up most of the time once he got past Kennebunkport. Rachel asked about the band. They were called Come the Rain and Michael had gone to high school with the guitarist; they'd been touring around New England and New York, and were finally playing back near home territory. Michael asked Rachel about some of the goings-on at the office, and she filled him in. Their drinks came, and Rachel wrapped her hands around the warm mug, held it to each of her cheeks, which were tingling now, coming out of their numbness.

"Are the white circles still on my cheeks?" she asked. "Is my skin turning black and peeling off?"

"No. Actually, your cheeks look good now. Red still. But in a more reasonable way."

"Reasonable red. That should be the name of a lipstick."

"Healthy red. Ruddy red. Nice, appealing, attractive red."

Rachel fluttered her eyelashes. Michael laughed into his tea, flushing again.

The restaurant was small and cozy: white-clothed tables, the walls color-washed a Tuscan-style terracotta, the light low. Heavenly smells of sautéing garlic emanated from behind the swinging doors to the kitchen, and the food, when it came, was very good: warm potato bread and focaccia in the basket, which they ate with olive oil; crisp Caesar salads for each of them, before their entrées. Rachel ordered a bowl of sweet potato gnocchi in a pesto cream sauce; Michael had fresh salmon and scalloped potatoes. Rachel declined any wine—alcohol was the last thing she wanted after the previous night—and Michael teetotaled right along with her. They split a plate of tiramisu for dessert, down to the mint leaf garnish, which Rachel tore in two. "To fight garlic breath," she said, handing half of the leaf to Michael. He took it, avoiding her eyes, but put it on his tongue and chewed.

She knew she was pushing things, but there was something about Michael's impeccable politeness and consideration that made her want to ruffle his surface a little, to provoke him into some definitive action. Her own private renouncement of commitment had freed her, she felt—she could flirt all she liked; she had nothing to lose. So she was happy when, as they were bundling up to leave the restaurant, and she'd put her mittens on before tying her earflaps down, he stepped forward without asking, and tied the strings under her chin for her, then held open the door. She took his arm as they walked down the sidewalk, and she felt him stand a little straighter.

They were early at the club—Come the Rain wasn't due to play for another hour—so they slid into a booth toward the back of the hall, some distance away from the opening band. Rachel sidled up close and Michael, after a moment of apparent internal debate, rested his arm on the back of Rachel's seat. They sat this way for quite some time, Rachel's head very near but not quite touching Michael's shoulder, his arm very near but not quite touching her opposite shoulder, listening to the band: bass player, guitarist, drummer, and female vocalist. The music was a blend of grunge, folk, and jazz, and sounded noodly and aimless, the vocalist "scatting" lyric-less syllables, achieving a sound that resembled an anemic horn, but without any real sense of rhythm. Eventually, Rachel turned to Michael to make a "yuck" face, and when she did, he leaned in and kissed her, abruptly, on the mouth—or, as it happened, halfway there; he misfired, got the corner of her mouth and part of her cheek.

He pulled back immediately. "Sorry. I—was that okay?"

"You're funny."

He looked disconcerted. "Why? What do you mean?"

"Funny in a good way. Sweet. Very sweet, Michael." She leaned in and kissed him again, making it last this time. He tasted minty and garlicky and warm. When she stopped, he laid his forehead against hers, his eyes closed.

"I've been wanting to do that for a long time," he husked.

"I'm glad you did."

"I wasn't sure you wanted me to."

"Well, now you know."

"Yeah." They kissed once more, and then he finally pulled her in close, and she rested her head on his shoulder, and they listened to the bad music like this, comfortably, interspersing their occasional comments about the band with more kisses. Rachel enjoyed his sandalwood smell. When a bartender asked them what they'd like to drink, they ordered ginger ale and water.

The bar filled up over the course of the hour with twenty-somethings, almost all of the men clad in plaid flannel, wool hats, and work boots, as if they were auditioning for a role as lumberjack, except they were all far too skinny for the part. The women were also thin, sporting zig-zaggy hair and tight jeans torn in strips, as though they'd wielded razor blades on the defenseless denim. Rachel watched them crowd the bar, order their beers, talk and drink and watch the band, their faces all affected ennui, which they apparently mistook for sophistication. She snuggled against Michael, glad for his blazer, his round wire spectacles, his shined shoes, and his palpable, unaffected, undisguisable intelligence. He was, she thought, one of the smartest people she had ever met.

Come the Rain, when they finally took the stage, was decent—much better than the opening band—but Rachel was distracted by the fans, who had now swarmed the dance floor and were bopping their heads to the music, the same bored look on their faces, like a bunch of anorexic zombie lumberjacks, and she began to yawn with increasing frequency, until Michael finally leaned in and spoke—loud enough to be heard over the music—in her ear, "Do you want to leave?"

Outside on the sidewalk, Rachel asked about Michael's friend—would he be disappointed he hadn't stayed to see him?

"He can't stand his own fans, either," Michael said. "He'll understand. He's sick of the whole thing, actually; this might be their last tour." He stepped closer. "I'm not really that big a fan myself. I just wanted an excuse to see you."

They kissed again, a longer one this time. Rachel was now exhausted. She wanted to get on the road, but she could sense Michael's desire. Still, there was no way she was going to make out with two guys, two nights in a row—that choice would truly depress her. So when Michael offered to walk her to her car, she refused. "It's just down the hill from here," she said. "I'll be fine."

"You sure? I mean, I know you're totally capable of taking care of yourself and everything. It's just—there's safety in numbers."

"Michael. This is Portland, Maine. I'm more likely to be attacked by a wayward puffin than a mugger."

He smiled and kissed her once more, gently. "Do me a favor, then."

"Sure."

"Call me when you get home. Okay? Just so I know you got there."

"Only if you'll call me."

"If I do, we'll just get a busy signal."

"Then we'll know we're both okay."

She waved goodbye, and walked to her car, turning once when she got to the parking lot. He was still standing in the alley where they'd parted, his shoulders hunched against the cold night air, watching. She smiled. She liked his concern. Maybe she'd never get married, but that didn't mean she couldn't spend time with smart, considerate, snappy-dressing, nice-smelling guys like Michael German.

3

The day of Don's party a week later dawned cold and snowy. It had snowed several inches in the night, and by the time Rachel picked up Michael at the bus station, the air had warmed enough so that a fine ice-mist coated the roads and the windshield. Rachel blasted the defrost, but still the ice collected, the wipers scraping across its surface. In the car, in between delivering directions—Michael had been to the Kurtzes' annual Christmas party before, and knew the back roads—Michael told Rachel the harrowing story of his ride up from Boston: how at regular intervals along the highway, cars were off the road, some of them overturned and balanced on their roofs, tires still spinning. He'd seen one pick-up truck do a 360 right in front of the bus, then keep going, as if nothing had happened. Rachel gripped the wheel tightly, driving the minimum admissible speed limit.

"You know what to do if you hit an icy patch, right?" Michael asked. "Just take your foot off the gas and gently pump the brakes—don't slam them, whatever you do. That's what causes accidents."

Rachel, who drove stick and preferred to downshift rather than apply brakes at all if she could help it, and who had been kicking herself all the way from her parents' place for forgetting to put the snow tires on, and who really very much *disliked* unasked-for advice on anything at all, but particularly on her driving, nodded.

Finally, they reached the Kurtzes' mailbox, a brick-red box on a post positioned at the end of a long, descending drive. "Jesus," Rachel muttered. "I hope they salted." She crept down the drive in first gear, the engine roaring its objection all the way.

Parked cars lined both sides of the drive, leaving a narrow alley between. Finessing the brake, Rachel managed to pull in behind a Hummer and come to a smooth stop. She turned off the car. The echo of the over-taxed engine died away, revealing the deep silence of the snow-covered country lawn beneath it.

"Nicely done," Michael offered, visibly relieved.

"Thanks."

"That's the kind of car you want in this weather," he added, gesturing to the Hummer. "I mean, I hate them and everything, they guzzle an obscene amount of gas, but at least you're less likely to die. Unlike the person you hit."

Rachel closed her eyes.

"Are you okay?"

"I will be in five minutes."

Her father had warned her earlier that day about going out in this weather, that it was not the kind of weather to mess around with. "Why not bring Michael back here?" he'd asked. "We'll make pizzas and play Monopoly by the fire."

Rachel had dismissed his idea, but now she had to concede that, as usual, he had been right. If this weather kept up, it was unlikely they'd be able to get out of the driveway, let alone get home. Plus, there was the prospect of facing Brian. He would undoubtedly be at the party. She hadn't seen or spoken to him since their debauched night the week before. She'd been telling herself she could handle it, that she'd just pretend everything was normal, that nothing had happened, that she'd just avoid him. But now that they were here—now that she was here *with Michael*—she felt less confident in her acting ability. She hoped Brian had done the smart thing and stayed home.

The cold from the darkening afternoon began to penetrate the car once the engine was off, so before five minutes was out, they were inching arm in arm down the ice-black driveway. Rachel noticed Brian's Subaru—hard to miss, with its Save Our Sturgeon and Phish bumper stickers—further up in the line of parked cars. So much for smart decisions.

The house was a large boxy colonial, impeccably restored, painted a deep pumpkin yellow with dark green shutters, each of which sported a cut-out of a crescent moon. Green piney boughs hung beneath each of the sashed windows, framing a single candle burning behind the glass. "Isn't that a fire hazard?" she asked, gesturing toward a window.

"The candles? Most definitely. But Stacy Kurtz likes to do things with integrity. That's what she told me last year. They even use real candles on their Christmas tree."

"She must come from money. No way Don could afford this place on his salary."

"She does. Southern money."

An enormous wreath, ornamented with pinecones and a big red bow, hung from the heavy red front door. There appeared to be no doorbell, only an iron knocker, wrought in the shape of a closed hand. Michael used it politely.

They waited on the narrow stoop, hearing voices rising and falling on the other side of the door, as well as strains of a canned Christmas chorale. The ice-mist had by now glazed their hats and the shoulders of their coats. Rachel plucked a thin frozen crust from Michael's shoulder and broke it between her fingers. He knocked again, louder this time, but still no one came, and finally Rachel pressed the old-fashioned thumb-piece that raised the latch, and pushed open the door.

They were greeted by the smell of mulled wine and fir. Clusters of people holding drinks clogged the foyer: men in blazers, coiffed women decked in holiday red. To their left, a small parlor was less clogged, but most of its space was taken up by an enormous Christmas tree, decorated, as Michael had said, with small lit candles in miniature aluminum candleholders, sitting unperturbed on the spruce boughs. Beautiful blown glass ornaments hung from other boughs, reflecting the candlelight. They stood awkwardly in this side-room—a kind of life-size display case—looking for a place to put their coats. A set of French doors opened onto a sitting room beyond, a big fire leaping in the hearth. Here Rachel recognized Don's back, clothed in a green woolen sweater. He was leaning against the mantelpiece above the fire, chatting with a startlingly athletic-looking woman in a snug red blouse and fitted slacks, her blond hair pulled into a severe ponytail. Don's elbow rested near a glass figurine: a translucent eagle in flight, connected by a flute of glass to a pedestal. One flinch and the thing would crash onto the hearth.

An older man with black hair and a deeply lined face waved at them from a wing-backed chair in the corner of the room. But Michael waved back, and finally Rachel recognized John Bonyers, the newly-elected president of the Penobscot tribe. They hadn't yet met, but she'd seen his picture in campaign photographs posted on telephone poles and in the tribal government building during her trips to the reservation this fall.

John stood stiffly, favoring one hip, and shook Michael's hand. "Michael German! Good to see you, my friend. How's the old alma mater treating you?"

Michael draped his coat over the back of a neighboring wing-backed chair, and sat down beside John, which, Rachel realized, was a calculated move to allow John—who was obviously nursing some significant pain in his leg—to sit back down without any loss of dignity. This considerate gesture did not escape Rachel's notice, and though it left her standing awkwardly behind Michael's chair, her hands still buried in her folded coat, she was struck once more by his thoughtfulness, and felt proud to be there with such a smart, decent person, comments on her driving notwithstanding. Brian, she thought, could go fuck himself.

Michael shifted in his chair, gesturing to Rachel. "John, this is Rachel Clayborne. She's the new Project Manager for the NRCM."

John moved as if to stand, but Rachel stepped forward. "Please, don't get up," she said, extending her hand.

"He's a hard act to follow, this one," John said.

"Oh, she's already outshining me, three months into the job. I've got nothing on her."

Rachel blushed. "He's exaggerating."

"Rachel!" Don was coming her way, a drink in one hand, his other arm extended as if readying for a hug. He embraced her with one arm, while she patted his back, bewildered. Don was not the hugging type. "I see you've met John Bonyers, here. He's going to be our new best friend."

"Looking forward to it," John replied.

"Hey there, Don," said Michael.

Don turned to face Michael, then made an exaggerated stagger-step backward. "Michael German! I didn't know you were coming!"

"Rachel brought me." Michael stood, smiling tightly, and shook Don's hand. No hug this time, Rachel noticed.

Don glanced at Rachel and back again at Michael, doing the math. "She did, did she? Well, glad you could make it. How's graduate school shaping up?"

They made small talk. Rachel sensed a tension between Michael and Don, and made a note to ask him about it later. Her eyes traveled around the room as they chatted: there were more glass figurines on the mantel, all of them a sculpture of some animal caught in mid-action—a leaping deer, a galloping horse, a pointing dog. Above the mantel, the stuffed head of a moose poked out from the wall, its antlers branching ominously into the room, as if they were still growing from the dead animal's skull. The fire looked as though it had just been stirred: its flames leapt and danced, licking at the mesh gate that balanced on the hearth tile. Half-full glasses of wine sat on two end tables on either side of a voluptuous sofa, as well as on the coffee table, which also held a carved wooden monkey, cupping its hands, full with pistachio nuts. A china bowl of discarded shells sat beside the monkey. People gathered and broke off, groups forming and separating like sparse schools of fish. Rachel watched the door for Brian's inevitable appearance. She felt as tetchy as a sturgeon in a net.

A woman appeared at Don's elbow—blond bob ironed straight, fitted carmine cardigan over a collared white blouse, perfectly applied lipstick to match her sweater, outlined, vigilant eyes. She stared at Rachel as if Rachel were modeling an outfit she was considering buying. "Don, dear," she said, her voice low and soft, with a slight Southern drawl, "won't you introduce me?"

"Oh, Stacy! I didn't see you there. Uh, this is Rachel Clayborne. Rachel, my wife, Stacy Kurtz."

Rachel offered her hand, and Stacy gave it a limp shake, smiling languidly. "Don has just not stopped talking about you, Rachel, ever since you stepped foot in the office. You just walk on water, according to him."

"Ha! Well."

"She's a great asset to the team." Don looked over Rachel's head, caught someone's eye, and excused himself.

"Thank you," Rachel replied to Stacy, who stood unmoving before her, statuesque in her petiteness. "You have a beautiful home, Mrs. Kurtz."

"Don isn't usually so easily *taken in*, which is why I was so eager to meet you, Rachel. He tends to be fairly critical, truth be told. But you've impressed him. I think I can see why."

Unsure how to respond, Rachel looked desperately at Michael, who was deeply involved in conversation with John Bonyers.

"I don't mean to make you uncomfortable, dear. I just like to meet the people my husband is fond of."

"Well, it's a privilege to work for him. It's such important work. I'm honored to be a part of it." Rachel stood tall, trying to garner some advantage from the few inches she had over Stacy, but Stacy was remarkably unfazed by her own shortness. She seemed somehow taller than Rachel, more present, more defined. Maybe it was her hairdo. She regarded Rachel unblinkingly, as if waiting for her to perform some kind of circus trick.

Rachel lifted her arms, still heavy with her draped coat. "Is there somewhere I should put this?"

"How inattentive of me. Please, this way."

Stacy gestured to a door. Rachel slipped Michael's coat from the back of his chair and then followed Stacy into a hallway, where she pushed open a door onto a small guest room, its bed piled high with parkas, sweaters, and long woolen coats. On the floor at the foot of the bed, two lines of purses waited like eager salmon at a fish ladder.

"I wish we had a closet to accommodate everyone. I hope you won't mind?"

Rachel was already dumping her and Michael's balled up coats on the pile. She swung around and almost knocked into Stacy, who was blocking the exit. Rachel, feeling big and clumsy, stepped backward into the side of the bed, almost falling onto the pile of coats.

"This is my son's room." She gestured to a picture on the wall—a high school yearbook photograph of a cocky-looking kid with an ear-to-ear grin and a buzz-cut. "He's off at school now. Duke University. Where my people are from."

"Ah."

"The house is just a godawful chasm without him around. You know? Well, you wouldn't, yet. Soon enough, though. The years pass so quickly."

"Ha, right. Though not me. I'm not having kids." She winced, immediately regretting the blurt.

"*Real*-ly?" Stacy pounced on the information. "You're sure about that, as young as you are? Why ever not?"

"Oh, well, I don't know. Just a feeling I have."

Stacy smirked. "You'd be surprised how feelings change." Rachel tried to edge past her, but she stood firm. "You're here with Michael German, aren't you? Such a smart man. I understand he's at Harvard now."

"Uh, yes."

"Don and Michael didn't always get along, sadly. But that's usually the way with powerful men working in close quarters. It didn't surprise me. I'm sure you'll have an easier time of it."

"My office is down the hall from Don's. I share it with two other women."

"But you travel together, don't you? Drive all over the state side by side? You're writing speeches for him, putting words in his mouth? I would call that working in close quarters, wouldn't you?"

The backs of Rachel's knees pressed against the edge of the mattress. "I'm not, um, *after* your husband or anything, Mrs. Kurtz. If that's what you're worried about. I'm there to do a job. That's it."

"What a thing to suggest! Goodness. Of course you're not." To Rachel's relief, Stacy turned toward the door again. Rachel stepped away from the bed and into the hallway again, behind Stacy, eager to get as far away from her as quickly as possible.

"Well, nice to meet you," she began, moving toward the door they'd come from, back toward the room where Michael was sitting. But Stacy gripped her forearm firmly. "Let me show you where the food and drink is, Rachel. I'm sure you must be hungry after your drive."

Stacy led them further down the long hallway until they emerged into an enormous expanse of a room, also filled with people. Immediately before them was the kitchen—terracotta tiles, wood-beamed ceiling, massive Viking professional oven. A marble-topped island marked the division between kitchen and sunken dining room, a long, farm-style table laid with tempting plates of food. The other side of the sunken dining room was marked off by a wet bar, complete with hanging glasses of all shapes and sizes over the bar, staffed by a white-shirted bartender, who smiled broadly at Rachel, as if he was auditioning for a part on *The Love Boat*. And behind him, the ceiling lifted away, opening onto an enormous living room, its far wall one enormous plate-glass window, looking onto a snow-covered sloping lawn.

"Wow," Rachel murmured. "This is amazing."

"We remodeled several years ago. It was hell, but I've been so pleased with the results."

Rachel, having moved closer to the windows, noticed an outbuilding at the edge of the lawn with two stalls and a fence bordering a paddock. "You have horses?"

"Two. Do you ride?"

"Not really. A little when I was a girl."

"Well, we'll have to have you back in the spring. There are trails all through these woods. We have forty acres, enough for a decent outing."

Forty acres, Rachel thought. *That's five times as big as the Farm.*

Seemingly satisfied by Rachel's envy, Stacy stepped away, gesturing in the direction of the bar. "Manny will be glad to fix you a drink, Rachel. And please do help yourself to some food. I always end up with far too many leftovers after this event." She said a few words to the bartender, and then drifted past the kitchen and disappeared into the hall.

Rachel smiled wearily back at Manny, who still sported the same sycophantic grin. Feeling chilled—maybe by too many minutes spent with Stacy the lizard queen—she moved toward another fire, this one blazing in a gigantic tiled hearth set into the wall behind the bar. She found an empty stool and sat down, holding her hands toward the heat. It was no wonder Don spent so much time at the office, she thought, and was always the first to suggest a Friday night out at the pub. Who would want to come home to Stacy? Even if you did live in a palace like this. So many people were walking advertisements against marriage. Infidelity, possessiveness, jealousy, out-and-out hatred . . . Her own parents were two of the most happily married people she knew, and even they bickered and acted basically indifferent to each other most of the time.

The noise of conversation in the great room behind her swelled, and she scooted her stool a little closer to the fire, as if trying to listen more closely to its communicative crackling and snapping. A group of people had gathered just behind her, walling her off from the rest of the room, and she was grateful for that, for this little ephemeral enclave. She shivered involuntarily, thinking of the fragile sterility of that parlor with the glass animal figurines and the stuffed moose head on the wall. Like surrounding yourself with death.

If Joe could see this house, he'd have something witty to say, she thought. Some good gallows humor about white people and their need to mount things like chemical-soaked animal heads on their walls. That's the difference between an Indian and a white man, Joe would say. An Indian would never even think to display another creature's severed head on their wall. I mean, what a waste of a pair of antlers. You couldn't find a better towel rack at all the Crate and Barrels in the world. She smiled ruefully at his ghost-voice in her mind.

"Hiding?"

She turned: there was Dr. Brian Speckel, all blazered up and freshly-barbered, confident and winky and fucking handsome as ever. Rachel's heart thrummed in her throat, and she turned back at the fire.

"So you're not talking to me?"

"I'll talk when I have something to say."

"Most people begin with the word 'hello.' Just to help you out."

Rachel, sweating with the heat of the fire and her own anger, pushed past him, only to see Sara—beautiful, blond, wholesome Sara, blithely gliding the edge of the buffet table, a plate in one hand, and innocent baby River on one hip, reaching for Sara's plate. Sara looked up and smiled. "Hi, Rachel! Isn't this spread *amazing*? The look of that turkey makes me wish I ate meat, but I'm consoling myself with my third helping of Camembert."

Rachel cleared her throat, wanting to say something polite and normal in reply, but nothing came out.

"Rachel's more interested in the spread behind the bar. Am I right? A good, strong stout sounds pretty good, right, Rachel?"

Rachel spun around, facing Brian's smug grin. "You're a prick, Dr. Brian Speckel. A manipulative, unfeeling, narcissistic prick. You call yourself passionate. Ha. You don't have the first idea of what passion is, of what it means to actually *feel* something *genuine* for another person. You and your cold-blooded sturgeon belong together. Don't ever come near me again." And she stormed past Sara's astounded face, squeezed behind a clatch of people blocking the hallway, and went straight out the front door.

The night was frigid. The sleet had stopped, but the cold had deepened, and she was immediately aware that she hadn't brought her coat. Her fingers, face, skin, the tip of her nose, all reached out to the cold, as if welcoming it into her skin, her body. The stoop and the walkway were slick with ice: she moved slowly across, gripping her thighs for a skid, until she reached the crusted snow, where she could allow her feet to break through to sturdy ground beneath. At least she'd kept her boots on. She shoved her fists into her pockets, and tromped down the slope, along the exterior of the house toward the backyard, watching each exhale embody itself and then dissipate into the air.

The Kurtzes' yard was large and bordered by dense woods. At the edge of the yard, Rachel noticed a shape in the dark—a small house with a peaked roof. Out of the arched entry trotted something, a shape, coming for her. A low bark, then two. She froze. The dog neared: a St. Bernard, trails of icy drool hanging from its ample flews. Rachel held out her hand, the dog sniffed, appraised her with its encompassing brown eyes. "I'm all right, girl," she said. "Or boy. Whichever."

She petted the dog's head and back a while, squatting beside it to warm by its body heat. The dog seemed to understand, and allowed Rachel to get up close, standing over her as she ran her stiff fingers over and through its thick coat, letting her nestle them in the mass of fur on its chest, where a working St. Bernard might have carried its flask. "Too bad you don't have a slug of whisky for me, baby," she crooned. "That might warm me up."

She stood and crunched through the snow again, further down the slope toward the horse paddock. The dog followed her, and Rachel reached down every now and then to set a hand on the dog's head, which came up to her hip.

When she reached the white fence that surrounded the paddock, she could smell the rich warm scent of manure from inside the stalls. It was quiet, deep woods quiet, the kind of quiet that seemed to creep like an invisible animal presence, surrounding her, the land, settling into the snow and the darkness all around. The muffled sounds of conversation that came from inside the house seemed only to accentuate the silence outside. She looked back through the plate glass to the living room, the people lounging on armchairs by the window or standing in tight groups, gesturing like mute actors in a silent movie. River lay on a sheepskin rug, with Sara sitting straddle-legged beside him, bicycling his feet. Brian stood a short distance away, talking with a man Rachel didn't recognize. The whole house glowed, a cold hearth. Rachel turned back to the stalls and the dog: dark but warm.

She whistled low and clicked her tongue a couple of times. Something moved within the deeper darkness of the stall. She clicked again, wishing she had a carrot or an apple. A low, lippy nicker escaped the stall, and then a high head moved into the open paddock: a gracious dark horse, breathing fog.

"Hi, baby." It nosed its face over the fence, snuffling at Rachel's hand, which was beginning to go numb with cold. She stroked the smooth plane of its cheek. "What's your name?"

A high whinny came from the other stall, and the second horse emerged, taller than this first, and gleaming auburn in the dark, as if from some kind of inner light source. The first horse moved aside, and the second stuck its snout in Rachel's direction, its lips nibbling the air. "Sorry, beautiful," Rachel purred. "I've got nothing for you but admiration."

The horse, as if it understood, haughtily turned aside, but allowed Rachel to pet its body, long and taut with muscle, warm beneath her freezing hands. The first horse returned now, snorting its hot breath onto Rachel's neck and ear, and she stroked it. The tall auburn horse moved away, loped a brief turn of the paddock, and then re-entered the dark warmth of its stall.

"I know," she crooned to the first horse. "It's cold out here, isn't it? I wish I could come in there with you. Bed down in the straw. Me and doggie here." She looked at the St. Bernard, who wagged its tail and stuck its cold wet nose in her crotch. "Hey," she laughed, pushing it away. "You're as bad as Mitzy." Mitzy was Grand's golden retriever, who greeted everyone that way. *Nuts-Knocker*, Derek called her. *There she is, good old Nuts-Knocker!* he'd shout, whenever they pulled up and Mitzy came running full speed from the house. *Guard your loins, folks! Guard the family jewels!*

"Rachel?!"

It was Michael, standing at the top of the yard, his body shadowed by the light from the parlor window. Bundled in his coat, he squinted in the direction of the woods. "Rachel?" he called again. The blanketing quiet scurried away.

She considered hiding from him, leaping over the paddock fence and tunneling in the straw and the shit with the horses. But the dog trotted purposefully in Michael's direction, and Michael turned and saw her and then came crunching through the crusty snow in big, leaping steps, as if he were traversing the surface of the moon. He carried something under one arm, and as he neared, Rachel saw it was her coat.

"Here." He held the coat out, gentleman-like, and Rachel gratefully slipped into it. He took both of her hands in his warm ones. "Didn't we just do this last weekend? You seem to have a thing for freezing yourself half to death."

"It's invigorating. Until your extremities go numb." She dug in her coat pockets for her mittens and hat, which she tugged down over her ears, slipped over her hands. She was shivering.

"Here, let me warm you up." He rubbed his hands vigorously up and down her arms, then her back, to little effect through the coat. Rachel, whose teeth were now chattering, moved closer to him.

"Stop. Not like that. Just, here." She began unbuttoning his coat, then slipped her arms around his body, pressing her cheek against his warm sandalwood-smelling chest. He wrapped the coat around her and held her against him. "That's the best way."

"I agree."

The dog nosed its head into the space between them.

"Stacy Kurtz is a vampire," she said.

He laughed. "A strong word."

"The woman obviously lives off the envy of her guests. It's disgusting."

"Is that why you came out here, then? To escape Vampiress Kurtz?"

"Partly," she started. Her skin began to prickle with new warmth. She looked up at him, hesitating, and he bent to kiss her.

"Your lips are freezing, Rachel. Let's go back inside and warm up by the fire. I'll keep Stacy Kurtz far away."

"I'm not going back in there. It's not just her. I can't stand to be near Brian." She swallowed, exhaled, and barreled forth. "I messed around with him, Michael. That night I was drunk and called you when I got home? Brian and I messed around with each other in his car."

Michael pulled away from her, stumbling on the crusty snow. The dog set itself just under his hand, as if to help him right himself.

Cold began to creep through her open coat. She wrapped it close and held it shut with folded arms. "Sorry. I should have warned you a confession was coming."

"Why did you—?"

"It was one of those stupid, stupid things you do when you're drunk. As soon as I was aware of it, I stopped. We didn't sleep together, if you're wondering."

He nodded and kept nodding, as if by nodding this news might work itself more efficiently into its proper place in his brain. "I was. Wondering. Not that it's any of my business."

"It is your business. I mean, if you're thinking of getting involved with me. You probably want to know the sort of person I am. Well, that's the sort of person I am. The sort of person who can get drunk and mess around in a parked car outside a pub with her happily married former boss."

"Hey, take it easy. You're being kind of hard on yourself, don't you think?"

"I'm good at that. That's another thing you should know about me." Rachel squatted to pet the St. Bernard again, sneaking a look up at Michael, who was staring at the dog, his face pained. Above his head, white moonlight hinted through a smudge of cloud.

"I kind of picked that up already." Michael squatted, too, and the St. Bernard wagged madly and licked his face, which made him sputter. "Listen, Rachel. It's okay. I mean, I wish you hadn't. I'm not happy about it. But it's not like I expected virginity or anything."

"Yeah. You missed that boat by a long shot."

"I appreciate you telling me about it. Thanks for telling me."

The snow between them glowed white now: the moon had pushed its way through the clouds and was shining bright, an almost-full disk encircled by gray-white icebergs. "Seeing Sara tonight was like . . . ugh." She picked up a handful of snow, and tossed it back onto the ground. "Makes me want to dissolve into a puddle of slime."

"Well. Sara's going to have to get wise one of these days. I mean, not to disappoint you or anything, but you're not the only one. I wouldn't exactly call them happily married."

"Why would that disappoint me?" She tossed another handful of snow. "So . . . who else has he . . . ?"

"Cleo."

"Cleo? No shit."

"And a former NRCM employee, Noelle. She left because of Brian."

"*Seriously?*"

"And a half dozen of his students. I've seen him with at least six different women over the years. Acting like it's part of his teaching duties."

"What a jerk."

"It's why I warned you when I first met you. Remember that? It was so easy to see what he was up to—I didn't want you to fall into that trap."

Rachel snorted. "Too bad I didn't listen."

Michael was quiet, and Rachel could tell he agreed. Too bad.

Mortified, she knelt, then fell backward into the snow. Her head cracked through the skim crust while her arms still hovered on top of it, too light to break the surface. She gazed up into the sky, the clouds moving now in ridged sequence over and past the moon, alternately blurring and revealing its brightness. She liked Michael. She liked him a lot. He was kind and thoughtful and he didn't condemn her right away, as she'd thought he might—he seemed sad, but not destroyed or disgusted over her dalliance, as some other guys might be. And it's not as though she'd cheated on him— they hadn't made any declarations to one another yet, and certainly hadn't as of last Friday night. Still, she did feel she'd betrayed him on some level:

that she'd knocked her own peg down a notch in his estimation, a thing which saddened her more than she'd anticipated. She wanted him to think well of her; she really wanted him to think well of her.

The St. Bernard came sniffing in her face, and she pushed it gently away. Behind it was Michael, looming over her like some sad giant blocking out the moon. He was holding a hand out to her, to pull her up.

"I like it here in the snow," she said, not taking his hand. "I might just sleep here tonight."

"You do and you won't wake up. It's supposed to go down to nine degrees."

"The dog will keep me warm. Right, Bernie? I'll call you Bernie." She patted its side.

Michael lay alongside her, propping himself on an elbow so he could look in her face. She turned to him.

"I hate that I disappointed you," she whispered.

"Hey. All you do is impress me, Rachel. More and more. I mean, you didn't have to tell me that. That took guts. You are a gutsy person. I really like that about you. And sure, I'm not happy about it. But I'm happy you told me. It makes me feel like . . . like I'm important to you. And maybe like you trust me."

She nodded. "I do. And you are."

They kissed again, long and deep this time. Michael moved his hand in between two of the buttons on her coat and held her ribs, his mittened fingers grazing the bottom edge of her breast. She arched into him, feeling like something he was shaping with his hands, a lump of clay he was pressing and smoothing into a pot, a beautifully contoured pot, to match a vision he held in his mind. She thought she would allow herself to be shaped by him, for a little while anyway. She was curious to see how she might turn out.

4

It took another two and a half years before jackhammers drilled their first holes into the Campbell Dam. The dam owners, backed by the power company, appealed FERC's decision, and so there were more hearings and more arguments and more reports to be written. Rachel traveled all over New England, visiting the sites of dams that had been demolished, or dam sites where fish ladders had recently been installed. She took dozens of photographs, documenting rebounding rivers, the striking renewal of salmon runs, the beauty of newly wild riverbanks. She interviewed fishermen on the Connecticut River who spoke of the jump in shad numbers since the local dam had come down. She raked through piles of documents, amassing statistics on the relative success of newly installed fish ladders versus newly destroyed dams with which to line her reports and Don's legal arguments. She logged hundreds of miles with Don in his VW station wagon, catching naps in the back of the car. The work took sticktoitiveness, a sense of humor, and a great deal of determination, all of which Rachel was blessed with. It also took patience, which she was not blessed with, but whenever she grew impatient with the obscene amount of money and time that was being wasted on the appeal—which everyone at NRCM knew was just a formality, that FERC wasn't going to change the decision—she called Michael and borrowed some of his.

She had moved by that time to a small walkup in Augusta, up the hill from the defunct mill, with a view of the river. She loved her apartment: it was long and narrow, with tall windows that flooded the front room with morning light and wide pine floors, scarred by years of dragged furniture and pointy heels. She bought gauzy curtains that blew in the summer wind and painted the walls cheery colors: sunflower yellow in the kitchen, deep orange in the living room, baby blue in the bathroom. Together, she and Michael outfitted it with thrift-shop furniture: a Papasan chair for reading, a brass reading lamp, a sand-colored terracotta bowl to set on the nonworking fireplace mantel—in it they put rocks they found on their weekend hikes. Their favorite purchase, though, was an old cast iron skillet—it made the best, most evenly cooked omelets either of them had ever tasted, and they joked about how if academia chewed them up and spat them out, they could open an omelet restaurant on the back of that one pan.

Rachel had decided by then that she wanted to go back to school in environmental studies. She was tired of the amount of busywork she had to do at the NRCM, and she was tired of Don's mercurial behavior. A graduate degree was necessary if she wanted to go beyond her current role as general Jill-of-all-trades. With Michael's encouragement, she'd applied to seven different graduate schools, all in the New England area—including Harvard, as a long shot—and by the time Campbell's appeal was rejected, and the first day of demolition had been scheduled, Rachel had gotten into every one of the schools she applied to, including Harvard. She was baffled and dismissive—she felt the schools' standards must be slipping. But Michael scoffed. Of course she'd gotten in, he said. Why wouldn't she have? They celebrated with a romantic Italian dinner in Cambridge and a stroll through the square to listen to the street musicians. Michael suggested, off-handedly, that she might move in with him in the fall, just to save money. "Sure," she replied, as if the question were no big deal. "Sounds like a good idea." Rachel bought some cigarettes, a treat she'd occasionally enjoyed in college, and smoked one while Michael avoided her eyes. Seeing how uncomfortable it made him, she threw the rest of the pack away.

They were different; both of them knew it. Michael's idea of a weekend together was working side by side at Rachel's kitchen table all day, then grabbing a bite at a trusted restaurant, and topping the night off with a rented foreign film and polite sex. Rachel preferred less work, more adventure—hiking a new trail, skinny dipping in a secluded swimming hole, experimenting in the kitchen, fucking in the woods. Forgetting about work for a day or even two. They had to joust a bit, trading favors: a morning of work for an afternoon of hiking. Rachel sometimes lost her temper at Michael for his workaholic behavior; he sometimes grew silent and broody at her recklessness (though he never once objected to fucking in the woods).

But the principle of attractive opposites kept them in each others' gravitational pull: the benefits of being with someone so complementary outweighed the tensions, usually.

On Demolition Day—Earth Day, 1997; a nice touch, they both thought—they picked up a breakfast of bagels and coffee on the way to the dam site. When they arrived, a crowd had already gathered on the shore, a small army of windbreakered spectators, wielding paper coffee cups. At least three different local news crews were out, wheeling their cameras into place, hovering long furry microphones above the gathered crowd. Yellow police tape marked off a boundary; beyond that parked the excavating equipment: two hydraulic jackhammers, a steamroller, and a giant dump truck.

Michael would have remained at the back of the crowd, but Rachel elbowed her way through, tugging him behind. As they neared, they saw the cast that had gathered behind the podium, a semi-circle of familiar faces: Don Kurtz, who waved to them, John Bonyers, who was busy talking with Dan Sheffield, one of the tribal elders, Clyde Jeffries, the president of the Kennebec Anglers Association, three different state legislators, and Congressman Franklin Black, their top advocate in Washington.

Michael nudged her and pointed to the gray-templed man next to the congressman. "That's the Secretary of the Interior. Nicholas Banks."

"Not a bad turnout," said a voice at her elbow: it was Paula, dressed in a light blazer and pearls, her butt-long gray hair French-braided for the occasion. Rachel gave her a quick hug, and noticed, a few heads down, Brian, his arm around his new girlfriend, a recent Colby grad. He and Sara had split up not long after Rachel's outburst at the Kurtzes'; Sara had gotten a tenure track position at a school in Florida. Rachel lifted a tentative hand, and Brian pretended not to see her.

Then a man stepped before the mic and began drumming on a feathered tribal drum he held in his hands, and the crowd hushed. He drummed and sang—an old, throaty Penobscot chant—and the whole riverbank seemed to stop and listen: the people quiet, the wind playing with their hair, the water gurgling just beneath them over the stony bank, sun darting and leaping from the waves like fish. When he was finished, Dan Sheffield stepped to the mic, his head wrapped in a gold and red band, topped by a crown of erect eagle feathers. As he spoke, he held another feather above the crowd, like a priest giving a benediction. Dan invoked the Great Spirit, and spoke about the importance of the river to the earth, how the freeing of the river here would help restore the salmon and shad and alewives and sturgeon who swam the river, and had swum the river for ten thousand years before anyone ever thought to put a dam on it. "The ancestors are smiling on us today," he concluded, and everyone applauded wildly. Rachel saw tears in Michael's eyes.

John Bonyers spoke next. He thanked the previous tribal administrations for their hard work in getting them this far, and all the various partner organizations who'd contributed their time and money and effort to educating the public, spreading the word. Don followed him, thanking everyone again, and the pattern continued that way for the next forty minutes: Clyde Jeffries said his piece, Congressman Black said his, and the Secretary of the Interior—each of them got up to repeat the same ideas about how auspicious the day was, how grateful they were, etc., etc., etc. Rachel leaned against Michael's side, and he put his arm on her waist, pulling her closer. The sun shone on their faces, the morning was warming up, and she felt she could fall asleep there, against his wiry strength, letting the voices from the podium blur into a drone. Until, that is, the Secretary let slip that, due to the huge efforts of Congressman Black, who'd led the charge in Washington, his department, in conjunction with the National Oceanic and Atmospheric Administration, was granting ten million dollars to the National Resources Council of Maine to go toward the purchase of the next three dams up the river, with the ultimate goal of freeing the river all the way to the headwaters. "This project is a model for not only the country, but the world," he said, "and we want to see it done well."

His announcement sent a hush of disbelief over the crowd. Someone whispered, "What did he say?" behind Rachel's shoulder. Then John Bonyers began clapping, and a few others joined, and soon enough, the clapping turned to cheering and hooting and slaps on the back. Don Kurtz actually lifted Cleo in the air. Paula was saying, "I can't believe it. I can't believe it," over and over again. Her face was pale; Rachel grabbed her hand and squeezed it. "You okay?" she asked. Paula just gaped at her.

Finally, once the crowd had calmed, Don stepped to the mic and announced the "big moment." Behind him, the jackhammers were poised ready to strike, their enormous drill bits hovering on arachnid-like steel arms above the dam. He asked the crowd to count down from ten, together, and once they reached the one, the great steel spider arms rose in the air and came down, slowly, the metal bit cracking into the dam wall, cracking and jostling, and sending clouds of concrete dust billowing into the breeze, spraying their faces, silting their tongues. People waved the clouds away, spat on the ground, but stayed in place, watching, spellbound, as the machines hacked away at the structure before them which, moments ago, had looked impermeable, permanent, a fixture on the river, and now was turning to dust and crumbled chunks of concrete, blowing away on the warm morning wind coming out of the west, blowing out to sea.

Rachel and Michael stayed to watch for another half hour or so, walking around to the other side of the dam, so they could see if and when any water would start moving. But there was no water flow yet. It was a sizable dam; there were many layers of concrete to get through before the pressure of the water began to melt the concrete away on its own. After a while, the bone-shaking chattering of the jackhammers grew wearing. Rachel suggested they leave, but Michael seemed reluctant to go. "Just a minute," he said, and he watched the jackhammers several minutes more, as if he expected something to happen.

"I don't think the water's moving today, Michael," Rachel said, with a gram of irritation.

"I know," he said, staring straight ahead.

"So . . . ?"

Most of the rest of the crowd had left; there were only a few hangers-on, smoking and staring, one man throwing a stick for his dog in the water. The dog swam back, the stick in its mouth, its head held high above the water. When it reached the shore, it dropped the stick and shook, droplets flinging off its back.

"Rachel." Michael was holding a box at his chest, a little padded box with a gold clasp. He lifted the lid: inside was a ring, its diamond glinting in the sun. "I thought we might as well go ahead and make it official." The box shook in his hands.

She looked at the ring, looked at his face. His heart was pounding so hard, she could almost feel its wake in the air. She looked at the ring again. She was totally, utterly stunned. "Whoa," she said. "Are you asking me to marry you?"

"Yeah." A nervous giggle.

A jackhammer drilled another deafening hole through the concrete.

"Say something."

"I'm just—surprised, I guess. I hadn't expected this."

"Well, I wanted to surprise you. I thought today would be the perfect day to ask. It's a good day for new beginnings."

"I don't know what to say."

He cut his eyes at the man and his dog, who were passing them now, the dog leaving wet prints on the asphalt. "Rachel, I love you. You're intelligent and brave and passionate and fun. I love being with you, and I want to spend my life with you. How about saying yes?"

Rachel felt uneasy, but she saw the fear rising in his eyes, and so quickly, to tamp it out, she said, "Sure. I mean, yes. Of course. Wow. Yes."

She kissed him, mainly to expunge her own jitters and erase the weirdness of the moment. When they parted, he took the ring out of the box and slipped it onto her finger. "How does it fit?"

"Fine. I mean, yeah. It's good." Her mind was spinning. She was thinking of the night of their first date three years earlier, when she'd stood by the dark, oily ocean and vowed never to marry. What, exactly, had happened?

❧

That evening, after they'd both calmed down a bit, they laughed off the awkwardness of the moment. Michael apologized for his nervousness, and Rachel marveled at how thoroughly he'd surprised her. When he kissed her goodbye ("Now I can call you my fiancée," he said), and puttered down the hill back to the highway and to Cambridge, their future home, Rachel sat in her darkening front room, the phone in her lap. She knew she should call her parents and tell them. They would be glad—they loved Michael. They would shout and laugh. Her mother would want to start planning, immediately. Next she'd need to call Derek, who'd joke about how he thought he'd never see the day, how Michael didn't know what he was in for. Then Grand, who would be equally excited, and who'd offer the Farm as the location for their wedding. There would be lots of joy and ceremony. But she couldn't make the calls. She was thinking of Joe, of those old dreams.

She dialed information. "Clinton, Wisconsin," she said, at the prompt, and then, a moment later, "Joseph Bishop." She waited. Finally, a real live person got on the line and told her that the only number for Bishop that was coming up in Clinton was a Diane. Rachel sighed, and said yes, she'd take the number. She wrote it on a sticky note and stuck the note to her finger.

She went to the dark kitchen and took a beer from the fridge door, pried off the top, and then walked back through the dark apartment and sat in the same chair, the sticky note still stuck to the tip of her index finger. She took a sip of the beer, set the bottle down, and dialed, her heart pounding. *Please be Joe*, she prayed, *please pick up, Joe. Please be Joe.*

"Hello?" It was Diane.

"Is Joe home, please?"

"Who is this?"

Rachel closed her eyes. "It's Rachel Clayborne. Is this Diane?"

"Rachel! Well, hi, hon. It's been a long while. How are you?"

"I'm fine. Doing great. How are you both doing?"

"Oh, we're just terrific. In the middle of the spring thaw, you know, so that always cheers us up. How's your grandmother? I imagine she'll be thinking about coming north pretty soon now, won't she?"

"She's good. Still the same old Grand, I guess." She laughed awkwardly, trying to hide her nervousness. "Um, I was just really hoping to talk to Joe. Is he around? I mean, assuming he still lives there and all . . ."

"Oh, sure. He still lives here, hon, but no, I'm afraid he's not here right now. What a shame. I'm sure he'll be sorry he missed you."

Rachel paused. "Do you know when he's due back? Maybe I could try back later."

"Actually, he's away right now. Won't be back for a couple of weeks."

"Really."

"Can I give him a message?"

"Does he use email at all? Maybe he's got an email address I could write to."

"No, sorry, hon. We haven't quite caught up to that trend yet."

"There's just something kind of important I wanted to talk to him about."

"I wish I could help you out, Rachel, but he's just unreachable right now."

Rachel took a pull on her beer. "I guess if you could just pass along the message to him that I'm engaged. That's really it. I just wanted him to know."

"Oh, for heaven's sake! Congratulations, hon! That's terrific news. I'll be sure to tell him."

"Thanks."

They hung up. Rachel sat in the dark, drinking her beer, watching out the window as the streetlights came on, one by one, the lighted windows of apartments and houses where couples were preparing dinner, helping their children with homework, watching the news, the river a swath of darkness beyond all the lights. Soon it would be moving, flowing free and unobstructed to the ocean. And she would be moving, too, in just a couple of months, down to Cambridge and to her new life—starting graduate school, living with Michael, dear, sweet, intelligent, kind, considerate Michael. And now, or eventually, they would be married. It was a dream life, an enviable life. So why did she feel so unsure?

BOOK THREE

I Have Not Yet Begun to Fight

June 2003

1

"Time for your vitals!" Diane swept onto the porch, starting Maddy awake.

"Oh! Oh, dear. I must have fallen asleep."

"Arm, please." She placed two fingers gently on Maddy's paper-skin wrist, and kept an eye on her watch, counting.

"Was there someone just here? I have this feeling."

"Twenty-nine, thirty..."

"It was Rachel! Where did she go?"

Diane finished her count. "Seventy-nine. Not bad for an almost-ninety-year-old. Rachel's out for a walk, hon. I saw her heading down to the lake a while ago." She slid Maddy's sleeve up her arm, revealing the fish-belly white of her forearm, then wrapped the blood pressure cuff around her upper arm. "Now you'll feel a hug," she warned.

"Oh, good. I'm glad she's getting out in the woods. She used to spend her whole day out there, when she was a girl. She and that boy. What was his name again?"

Diane squeezed the bulb that pumped the cuff tighter around Maddy's arm, her eye on the monitor. "Joe, hon. My son, Joe."

"Of course! Goodness gracious. Your son. How could I not remember that?"

"One-twelve over seventy. Also not bad." Diane ripped open the cuff's Velcro and marked the figures on Maddy's chart.

"You know, Diane. I hate to contradict you, but I think you might be mistaken about Rachel and her feelings about the Farm. We were just talking here, just a little while ago, and she was telling me how much she loved this place. I must admit, it gave me pause."

Diane wrapped the rubber cord around the blood pressure cuff. "I never said she didn't love the place, Madeline."

"Didn't you?"

"No, hon. Not once. I'm sure she does love the place. But loving a place and doing what's right are not two mutually exclusive things."

Maddy nodded slowly, considering. "I suppose that's true. It's just . . . well, I hate to think that Rachel won't be able to come up here and enjoy these woods after I'm gone. I think that would just be such a shame."

"It's your choice, hon. You know I've said that from the beginning. It's entirely your choice."

"I know, dear. And I've already made it, haven't I?"

Diane looked out toward the stand of birches just off the porch. The sky was beginning to darken, and the white of their bark stood out like ghostly skin against the dark woods. "I'm going to go change your sheets, hon. It looks like rain's coming, and we don't want you out here on the screen porch in the rain."

"Again?" Maddy craned her neck and looked toward the woods. "Goodness. What a wet spring we're having. I certainly hope Rachel doesn't get stuck in the rain."

Diane tucked the blood pressure monitor and clipboard on the corner table in the office, and climbed the stairs heavily. Rachel was telling Maddy how much she loved the place. She knew it—she could see this coming, from the moment Rachel stepped out of her Prius early this morning. Just like the bumper sticker on the back of her car: if you want to make God laugh, tell her your plans. God was having a good laugh now.

She'd seen this sort of thing before, and it always made her sick. The long-lost relative—the prodigal granddaughter, in this case—swooping in at the last minute, making eloquent professions of love and apology, rubbing hands, licking lips. *If you wouldn't mind just whipping out your will, I've got a notary public right outside the door . . .* It was sick and unfair, but it was the way families worked. She had no call to be surprised. No call at all.

At the top of the stairs, she went to the linen closet, where she selected a set of clean sheets with a faded floral design. She closed the closet door, then froze, her hand on the knob. The Claybornes would see her as manipulative, a gold-digger, even. Maybe Rachel already did. Diane rested her forehead against the closet door, catching her breath. She'd rather die than be thought of like that. She was going to have to figure out how to set things straight.

Walking slowly, she brought the clean sheets to Maddy's bedroom, where she laid them on a chair and began stripping the dirty linens from the bed. The thing was, she understood Maddy's feelings completely—her unbridled love for Rachel, her desire to give the girl just what she loved: these woods, this place. If she were in Maddy's position, she would feel the same way.

She balled the dirty sheets up and tossed them on the floor by the door. Out the window, gray clouds were gathering above the lawn. She worked more quickly, snapping open the clean fitted sheet and tugging it into place over the mattress corners. What the Claybornes were going to have a hard time understanding was that the whole thing had been Maddy's idea. Maddy had been the one to suggest it. All Diane had done was tell her the story of how the land came to the Clayborne clan in the first place: How the Bishop family's allotment had once upon a time been a decent acreage near the old river, how her great-grandfather had hunted on that land and cleared a portion of it to farm, and then, how he had fallen sick with tuberculosis, and his daughter, Diane's grandmother Mary, pregnant and poor, had tricked him into selling it. Mary had told the old man she was taking out a loan, and she needed his signature on a promissory note. And so he'd made his "x" on the line, leaving a spray of bloody spittle on the page (Diane had seen the thing herself). Luckily, he'd died before finding out that what he'd signed was not a note but a deed, because the knowledge of his own daughter's cold-blooded betrayal probably would have killed him. And the person he'd signed the land over to was Benjamin Turner, Maddy's father, builder of the Old Bend Dam.

Maddy had listened to this story, rapt and open-mouthed, and when Diane had finished, she'd declared, in a voice edgy with righteousness, "Well, there's no question what the right thing to do is. I'm just glad I'm in the position to do it."

"And what's that?"

"To give it to you, of course!"

"That's very kind of you, hon," Diane had demurred, "But I don't want to make any enemies."

"What on earth do you mean? What enemies?"

"Don't you think Christopher and Linda might resent that?"

"Well, they don't want it. They've told me again and again that it's too much of a burden. So, they've had their chance. What do they expect?"

Was it wrong of her, then, to accept Maddy's freely given gift? Was it manipulative of her to rejoice and support this old woman's dying wish— that justice be done, that the land be restored to a family who'd been tricked out of it generations before? Why shouldn't they do what they could to keep the moral arc of the universe bending toward justice—to quote one of Maddy's most revered idols? Why should she feel so wretched for doing what was right?

The bed finished, she sat on its edge, pulled her phone from her pocket, and dialed Ramsay's number. Ramsay was the medicine she needed right about now.

"Hey, babe," she spoke into his voicemail. "I've got my day off tomorrow and I want to spend it with you. Let's meet for lunch at the Hunter's Haven, my treat."

She closed the phone, dropped it in her pocket, and bent to pick up the balled sheets. She'd start a load of laundry, then help Maddy upstairs, out of the coming rain.

⤙⤚

That night, Deirdre down, Rachel called Michael, feeling apologetic for how she'd left. She gave him a summary of the day—Grand's strange incoherence, her suspicions about Diane, the phone call from her father, in which he declared he was going to be selling the Farm after Grand died. Everything but Joe's appearance, and then weird disappearance—this she left out. No need to put him on edge anymore than he already was.

"Well, I can't say it surprises me," Michael replied, after listening to her rant about the idea of selling the Farm.

"What do you mean by that?"

"It's nothing against your father, Rachel. I think his plans are very practical, to be honest. It's true that you guys don't use the place anymore."

"Thanks to you." The apologetic impulse that had compelled her to call him had vanished.

"Rachel. Please don't start with that again. Anyway, my feelings—*our* feelings—about the Farm don't have anything to do with the rest of your family's attitude toward it. And they've stopped going. They've moved on."

"Okay. Fine. But the thing is, Michael, what I'm realizing, is that I haven't. I'm not ready to give this place up. I want Deirdre to have a chance to spend her summers here."

Michael paused. "I thought we were in agreement on this."

"In principle, yes. But this is reality."

"But don't we want reality to match our principles? Isn't that what principles are for, in the end?"

Rachel rolled her eyes sumptuously, staving off an urge to throw the phone against the wall. "Anyway," she said, "I'm going to fight this thing."

"How?"

"Talk to Grand. Try to get her to see things my way."

"And won't that be exactly what Diane has done, what you're so angry at her about? Exerting too much influence over a vulnerable, dying woman? I mean, forgive me, Rachel. I know you're upset about this. But I don't want you to do anything rash. It sounds like Grand is not totally in her right mind anymore. It's possible that it might be difficult for her to make a clear-headed decision about all of this, particularly if she's being lobbied."

"But she's already been lobbied, hard, Michael! It's Diane's lobbying that's put us here!"

"I know, Rachel. I know it probably feels wrong to you. But Diane and Grand have a relationship, right? They've been friends for a long time. And it's entirely possible that Grand's decision about the Farm might be based, at least in part, on that friendship. In addition to the idealism behind it. She might *want* Diane to have it."

"I don't believe that. I think she wants her family to have it."

Michael sighed, and Rachel heard condescension in his sigh. "But if she leaves it to her family, your father's going to just turn around and sell it, Rach. So what does that accomplish?"

"Not if I have anything to do with it."

They went on like this for some time, each of them digging deeper into their own argumentative trench. Finally, after a prolonged, angry silence, Michael attempted to change the subject.

"I heard they got a lead on the mother of that abandoned baby."

"Really?" Rachel said, anger giving way beneath a sudden rush of concern. "What?"

"Someone at a Walmart in Ohio said they saw a woman who looked like her buying some groceries earlier in the day. The police are swarming the town now, beating the bushes."

"Poor thing."

"They'll probably find her by the morning."

"I hope not."

"Well, at least if they do, she'll have shelter and food. It's hard, being on the run."

"Better than being in jail."

They said goodnight—Rachel claimed exhaustion, which was very true—but the moment she got off the phone, she went downstairs to the den and turned on the TV. Grand hated TV and had always maintained a no-TV policy on the Farm—though Grandpa Jacob would sometimes turn on his thirteen inch portable at the end of the day to watch McNeil Lehrer—but when Diane agreed to be Grand's live-in hospice nurse ten months earlier, she had demanded they install a Dish. Normally, Rachel would have stood with Grand—TV on the Farm was sacrilegious, an abomination; the whole point of being here was to get away from the corrupting influences of modern life, to fall into more natural rhythms, let the news be what the birds sang in the morning, and what the loon called each night, etc., etc.—but since Dee had been born, the twenty-four-hour news cycle had become her guilty pleasure, and she was glad to indulge it. She was grateful to Diane for the gift of MSNBC, if nothing else.

She waited through a report on the latest soldiers killed in Iraq (Mission Accomplished! Bush had declared a month ago, in his goofy flight suit, after landing a plane on board the *USS Abraham Lincoln*), and another on Israeli Prime Minister Sharon's recent controversial swerve to the left on the matter of the West Bank and the Gaza Strip, waiting for an update on the missing mother. Eventually, the image of that lonely cabin in the woods appeared, and then the sad picture of the teen mom with too much eyeliner and bad teeth, and Rachel sat up straight on the edge of the couch. Up flashed an image of a band of cops, their high-power flashlights beaming into a spindly woods, preceded by a team of German Shepherds nosing through leaf debris. They were still looking.

"You go, Mama-girl," Rachel whispered. "Keep running."

"Rachel." Diane stood at the doorway in her robe and slippers, her face shiny beneath a layer of moisturizer.

Rachel jumped. "You startled me." She turned down the sound on the TV.

"I just wanted to let you know that tomorrow's my day off. The relief nurse comes at nine. Just in case you got up late and didn't find me."

"Oh, I'll be up way before nine. Dee will see to that."

"Well, anyway. She'll be here all day." Diane turned to go.

"Wait. Why don't I just take care of Grand? That's what I'm here for, right?"

Diane smiled tightly. "I think it's best the nurse come. She knows the procedures."

"Seems like a waste of resources. I'm perfectly capable."

"I'm sure Maddy will enjoy your company while the nurse takes care of the chores."

Rachel shrugged in a surly way. "All right. Whatever."

Diane lasered her eyes at her. *Whatever* was her least favorite word. "Goodnight then."

"Goodnight."

Rachel watched her slide toward the stairs, her back padded by the quilted fabric of the robe. Something about the way she climbed the stairs made Rachel bristle: her regal stance, her hand caressing the curved wood of the banister, as if she owned the place.

2

Diane's morning started with an early phone call from the relief nurse. Something had come up at home, and she was going to have to be late. "I'm so sorry," she repeated. "It's just one of those things."

"No problem, hon," Diane assured her. "We'll be fine." But inwardly, she was moaning with disappointment. She'd woken much too early, excited by the prospect of a day to herself, and had laid in bed a full hour, listing all the things she would do, starting with an early morning visit to Joe. It was the only way she was ever really able to talk to him—in person, at his place, where he was at his most relaxed. She wanted to be with him in an easy way: walk the dog together, watch the sun wink off the waves. No agendas, no recriminations.

"I can watch Grand, Diane," Rachel offered again, when she mentioned the situation at breakfast. "Really, I can handle it. It's only going to be an hour or two at most, right?"

And Diane, after a moment's hesitation, agreed. "Better to just let her stay in bed—it'll make things easier on both of you. Unless of course she has to go to the bathroom. Then you've got to help her onto the toilet."

"No problem."

"It's tricky—she's heavier than you think, and she really leans her weight into you. You've seen me use her pink belt, right, to help her up and down, and just give her stability?"

"You showed me yesterday."

"Mid-morning, if the nurse still isn't here, you'll need to give her her pills, which are in the pillbox on the counter downstairs. And if there's some kind of emergency, God forbid, then call me right away. I'll leave my number on the counter. *Don't* call 911. If you call 911, the hospital will send an ambulance out, and once they do that, they have to follow through, and she has explicitly said she doesn't want to go back to the hospital. She wants to die at home."

"Okay, I know. I won't call 911."

"Maybe I should just do these errands another time."

"Diane. We will be fine. Please, go. Enjoy yourself. It's your day off."

Leave us alone, why don't you? was what Diane heard. "I'll just go say goodbye to Maddy."

Upstairs, Maddy was leaning against her stack of pillows, staring out the window across from the bed, as if at some disturbing scene transpiring on the other side of the glass.

"Knock knock," Diane sang out.

"Who's there?" Maddy turned stiffly in the direction of the voice.

"It's just me, hon. Diane. Is your neck okay?"

"Something's funny. I slept on it funny."

Diane rubbed it a little at the shoulder, and Maddy closed her eyes and hummed. "Better?"

"Yes, thank you. Much."

"Listen, hon, I wanted to let you know that today is my day off, so I'll be out for the day. The relief nurse, Cindy, is coming a little later. You remember her?"

"Cindy," Maddy repeated.

"The young nurse with the pretty red hair? You like her."

"Okay."

"And in the meantime, Rachel's going to stay with you until Cindy gets here. She's got your monitor, so if you need anything, all you have to do is say the word, and she'll come help you out, okay? I'm sure she'll be in soon—I think she's just changing the baby."

"The baby?"

"Her baby, hon. Deirdre. Your great-grandchild."

"I don't know any Deirdre."

Diane smiled, put a comforting hand on her shoulder. "You'll recognize her when you see her, hon, I'm sure."

"All right. I'm not dead yet."

"That you're not." Diane kissed the top of her cloud-white head. "I'll see you this evening."

And Maddy nodded into the empty space of her room. "Evening," she said to herself, then closed her eyes.

∞×∞

Diane took the curve to Joe's, passing the thrown corpse of a deer, fat with bloat and gathering flies, and down-shifted to second as she drove down the muddy access road to the dam parking lot, where she parked next to Joe's pickup. The rain had started up again, a mist for now, but it looked like it wasn't going anywhere for a while. She got out and slammed the door shut. The noise echoed through the silent bowl of lake and woods. A moment later, Sally came to greet her, a barking run that turned into a joyful wagfest. Diane squatted to let the muddy creature lick her face.

"Where's Joe, Sal?" she asked. "Where's your master, huh?"

Diane walked toward the dam office building, figuring she'd try there first, but a moment later, the door to the control house opened, and Joe stepped out. He was dressed in chinos and a blue button-down shirt, and his hair was freshly washed and combed. Even his face looked better—clean-shaven and scrubbed, a little less lopsided than usual.

"Hey, Ma," he said, loping toward her.

"Don't you look nice. Do you have a job interview or something?"

He threw her a look. "No. I have a job, remember?" He shouldered on a rain jacket. "What'd you do with old Mrs. Clayborne? Pack her in the trunk?"

Diane smirked. He was dodging the question. "It's my day off, hon. She's covered." She dug in her purse and pulled out a sealed envelope, which she handed to him. "Some grocery money."

He took the envelope and shoved it in his coat pocket. "Thanks."

"You have time for a coffee over at the café? My treat."

"Nah. I've got other plans, Ma. Thanks, though."

She swallowed her disappointment. "So where you going, mystery man? You meeting Susan?"

"It's really none of your business, Ma, but if you must know, I thought I'd drive over to the Farm. Move that furniture finally."

Diane pursed her lips. "You need to be careful, hon. She's married, remember."

"Oh, for chrissake, Ma. Have some faith, would you?" And he stomped over to his truck, the envelope full of cash sticking halfway out of his pocket. Looking like it would fall out any minute.

He spun the truck around, mud spraying in a thin arc, and tore up the road.

Diane stood in the new silence, the mist coming wet on her cheeks. Sally nosed her in the thigh, and she patted her absently on the head, then turned and strolled onto the dam bridge. Sal followed.

The lake freckled in the light rain. It looked full, fuller than she'd seen it in a while, and she wondered if Joe had noticed, then scolded herself for the thought. Of course he'd noticed. He was the damkeeper here. He'd been doing this job for six years. He was good at it—careful, steady, conscientious. She was too full of doubt.

She walked the length of the pier and leaned out over the railing on the end, thinking, as she often did when she came here, of Thomas, Joe's father. Thirty-one years ago this August they'd met just here, on this very dam. Skinny Thomas, bare-chested beneath his fringed leather vest, that red bandana tied around his head. A sad smile crept to her lips. God, but those were the days. Alcatraz and the protest there spread across Indian country like a prairie fire, and they'd all huddled around their TVs, mouths gaping at each image: the huge graffiti lettering sprayed across the concrete block at the Alcatraz boat dock reading "You Are On *Indian* Land," the young Richard Oakes, looking like a Mohawk Elvis Presley, his hair blown back from his forehead by the Pacific winds, the crowds of rag-tag Indians huddling on the pier, waiting for the next boat out, and the Rock itself, rising up out of the bay, stark and cliffy, bedecked with white industrial behemoths of buildings. She and her friends had followed the story in a giddy daze, trading details with each other to confirm them—*did you hear they offered the government twenty-four bucks for the whole rock? In beads and cloth. Yeah, and they're setting up a BCA, Bureau of Caucasian Affairs. To educate the white savages in our life-ways.*

After Alcatraz, it was like a fever had caught: a fever of hope and promise and possibility. If they could take Alcatraz, well . . . And so they'd held their protest here, right here, on the Old Bend Dam. 1972. The power company's lease was up for renewal, and a group of them wanted to deny it. To take the river back. They were just a dozen, maybe, with their long hair, their bellbottom jeans and homemade signs, their guitars. They invited the TV stations. The tribal president gave a speech. And then out of nowhere, a caravan of cruisers with Minnesota plates came putt-putting down the road, full of A.I.M. guys in braids, looking the part. Thomas was one of them, Cherokee-Cree from the twin cities driving a beat-up Pinto, skinny as a teenager, sexy-voiced and a smooth-talker. They turned the protest into a three-day occupation—camping by the lake, smoking whatever anyone had to smoke, singing and drumming late into the night. Thomas whispered utopian fantasies in her ear. She fell in love—with Thomas, with all of it, the whole scene. The third night there, they hiked over to Old Bend Island and lay naked under the stars, tangled up in each others' limbs.

She shook her head now at the memory. What a fool she'd been. They all were, back then. Beautiful dreamers. Except it wasn't foolish, in the end—the tribe won. Got the dam back, and now *they* leased *it* to the power company. Justice won out, that time. But love, well ... Thomas stuck around the rez a while, picking up odd jobs and sleeping on her parents' couch, and then finally he left to join the Trail of Broken Treaties, that coast-to-coast caravan of fed-up Indians, veteran civil rights fighters, and assorted unemployed drifters. He promised he'd return when the fight was won, whatever that meant. She stayed home, bereft and big-bellied. Her parents kept her in oranges and commodity cheese all the way through Joe's birth, infancy, and toddlerhood, when it finally became clear to her that Thomas wasn't coming back. And by that time she didn't care: she'd carved a life out for herself at home, with her parents and two sisters and all their children—Joe had family enough to go around. Uncles and cousins aplenty who had stepped in when needed, to do the things dads did with their sons. Thomas sent checks for a while, and then didn't, but they'd managed. She'd been better off without him. When Joe used to ask about him, she told it to him straight: said his dad was a freedom fighter, a man who loved justice. That Joe should be proud of his work. That sometimes men and women got together just to bring a child into the world, and that the universe smiled on those children. That they were the special ones. And that she loved him enough for father and mother both. And she did. He was a happy, well-adjusted kid, an A student with a bright future. Graduation day, she remembered him: black robe and mortarboard squashing his curly clown's head of hair (unusually curly; Thomas was obviously not the full-blooded brave he had claimed to be), brandishing his diploma, his smile as bright as the sun glinting off the lake. College-bound and proud, after the Army; they were giddy with the promise of it all.

And then came the war and the helicopter accident, shattering his jaw, and all their hopes and dreams with it.

Well, they'd adapted. Changed course. Their dreams became more immediate, for a while: to get through this next operation, to complete the next course of jaw exercises, to regain comfortable motion in the new joint, to get the hell out of the hospital. Step by step, they'd gotten through it, achieved each little victory, enacted each little dream. But Joe was changed. All his wide-eyed ambition and imagination had drained away, as if the helicopter blade had sheared through the locus of his spirit, too. And there were no surgeries to restore that. Diane had to pick up the slack, to do the dreaming for him for a while. And she had; she'd devoted herself to it—doing all she could to ensure he had a future, as bright a one as possible. And part of that job had meant keeping Rachel Clayborne far, far away from her boy.

Those had been his instructions. That day after the fourth or fifth surgery, when his articulation was clear enough to be understood over the phone, Diane had dialed Rachel's number for him, and then left the room to give him privacy. When she returned, the phone sat in the cradle, and Joe's face was to the wall. He wouldn't talk at all then, for three days. When he finally did, he said he never wanted to speak to Rachel Clayborne again as long as he lived, and he asked her to make sure he never did.

She'd taken him at his word. When Rachel called back a week later, after Joe had been moved to the rehab center, and was learning how to use his new tongue and jaw, how to form a believable "s," how to sip from a straw (no chewing yet), Diane had simply done for him what he'd made clear he wanted. She'd made things easier for him. The only important thing at that point had been his recovery, and if Rachel was getting in the way of that, then Diane was going to make sure she stayed out of the way. Phone messages and letters—all the dozens of letters—included.

Later, after the last surgeries (a grand total of eighteen) and the months of physical rehabilitation, after Joe had been released to her care and they were back home, Diane had asked him, once, about Rachel. He was already sliding into addiction then, spending his days drinking in front of the TV set, and she'd begun her years of fearful worry. It had occurred to her that maybe what he'd said about never wanting to speak to Rachel again had simply been one of his pronouncements. He'd been prone, as a teenager, to making ridiculous pronouncements, enunciating pre-cut phrases that he'd picked up from books or television shows that seemed to fit the occasion. *I have not yet begun to fight* was another he was fond of back then, when he was still insisting he wanted to go back over to Iraq and actually use some of his training. *The war's over, hon*, she'd say. *There's no need.* And he'd grit his new teeth and give a lopsided grimace and utter his phrase: *I have not yet begun to fight.* And then he'd take a long pull on his beer.

One morning, after she'd spent a sleepless night worrying that maybe she'd done wrong by keeping Rachel's messages from him, she'd asked him what Rachel had said on the phone that time that had upset him so. When he told her—in a bitter voice, his new mouth twisted in pain—Diane had felt the anger and shame with him, and knew she'd been justified in keeping them apart. No kind of apology could take that away. In fact, she had been so angry at Rachel, that she'd cut off all contact with the entire Clayborne family for a good year or two.

By that time Joe was in the thick of his addiction. His six-packs of beer in the evening had turned to whisky in his morning coffee, and he'd started drifting, staying out all night. Joe never mentioned Rachel when he was sober (the rare occasions when he *was* sober), only when he was deep in his cups, but it happened frequently enough that Diane began to see how deeply the girl had insinuated herself into his skin, how much he'd loved her, and how much her rejection—or what he believed to be her rejection—had hurt him. At that point, though, she just couldn't bring herself to change the story. It was too late, she was ashamed, and Joe was too far gone to get it, anyway. Truth be told, she was afraid of his anger, magnified by the liquor as it was. He would never hurt her—this was Joe, alcohol or no—but he might cut her off, disappear forever. So she stayed quiet. Eventually, word came of Rachel's engagement. And Joe had lain his soggy head on the railroad tracks before the morning train. If it hadn't been for that night watchman who'd found him . . . well, she didn't like to think about that.

That had been the bottom, the very bottom, as well as the beginning of his sobriety. Since then, she feared that any admission of regret on her part, any change in the story—or even any mention of the story—might send him back to the train tracks and the whisky bottle. So she'd kept quiet, and Rachel had, thankfully, kept out of their lives. Until now.

The mist began to turn into a drizzle. A rivulet found its way down Diane's temple to her mouth. She wiped it away, rubbed her fingers through her soaked hair, and lifted her hood over her head. "That Rachel Clayborne better be good to him, Sal. Right? She better be nice, otherwise I'll sic you on her. God knows she doesn't want to mess with you when you're angry." Her hands buried deep in her raincoat, she walked back down the causeway to her car, gave Sal a final pat on the head, and drove up the hill.

3

With Diane gone and Grand taking her morning nap, Rachel took Deirdre outside to examine the garden, maybe do a little weeding. The day was gray and misting, but warm. Rachel let the porch door slam shut behind her—Deirdre flinched at the sound—and walked around to the herb garden on the south side of the house. Normally a well-tended arrangement of rosemary, basil, oregano, sage, and mint plants in a mulched patch under the kitchen window, it had grown into a neglected forest of rampant tarragon and mint. The sage had bushed out, the rosemary seemed to have died off in a frost, and the basil had not been planted. The chives were spiny, calling out to be cut, a few of the thin stalks even culminating in a bud. But at the edge of the plot, the rhubarb patch was thriving: three plants brimming with lush, Cretaceous-era leaves and stems the width of racquet handles. The sight of it saddened Rachel: each sprawling herb, each uncut rhubarb stalk spoke of Grand's decline.

When Rachel had first moved in with Michael, she'd planted a rhubarb patch like Grand's in their postage stamp of a yard. Years later, on the night of their first wedding anniversary, when they were still early enough in their marriage to be enthralled by their own love story, Michael confessed how happy that rhubarb had made him. *It was so domestic*, he'd said. *Even though you didn't end up using it that much. The fact that you put it in at all: it meant you wanted to stay.* And the first time she'd brought Michael up to the Farm to meet Grand, Grand had fed him rhubarb pie. Michael's courtly manners—plus a couple of G&Ts—had charmed Grand into talking about her past, and Grand had gone on and on, describing her father's thwarted ambition as a gentleman farmer, her mother's disdain for the messiness of farm life, her sister's illness that had brought them north in the first place. Grand had talked for close to an hour, revealing things about Rachel's family that she'd never before known, and then they'd eaten the pie, warm, with vanilla ice cream. In the bathroom that night Grand said through a mouthful of toothpaste, "He's a good one, Rachel. Hang onto him."

And she'd been right. He had been. And he still was. It was Rachel who'd changed; she'd grown impatient, easily irritated, desperate for space, to be alone, to be anywhere he wasn't. Motherhood had transformed her basic state of mind from sunny to gothic. Every object, moving or stationary, had become a hazard: passing cars, tree branches hanging over power lines, the neighbor kid on his bike. The sun: a purveyor of skin cancer. The bathtub: a drowning device. The screened-in three-season porch, where she and Michael used to sit for breakfast, dreamily entering the day: a poisonous den of chipping lead paint.

Really, from any objective point of view, Michael had been a saint through these last months, coming home early to hold Deirdre so Rachel could shower, putting dinner in the Crock-Pot before he left in the morning. Taking more days off than was wise for his tenure case. Really, he was a prince. You couldn't argue otherwise. And yet somehow, his saintliness made it worse. Beneath his selfless actions seethed an undercurrent of judgment and reproach. He was so concerned with doing everything correctly, so obsessed with achieving parental perfection, that Rachel couldn't help but feel him steaming behind his furrowed brow at each half-measure she took—skipping Deirdre's bath, letting her wear the poop-stained onesie, because she just couldn't deal with another change. Michael would offer, with thinly veiled annoyance, to change Deirdre himself, and then would wear her in the front pack while he vacuumed so Rachel could get some work done (there was judgment here, too: he couldn't understand why she'd grown so lax about her coursework; she'd gotten a B- in statistics last semester) and basically, she was starting to feel like the woman in "The Yellow Wallpaper," that short story that had so freaked her out in college: the "hysterical" woman whose husband confined her to the bedroom, where she crawled around the walls like a lunatic. This was how Michael made her feel, like a lunatic, someone to be humored and coddled, while poor, gentle, sensitive Michael kept the family together. And meanwhile, Deirdre was getting bigger and bigger, and soon enough she would be old enough to ask daddy what was wrong with mommy, why was she so sullen and angry all the time, and daddy would make some comment like "Mommy has a sickness that makes her sad," and Rachel would lose it, would just completely *lose it*.

She sighed. The idea of returning home, to her life there with all her papers and books and the daily demands of the household, to their prim, buttoned up neighborhood and Michael's oppressive care, filled her with panic. She'd been right to leave. The Farm and Grand were saving her, as Rachel had known they would. Grand, who cared not about what you achieved, but how you cared for the people who depended on you. Grand, whose joy in life derived not from reaching for perfection, but from delighting in her surroundings and carrying out whatever tasks the day required. Grand's way of life seemed closer to the earth's pulse than the life she'd grown accustomed to living. She felt that pulse beating up here on the Farm, and she wanted to grab it, to hold its vital rhythm, to never let it go.

She turned back to the herb patch and to Deirdre, who was lying on the grass. Before her, the rhubarb stalks beckoned. She knelt and fingered one: it was taut with life and, undoubtedly, flavor.

"Deirdre," she declared, "we're going to make a rhubarb pie."

Rachel grabbed a serrated bread knife from the rack in the kitchen, tramped back out to the herb patch, and sawed through the bases of eight of the thickest stalks of rhubarb. Inside, she found Grand's card catalog of recipes—tacky with decades of accumulated sugar—and riffled through it until she found the card for rhubarb pie. She pulled out the ceramic bowls, the hand mixer, the plastic spatula, the rings of metal measuring spoons and cups, and the ingredients: the yellow and white tin, circa 1943, that held the flour (still in the bag, thankfully, so it hadn't absorbed the rust that had corroded the tin's seams), the container of Crisco (circa God-knows-when, but Crisco never went bad), the sugar tin, the salt. Heroically, she measured the flour, cut in the Crisco with the steel pastry cutter (the handle also seamed with rust), spooned in drops of water and extra handfuls of flour until she had something that resembled a dough, and then, in the final stages, mixed the dough with her hands on the butcher block counter.

By the time she'd finished, the kitchen was a disaster—bowls scattered over the countertops, the rolling pin encrusted with dough, and flour dusting every surface in sight, including Deirdre's nose and the front pack she was nestled in—but Deirdre was squealing with delight and the dough itself appeared pretty convincing: pliable, rolled thin, and mostly round.

And all through making the pie, Rachel had been thinking. If she wanted to, she could change things completely. She could quit her PhD program, move up here to the Farm, and start a new life as a do-over Grand, a Grand for the twenty-first century. She'd plant a garden, keep chickens, forage for fiddleheads and mushrooms in the woods. She'd raise Deirdre in the great outdoors, teaching her the names of all the plant and animal species that surrounded her, teaching her to think of herself as only one organism among a dazzling array of organisms. Maybe she'd even become one of those fringe-y homeschooling mothers, growing her daughter's brain on a steady diet of environmentalist literature: E.O. Wilson, Thomas Berry, Roderick Nash, Aldo Leopold. She'd teach her the *right* values, values that had little to do with achievement or perfection, but had everything to do with *care*. Together, she and Deirdre, would care for each other and for this place, the land they would live on and work together, the land that Grand had once cared for so tenderly. And at night in the summers, they'd huddle together on the porch and watch the stars poke through the black canopy of the sky. She could even write a memoir about it ten, fifteen years down the line, take it to the Oprah Winfrey Show: *How a Family Legacy Saved my Life: One Woman's Incredible Journey from the Soul-Sucking Grind of Academia toward the Peace of Care-ful Living.* Except probably she'd scratch that play on *careful*; that stank of too-clever academ-ese.

Energized by her fantasy, Rachel lifted one pie crust into the pan, leaving a draped edge for crimping, and then began to chop the stalks of rhubarb—using her best Food Network technique—when the monitor, sitting on the windowsill above the sink, buzzed with static.

"Diane?" Grand's voice came through, weak and plaintive.

Rachel set the knife on the counter, wiped her hands on a dishtowel, and (capably, oh so capably!) marched up to Grand's bedroom.

"It's me, Grand. Rachel," she said in response to Grand's bewildered stare. "Did you have a good rest?"

"You're going to have to teach her how to eat properly," Grand said.

Rachel laughed, brushing the flour from Deirdre's nose and the front of the baby pack, creating a small maelstrom of dust. "We're making rhubarb pie," she said. "Just like you used to do."

"Oh!" Grand said, brightening. "That's wonderful. Where's Diane?"

"It's her day off. She'll be back this evening."

"Oh. Oh, dear."

"It's all right, Grand. I'm here. What do you need?"

"Well, I don't know, dear. I—Diane usually—"

"I'm taking Diane's place, just for a little while, Grand. Just let me know what it is—I can help."

"I've got to use the bathroom."

"Right. Okay, that's no problem." Rachel pushed Grand's walker toward the edge of the bed. Diane had shown her how to help Grand up—the business with the belt and making sure to keep her steady—and Rachel had done it once before, but now she had Deirdre buckled in the pack and the angle of purchase wasn't right—it would be too much weight in front, and Rachel might end up tipping over onto Grand and Deirdre. "Wait a second," she said. "I'm going to have to put Deirdre down."

"All right," Grand said, her voice tinged with worry.

"It'll just take me a second." Rachel unlatched the front pack and slipped Deirdre out, brushing some undiscovered flour from her thighs and feet before laying her in the center of the bed, far away from the treacherous edges.

Meanwhile, Grand was trying to slide her legs over the side of the bed.

"Whoa, whoa, wait a minute, Grand. Wait for me."

"I can't wait, dear." Grand's voice was sharp.

"All right. Just let me get a hold of you—" she grabbed the pink belt. "Ready? I'm going to count to three, and on three, you stand, okay?"

"I know how to stand up, for Pete's sake!"

Diane had said she might get like this, Rachel reminded herself. Just breathe. "One, two, three," and she pulled and Grand stood, and for a horrible freakish moment Rachel felt her grip on the belt slip, and Grand tipped precariously back toward the bed, which was, suddenly, a long way down. Grand squealed and grabbed at the walker, and then Rachel regained her grip and equilibrium was restored. "Phew," Rachel said. "That was a close one."

The monitor that hung from Grand's neck danced on its strap.

Chagrined, Rachel led Grand carefully over the rug, which bunched under the walker's wheels. "A little step here, Grand," she said, guiding the walker over the threshold.

Grand sighed—with relief or annoyance, Rachel wasn't sure.

Once over the hurdle of the bedroom threshold, they were confronted with three shallow steps leading up to the bathroom hallway. Grand sighed once more.

"How does Diane do this, exactly?" Rachel wondered aloud.

"Much better than you do," Grand said.

A finger of hurt clenched in Rachel's throat. "Okay, Grand. I'm just learning here. Cut me some slack. We'll go slow."

"I can't go any slower. I've got to use the toilet."

"We're almost there."

Rachel decided to abandon the walker, unsure how to navigate the steps with those wheels, and instead, had Grand lean into her. One foot up, then the next, they climbed the steps together, Grand's weight heavy on Rachel's arms. At the top of the third step, they rested.

"Where's my walker?" Grand asked.

"At the bottom of the steps, Grand. I didn't want it to slip."

"Well, how am I going to get to the bathroom without it?"

"I'll be your walker for now, okay, Grand? Just keep leaning on me." And Rachel tightened her grip on the belt, and with one arm around Grand's middle, helped her on her painstaking way down the interminable hallway until finally, finally, they reached the bathroom.

"Okay," Rachel said. "Now, do you need me to help you with your pants?"

"I'm afraid so, dear."

"Here, hold onto me, and I'll pull them down." And they managed. Grand was wearing a diaper, a kind meant to lend dignity to the elderly— better described, really, as absorbent paper underwear. The crotch of the diaper was heavy with urine, and Rachel wondered whether she should change it. But how to ask Grand without insulting her? How to carry it out, exactly? She decided against it. Those things could absorb gallons of pee without breaking down. Grand would be all right, at least until the relief nurse arrived.

Grand settled herself on the toilet and immediately, an explosion with the force of a small firecracker sounded in the bowl. Rachel closed the door, catching the look of blissful release on Grand's face.

After checking on Deirdre, who was happily bicycling her legs in the air, Rachel remembered the pie. She was minutes away from putting it in the oven. Grand might be a while. Might as well be efficient.

Rachel thundered down the steps into the kitchen, tossed the rhubarb and the sugar into the bowl, and mixed it with a few swift strokes of the spoon. All was quiet upstairs. She threw a handful of flour on the butcher block counter and began to roll the second ball of dough into a lopsided circle. Through the monitor, she could hear Grand fumbling with the toilet paper roll. Deirdre began to cry.

"Just a second, Dee!" Rachel shouted, rolling faster. "I'm coming!"

"Rachel?" Grand's voice came through the monitor. "I'm finished."

"Christ," said Rachel. She should go immediately, she knew she should. What was the big deal about the pie? But for some reason, she couldn't, not yet: she had to get this pie in the oven by the time the relief nurse arrived. It was to be the measure of her success, and, by extension, of her eligibility as a caretaker: the ability to make a pie while caring for two incontinent dependents. She spooned the sugar-coated rhubarb into the bottom crust, and then palmed the second crust—still lopsided—on top of the pie and hastily crimped the edges with her fingers, One side of the pie gaped open; the other side had a slab of crust far too thick for its own good.

"Rachel? I need your assistance please."

Deirdre's cry became a wail.

"Just a minute, just a minute," Rachel shouted, though she knew neither Grand nor Deirdre could hear. She pulled off an edge of the bottom crust and draped it over the gaping hole, patting it into place and, though the pie looked like someone had formed it out of play-doh, she carried it in one hand to the oven, which was cold. "Shit," she said. She could have sworn she'd preheated it. The dial was at 350 degrees. "What the fuck?" She stuck her head into the oven, balancing the pie on one hand.

"Probably not the most effective method," a man's voice said from behind. Rachel, startled, whapped her head against the edge of the oven.

"Ow!" she yelled. Joe stood beside her, his face liked a dried-up river basin. But he'd dressed up, she noticed. His blue button-down was tucked neatly into his jeans, showing off a trim waist.

"You all right?"

She rubbed her head with one hand, the pie in the other.

"I was going to say try a bottle of drugs if you want to go out unconscious."

"Very funny."

"It would have been funnier if you hadn't hit your head."

"So you're back."

"The cat came back."

"I got the crib put together. No thanks to you."

"I thought you could handle it."

"Your mom's not here. It's her day off."

"I know. Where's the baby?"

"Rachel? Diane? Is anyone there?" Grand's voice from the monitor. Deirdre screamed.

"So, they're both yelling and you're making pies?"

"Listen, smart-ass." She handed him the pie. "If you're so smart, why don't you fix that oven?" And she ran upstairs, her hands still coated with flour.

Deirdre's feet were straight up in the air, her belly tight with the pressure of her wails, but other than looking uncomfortable, she didn't seem to be in immediate danger. "Priorities," Rachel whispered, and then shouted to Deirdre on her way to the bathroom, "I'll be right there honey, just one minute." Her heart pounded a steady drumbeat: Joe, Joe, Joe, Joe, Joe.

Grand was leaning forward, trying to wipe herself, leaving streaks of shit on her bare butt. "Oh, Grand, let me help you with that," said Rachel, taking the dirty paper from her and dropping it in the toilet.

"I didn't know where you were," she said, in an offended tone of voice.

"I was in the kitchen. I'm sorry." Rachel wadded up a new section of paper and wiped the streaks from Grand's leg and bottom—all the while feeling each of Deirdre's screams like a spear in the gut—before helping her to stand and pulling up her heavy diaper and pants. At the sink, Rachel washed both their hands thoroughly, and then walked Grand step by maddening step, along the hall toward the stairs. When they reached the first step, Deirdre stopped crying.

Once again, Rachel held Grand as she descended the three shallow steps to the level, where the walker was waiting. Grand grabbed the walker, Rachel held her belt, and together they moved over the threshold into the bedroom. Joe stood by the bed, Deirdre nestled against his shoulder, her little body shuddering with her quieted sobs. Rachel looked at him in astonishment. "Thank you," she said.

He smiled proudly. "I figured I couldn't make it any worse than it already was. Good morning, Mrs. Clayborne."

"Good morning, Joe. Did you bring your mother with you?"

"I sure didn't, ma'am."

"She'll be back later, Grand," Rachel said. "Let's get you back into bed where you can relax."

"The pilot light was out," Joe said, one large hand spread against Deirdre's back. "That was all."

"Oh, thank goodness," Rachel said. "I thought I was going to have to roast the pie over the fire."

"Mmm. Blackened rhubarb."

Haltingly, Rachel lowered Grand back onto the bed, pulled the covers up, and then set her walker against the opposite wall. "There," she said. "Are you comfortable, Grand?"

"Yes, thank you, dear. I hate to be a bother."

"No, Grand," sighed Rachel. "No bother at all."

She turned to Joe. "Seems like you two have a good thing going there." She walked around behind him, so she could see Deirdre's face. Her eyes were wide open, her nostrils dilating with each breath. "Hi, baby," she said. "You like your uncle Joe?"

"I rescued her. She loves me now. Don't you, little one? Huh?" He held her out from his chest to look at her. Her face crumpled in terror. "Aw, she's just acting," he said, passing her to Rachel.

Rachel took her, feeling a warmth spread across her forearm and drip down her wrist: mustard-colored baby poop, all down Rachel's hand and arm, squirting out the sides of Deirdre's onesie, smudged up her neck into the wisps of hair at her nape. "Oh, good God," Rachel said, holding Deirdre at arm's length. "You might want to check your clothes, Joe. She's covered in poop."

Joe examined his arms and his shirt, which, somehow, were pristine. "Smart kid you got."

"Unbelievable. I'm going to rinse her off in the bath. Can you sit with Grand?"

"No problem, Sarge." He saluted.

Still holding Deirdre at arm's length, Rachel waddled back to the bathroom, where she stripped both Deirdre and herself and climbed into the bath, nestling her poop-covered baby between her legs, while the porcelain tub warmed with the water. "Oh, Dee," she said, squirting baby shampoo into the fine black fuzz on Deirdre's head. "Dee Dee Dee," she hummed absent-mindedly, her mind on Joe. He'd come back. And not to see his mother. He'd come back to see her.

After they were both clean and dry, and she'd outfitted Deirdre with a lavender sundress and herself in clean jeans and a black T-shirt, Rachel went back to Grand's room. Joe was sitting in the rocker next to the bed, one ankle balanced on the other knee, listening to Grand narrate a slow, meandering story. Rachel sat down on the end of the bed and bounced Deirdre on her knee.

"Is Diane here?" Grand asked.

"Not yet, Grand. But Cindy's coming soon."

"Who's Cindy?"

"Diane's sub, Grand. The same one who comes a couple times every week. You'll recognize her."

Grand began to pluck at the blanket that covered her chest.

"All clean!" Rachel said cheerily.

"You sure she's yours?" Joe asked, standing up to get a closer look at Deirdre. "She doesn't look anything like you." Deirdre clung tightly to Rachel's arm.

"Pretty sure," Rachel said.

"Well, of course she's hers," Grand said, again in that offended tone of voice. "Whose else would the child be?"

"It's all right, Grand. He was just making a joke."

"So," Joe began.

Rachel nodded encouragingly.

"I brought you something." From the back pocket of his jeans, he dug out a crinkled brown paper bag.

"This is for me?" Rachel said, taking it.

"Yeah. Well, for the baby. You know. A gift to welcome the baby."

"Thanks, Joe. That's really sweet of you." Rachel opened the bag and pulled out a Gerber baby rattle, light blue, in plastic packaging. It was the sort of thing that you could find in just about any grocery store, hanging next to the disposable plastic baby spoons and the Desitin. Rachel had the very same one at home.

"Hey, great," she said, "just what we needed." The price tag was still affixed to the back: $3.95.

"Can I see? What is it?" Grand asked.

"A rattle," Rachel said, holding it up.

"How nice," Grand offered. "The cat will love it."

"She's having a hard day today," Rachel said in an undertone to Joe.

"It happens."

"So," Rachel tried again. "Why'd you take off like that yesterday?"

"The pie's burning," he replied.

Rachel ran to the kitchen. She set Deirdre down on the rug and opened the oven, and a thin wisp of smoke emerged. Its source was not the pie, though, but an oozed bit of filling that had dripped onto the bottom of the oven. The pie looked fine. She set the pie on one of the stove burners to cool and turned off the oven.

"Looks good," Joe said, at her elbow.

"You've got a good nose."

"One of the few parts of my face that survived," he said.

"That's not what I meant."

"I know."

A pause, during which they both looked anxiously at Deirdre for help. Deirdre obligingly yawned.

"She's getting ready for a nap," Rachel said.

"Oh, okay. Well, I can come back another time."

"No, no. I didn't mean that. She's always getting ready for a nap, or coming out of one. I was just—making conversation."

"You call that conversation?"

She laughed. "That's about as scintillating as I get these days."

"Listen, I'm sorry I disappeared yesterday. It's just that it's a little strange seeing you again. After all these years."

"Tell me about it."

"I was mad at you for a long time."

"I don't blame you," she said quietly. "I was mad at myself. I still am."

He swallowed. "Well, it was a long time ago."

She put a hand on his arm. "Listen, Joe, for what it's worth, I'm sorry. I mean, I'm more sorry than you know. I know it's probably too little too late . . ." she trailed off.

"Okay." He stared at her a long moment, making her blush. "That's good to hear. Thanks."

"So, can we start over? Just pretend we didn't have that weirdness yesterday or today, and that you're just arriving now? Can we do that?"

"All right."

"All right. So. Hi, Joe. Boy, it's good to see you."

"It's good to see you, too. Been such a long time."

She laughed.

"So where's the hubby? I was hoping I'd get to meet him."

Rachel lifted an eyebrow. "He had too much work to do back home. He might come up in a couple weeks or something."

"You staying that long, then?"

"As long as I can. I wish I could stay my whole life." Immediately, she regretted her words. They'd barely just laid eyes on one another and here she was letting fly her current, most intimate desires.

Joe smirked—or was it a smile? The deformity of his face made it difficult to see exactly what he was thinking. She used to be able to read his face in an instant. Sometimes, she didn't even need to look at him to know what he was feeling. It was a kind of aura he wore that she sensed whenever he came near her: melancholy, often, but when he was angry or feeling righteous about something, she could sense that, too, and she'd feel her own body responding in kind, preparing itself for whatever emotional offering Joe was about to make to her. She'd forgotten.

"I just mean," she corrected herself, "it's good to be here."

They continued with their small talk, feeling each other out—Rachel asked about his job, and he described it to her briefly, mentioning that he lived alone. Rachel told him about her work—the daily grind of graduate school, the occasionally painful, occasionally entertaining undergraduate teaching. She told him about Michael's work in Native studies, his research on the long-reaching detrimental effects of the Dawes Act and the general allotment policy, and Joe refrained from making any smart-alecky comments. It was all very polite and aboveboard until Joe asked about motherhood.

"It sucks," she said.

"Well, don't hold back now," Joe replied, surprised.

And there, in the kitchen, Rachel unloaded it all, telling him everything—the exhaustion, the secret wish that she could turn back the clock, take Deirdre back to the hospital, get back her life, and then the self-excoriating guilt she felt for even thinking such a thing, the occasional moments of happiness when she saw how truly beautiful her daughter actually was, and how lucky she was to have her, and then the passage of those moments and the return of grim reality, the feelings of imprisonment, as if she were on perpetual house arrest, except her ball and chain was a baby girl. This was motherhood: being forever chained to a crying, pooping, spitting-up blob of living flesh. Long mind-numbing afternoons of bouncing and sitting and rocking and walking, of glazing over into catatonia while the baby ate and ate and ate. Sore tits and a flabby belly and drudgery.

Joe listened and nodded, and Rachel bitched and cried a little and bitched some more. And then, feeling awful about everything she'd said, she took it all back. "You probably think I've turned into a witch, don't you? Maybe I have."

Joe just shrugged. He looked at Deirdre, who had, amazingly, drifted off to sleep right there on the kitchen rug. "Anyway, she sure is cute."

4

Diane lived in a quiet sixties-era development on the outskirts of Clinton, about a half-hour's drive west of the dam. Her street—freshly-tarred and well-shaded by mature trees—wound in a long gradual curve from its intersection with the county highway at one end to a more densely-populated grid of streets at the other. Cookie-cutter one-story ranch houses presided over the modest front yards, each one sporting a variation on a theme: a spread of lawn, an arrangement of hedge and hosta and honeysuckle, a collection of day lilies and daffodils, of lilac and wild rose and burning bush. Diane knew her neighbors well, and relied on them to keep an eye on things while she was living over at the Farm. Marcy Minsker next door took care of the cats and brought in the mail, and her husband Stan mowed the lawn. Diane had done the same for them over the years, when Marcy's back went out or they were on vacation. It was what neighbors did.

Pulling up the slope of her driveway, she was calmed by the sight of her own cozy little house—the yellow flowered curtains in the windows, the viburnum bush (looking overgrown already, she'd have to get out the pruning shears), the word Welcome spelled out in colorful wood-block letters on the front door. As she climbed the steps, she felt her worries recede a little, loosening their hold on her. Home sweet home. She turned the key in the lock and pushed open the door, greeted by the smell of kitty litter in need of a change. Marcy promised Diane she spent plenty of time with the cats, but still, they always acted as though they hadn't seen a human being for a month whenever Diane came in. Romeo pounced on her from the windowsill and Juliet tangled herself in and around Diane's legs, purring like a stalled motor. Diane dropped her purse on the floor and cooed and petted them for a while, feeling the tension she'd stored up draining away with each pass of her hand over their warm, needy little bodies. Carrying one cat in each arm, she went to the kitchen, where Marcy had left the mail: one pile of magazines and catalogs, sliding sideways, and another stack of envelopes, neatly bound with a rubber band. Diane sighed at the sight of it: mostly bills, red tape. She would deal with it after lunch.

Feeling dazed, she poured herself a glass of water and drank it standing at the sink, while she looked out the window at the back yard: the empty bird feeder which the birds had long since given up hope on, the garden beds, already greening over with weeds. She hadn't yet had a chance to plant anything this year, and probably wouldn't get to it at all, the way things were going. Oh, well. There were worse things than letting the garden lie fallow for one summer.

She set the empty water glass in the sink and went over to the kitchen table, the cats winding in and out of her legs. There was a light blinking on the answering machine, and she pressed the play button. The voice of Eleanor, one of the receptionists at the hospital, spoke into the quiet room. Eleanor was a fortyish busybody who lived over near the Farm and felt it was her duty to keep an eye on everyone's comings and goings. Joe had gone out with her a few times, out of pity—though Eleanor probably thought she'd been doing *him* a favor—and since then, Eleanor seemed to think she had some special relationship to their family. So she'd call periodically with any little bit of gossip she thought would interest them.

"I just thought I should let you know," came her voice, high and breathless, "that it looks like there's a stranger visiting the Farm. A car I don't recognize—one of those new hybrid electric kinds—has been going up and down the lane over the last few days. Maybe you know this already—but just in case you don't, I thought I should inform you. Give my best to Joe!" And she signed off. Diane, shaking her head, pressed the delete button.

The next message was from Ramsay. He was constantly mixing up her cell and land line numbers. "Welcome home, babe," he said. "Give me a ring and let me know when you'd like to meet up."

Diane picked the phone up from its cradle and brought it into the living room, where she fell onto the sofa, the phone in one hand. The cats leapt up after her, climbing onto her lap, snuggling into an oversized nest of fur on her belly. She closed her eyes a moment, feeling the last of her tension slip away, letting the deep quiet of her house surround her. The last thing she felt like doing right now was going out again, even if it was to meet Ramsay. She didn't want to move an inch from this sofa for a good while. She dialed his number and held the phone to her ear, closing her eyes again.

"Ramsay here," came his voice, deep and rich and sexy.

"Hi, hon."

"How you doing, beautiful?"

"Exhausted. I think I'm going to crash and it's not even ten in the morning."

"Hey, that's your prerogative, Di. That's what a day off is for."

"Listen, would you mind coming here for lunch, maybe picking us up something on the way? Hunters' Haven does take out, don't they? I just don't think I can move."

"Room service it is. Around one?"

"That sounds perfect. I might still be right here on the couch."

"Mmm. You and a couch sounds just about right."

She smiled. "Don't get carried away now, hon. I've got some things I want to talk to you about."

"Uh-oh. That sounds serious."

"Don't worry—nothing bad. I need your professional opinion. There might still be a couch in your future."

"All right. Professional advice for a spin on a couch. That's a deal."

They hung up. Diane let the phone fall to the floor, and two minutes later, she was asleep.

❧

When Ramsay pulled his Silverado pick-up into the driveway a few hours later, Diane had napped, showered, sorted the mail, and was going at the viburnum with her pruning shears, her hands encased in a pair of green rubber gardening gloves. She set the shears on the front steps and peeled off the gloves as Ramsay—burly, thick glasses, long black hair fastened into a ponytail—approached, a white shopping bag smelling of burgers in one hand.

"Well, Mr. Ramsay Lawrence Flynn," Diane purred, feeling as curly as one of her cats. "You're a sight for sore eyes."

"Hello, beautiful." Ramsay deep-kissed her right there by the viburnum, one hand reaching down to her butt for a squeeze, for all the nosy neighbors in the world to see. "It's good to see you."

"Oh, hon, I can't tell you how good it is to see you." And it was. He wore a Green Bay Packers baseball cap and a pair of mucky work boots under his jeans—he'd probably been thinning out his woods all morning, an obsession of his—which made him look like a Scandinavian-descended dairy farmer, except for the width of his face and his coppery skin. Ramsay was a retired lawyer, in his sixties and showing it—he walked with a limp because of his bad hip, and his hand shook a little, holding the takeout bag—but he had a looseness about him that Diane loved. With Ramsay, anything went. He asked nothing of her other than her company when she was willing to give it, and when she wasn't, he knew how to make himself scarce. He wasn't simmering inside much of the time, like she was. Being with him was easy, a relief from her own self. It was, indeed, good to see him. "Let's eat," she said happily. "I'm starving."

She led the way into the house, holding the door open for him. The cats appeared at their feet again, meowing for attention. Ramsay knelt for Juliet, who leapt into his lap. He carried her into the kitchen and set the bag of food on the table.

Diane had opened all the windows to air the place. Now she opened the fridge and pulled out a couple of Diet Cokes, which she set on the table, along with two plates and two glasses. She poured the pop while Ramsay pulled out the boxes of food: burgers, French fries, a tub of coleslaw, and a chocolate-chip cookie as big as her head for dessert. They ate and chatted a while—he told her about the recent trip he'd made to Minnesota to visit his daughter and her family, and she told him about Rachel's arrival and Maddy's spiral into dementia. He wasn't the type to pry, but Diane knew he was waiting to hear what she'd mentioned on the phone, and so, finally, fed and rested and content, she began.

"It's kind of a long story."

"I've got nothing but time."

So she told him what she hadn't yet told another living soul, all about the question of the Farm: the fact that Maddy's children didn't want it, that Maddy didn't want to sell it, and the solution they'd landed on. "It was Maddy's idea," she emphasized. "As soon as she heard the story of the sale, *she* was the one who said our family should have it back. I didn't even suggest it to her."

"But you told her the story."

Diane's skin tingled with a reflexive defensiveness. "I thought she should know, Ramsay. I thought she should have all the information."

"All right."

She continued, describing Maddy's apparent satisfaction with the idea, the drafting of the will, everything. And she explained how she'd been hoping Maddy would tell everything to Rachel, get her on board with the idea, so that then Rachel could help tell the rest of the family. But Maddy was losing her marbles, and Rachel was obviously not the ally Diane had thought she might be. Then she stopped, her story told, and watched Ramsay for his reaction.

He leaned back in his chair, took off his hat, smoothed his hair back, and replaced the hat on his head. "Sounds complicated," he said finally.

"That's for sure," Diane replied. She was feeling unsure, an unfamiliar emotion for her. Usually she was unflappable in her sense of right and wrong. But somehow telling everything to Ramsay—the man she respected and loved, the man who'd known her for twenty years, who knew just about everything there was to know about her—somehow she found herself afraid of his judgment. She hadn't been prepared for that.

He cleared his throat, took a sip of his Diet Coke. "Well, they'd have a case," he said, setting the glass back on the table. "If they wanted to bring it."

"But she had two witnesses in the lawyer's office sign the will, attesting to her being of sound mind and all that."

He nodded soberly. "Yes—that's all above-board. Their case would hinge on the question of undue influence. For that, they would only have to prove that the testator was sufficiently vulnerable to—" he paused, "to you."

Diane felt sick to her stomach. "That's what I've been worried about."

"Let me ask you this, Di. This property is not cheap, right? Have you considered how you're going to pay for the taxes?"

"Maddy's providing for that. She's set up a trust in the will."

"Which will be another sum of money that her family won't see."

Diane's face grew hot. Ramsay was doubting her, she could tell. And if he was doubting her—the man who understood her the best out of almost anyone else in the world—then the Claybornes certainly would doubt her. "I know it looks bad, Ramsay, but it's the right thing to do. The *just* thing. I mean, the land never should have left our family in the first place! And now, to have to ask myself whether or not I'm offending the people who've basically made their lives off of my family's property—I mean when in the history of the planet have white people *ever* asked themselves this question? Do you think Benjamin Turner asked himself whether or not he was doing the right thing when he signed that deed? Of course not! He was looking out for his family, *his* tribe. Why should I have to do anything differently?" She glared at him, as if all of this were his fault, her heart thundering in her ears. Ramsay met her gaze impassively, giving her nothing back except his own calm attention. She took a breath, let it out, started again.

"Anyway, it was Maddy's idea. She's giving it freely. All I did was tell her the history of the place, the *truth*. She's the one who came up with the idea of giving it to me." She stopped, hearing the tinny ring of excuse-making in her voice.

"You finished?"

She nodded, rolled her eyes once, a final gesture toward revolution. "Yeah."

"I thought you'd grown out of your angry phase."

"Yeah, well. Apparently not."

"You don't have to lecture me about justice, Di."

"I know it." He'd spent his life defending downtrodden people, had delivered countless arguments of his own on the question of land tenure and Native rights.

"I've got no argument with your logic, or with Maddy's decision. It's a magnificent gesture. The thing I'm concerned about is whether they'll be able to prove undue influence. And I'm saying that I think they'll have a pretty good case. You asked for my professional opinion."

"That I did."

"So." They sat in silence for a while, Ramsay tapping the metal tab of the Diet Coke can against the tabletop. Then he set the tab down. "Can I ask you a personal question?" he said, meeting her eyes.

"Sure, hon. Always."

"Why do you want this land so badly? You've got a nice place right here, a good life for yourself. Don't you? Why get yourself caught up in this?"

Diane looked down at the table, at her plate with its scattering of uneaten French fries, its trails of ketchup. Once again, her mind went to Joe, and the bad time he'd had after the war. Last night, trying to get to sleep, Diane had lain awake, helpless before the train of images processing like a slow cross-country freight across the black night of her mind: Joe on his hospital bed just after the war, blotto with painkillers, his face a bloody jelly; Joe, in the car with her on their way to yet another surgery, staring dismally out the passenger-side window; Joe, systematically cutting to pieces each of the notebooks he'd kept since he could write, notebooks that documented in meticulous sketches and careful prose each of his obsessions through the years: comic book heroes, lists of the scientific names accompanied by sketches of all the species of snakes, spiders, and lizards one could find in Wisconsin, proto-blueprints for spaceships and rockets he planned to design, song lyrics—and much more; he'd stopped showing them to her after a while. She'd been so horrified, she'd tried to snatch the scissors from him, but he'd only deflected her and kept right on cutting, his face that same blank page, that unreadable map. And finally, the worst of them all: Joe, sprawled across the train tracks outside of Clinton, dead to the coming dawn and the early morning freight.

That had all been ages ago, of course. Joe was sober now. And he hated for her to worry about him. But if life had taught her anything, it was that anything could happen. And when anything happened, you needed someone—or some*thing*—to fall back on.

She looked up at Ramsay, who was watching her with his kind, intelligent eyes. She cleared her throat. "For Joe," she said. "I want it for Joe."

He nodded, as if that's exactly what he'd expected her to say. And then, gently, he asked, "And what about Joe then, Di? Have you talked to him? Does he want the Farm?"

She smiled ruefully. "You know I haven't, Ramsay. Not yet. And I know what he would say—he would say he doesn't want it. But he's young yet. He's only thirty-one. He thinks he can live the way he's living for the rest of his life, but he doesn't know what that *means* yet. He just hasn't lived long enough. Having the Farm, well, it would be ready for him when he needed it, *if* he needed it, later in life. You know, in case."

"In case you're not around to help him out anymore."

She felt a rush of tears pricking at her sinuses and inhaled sharply to stop them from falling. "Yeah. Something like that."

That was it, of course. She was and had always been Joe's back-up. Any time he needed anything extra—a high medical bill, an expensive part for the truck—he came calling on her. And she'd lay out the cash. She was happy to do it: it's what families were for, in her opinion. But she'd had her own back-up, all her adult life: Madeline Clayborne. Maddy had helped her with nursing school tuition, helped finance Joe's college degree, loaned her the money for the down payment on this house. Maddy had been her rock, financially speaking. And in a few short weeks—or sooner, possibly, any day now, really—that rock would melt into the earth, and she'd be left standing on shifting silt.

Ramsay, seeing her fragility, covered her hand in his larger one, and spoke to her in a gentle voice. "You do have some options, Di. There are arrangements you can make, legally, that would maintain the spirit of Mrs. Clayborne's wish to restore the land to Indian ownership, but might also soften the blow to the rest of the family a little bit, make it not quite as stark a deprivation for them."

"They're hardly deprived," Diane quipped automatically.

"No, but it'll *feel* that way to them. And that's what counts. That's what makes people sue. How it feels."

She nodded.

"It's contiguous to the reservation, right?"

"Yes. Why?"

"Well, I'm just thinking . . . a better solution might be to leave it to the tribe. That way, you wouldn't have to worry about the property taxes and it would still revert to Indian land."

"I suggested that, but Maddy said she didn't want to deal with the tribal politics."

Ramsay shrugged. "What politics?"

"What politics? Come on, Ramsay."

"With something like this, there isn't a whole lot to fight about. The tribe gets more land. Who can argue with that?"

"I don't know, hon. She thinks it would be too complicated that way."

He waved a hand in the air dismissively. "It'd be simple. I could do it for you. And you could draft a clause in the agreement, a life tenancy clause, that provided for you—and Joe, for that matter—to live there, as long as you didn't diminish the land in any way. You know David Warren? He handles land tenure issues in the tribal office, and I can tell you, he would be all over that. Any opportunity to increase tribal land holdings is Christmas morning to him."

Diane nodded again, feeling the weight of it all like a sandbag in her lap, on her chest. She was in deep. "Honestly, Ramsay, I don't even know that I *do* want to live there. I love my little house."

He nodded, waiting.

She sighed. "I guess I've got to talk to Joe."

"Probably a good idea."

"But hon," Diane started, seized by a panicky realization. "Even if this plan is the better way to go, we still have the same problem. Maddy is getting worse and worse. Even if I could get her to understand and agree to this new plan, even then, I don't think we could get witnesses to agree to sign off on the will. I mean, her mind is not sound anymore." At this, Diane surprised herself by leaking out a tear, which was quickly followed by a succession of several more.

Ramsay held her hand while she silently cried, stroking her forearm with his finger. After a few minutes, she collected herself. "I guess I'm going to miss her more than I realized," she said, wiping her cheeks.

"She's a good one."

"She is. She's been a good friend for a long time. And all this shit about the Farm is complicating things. I mean, I'd take Maddy alive and healthy any day over some piece of property. I know that, she knows that. You know that." She squinted at him: did he?

"I do. I know that, Di."

"But everyone else is going to think I planned all this from the start, that I *schemed* to get Maddy to leave the place to me, that I'm a parasite, a sponge. That's what gets me, Ramsay. People are not going to understand." With sudden purpose—she'd had enough of her own whining—she stood and strode over to the coffeepot, which she rinsed and filled with fresh tap water, then poured the water into the back of the coffee maker.

"Since when do you care what people think?"

"Since now, I guess." She scooped the grounds into the filter, sending a spill skittering across the counter. "You're right, hon. Why should I care what people think? As long as what I'm doing is just—and legal."

"That's the rub."

She wiped the spilled grounds into the sink. The coffeemaker began its cheery gurgling.

"Talk to the family, Di. It sounds like Mrs. Clayborne is too far gone. But it's going to take the family a while to get used to the idea, and things will go much better if they can talk with Mrs. Clayborne about it, even if she isn't firing on all cylinders."

"Yes. You're right. I'm working on that."

Ramsay stayed a while longer. They shared the chocolate chip cookie, drank the coffee, and then went to snuggle on the couch a while, the TV flickering in the afternoon light. Outside, clouds began to gather. The sky grew gray and then charcoal. The light from the TV played a changing rainbow of hues across the furniture, the walls, their faces. Diane barely noticed the increasing darkness. She was too caught up in Ramsay—his baggy neck, his warm, wet mouth, the feel of his quiet, stately hands—to be aware of the coming rain.

5

But the rain came. It fell on the roof of Diane's little house, pummeling it with its tiny rain-fists, making the interior of the house sound like a drum circle. It fell on the street outside her house and the busier county roads outside of town, slicking the surface of the summer tar, causing a sedan to skid off the road onto the muddy shoulder, where its driver stayed put for a long while, waiting it out. It pooled in enormous puddles on the roads, pools which then fanned themselves into majestic arcs of spray every time they were penetrated by a set of whizzing tires. The rain fell on side streets and dirt roads and old logging trails deep in the woods, creating washouts, mud streams, rushing rivers of dirt. It fell on the dairy farms, pelting the hides of the cows, who found shelter in the barn—the lucky ones—or under a tree, or else just endured it, masticating the sweet soaked grass. It fell on the gravel roads and driveways, deepening sinkholes in the subsurface soil, repuddling patches of exposed earth, making circles of ever-expanding rings in the new and fast-growing puddles. It rained on the treetops, the forest canopy—the white pines, the cedars, the tamaracks and spruce boughs, the needles shedding water as fast as it fell, the drops collecting in the crevasses of the wood, on the leaves of the second-story species, the spreading oaks and maples, the birches and beeches, the saplings—wetting both the strong and the doomed. It painted to darker hues the windward side of the trunks; it dampened and softened the fallen pine needles and rotting deciduous leaves that littered the forest floor, tamping them toward their inevitable verge: that intimacy with their microscopic decomposers, the earwigs and centipedes, the ants and sow bugs and earthworms, the spiders and millipedes and beetles, those dumb agents of reincarnation, whose eating and defecating would bring the fallen glory of the giants above them to meet their eventual fate as soil. It rained on the mushrooms, the fungi that grew out of the downed tree trunks, the white spreading fungi with tentacled stalks, the little cities of umbrella mushrooms with their crenellated undersides.

It rained on the Farm—on the Eliza tree and the eagle's nest, wetting the wings of the eaglet and the matted dropped feathers in the nest's bowl. It rained on the overgrown apple trees, the gnarled branches, the early blossoms trembling and tearing and falling to the saturated ground. It pounded the garage roof, drummed on the old icehouse, pocked the surface of the tennis court, spattering the clay. It rained on the farmhouse itself, where Maddy slept obliviously in her bedroom, encased in the protective sheaths of bedspread, walls, ceiling, roof—leaky as it may have been—and where Rachel and Deirdre and Joe huddled on the back porch, watching the water sheet down, feeling the cool thrill of spray through the screens, stepping a little closer together, closer to the center of their dry interior. It rained on and on, pocking the surface of the flowage—that great puddle—creating mad geometries of ripples, ring crashing into ring, until the circles became fragments of circumference, interrupted arcs, aborted parabolas. The flowage seethed and foamed, the ripples became waves, which became whitecaps, which knocked against one another with ever-increasing vigor, startling the bass and the trout and the crappie, who swam deeper beneath the surface, down toward the sunken village, toward the drowned graves, the flooded boneyard. The rain came down on the muskrats and the otters, who found shelter under overhanging branches, in muddy burrows, in hidden caves. It rained on Joe's yurt, peppering the canvas and the plastic windows, streaming down the slick surface. It rained on the dam, the sturdy and reliable Old Bend Dam, on the causeway and the bridge, the splashwalls and the gatewheel, and it rained on the rocks below the dam, where the eagle liked to fish. The river grew wild and rushy; the river liked the rain. A catfish darted, a bluegill dove, a crayfish scuttled under a rock. It rained and rained and rained, and the water accepted itself into itself, and rose, increment by increment, even as the gates rushed with water and the penstocks echoed shootingly beneath the drumming of the rain, and the levels, mark by mark, began to rise.

6

Several days passed. The sky was a perpetual cloudbank, and the rain fell steadily, pimpling the lake with colliding rings. Joe, nervous about how high the water was getting, didn't stray far from the dam. Maddy slept more than usual, allowing Diane to sneak in an unheard-of catnap one afternoon. Even the eagles huddled in the nest, making only the necessary fishing flights when the juvenile's squawking could no longer be tolerated.

Rachel was finding it next to impossible to talk to Grand about the Farm. When Rachel wasn't busy with Deirdre, it seemed that Grand was either incoherent, asleep, or Diane was hovering, moving in and out of the bedroom: giving her medicine, checking vitals, bringing a tray or taking one away. During the rare moments when Grand was coherent and Diane nowhere in sight, Rachel found herself tongue-tied. She couldn't find the right way to broach the topic without coming off as selfish and grasping. Michael's warning—that by lobbying Grand in her current state she'd be no better than Diane—rang in her head every time she opened her mouth.

Still, despite the gloomy weather and the current prognostications about the Farm, Rachel felt more or less okay, happier than she'd been in a long while. She woke with Deirdre beside her in bed (she'd decided to give up the crib altogether, despite what the sleep-training books said—and why not? They both preferred each other's warmth), breakfasted on muffins, read the paper to Grand while the lake breeze blew up, and, when Grand closed her eyes to doze, suited up in Grand's old slicker and rain hat and galoshes, popped Dee in the front pack and hiked through the dripping woods. One morning she bent to collect a patch of tender fiddleheads—Deirdre swatting at the curled fronds with a misaimed hand—and fried them in butter for lunch; another they picked a bouquet of Indian paintbrushes and white daisies that had sprouted up beside the road and brought it back for Grand; on a third they watched a neighbor kid tear through the soggy meadow on his ATV, spraying clods of mud and leaving wide tire-treaded ditches. Deirdre napped in the pack as they walked, snug against Rachel's chest, and Rachel walked and breathed and poked around, and step by step felt herself filling up with freshness.

She and Michael spoke most days, checking in, and she reassured him that all was well, that Deirdre and she were both thriving, that she was loving spending time with Grand, that being up at the Farm was just what she'd needed. She thanked him for understanding, for not freaking out too much about her having left, and in general, made him feel as good and secure as she could about the fact that she'd essentially kidnapped their daughter and removed her from his care for an indefinite period of time. And Michael was, as usual, remarkably understanding. He told Rachel he was glad she was feeling better, he was glad Grand was getting to spend some time with her. One morning, when Deirdre had risen shockingly early, Rachel brought her out to the chilly porch (well-wrapped in a sleep sack), and laid her on a blanket on the floor while she painted the sunrise in watercolor. Later, when the paint had dried, she slipped it into an envelope with a daisy she'd picked and pressed between Webster's Tenth Edition and the massive old bible Grand still kept on the library shelves. "Here's a little bit of the north country for you, sweet man," she wrote on the back of the painting. "Mommy and baby miss you."

As for Diane, the rain made her sluggish and uncharacteristically indecisive. She knew she should insist on sitting Rachel down and coming clean with her about Maddy's plans for the Farm, let the chips fall where they might. But it seemed that every time she entered the same room as Rachel, the girl found some pressing reason to leave, as if she knew what was coming. Somehow the close sky and the constant rain made it easier to skate along just as she had, without taking any action, as if the rain had suspended time.

Eventually, it cleared. On that first sunny morning, Joe was back, with a bag of Krispy Kreme donuts. Diane greeted him at the door.

"I was out this way," he lied. "Thought I'd see how that roof was holding up in all this rain."

"Roof's fine," she said. "How's the dam?"

"Still there." He held up the bag of donuts. "Brought your favorite. Boston Crème."

"Well, come in." He followed her into the kitchen. "Want some coffee?"

"Thanks," he said, setting the bag on the counter. She handed him a steaming cup.

He took a donut out of the bag and ate half of it in one bite. "That furniture still need moving?" he asked through a mouthful of powdered sugar.

Diane sipped her coffee. "I don't see any other big strong men around here, do you?"

"All right, Ma. Take it easy. I'll do it today."

"That would be nice. Medical supply delivered a hospital bed the other day that's just sitting in the downstairs office, but I can't move her in there yet until we clear out the desk and sofa and make it livable." She dumped the rest of her coffee in the sink. "Actually, I'm glad you're here. There's something I've been wanting to talk to you about."

"Where's Rachel?"

"What?"

"I thought I'd get Rachel to help me. She around?" He put his mug in the sink and wiped his mouth on a dishtowel.

"Somewhere around here."

He pulled another donut by its paper wrapper out of the bag, then ambled hopefully through the swinging kitchen door.

Unbelievable, Diane thought. *The boy has a one-track mind.* She moved to the bakery bag he'd left on the kitchen counter. There were two donuts left; he'd brought one for Maddy, too. She took out the Boston Crème and tore into it, letting her mouth fill with sweet cream. *The hell with it. It's his life. He can screw it up however he wants.*

Joe and Rachel worked all morning side by side, first removing a set of old file cabinets, then an ancient sofa, penetrated with dust, and finally, the big pine desk in the corner. They cleared all the old games—the Sorry!, Parcheesi, and Scrabble that had been untouched for decades—out of the game cabinet, leaving the shelves empty for Maddy's clothes. In the process, Rachel discovered an old Earth, Wind, and Fire record, one they used to listen to together as kids. She put it on the stereo, which still had a working turntable, and they grooved to it as they dusted the room, singing along. Finally, after they vacuumed up the skeins of slut's wool that had been hiding beneath the furniture, they rolled in the hospital bed and set it up by the window. Maddy would be able to sit up in bed and watch out the window for the eagles or morning robins or any other creature that might wander by.

The job took the bulk of the day. Joe left late that afternoon, promising to come back the next day to see how Maddy liked her new room. Diane never managed to buttonhole him; it seemed he was always with Rachel, and the few moments when she knew he was alone—when Rachel was feeding the baby or putting her down for a nap—Diane lost her nerve. She knew, more or less, what he would say: that he didn't want to live on the Farm, that he was perfectly happy where he was, etc., etc. And if she tried to argue at all, or not even argue, but present an alternative point of view—that maybe he wouldn't feel the same way in five or ten years, that maybe, once he settled down, he'd like something a little more permanent—she knew he'd blow his top, accuse her of trying to control his life, etc., etc., etc. It would be the same old argument they'd been having as long as she could remember. And she hated to dredge all the old business up again, especially now, when he was looking so happy, when he was clearly enjoying himself in a way she hadn't seen in a long time. Being with Rachel. She could see the hope rising in his eyes, and she didn't want to spoil it. Even though she knew it was just a matter of time before all that hope overflowed its banks and left him empty once more.

⁂

That evening at dinner, Rachel announced to Maddy that her new bedroom was ready. "Joe and I worked on it all day. You can even sleep in it tonight, if you want. Your bed is right by the window, so you'll be able to look out at the moon before you fall asleep."

Confused, Maddy looked to Diane for help, but Diane was too busy glowering at Rachel. "We'll think about that tomorrow," she seethed.

"Why not tonight?"

"That's kind of you dear," Maddy murmured, "but I don't need to see the moon. I'm perfectly happy just where I am."

Rachel, quelled by Diane's gaze, said nothing more about it.

Later, after they'd finished dinner, and both Maddy and Deirdre were asleep, Diane found Rachel sitting cross-legged in the living room next to one of the cardboard boxes that had come out of the office, a collection of sepia-toned photographs spread on the floor in front of her.

"I'd prefer if you let me approach Maddy tomorrow morning about the bedroom," Diane began, trying for civility. "As you can see, she's not wild about the idea of moving, and we're going to have to handle it carefully."

"Fine," Rachel said. "You could have said something before, though. I thought she knew all about it already. I didn't realize she wasn't in on the plan."

"People Maddy's age, well, they don't always respond well to changes."

"I can see that."

"Thankfully," Diane continued, "it seems she forgot all about it after dinner. So here's what we'll do. Tomorrow morning, when she's fresh, I'll get her dressed. You can go out and cut some flowers or pine boughs or something and make the room look appealing. Then I'll bring her down and we can show it to her. We'll have breakfast in there, let her nap in there. Eventually, she'll see it's easier and more comfortable."

"What if she objects?"

"Oh, she will. But I'm afraid she doesn't have a choice."

"Jesus, I never want to get old. You lose all control over your own life." She turned back to the photos.

"Well, you can let me know when you find the fountain of youth," Diane snapped.

She was about to stalk off, but she caught a glimpse of the picture Rachel was holding. It showed a younger Benjamin Turner—he was still mostly bald, but his face was smoother than the face that presided over the upstairs hallway. In fact, this Benjamin Turner seemed an altogether different man. He was wearing only a white T-shirt and a pair of linen pants, and his mouth was open in a good-humored laugh, as if someone had played a joke on him, and he'd only just gotten it. It was a picture Diane hadn't seen before, and she'd thought she'd seen every picture in the house. "Where'd you find that?" she asked.

Rachel gestured to the cardboard box. "In the office, tucked away in the back of the game cabinet. God knows how long it's been there. It's probably been ages since anyone's looked at these."

"I bet Maddy would like to see those."

"I was thinking I'd show them to her tomorrow." Rachel set the photo down, picked up the next one—a beautiful portrait of a teenaged Maddy, her hair sandy and curled in a wave off her forehead, her face apple-cheeked and smooth. She wore a dark blouse buttoned at the throat, and on her chest a silver latch-key with a chain hanging from each end.

They lingered over the photo, Rachel absently rubbing the edge of the matte paper with her thumb.

"She was a beauty, wasn't she?"

Rachel nodded. "I think this was her high school graduation." She flipped the photo over. The year was scrawled on the back in black ink. "1933."

"Ten years after the dam went in."

Rachel looked up, surprised.

Diane went on, seizing the moment. "She was there to watch it fill. She was young, but she still remembers. How people resisted, didn't want to leave their homes. Her father—your great-grandpa—had to go around convincing people to leave, even as the water was licking at their stoops. Some people just did not want to budge."

"Wow," Rachel breathed. She flipped to the next photo, and there was the dam itself, all trim and spanking new, even in grainy black and white. And behind it, the brand new reservoir. "There it is," Rachel said. "The Old Bend Dam."

"For years after that thing went in, bones were washing up on the shore. Thigh bones, vertebrae, even skulls. On the beach. People would cast a line and hook a collarbone instead of a fish."

Rachel gaped at Diane. "You're joking."

"I wish I were. The reservoir flooded out thousands of graves. The riverbanks were the traditional tribal burial ground for generations. And bones float."

"I never knew that." Rachel stared at the photo of the dam. "Jesus, what a legacy." She turned back to Diane. "Can I ask you something?"

"Yes."

"Grand told me the other day that your family used to own this land. Is that true?"

Diane took a deep breath. "Yes. It used to belong to my great-grandfather. Mr. Turner," she gestured to the picture Rachel had set aside, "bought the land from him."

"Grand said he bought it from Mary."

"Well, sort of. Mary tricked him into selling it. Told him he was signing a promissory note for a loan when really he was signing the note of sale. She thought they needed the money more than the land. She was a hard woman."

Rachel returned to the picture.

"Did Maddy—" Diane began, her voice cracking. She cleared her throat, started again, "Has Maddy spoken to you about her intentions for the Farm? I mean, after she dies?"

"Not directly, no," Rachel's voice grew sharp. "But I know what's going on."

"What do you mean?"

"I mean, I know she's leaving it to you. It's obvious, from the things she's let slip."

Diane sat down on the edge of the wicker rocker. "I was hoping she'd be alert enough to talk to you about it herself. But it appears that window may have passed."

"I guess."

"It's very important that you understand, Rachel, that this gift of Maddy's was her idea. It did not come from me."

Rachel was staring daggers at the photographs in her lap. "I find that a wee bit hard to believe, Diane."

"Why?"

"Why? Isn't it obvious? Here she is, alone with you, day after day, basically captive to you and any ideas you might plant in her mind, feeling abandoned by her family—"

"Well, that's not my fault."

"We all live hundreds of miles away!"

Diane took another deep breath, then spoke with evident restraint. "I know. I know this isn't easy for any of you. Losing a loved one never is. But I thought—*we* thought—that you would be the one person in the family who might best understand Maddy's reasons, that you might even support the idea. Your stance on the Farm—which I very much respect, by the way— is part of the reason she *made* this decision. You and Michael have helped her to see beyond sentiment to truth. To what's right."

"God, I'm so fucking sick of doing what's right." She tossed aside the photo of the dam. It sailed like a Frisbee into the leg of the rocker, just missing Diane's ankle.

"Okay, well." Diane stood up. "It's late. Not the best time to get into this. We can talk more in the morning."

Rachel, glaring into space, waited until Diane's footsteps stopped before she crawled over to retrieve the photograph she'd thrown. She checked it for damage—only the corner had chipped—then laid it on top of the pile next to her.

Most of the photos were still fixed to pieces of paper that looked as though they must at one time have been organized in an album. The pages were now brown as toast and just as brittle, cracking easily at the edges. Some of them were empty, showing only the residue of adhesive that had long since lost its stickiness. Rachel handled them carefully. They dated from an earlier period on the Farm, some of them evidently from as far back as when Great-Grandpa Turner had first bought the place, for there were several shots of the partially-finished farmhouse—one of the stone foundation, presumably after it had just been laid, another of the still unpainted siding, a third of an unfamiliar man, shirtless and with a cigarette on one lip, brushing on the first coat of white.

In all of these pictures, Rachel was struck not so much by the house itself, but by the appearance of the land that surrounded the house. It was barely recognizable—so sparse and scrubby! There were trees, yes, but they were spindly and new, and between the few ambitious saplings that were beginning to reach the height of the house, there was nothing but open air. So different than the thick woods that bordered the lake now. The only part of the woods she recognized was the stately old Eliza tree, still towering over the house, and its three skinnier followers, marching as if in a line up from the lake.

She examined a picture of a woman in tennis whites who looked like Grand, though it was hard to tell from the angle, swinging an axe over a log, and admired another of a fit young Grandpa Jacob standing by a bevy of shirtless boys and girls, all of them squinting into the sun. There was another trio of photos of a thirty-something Grand getting up on water skis: first the squat as the boat pulled her from the water, then the moment when the skier either finds her balance or doesn't—Grand looked like she was struggling to feel the right lean, the proper amount of counter-force to balance the boat's pull—and, finally, a shot of Grand up and skiing, her long-legged hourglass figure silhouetted against the bright sky. Rachel admired that one a long while—the grace in Grand's stance, her broad, exhilarated smile. Then, she flipped to the next picture, which took her breath away.

It was a very old shot, one of Grand and her sisters. Grand looked only two or three years old. Great Aunt Jennie—the one who'd almost died as a girl, Rachel remembered—stood tallest, wearing a white blouse with a green tie around the neck and homemade knickers that poufed around the thighs and stopped at the knees. She must have been around ten or so. Next to her stood a very young Great Aunt Dorothea in a white dress with socks drawn up to her knees, a crooked bow in her hair. And beside her, half-turned from the camera, was little Grand, her hair loose and knotty, her dress lopsided, the tie at her waist undone. They stood in front of a very old cabin. There were two floors; the top one was sided with new cedar shingles, but the bottom was made from unmilled, roughly-hewn logs with the bark still on them. And in the corner of the picture, half out of the frame, stood a woman with long dark hair and a dark blue dress, wearing a sober, squinting expression. The woman looked just like Diane.

7

The following morning, while Diane was helping Maddy get dressed, Rachel cut a fresh rose from the bush outside the office window and set it in a vase. She placed the vase on a side table she'd set up at the head of Maddy's bed, along with her reading glasses, a copy of the latest *New Yorker*, a coaster (for the cup of hot coffee she intended to bring), and the folder of photographs she'd found the night before.

Upstairs, Diane was in the process of pitching the move into the new bedroom to Maddy as a great adventure. "Do I have a surprise for you today!" She opened Maddy's shades, letting in a flood of sunlight.

Maddy blinked. "What is it?"

"It's something Rachel and Joe have done for you, and I can promise you, you are going to love it. Up, now."

Diane jollied Maddy through her morning toileting and dressing routine, then helped her downstairs for the final time. Rachel waited at the bottom with a mug of coffee, Deirdre kicking happily in the front pack. Maddy grabbed the walker that Diane had positioned within reach, then smiled at Deirdre. "How's that beautiful baby this morning?"

"Just fine. Happy to see you."

"I hear you've made a surprise for me. You didn't have to do that, darlin'."

Rachel swallowed her guilty feelings and led the way to the office, Diane guiding the old woman behind.

When they reached the doorframe, Rachel threw her arms open. "Ta-da! Your new bedroom!"

"Rachel and Joe fixed it up just for you, hon."

The excitement of the surprise faded from Maddy's face. "But I thought I told you," she said. "I don't want a new bedroom. I'm fine just where I am."

Rachel set the hot coffee on the coaster while Diane moved Maddy across the floor to the bed. "I know, Grand. But look. It's a perfect spot. You can sit here—" she plumped the top pillow of the waiting throne "—and look out the window. And there's a beautiful rose here, in this vase right next to you. You'll be able to watch it bloom."

"Well, it's very lovely, dear. But really, you didn't need to go to all this trouble."

"And look!" Rachel opened the doors to the old game cabinet and revealed Maddy's new wardrobe—she'd emptied the contents of her dresser upstairs and rearranged them in here, making piles of pants and loose knitted blouses, nightgowns, and three different pairs of green satin PJs, her favorite outfit. "See, all your clothes are right here. You'll have everything you need. And look, over here—" she pointed to a shelf by the opposite wall, where she'd lined up several books and a stack of old *National Geographics*. "I've arranged some things for you to read, or that I can read to you when you get bored."

"Well, goodness, dear, it's certainly a lot of work—"

"And look. This is the best thing. Look at this. I found this yesterday, Grand." And she picked up the red folder with the photographs she'd discovered the previous night, sat down beside Maddy—whom Diane had helped to lean back against the throne of pillows—and opened to the first one.

That did it. Maddy ceased her protesting, and gazed at the photo. It was a picture of a Gatsby-style cocktail party out on the lawn. Women in long, drop-waisted skirts and cloches pinned to their bobbed hair and men in shirt-sleeves and pleated pants congregated around a few outdoor tables by the tennis court, drinks in hands. The grass grew long and wild. After a long moment, Maddy said, "Oh, my. Father was away a long while that summer, and the hired man just never cut the grass."

They spent the next half-hour going through the pictures together, Maddy alternately exclaiming in delight or moaning with embarrassment, occasionally trying to dig far back enough in her mind to put a name to a face. Deirdre began to fuss, so Rachel unclipped her from the front pack. Diane offered to hold her while Rachel showed Maddy the pictures, and Rachel—who was speaking as few words as possible to Diane—reluctantly agreed. As Maddy lifted each photo with a shaky hand, Rachel listened hungrily to her stories. Diane stood and jiggled Deirdre, looking over Maddy's shoulder.

Finally, they reached the picture of the children in front of the old cabin and the woman who looked just like Diane.

Diane gasped. "Good Lord, that's my Grandmother Mary. I didn't know you had a picture of her."

"That was her name! Mary. Oh, was she a tough old bird." Maddy stared at the photo, shaking her head in disbelief.

"You said it," Diane agreed.

"Just like you, Diane," Maddy joked, surprising both Rachel and Diane with the sudden return of her teasing humor.

"That's what my mother always used to say," Diane admitted. "'You're as stubborn as your Grandma Mary,' she'd say, when she was angry with me. She didn't like her one bit."

"Of course, I probably gave her fits," said Maddy. "Look at me. Such a scallywag."

Rachel watched Grand and Diane, noticing their jokey intimacy. When Diane caught her staring, Rachel turned to another photograph, this one of Mary and a strange white man, standing in front of a cottage. "Mary was your cook, right Grand? When you were a girl?"

"Oh, yes. She was a little bit of everything, really. She would look after us and tend the garden and keep house. Whatever Mother needed, I suppose. She lived with her family in the old caretaker's cottage down the way. Her husband was the hired hand. What was his name?"

"Tobias," Diane answered. "My grandfather."

Maddy sighed and closed her eyes. "Tobias," she murmured. "That was it."

"He's blond," Rachel observed.

"So?"

"So nothing. I just didn't know he was white."

"He was."

"So you're . . ."

"I'm a half-breed, Rachel," Diane snapped, "if that's what you're thinking. It doesn't make me any less a member of my tribe."

Rachel sat in silent shock, as if Diane had slapped her in the face.

Diane turned righteously to Grand. "Have we worn you out, hon?"

"Oh, no, dear. I'm just resting my eyes a moment."

Abruptly, Rachel stood, the red folder of photos sliding from her lap to the floor, and stalked from the room.

Diane followed her into the library, a clump of her hair in Deirdre's fist. "Rachel!"

Rachel turned, eyes flashing.

"I'm sorry about that back there," Diane said. "I lost my temper."

"Give me my baby." She lunged forward and grabbed Deirdre from Diane's arms. Deirdre went, along with the fistful of Diane's hair.

"Ouch! Could you *wait* a minute?"

Rachel stood fuming while Diane peeled Deirdre's fingers open. "I guess a good night's sleep hasn't made you see reason," Diane said.

"Reason? That's a good one. Oh, yes, this whole thing is entirely reasonable."

"Rachel. Listen. This solution has given her peace. You haven't been here these last ten months. You haven't seen how she's agonized over this question of what to do with the Farm. She couldn't stand that no one wanted it. She couldn't stand the idea that it would be sold to strangers. She was absolutely torn up about it."

"Well, it's certainly convenient for you."

"All I did was tell her about my family history. She had a right to know."

"Don't give me that, Diane. You knew exactly what you were doing."

"What happened to all your high-minded ideals? Those have all disappeared now, all of a sudden, is that it? Now that you stand to gain? Now that the Farm is on the auction block?"

"That's not fair."

"Maddy cares about this place," Diane went on. "She wants it to go to someone who cares about it as much as she does. *And* she cares about justice. This way she gets both things."

"I care about it, too! I care about this place more than anywhere else in the world."

"And I think that's too little come lately. You didn't care about it for eight long years."

"That's not fair," Rachel protested again, louder this time. "There's more to it than that."

"Oh, tell me all about it," she replied, her voice rising until it was just under a shout. "A pretty, educated white girl like you, who drives a Prius and works in the Ivory Tower and cares about wild animals and Indians, as long as they stay poor and shitfaced on the reservation—you go right ahead and tell me about what's *fair*."

"Jesus, Ma," came a voice from the dining room. Both Diane and Rachel swiveled in its direction. "Why can't you ever learn to take it easy?" Joe glared at Diane.

Maddy's voice keened from her room, "Diane? Rachel? Hello?"

"Good God," Diane muttered, turning on her heel and returning to Maddy.

"Boy, a guy stops by for a visit and ends up facing down World War Three. What the hell's going on?"

Rachel stood in the middle of the living room carpet, dazedly clutching Deirdre to her chest, her eyes on a small framed picture that hung on the wall a few feet away. It was a miniature silhouette of a pine tree, carved out of cork. Grand had carved it herself, many years ago. As a kid, Rachel had asked Grand to teach her how to do it. Grand had found some corkboard and a couple of paring knives, and they'd sat together on the porch, each carving their own design. She'd been proud that Grand was letting her use a sharp knife—something her parents wouldn't have done—but also frustrated at not being able to carve the design she wanted to carve. Savagely, she slashed her piece of cork with the knife. At home she would have been scolded for an outburst like that, but Grand didn't scold. Instead, she picked up her own piece of corkboard, on which she'd carved an eagle in flight, its wings reaching from corner to corner, and broke it into pieces, bit by bit. Each break in the cork made a soft crunching sound, like teeth tearing into a taut piece of fruit.

"But yours is good!" Rachel had exclaimed, dismayed.

Grand only shrugged. "So was yours. But you know what? We can make new ones."

A pulse beat in her head as the walls of her mind seemed to close in on themselves, her perspective narrowing. She felt dizzy, as though she were traveling at a height over a vast distance, flying quickly on the spread wings of a bird, over deserts and plains, over emptiness. There was nothing to see. It was a barren landscape. Nothing but blank sand.

"Rachel?" Joe took a step toward her and put a hand on her elbow.

"Grand is leaving the Farm to your mother," she got out. "After she dies."

Joe dropped his hand. "Whoa," he said. "You're kidding."

"No. Not kidding."

"That's radical."

"That's one word for it."

"I gather you're not happy about it."

Rachel shot him a dirty look. "Your mother can be pretty persuasive."

"You think my mother made her do it?"

"I think she had something to do with it, yeah. It's not the kind of decision Grand would make on her own."

Joe's eyes lifted from Rachel's, and Rachel turned to find Diane standing outside the door of the office-bedroom, glaring at her. "Your grandmother wants to see you."

Rachel stormed past Diane into Maddy's room.

Diane remained where she was, withstanding Joe's inscrutable gaze. "I was trying to find a time to talk to you, hon," she started. "But you've been so . . . preoccupied."

Joe blew out a poof of air. He put both hands on top of his head, then dropped them to his sides again. "Wow, Ma," he said. "Whoa."

"This wasn't how I wanted you to find out."

He walked to the nearest chair—the wicker rocker with a flowered cushion—and dropped into it. Diane stifled a wince as the chair creaked beneath him. She perched on the couch, a few feet away. "I know it looks bad, hon. But I promise you—this was Maddy's idea. She was at her wit's end with her kids—they don't want this place. They were going to sell. All I did was tell her the family story." She was getting tired of repeating the same information.

Joe let his head fall back against the chair, his legs sprawl open. She snuck a moment to admire him: his brown neck, his thick black hair lifting off his forehead. He had a lot of Thomas in him. Sometimes, he could take her breath away—the beauty of his body, his ease, the complete Joe-ness of him. He still moved like he was sixteen years old. It caught her off guard, sometimes, how young his body was, how it didn't seem to match his face, that undeniable reminder that time had passed, that he was no longer sixteen, that he would never be sixteen again.

"Well, Ma. What do I say? Congratulations, I guess. You'll be a wealthy woman."

"No. No, I won't. It'll cost me, actually—paying the taxes, the maintenance. She'll help with it, but still."

Joe snorted unkindly. "I guess I shouldn't be surprised."

"What's that supposed to mean?"

He shrugged. "Nothing. Only that this is so totally you, Ma. Poetic justice, your trademark. A wrong brought right."

"And what's the matter with that? Excuse me, but I was under the impression that justice was something worth working for."

"But this isn't our land anymore. It never was our land."

"It *was*, Joe. It *was* our land—it belonged to our family."

"Yeah. And before that it belonged to the tribe. And before that it didn't belong, it just *was*, Ma. But that was a long time ago. A long, long time ago."

"So? Does that mean we should just give up, just because an injustice happened long ago? I don't think so."

Joe jiggled his knee, up and down, up and down. "I don't know. I guess not."

Quietly, knowing it was now or never, Diane said, "I wanted the land for you, hon. I thought maybe, in the future, you might—"

Joe jumped to his feet. "Oh, no you don't, Ma. Don't put this on me. I don't want anything to do with this place."

"Joe. Just hear me out."

"No, Ma. You listen to me. I am not moving onto this funny farm. Not in a million years. You can just get that idea out of your head right now."

She closed her eyes. God, what a disaster. The whole thing—one enormous, out-of-control disaster. "So you think I should decline Maddy's offer? I should say 'no, thanks' and then just let her die, knowing her family's going to sell the place she's spent her life caring for to a complete stranger? She *wants* to give us the land, Joe. She thinks it's the right thing to do."

"Do whatever you want, Ma. Just don't involve me." He stood with his legs straddled, as if caught between two forces pulling at him from either direction. He glanced toward the office-bedroom. "Rachel's pissed," he said.

"I should have known you'd take Rachel's side."

"Whoa, calm down, Ma. I'm not taking any sides. I'm just stating a fact."

"She's not as happy with the idea as I thought she might be, no."

"Why did you think she'd be happy?"

"She and Michael have boycotted this place for years, Joe. You know that. In the name of indigenous rights. This whole idea is just walking their talk. But I guess for her it was just talk. Justice is all well and good in the abstract, isn't it? But when it comes to actually making some kind of sacrifice..."

"Rachel loves this place, Ma. *You* know *that*."

"She used to."

"You don't ever stop loving a place. It gets in your bones."

Diane stared at him, feeling herself swell with emotion. He was so young still, so innocent. So vulnerable, despite all his posturing. "What do you think you're doing, anyway, Joe? With her."

"What do you mean, what am I doing?"

"Getting involved like you are. She's a married woman. She's got a baby. You don't need that kind of complication in your life."

"Hey, look, Ma. I'm not *involved*. I'm just being a friend is all. She's having a rough time right now."

"What do you mean, a rough time? Is she breaking up with Michael?"

"No. I don't know," he stammered. "Just adjusting to being a mother is what I mean. Turns out having a kid is a lot harder than it looks."

"Oh, that's a news flash."

Joe rolled his eyes.

"You may think you're just being a friend, but it's more than just that. *She's* getting involved. And she shouldn't be. I just don't want you to get hurt again, Joe. Maybe you could stand it, but I couldn't."

He glanced once more toward the office-bedroom. "This is all a little too fucked up for comfort." He turned on a heel. "I'm going home."

Meanwhile, in Grand's room, Rachel sat on the edge of the hospital bed, balancing a nursing Deirdre on her knee while trying to reassure Grand and stabilize her own careening emotions at the same time. "You've done nothing wrong, Grand," she said. "Don't worry."

"But I feel as though I have! I'm afraid I've done something terribly wrong!"

"No, you haven't." Rachel stroked Grand's hand, as if she might stroke back the minutes, the days, the years. She could feel Grand's pulse beating wildly, and she encircled her wrist with her own hand, trying to calm the pulse, slow the blood. "You haven't. It's just—I was surprised. I wasn't expecting it."

"Of course you weren't, darlin'. Who would expect such a thing?"

Deirdre swallowed, humming contentedly.

"I wanted to keep it in the family," Grand continued, "but neither your father nor your aunt Linda were interested. I thought often of you, but, as Diane reminded me, you've been, well, against it for a long time. This seemed to me the next best thing."

Rachel marveled at how Grand's mind flickered in and out of clarity, like a flame in a fickle wind. "I know, Grand. I understand. It makes sense. It's just—" she stopped herself.

"What, dear? It's just what?"

Deirdre smacked her lips so comically loud it would have made them both break into guffaws at any other time. Rachel inhaled deeply, feeling torn between two courses of action: telling Grand the truth or pretending to be fine with it, with everything. Just brushing the whole thing off. She knew what she *should* do, what Michael would want her to do. This is the perfect solution, he would say. The whole weight of history is behind this decision. Grand is doing the right thing, the just thing, the thing they'd said all along that should be done. Why should Rachel be upset? What right did she have to think even for a minute that the land might belong to her? It never should have gone to her family in the first place. She knew all of that. But she was tired, so tired of doing the right thing, bending to the will of the expected, prostrating again and again to the power of the Should.

"It's just that I love this place a lot, Grand. I didn't realize how much until now. And I can't stand the idea of losing it."

"But I thought you didn't like the Farm."

"No, no, not at all, Grand," Rachel countered, trying to stem her rising frustration. "I've been trying to tell you. I love it up here. Michael's the one who objects to it. And it's not that he doesn't like it exactly—it's just—" She hesitated, but then figured she might as well speak her mind. She had nothing to lose. "I've been fantasizing, Grand. About what it might be like to *move* up here. Permanently, I mean. To live. Just like you did after Grandpa died."

"I see. Oh, what a lovely dream, dear. But what would Michael say?"

Rachel pressed her lips into a thin line. Here was the question she hadn't yet faced, the one she'd been avoiding. Out of all her fantasies about this place, about making a new life up here, or, as she preferred to think of it, reclaiming the life she might have had, none of them included Michael.

Grand, lost in a world of consternation, didn't press the point. "Well." She looked at Rachel's hand and then up again into her face, then back down once more. "Well, this *is* something. I don't know what to say."

"I just can't stand the thought of losing this place, Grand. I know it's completely impractical but, I don't know—I just can't stop thinking about it, about living up here, maybe starting my own little farm, raising

Deirdre here. It's the kind life I want to lead, you know, Grand? The life I've been leading—I don't know, it seems so *irrelevant*. So soulless and pointless. I don't think I can go back to it." Her voice dropped off, quieted by the gravity of what she'd just said.

She became conscious of a presence outside the door, a presence that she realized had been standing there a good while. "You might as well come in, Diane. Join the discussion."

Diane stepped into the doorway. Even from across the room, Rachel could feel the energy coiled like a snake within Diane's small frame. Her hands were fists and she stood on the balls of her feet, as if ready to leap into the air.

"All right," she said matter-of-factly, not at all embarrassed, apparently, that she'd been caught eavesdropping.

"Oh, Diane!" Maddy said, startled. "I didn't know you were there."

"Evidently not."

"Well," Maddy continued once more, then stopped, caught in the conundrum of the moment, in the midst of her divided loyalties. Her eyes grew wide and began to dart, the consciousness behind them coming unmoored.

"Grand!" Rachel grabbed her hand.

"Rachel, if you'd come out here, please, I have something I'd like to talk to you about," Diane said, her voice strained and even.

"You can talk to me right here."

Diane's eyes went to Maddy, who bunched the covers into a fist, then let go and rummaged in them, as if looking for a dropped earring, some lost treasure.

"I think it would be better if we talked out here."

"Why? So you can pull another yard of wool over Grand's eyes?"

"Oh, dear," Maddy said.

Diane, in her steeliest voice, replied, "I have not pulled a stitch of wool over your grandmother's eyes. All I have done is tell the truth."

"Well, that's all I'm doing right now. I'm telling my grandmother the truth. And I don't appreciate you barging in."

"Now, now," Maddy said vaguely, to the air.

"You were asking for an inheritance."

"You have no right to listen in on our conversation!"

"Please!" Maddy shouted, and her voice startled both Rachel and Diane into silence.

"I can't hear myself think," she added. Her eyes bulged wetly, the blue irises pure and translucent. She held her hands aloft, and they shook with the effort. "I—I—I thought we were having a conversation," she managed, finally, though it wasn't clear that that was what she had intended to say. "Rachel and I. I don't—I don't understand what happened."

"We were," Rachel nodded. "A private conversation. You're absolutely right, Grand." She glared at Diane.

Diane swallowed, looking at Maddy—the wide glistening eyes, darting with anxiety, the lopsided thunderhead of hair. "I apologize, Maddy. I lost my temper. Forgive me. I'll leave the two of you alone." And she spun on her heel and left the room.

"Thank God," Rachel said.

"I don't understand," Maddy continued, her eyes on the door, shaking her head. "I just don't understand."

"It's okay, Grand. She's gone now."

"I have a terrible feeling, as though I've done something very wrong. But I just can't put my finger on what it is."

"It's all right, Grand," Rachel said again, sitting back down beside Maddy's thin, blanketed legs, taking her hand. "You haven't done anything wrong."

"I wish I understood. I wish I understood what I've done."

"You haven't done a thing, Grand. Please don't worry. You haven't done a thing at all." Rachel sat with Grand, stroking her hand, soothing her, until she fell back against the pillows and closed her eyes. And she kept stroking her hand while she slept, her mouth hanging open, her breath coming hard in her nostrils. Then she laid Grand's hand gently on the covers and left the room.

Closing the door behind her, she looked for Joe in the living room, but he was gone. Water was running in the kitchen. Rachel went upstairs.

She laid a sleeping Deirdre in the crib, then slid her duffle out from underneath the bed. Quietly, she opened dresser drawers and pulled out shirts and pants, stuffing them in the duffle. Deirdre began to stir. Rachel watched her squirm in her sleep, her little face crunch into a grimace of irritation, and then release into sleep once more. Rachel turned back to her packing, filling the bag until it bulged at the zipper.

Then, the bag over one shoulder, she leaned over the crib and gently lifted Deirdre out. Deirdre squeaked and fussed, but Rachel shushed her. "You can sleep in the car," she said. She made her way downstairs, jiggling Deirdre as she walked, the leather straps of the bag digging into her shoulder.

Diane looked up from the sink, her face drained of its former hostility, now just tired and sad. "Where are you going?" she asked.

"None of your business," Rachel said.

"I'd like to know what to tell your grandmother when she asks after you."

"Why don't you tell her that I left because I don't give a shit about her or the Farm. Just what you've been telling her all along."

"Oh, please. Let's be adults, for God's sake."

"What does that mean, exactly, being an adult? I'd like to know."

"I mean be reasonable. You're acting like a teenager."

"I'm sick of everyone telling me to be reasonable! I've been reasonable for thirteen years, and look where it's gotten me. I'm done being reasonable!" And she swept out the back door and marched across the lawn to the garage, Deirdre wailing all the way.

BOOK FOUR

COME THE RAIN

June 2003

1

Joe parked the pickup by the dam office. Sally ran up to meet him. A breeze blew off the lake, and water crashed beneath the gates a short distance away. The rain still fell from the slate sky, steady and businesslike, pocking the surface of the slate lake. If it weren't for the trees rising up from the shore on the opposite bank, sky and lake would seem to be one continuous surface, as gray and monotonous as the end of the earth.

Joe slammed the door behind him, still fuming. He was disgusted with his mother, with Rachel, with the crazy Clayborne family and their precious Farm. He wanted nothing to do with any of it. His mother and Rachel and Mrs. Clayborne could battle it out among themselves until the last woman was left standing as far as he was concerned. He was not setting foot on that property again, family history be damned. He was staying put in *his* territory: his yurt, his dam, his good, simple, peaceful life. He would make his own history here.

He headed for the control house, letting the rain soak his body, making his shirt cling to his shoulder, his chest and back. Sal ran ahead to the door and then turned, waiting for him. He dialed the key ring hanging from his belt loop until he found the right one, unlocked the door, and stepped inside. The room smelled of damp cement and dust. He tossed the keys on the table with a *chink* and dropped heavily into the rolling chair, his weight propelling him halfway across the room toward the gauges. He gave a cursory glance at the water level gauge and then looked at it again. The gauge seemed to claim that the water had risen almost two inches in the time he'd been gone, a startlingly steep rise.

Cursing, he tramped back outside, holding the door for Sal, and made his way down the asphalt of the causeway to the pier that jutted into the reservoir. Attached to the pier on one side was the staff gauge, a long ruler riveted to the concrete, now mostly submerged. Kneeling on the asphalt, he eyeballed the number at the line where the water licked the gauge, then sat back on his heels, dismayed. The gauge in the control house was right. The lake had risen about one and three quarters of an inch over the past few hours, edging closer to flood stage. One more foot and he'd be calling the county.

Sally licked his ear, and he patted her absentmindedly, then stood and strode toward the dam office and the phone. At his feet, waves slapped the concrete in irregular rhythms. Off in the distance, a loon called. Joe eyed the surface of the causeway as he walked, looking for any new cracks, any disturbing pooling. There were puddles here and there, but nothing out of the ordinary, given the rain.

In the office, he took off his soaked shirt and hung it over the chair. Sally plopped into a wet curl in the corner. The small room smelled wet: wet dog, damp carpet, the faint hum of mold. A red message light blinked on the phone. Joe picked up the receiver and punched in some numbers, then listened to the voice of George Perrin, the damkeeper upriver, at Woodbridge. "I'm inclined to open the gates a bit, relieve some of the head we've got here. Give me a ring with your yay or nay." That message was at 8:47 this morning. The next came at 9:11, George again. "Just trying you again, Joe. I tried your cell with no luck. Give me a buzz." And the next at 9:52: "You're a hard man to get a hold of, Joe." Then, finally, a last message at 10:38, nothing but a click. Joe punched in George's number immediately and apologized for being unavailable. George grunted. "Well, I went ahead and raised the gates half a foot. I figured if we flood out, I wanted it on your head, not mine."

"Fair enough," Joe replied. "Tell you the truth, it's a bit of a relief to know what happened. I was on the verge of calling in a Level One to the county."

"Yeah, well, people were getting worried up this way. You know how they are. They start talking to each other, getting riled. Pretty soon they're phoning in complaints to the power company. Better to nip it in the bud."

"Right you are, George."

"Some rain, though. Worse than I've seen in twenty years. And we're just in for more of it, looks like. Better not stray too far, Joe. Just in case."

"Got it, George. I'm here now, and I'll stay here, you have any problems."

"Good man."

They signed off. Joe immediately called Frank, his supervisor at the power company. Frank picked up on the first ring, and Joe reported the new levels, the action George had taken, and his recommendation: to open the gates about a foot to draw down the reservoir and relieve pressure on the dam. Frank okayed it, as usual—the obligatory call was not much more than a formality—and they exchanged a few words about the rain before hanging up. Sally jumped up as Joe rose from the chair and followed him out the door toward the control house. The rain lashed his bare chest.

Passing the pier, he paused a moment, eyeing the staff gauge once more as waves lapped the numbered lines. It seemed almost a pity to draw the lake down, just as it was getting somewhere. It was as if he could feel the water egging him on with each slap against the concrete, daring him to let it fill, *just this once*, to let it have its way, to reach its upper limit, fulfill its potential.

As part of his training course for this job, he'd had to watch hours of footage of dam breaks—video after video of failures: huge discs of earth sliding down the sides of earthen dams, cracks the size of pencil lines widening into highways of water in seconds, huge structures melting beneath the reservoir's powerful weight like sand castles in a rising tide. The videos were intended to scare responsibility into him, and they did that, but they did something else, too: they awed him, planted in him a secret wish that he might see such a spectacle himself someday. There was something primordial about a freed river, something sublime about a forty-foot wall of water barreling into banks, squashing levees flat, uprooting century-old maples, tearing houses from their foundations as if they were toys. It was a dramatic, deadly object-lesson in hubris, in peoples' apparently ineradicable belief that they should be able to build wherever they liked, that nature should always bend to their will. Again and again throughout history, disasters illustrated this lesson in plain language: Mill River Dam, Williamsburg, Massachusetts, 1874, internal erosion, 138 people died. Time elapsed from the first slide of earthfill to total dam failure: twenty minutes. South Fork Dam, Johnstown, Pennsylvania, 1889, overtopped in a quarter-century storm, 2209 people died. Floodwater was 70 feet high in some places. Saint Francis Dam, Los Angeles, California, 1928, foundation failure, 420 people died. Vajont Reservoir, Italy, 1963. Major rockslide into the reservoir sent up a splash-wave 820 feet high, 2000 people killed. Macchu II, India, 1979, catastrophic flood, gate malfunction, dam overtopped, another 2000 died. Yet people didn't get it; they didn't understand the language. Again and again, they built the dams, repaired the levees, filled in the wetlands, tore up the forests, and basically asked for it.

So, on a strictly theoretical basis, Joe rooted for the rivers. But here he was, the keeper of this particular dam, the protector of these shores and of these people—the few and far between—who lived downstream. The floodplain map showed twenty, maybe twenty-five homes that would be compromised in a dam failure, but even just one was enough to qualify the Old Bend Dam as a high hazard dam, enough to snap Joe out of his impish fantasy and back to the imperatives of the moment. He knew the folks downstream. A few of them fished off the pier here regularly. Almost all of them had shown up the year the fallen white pine had drifted down the reservoir and started banging against one of the gates like a gigantic battering ram. The sound of that pine bashing against the steel had echoed through the woods as if the trickster-hero Wenebojo himself were drumming a massive drum, and people from both downstream and up-reservoir had come to see where the noise was coming from. They'd brought brooms and pikes and long sticks and together a group of them had diverted the enormous log, moving it out of the current toward the shore. Several of the men had waded out to haul the log ashore with chains, had lashed it fast to a couple of sturdy oaks, and had kept watch over it until the Name River Construction Company could get out there and haul it away. They were good folks downriver, worthy of protection.

With these civic-minded thoughts, Joe hiked back to the control house, where Sally waited for him, wagging. Inside, he turned the dial and pressed the button that started the great winches beneath the floor turning. He stood, feeling the vibration in his feet, listening to the satisfying creaking and groaning of the iron cables against the great spools of metal, and felt at ease. It was all right. The gates would open, the water flow, the lake dip again to a more comfortable level. All would be well. Eventually, this rain would pass, and then they could all relax.

At least, he thought, he could do this much well; he could be a decent damkeeper. He might have a fucked up face and a crazy mother, he might be stuck in the past, getting in too deep with an old girlfriend who was bound to toss him on his ass again, he might be just as stupid about that old girlfriend as Sal was about carcasses in the woods, rolling in stink and coming back for more, but at least at this one small thing, he was all right. At least he could take care of this one thing, this one place, this one dam pretty damn well.

2

Rachel slowed the Prius to a stop before turning onto the dam access road, squinting at the sign. "Do Not Enter," it read, and then, in smaller lettering, "Any unauthorized access will result in a fine of $500 and/or imprisonment."

She sighed and shifted into park. "What do you think, Dee?" she asked. Deirdre stared out the side window at the dark web of green outside. Rachel opened the door—the car *binged* cheerfully—and stepped out into the rain, which had slowed to a sprinkle. She read the sign once more, then walked a few paces down the road. Wide muddy tire tracks descended the tarred surface until the road curved and they disappeared from sight. A wind blew, shaking the overhanging branches, which showered her with rainwater. She looked back at the car: the door yawned open, the binging sound insisting on its own importance even in this wet wilderness. She had driven deeper and deeper into the woods, farther and farther from civilization. She would not have been surprised to come across a candy house, a welcoming witch at the door.

She turned back toward the road, trying to see down its slope to the bottom. The curving road and thick forest cover on either side of it prevented her from seeing much of anything, but she thought—or possibly imagined—she could just make out a slice of lakewater in between the trees. "Joe?" she said, in a voice that only the trees heard, and then again, louder, "Joe? Are you there?"

She trudged back to the car, feeling ridiculous. What was she so worried about? The sign was there to scare off the loonies, the unsavory few. There were no cops around anyway. She got back in the car and rolled forward, the wheels spinning before she gained traction.

Halfway down the slope, the macadam became dirt, and the soporific drone of tires on asphalt that she'd endured the whole way here changed to a more irregular crackling and squelching as the tires met the muddy surface. Deirdre gurgled. Rachel pumped the brakes and rounded the curve. The thick woods opened. She saw Joe's pickup parked at the base of the hill next to a small white shed. The road forked: to the left, it dead-ended at a level unpaved parking area, with enough spaces for maybe four cars; to the right, it continued on, past the shed and over the lake, tossing gray and white in the wind. This road, she realized, continued right over the dam. On one side was the lake and on the other a drab complex of buildings: one close by, on the shore, another about halfway down the road, and then, extending parallel to the bank, a long wooden wall, the top of which sloped gradually toward the riverbed, some distance away. This was it, then. The dam that Granddaddy built, the one her family had made their yearly pilgrimage to every summer, the one her father had talked into legend from the lookout. Nothing more than a road over a lake.

She parked the car and got out. The sound of rushing water rose in her ears, and she looked toward its source, but her view of the downstream side was blocked by the building on the shore. All she could see was a cloud of mist hanging in the air.

Deirdre was complaining, so Rachel unstrapped her from the infant seat, then nestled her face against her own throat. Deirdre began to root around, gumming and sucking on Rachel's clavicle.

"All right, baby," Rachel murmured. Seeing nowhere else to sit, she backed into the passenger seat, reclined it to semi-prone, and settled Deirdre on her breast. As the milk buzzed forth, Rachel felt herself relax. All the pent-up emotion—the anger and pain and sorrow that had taken hold of her, hard, and hadn't let go the whole way here—began to release its grip. She closed her eyes, listening to Deirdre's regular hums as she swallowed and the rushing water in the background, and behind that, the deep silence of the woods. Her breath came long and slow. Amazing, she thought. Just when it seemed like the entropy monster was sinking its fangs into your flesh, the universe sent you a moment you could tolerate.

Rachel let her thoughts drift back to another rainy June, years ago, when she and Joe had first crossed over from childhood friends into new territory. They had been out tramping through the old field beyond the barn. The rain had been light, barely noticeable, but it had soaked the grass, making the cuffs of their jeans wet and heavy. Rachel had taken off her shoes and socks.

They'd been arguing that day about the Marines, about Joe enlisting. He was off to basic training at the end of the summer, and Rachel didn't want him to go. She took it personally, his decision. It was as if he was choosing a life that was beyond her ken, and in doing that, he was rejecting her. They walked through the wet grass, the mud squelched through her toes, and she felt sadder and angrier than she'd ever felt in her life.

And then the rain got harder, and they'd taken cover in the old chicken house on the far side of the field. It had been years since any chickens had roosted there; the floor was long swept clean of hay. They sat on the edge of the entrance, amid the bat droppings and the close smell of moldering wood, and she cried, feeling both truly sad and simultaneously moved by the depth of her own sadness. Joe had put his arm around her shoulder. It was something he'd done before, though in different situations—jokingly, pretending he was in control, pretending to be a man—but in that moment, it was real, and she felt that what he had pretended to be was suddenly what he was. The weight of his arm on her back, the way he pulled her into himself, the smell of his clean skin beneath his T-shirt—suddenly, she understood that he was becoming a man, right before her eyes, and that she wanted to be with him, to watch it happen.

She'd rested her head against his chest and let him hold her. And after a little while, he'd put the other arm around her, too, and pulled her closer. And she'd looked up into his face and kissed him. She remembered how soft his lips had been, softer, it seemed, than the lips of the boys she'd kissed back home. She'd kissed him again and again, loving the taste of his mouth, loving, too, that this was Joe she was kissing, feeling as though suddenly her entire childhood made sense in a way it hadn't yet. "Your face is like the moon," she'd said, overcome, and he'd pulled back, startled and muttered something sarcastic like, "Thanks a lot," but she'd pulled him back to her mouth and assured him with her kisses—on his wide cheeks and broad sloping cheekbones—that she meant well, that she loved his face, that to her it was the purest, most beautiful shining thing there was.

She wondered what his lips might feel like now, marred as they were by scar tissue and skin grafts.

A wet tongue on her arm startled her out of her reverie. Sally wagged at the door of the car. Beyond her came Joe walking in his easy way, his shirt off, his jeans hanging low at his hips, looking like a young Hemingway or Jimmy Dean, if you squinted.

Shit, she thought. She was getting into trouble.

"Hi, girl," Rachel said to Sally, letting her lick an outstretched hand. As Joe neared, she smiled wearily up at him. The rain seemed to have ceased, but his hair was still dark-wet, slicked to his scalp.

"What are you doing here?" he barked.

She straightened up, taken off guard. "I—uh. I wanted to see you. You left so suddenly."

"I was a little uncomfortable with that whole scene back there."

"You're not the only one."

He looked away, rubbed one hand through his hair, looked back again.

"Look," she said. "I don't want to bother you. I just thought—you know…" she trailed off. His face was a blank wall. "I can leave, if you want. As soon as she's done eating." She nodded to Deirdre.

"Oh." He backed up a step, looking embarrassed. "I didn't realize."

"It's fine, Joe. I'm not hanging out or anything. You don't really have to worry about that with boobs the size of mine."

He snickered, then snuck a quick glance at Deirdre, her mouth pressed against the curving flesh, before he met Rachel's eyes again.

It was nothing—a tiny flicker of the eyes, barely noticeable—but this one impropriety, this little invasion of Rachel's privacy, lit a flare in her groin. Michael always averted his eyes when Deirdre was nursing, as if the sight of a baby—*their* baby, for Christ's sake—at her breast was a dirty thing, an inappropriate thing, unworthy of being acknowledged. This reaction she knew was just another manifestation of Michael's refinement, his reflexive, almost Victorian politeness. It was—like everything about Michael—well-intentioned, meant to be respectful, to restore to her some dignity, a thing she had been stripped of since becoming a mother. Usually, she understood it as a gesture of love, but now, at the moment, it seemed more like frigidity. This, Joe's interest, this she liked better.

"You see anything?" she teased.

He blushed. "Caught some skin. That'll keep me going for a while."

They fell silent, both of them embarrassed. Joe leaned awkwardly against the car, looking out over the flowage.

"Stopped raining," he offered.

"Finally."

"So what did I miss? You and Ma have it out or what?"

Rachel snorted and switched Deirdre to the other breast. "I don't feel like talking about it right now."

"Okay, good. I don't feel like talking about it either."

They stared at the water and the woods for a few minutes in silence. A fissure opened in the cloudbank, and a single ray of sunlight beamed onto the surface of the lake. Joe pointed at the sky and, turning to Rachel, gave a thumbs-up sign.

"Joe," she said. "Don't be a wise ass."

"Me?" He mugged, wide-eyed, though the effect was hampered on one side by the scar tissue. "I wouldn't dream of it."

Deirdre's earnest sucking had tapered off to an idle tongue-fluttering, so Rachel unlatched her from the second breast and snapped her bra back into place. In one motion, she shifted Deirdre to an upright hold against her shoulder, swung her legs around, and stood up. "How about you give me a tour?"

"All right," Joe said, hesitating. "Though I don't know that there's that much to see."

"Hold the baby a minute, would you?"

Joe accepted Deirdre, who immediately began to fuss. "Oh, don't cry, don't cry, baby. Look! Look at the pretty water." He walked a few steps toward the waves.

Quickly, while Joe's back was turned—she didn't want him to see that she'd packed a bag—Rachel opened the trunk and rummaged in the duffle until she felt the hard plastic clasps of the front pack. She slammed the trunk shut, then slipped her arms through the loops and centered the crosspiece in the middle of her back. "Ready!" she sang out.

"She likes the water," Joe said as she came near.

Rachel tucked Deirdre in the pack and latched the second clasp in place. Deirdre, watching her, let out a delighted sigh. Both Rachel and Joe laughed. "She likes her momma even better," Joe said, and Rachel warmed with pride and relief. Things were all right. Maybe it didn't matter so much about the Farm.

But the hollow sensation in her gut persisted. "So tell me something about the Old Bend Dam. About the environmental destruction my great-grandfather wrought." They walked down the causeway, Sally trotting contentedly beside them.

"Oh, all kinds of destruction. He was a regular Hun, that great-grand-father of yours."

"I thought it would be bigger somehow."

"You've never seen it?"

"Only from the lookout." She pointed toward the hill that rose above the river. "Way up there. Though it never looked all that impressive from there, either, come to think of it."

"Well, it's not Hoover or anything. But it's a good, solid dam. Well-engineered."

"You're just saying that to make me feel better." And she pitched her voice higher, mimicking him. "'It's okay, Rachel. It's a very *well-built* agent of environmental destruction.'"

Joe laughed. "All right. Feel as bad about that as you want."

"Thanks, I will. What's this little building here?"

Joe pushed open the door of the dam office, displaying his desk, computer, and the metal shelving unit full of files against the opposite wall. "My office. Home of paperwork and drudgery."

"Cozy," she said. The computer screen displayed an endless drifting sequence of neon-hued caterpillars. Sally bumped into the space, her tail thumping the wall, Joe's legs, the chair. He picked up the key ring he'd left on the desk earlier and hooked it back to his belt loop.

"Come on, girl," he said to Sal, and they stepped back onto the causeway. He led Rachel to the pier, which was bordered by a laughable metal railing. They walked the length of it, the water smacking the concrete on both sides. At the end, they stood looking out toward the opposite shore. "This is a pretty good fishing spot here. People come out early mornings, evenings, catch crappie, bluegill, some walleye."

"Musky?"

"Some. Sometimes you can see them sunning themselves on the sand in the shallows."

"Muskies were always my dad's coveted fish, back when he used to fish. He never caught one, though. But Granddaddy did. We've got it . . ." she trailed off, hearing the new false note in that word "we."

"Stuffed and mounted," Joe said, finishing her sentence for her. "I've seen it in your dining room there."

"Yeah," Rachel said. "It always freaked me out a little when I was a kid. A dead fish on the wall. And so huge, with those sharp teeth. I used to have nightmares about it coming alive and devouring me."

"Muskies are nothing compared to the sturgeon, though."

"No more sturgeon in this river."

"Used to be. Fresh-water sturgeon."

She stared at him, struck suddenly by the chasm of unshared experience between them. "I had a job tagging sturgeon once. Just after college. On the Kennebec River."

"Really?"

"Atlantic sturgeon mostly. Some shortnose. They're amazing animals."

"Indians used to spear sturgeon from these banks. So they tell me, anyway."

"Before the dam went in." She felt the familiar queasiness spread through her gut, her faithful reaction to ecological disaster. The wetlands, bogs, and swamps once bursting with aquatic life—myriad species of frog, toad, turtle, and snake, the humming dragonflies, midges, damselflies, mosquitoes, and gnats, the ducks and terns, cranes and herons, wrens and gnatcatchers that thrived on such plentiful prey, and the fish that liked the shallows: the pike and largemouth bass and pumpkinseeds—now inundated with stalled and stagnant currents, all the jumping, sucking, oozing, swimming, buzzing, rotting thrum now mute beneath the reservoir. And the dammed river itself, once cool and clear and moving, filtered clean by the sedges and marsh grasses, bending to the whim of its own flow, now cloudy and slow with silt, choked by algae, over-warm. And of course the massive fish die-offs. Just another way that people were contributing to the growing list of extinctions, just another manifestation of anthropocentrism, courtesy of the planet's most destructive and rapacious species of all. She knew well all the sickening details.

And yet, this was the Turner Flowage, *their* lake. She'd always thought of it that way—as belonging to her and her family. Not in a proprietary way, but in an affectionate way, the way families belonged to one another. She didn't like to think of it as just another reservoir, another constructed environment, a man-made "natural" playground, engineered purely to serve the people who made use of it: the power company, the vacationing outdoorsmen, the jet-skiers and boaters and hobby sailors who frequented it. Yet here she was, standing on the dam that had created it, which made it hard to avoid the stark reality of that fact: that the Turner Flowage *was*, first and foremost, a flowage, a dammed-up river, its primary purpose the farming of energy. Something created for the profit of one—company, species, class of creatures—to the loss of another.

Rachel looked around. "Where's the power plant, anyway?"

Joe turned and pointed at the cement-block building on the shore, near where Rachel had parked.

"That's it?"

"It's a pretty minor contributor to the grid. Only three generators, about 1.3 megawatts. Nothing the power company couldn't live without."

Rachel walked restlessly down the pier, thinking of the Campbell Dam, which had been much bigger, supplied three times as much energy to the grid. "Dad used to talk about this dam so proudly, like it was this grand civilizing project, bringing electricity to the hinterlands. But here it is, this puny little thing, as dams go."

"I don't think the energy it produced back then went to this area, anyway. I think they exported it to Milwaukee and Madison."

Out in the water, close to the dam, a chain floated on the surface, marked at either end by two orange buoys. "What's that?" Rachel asked, pointing.

"That's just to signal to boats not to come any closer to the dam. Unless they want to get sucked under."

"Ah."

"You'd be surprised how dumb people can be," Joe added. "They're curious, you know, so they paddle right up here, looking around. I can't tell you how many times I've had to chase people off. Even the damkeeper is never supposed to enter the water around the gates. Rule number one."

He led her back down the pier and across the causeway to the other concrete block building, this one a little bigger than the dam office. Rachel waited on the top landing of a metal staircase that hugged the building while Joe fiddled with his keys, then unlocked the door and held it open. Sally pushed in first.

This room was also narrow, with two parallel control panels flanking the longest walls. The short wall at the back of the room held an array of meters and gauges, shaped like clock faces and thermometers, decorated with ranges of numbers. "This is the control house," Joe said. "This is where I read the water levels." He pointed to each meter and gauge in succession, rattling off their respective functions. "This one shows the flowage's water level electronically. This one gives me the water temperature, and this one the inches of rainfall. I have to write all this down in the log. Then there are the readings over in hydro, about fifty of them—voltage, current, frequency, hydraulic oil pressure, water pressure." He looked back at her, then stopped. "I'm boring you."

"No, no. This is just the way my face is."

"Well, check this out. This is more exciting. If the water level gets to this point—" Joe pointed to the highest number of one of the vertical gauges on the wall, "then we've got problems."

"Like what?"

"Like potential dam failure."

The water level looked to be very close to where he'd pointed. "But you're almost there."

"Well, not quite. The difference between here and here is actually pretty substantial. But, yeah, we're getting close." He grinned again, as if this were good news.

"So what do you do if it reaches that point?"

"Oh, there's a whole plan. Main thing is to open the gates all the way, let the water out under the dam, rather than over it. Ideally, I do that gradually, so the downstream channel can manage it. But in extreme cases, I might do it all at one go. You'd get some flooding then, probably, but not as bad as if the whole thing broke."

"And if that doesn't work?"

Joe smirked. "Run."

"You're kidding," Rachel said.

"Not really. If the water wants to get high enough, there's not a whole lot we can do. But, like I said, this is a solid dam. Built for the 500-year flood. In other words, it doesn't often happen. Hasn't happened yet, anyway."

"Well, that inspires confidence."

"Yeah. I'll tell you what else, too. If a dam decides to go, it *goes*. I mean, fast. Within minutes, even. One little crack in the structure, and the water rushes in to fill it, and the force of all that water is like a massive pliers just prying the whole thing apart."

She thought once more of Campbell, how it had taken almost a full week before the water started leaking through the concrete where the jack-hammers had drilled. She and Michael had both been surprised at how long it had taken for the water to start helping the job along—they'd been expecting something more spectacular, more like what Joe was describing. But then there'd been a cofferdam in place, which took off much of the head pressure, and which probably explained the anemic pour once it did start flowing. She remembered how disappointing it was, the breach—too controlled, like water pouring from a large pitcher. That had been ten days after Michael had proposed.

Joe pushed the door back open, letting in a rush of fresh humid air. They stood on a metal landing that flanked the control house. The earlier chink in the clouds had opened into a blue swatch of sky over the river. Below them, a set of stairs descended, following along the length of a tall wooden wall buttressed by steel girders and struts. Rachel put her hand against the wooden boards. "Is this all there is between us and the water?" she asked.

"That's it. That's the splashwall."

"It seems kind of flimsy."

"You worry too much, you know that? You never used to worry this much."

"I do know that. I'm well aware of that fact."

"It's called a splashwall because it's made mainly to contain splashing water, not torrents of water. Normally, the rate of flow at the gates is controlled. The water doesn't get high or fast enough to even make it anywhere close to these walls. There was one time, back in the eighties, when they were repairing two of the dam gates, when the water was coming so fast it blew out one of the splash walls. But that was a fluke. If the gates are working as they should, the splash walls don't get tested."

"That's a big if."

"Hey, life's a big if."

They descended along the length of the splash wall. The metal was still wet, and Rachel held tightly to the railing with one hand, the other pressing Deirdre close. She trained her eyes on the sharp edges of each step and the steep grade of the bank that fell away beneath the stairs.

The sound of the rushing water was much louder at the bottom, so loud she could barely hear Joe's voice above it. Deirdre's eyes opened wide.

"Here's where it gets more impressive!" he shouted, as they walked the rocky bank. "The water's almost at about 5000 cubic feet per second! Usually at this time of year, we're at around 400, maybe 500 CFS! So, things are a little dicey!" He stepped onto a pile of downed birches, and climbed along their length to a more stable spot, higher up, away from the rushing river. Rachel, nervous, didn't follow.

"Come on! From here there's a good view of the water through the gates!" He stood above her, his bare chest as smooth and strong as the inner bark of a birch.

She swallowed. "I don't trust those logs!"

"Here!" He stepped back across the pile and reached his hand out to her. Reluctantly, she grabbed it, and let him pull her forward, stepping carefully on the thickest part of each log until she made it across. Trembling, she turned and looked where Joe was pointing.

Extending out from the causeway they'd just been standing on were four massive slabs of concrete, maybe thirty or forty feet high. Three steel gates spanned the space between the slabs, their great arms fanning out from a central trunnion nestled within each slab. The arms of each gate reached to support a convex face, each of which arced skyward, thick curved planes of steel against the bright blue sky. Now and then, the view of the gates disappeared behind a shifting curtain of dense spray thrown up by the water pouring out beneath them, glassy in freefall, frothing a tannic foam as it slammed into the spillway below. It churned forward, roaring and roiling, as if the newly released droplets were mad to be free, leaping to their airy escape, blindly bumping and jostling into others with the same goal, until, some distance on, the froth dissolved once more into the body of the river, seething forward, raucous and high along the banks, half drowning a patch of young ashes on a downriver island. The water seemed to send up an almost electric scent, a freshness that buzzed in the nostrils.

"This is the best view of the dam!" Joe shouted over the thundering water. "Though with the high water, you can't see as well! Usually, you can get a good view of the gates from here! These gates are used all over the world, designed by a Cheesehead, believe it or not! Jeremiah Burnham Tainter! He invented them for the lumber mill dams down to Menomonie in the 1800s!"

"You know a lot about it!"

He shrugged. "I've got time to kill!"

Even from this distance—they stood maybe a hundred yards away—Rachel could feel the mist on her face. Deirdre danced her limbs in the air and aahed an echo of the water. Rachel touched Deirdre's cheek and brought her fingers away wet. She thought of the sturgeon that used to frequent the river before the dam went in, then of the human bones Diane had mentioned washing up on shore. If Granddaddy Turner had known what would happen, she wondered, would he still have built the dam?

They admired the view in silence. The water glimmered and winked. On the opposite bank, a young white pine leaned over the water, as if yearning to dive in. A kingfisher flew over the water before disappearing into the leafy cover of the woods. Surrounding them was nothing but wilderness—the cool, dark woods, the rushing water, the sweet electric air. If you turned away from the dam and watched downriver, you could imagine you were standing in the midst of a primeval forest, untouched, uncut, unmeddled with. Any moment a cougar might appear at the river's edge for a drink, or a beaver waddle forward, towing a fallen log. Maybe a roaming pack of wolves could be glimpsed, dashing in between the trees. In a place like this, the only thing that mattered was instinct and survival; in a place like this, there was only the moment at hand to consider. Time was irrelevant; there was no time. There was only now and now and now.

"God, Joe," Rachel whispered. "This is not bad."

Joe beamed. "Yeah. It's pretty great. You haven't even seen the best part yet."

"What's that?"

He held out his hand again, and led her back across the treacherous fall of birch logs to safer ground.

It was about a ten-minute walk down a narrow footpath from the causeway to the yurt. Deirdre, exhausted by the loud water and the bright sun, fell asleep against Rachel's chest. They walked in silence, Sal close on Joe's heels and Rachel following behind. The footpath bordered the lake, leading them through tall cattails and reed canary grass, up over tree roots, some of which poked through the sandy soil like elbows or knees. Sally rushed on ahead of them once they got up the incline and the yurt appeared: a round bone-colored canvas tent, with a black stovepipe chimney. A pile of wood was neatly stacked against a plywood lean-to; an axe hung from a nail on the outside of the shed. A twist of wires snaked from beneath the shed door and followed beneath the yurt's canvas.

"So you're not off the grid, I gather?" Rachel asked, pointing to the wires.

"That would be ironic, working at a hydro plant. I'm too attached to my media, anyway. Do have a composting toilet, though." He pointed to another shed about fifty yards from the yurt.

"Wow. You're hardcore."

He pulled back the canvas flap that served as the door to the yurt, and stood chivalrously aside to let her pass.

Rachel stepped inside. It was surprisingly bright. Sunlight penetrated the vinyl windows and reflected off the white canvas walls. The floor—evenly milled hardwood boards—was in better shape than her own floors at home, freshly finished and varnished to a shine. Joe had organized each section of the large circular room into its own separate space. The bedroom consisted of a mattress on the floor, covered by an unzipped sleeping bag, and framed by a stereo mounted on a milk crate (a set of headphones still plugged in) and a white dresser with oversized knobs. On the other side of the dresser, you entered the "office" space: a simple wooden desk, a straight-backed chair, next to a tall well-stocked bookshelf. Then, beyond the bookshelf, there was a round table with two diner-style chairs (chrome legs and back, red plastic seat), and finally, rounding out the circle, the kitchen: a metal shelving unit filled with jars of rice and beans and dried fruit and other unidentifiable containers, a sink, and a small half-size refrigerator, on top of which sat a dish drain and a butcher block cutting board. A wood stove squatted in the middle of it all.

Joe went to the dresser for a fresh T-shirt, which he pulled over his head. Then, taking an electric kettle from the shelf, he asked, "You want some coffee? Or tea? I've got some Lipton."

"Sure," Rachel said.

He filled the kettle with water while Rachel walked slowly around the space, marveling. "This is lovely, Joe," she said. "Really. Cozy and roomy at the same time."

"Works for me."

"How did you even know what a yurt was?"

"I knew a guy in Iraq who lived in one. He was kind of a freak show, actually. An end-times fundamentalist, believed in the rapture, the whole bit. He was from Montana."

"How does it hold up in the rain?"

"Stays dry."

"And in winter?"

"The stove keeps me warm. I wear layers."

Rachel shook her head. "Incredible." Joe set the full kettle on the butcher block, then bent to plug it into a thick orange extension cord on the floor. He pulled the box of Lipton and two mismatched mugs from another shelf, unwound the string from two tea bags, and dropped one into each mug. They were simple tasks, but something about the way he completed them—with such unconscious ease—astonished Rachel. He looked up to catch her staring.

"What?" he said.

"Nothing. I'm just having a moment."

The kettle began to bubble. Joe turned it off, then poured the steaming water into the two mugs. He handed one to Rachel, who held it well away from Deirdre's sleeping head.

"Hot liquids and baby," she said. "This is the sort of thing they warn you about in parenting magazines." She set the mug on the table then knelt by the mattress. Gently, she slipped the clasp of the front pack open and then eased Deirdre onto the bed. Deirdre's head rolled to the side like a ragdoll. She moved her mouth in a phantom sucking motion a few times, and then stopped. Rachel's skin was damp where Deirdre had been pressed against her. She shook the hem of her shirt, unsticking it from her chest.

"Wow," Joe said. "That took some skill."

"It's a lot easier when the bed isn't all the way on the floor." She picked up her mug again and blew across the surface of the tea, feeling the steam warm her nose and chin. Tea was suddenly the last thing she wanted; it was hotter in here than outside. She set the mug back down on the table.

"So," said Joe. "Is your moment over?"

She smiled and shook her head.

"Is it a good moment?"

She nodded.

"Well, then."

Something had shifted. They both felt it. They had left the wild thundering water and the lush forest behind them and entered this silent, well-ordered space together, and in doing so they felt as if they'd crossed over some invisible boundary, entered some strange and sacred new land. Deirdre's breath came and went, soughing in and out of her lungs, echoed by the wind in the branches outside. Rachel sat in one of the chairs; the seat *foofed*, exhaling as it accepted her weight.

Joe sensed that Rachel was moved, and though he wanted to know why, he respected the privacy of her emotion. He went to stand by the window and looked out at the lake. He knew it wasn't trivial, the fact of her marriage, her nascent family. He respected commitment. In principle. And he was well aware of the pain and suffering that resulted from broken families. He'd seen divorced friends turn bitter and angry, their kids cynical and depressed. He didn't want to be party to that. If it had been any other woman, he could have easily walked away, told himself it wasn't worth it, that they could pick things up again after the marriage broke up and everybody cooled down. He'd even half-convinced himself that he could do this with Rachel. This would be the peacemaker's way; this would be the heroic thing to do.

But she'd shown up. She'd shown up in her fancy little Prius, the baby nuzzling her breast, and all his high-minded moral resolve had evaporated. He didn't care what was right; he didn't care who got hurt. He wanted Rachel. It seemed he hadn't grown out of that desire, even after all this time, all the agony. Wanting her was just a part of who he was; he'd wanted her all his life. As a kid, watching her balance on the gunnels of the canoe, her bare feet gripping the metal, her arms outstretched in a perfect T, goosebumps raising the blond hairs on her thighs; as an eighteen-year-old, nestling his nose in the sweet bread-smelling warmth of her neck, traveling, with stunned and clumsy fingers, the contours of her collarbone, her ribs, the impossible swells of her breasts; and now, as an adult, witness to the faint lines circling her mouth, weighing its corners into a perpetual frown, watching her trace a finger along the fresh hair on Deirdre's scalp, plant an absent-minded kiss on her ear, watching her lovingly lay the baby on the bed. This adult Rachel, this Rachel as weary and imperfect mother, this Rachel was an opportunity, his one major missed opportunity, opened up once again for him. Second chances, in his experience, didn't usually happen. But here was his, sitting at his table, pressing her fingers to her eyes. Sniffling.

He plucked a box of Kleenex from the pantry shelf and set it on the table in front of Rachel. She nodded gratefully, swished one out, blew her nose. "Sorry," she said. "Sorry. God. I'm making myself sick."

"Hey now. Take it easy."

"This is what I do now. This moaning and crying bullshit."

"It's okay," he said. He pulled out the other chair and sat across from her. He thought about taking her hand, but decided against it. Rachel didn't like to be caught in a weak moment. Better to let the squall pass.

"I don't even know why I'm crying. It's this yurt, this place. It all seems so perfect, Joe. The perfect life, you know?" She sniffed again, and took another Kleenex.

"Wow. You should tell that one to my mother."

"Oh, fuck your mother." Immediately, she took the tissue from her eyes and stared at Joe. "Sorry. That was incredibly obnoxious. I didn't mean that."

"Okay," he said, a little warily.

"What I meant was, you've achieved something here with this place, this life that so few people even *think* about achieving. It's so peaceful here, Joe. People have these ideas about success, about what makes a meaningful life, that are just so *bogus*. You know? I mean, everyone I know back home is buying minivans. Christ!" She took a deep, shaky breath, then let it out slowly. "I'm babbling."

"No, go on. This is good for me to hear. I don't get people telling me stuff like this much."

"I don't know, Joe. I just kind of feel like I missed the boat somehow. I'm living this life that doesn't feel like mine. It's a good life in the abstract, but it doesn't feel like *my* life. I guess that's why I've been fantasizing all week about moving up to the Farm, kind of starting over up here. Like maybe I could create something kind of like what you've got here."

Joe stared into his teacup, his blood thrumming at his temples. He had no idea how to answer this. Was she hinting at something? Making some kind of request? Was she saying she was leaving her husband? He sipped his tea, buying time.

"So your mother doesn't like the yurt, I gather."

"She thinks I'm pissing away my options with this job, living out here. She wants me to go back to school, get a decent job, get married, etc. The full-on American dream."

"The full-on American nightmare." Reflexively, Rachel looked at Deirdre. "Well. Not totally."

"The weird thing is that despite my mom's politics, her red-warrior credentials, she dreams in white. The Clayborne kind of white. I mean, no offense, but she wants your life for me—stable job, decent income, a house, a marriage, kids, etc.—except she wants me to still be Indian. The grandbabies have to be Indian, otherwise the whole thing's a bust. But one of the things that makes a person Indian, in her mind, is being not white. Being opposite from white people—*not* having all those things, and suffering for it."

"In order to be Indian you have to suffer."

"Mightily. But the trade-off is that you get to suffer along with all your relatives and friends. You get to share the misery."

"But everyone suffers. I mean, that's just part of living, right?"

"Sure. But Indians, we're supposed to suffer in a very specific way. You know: poverty, alcoholism, suicide. The works."

"Jesus."

"So the message she's always sent me is mixed. It's something like—you're smart, you're capable, so you should get out of here and go after all the things white people have, but make sure you don't forget for a minute where you come from. I guess that's why I just kind of dropped out, you know? Moved out here. It seemed like whatever I did, whatever choice I made, something was going to piss her off."

"Well, I think you made a good choice."

Joe smiled. "Thanks," he said. "Most days I think so, too. Some days I think I should just dump all this and reenlist. Go back to Iraq. Get myself blown up by one of those IEDs that are lying around all over the place over there. Then she'd really have something to suffer over."

Rachel looked at him sharply. "You're joking."

He smirked. "Mostly."

"God, Joe. Why on earth would you ever go back? I mean, you've given enough." She gestured vaguely in the direction of his face.

With one hand, he turned his mug in a clockwise circle, then back in the opposite direction. The base of it slid a little to the right, revealing a wet trail of condensation on the table. Joe wiped it with the flat of his hand. "Lots of reasons. I'm trained, for one. And they're short on soldiers. I'm replaceable here—anyone can do this job. I don't have a family I need to support, like a lot of other guys who are over there. And part of me still wants a piece of the action. I mean, I know how to fire an M-16. Don't have much opportunity to make use of that skill on the job here."

Rachel rolled her eyes. "You're just saying that to piss me off."

He grinned. "Maybe." Then, more seriously, he said, "To tell you the truth, Rachel, I have a hard time shaking the feeling that I got away with something over there. Like I cheated. I mean, the Marines poured a hell of a lot of time and effort into training me, flew me over there, had me ready to fight, and what do I do? I stand in the wrong place at the wrong time and get a flying helicopter blade in the face. What a waste. A stupid, meaningless waste."

"Is that what happened?"

"That's the short version."

"What's the long version? If you don't mind my asking."

He took a deep breath. "One of my jobs in Kuwait was to help direct the helicopters to a safe landing. Airfield stuff, you know—I was one of those guys with the wands out on the tarmac. Anyway, one of the blades was loose on this one copter. Flew off while it was landing and sheared into my face. One minute I was standing, the next, I was on the ground, my jaw like a bag of rocks in my mouth. Then I passed out."

"Jesus," she said again.

"Next thing I knew, I was back stateside, all doped up and no place to go."

"Oh, Joe." Tenderly, tentatively, she reached out and ran a gentle thumb over the taut skin of his cheek. He closed his eyes, inhaled the closeness of her, the clean smell of her skin. "I'm so sorry I wasn't there to help you through that," she whispered.

He opened his eyes, snorting involuntarily. "Yeah, well. Me, too."

She took her hand away from his face, tucked it between her thighs. He was staring at her with a startling intensity.

"What happened back then, Rachel?" he asked, finally. "We had something so amazing, so fucking amazing. Why did you—?" He paused, noticing his knee was jiggling up and down like a runaway washing machine, and stopped it. "Why did you *act* like that? Send me those shitty letters? Chew me out when I called you from my hospital bed? I mean, my God—" He barked a pained laugh. "You just completely tore me a new one. And there I was, lying there on my fucking gurney, my face like a bowl of mashed potatoes, doped halfway into the next world. Christ, I couldn't believe it. I couldn't fucking *believe* it."

A flush flooded Rachel's chest and face, and the blood beat in her ears. She swallowed. "I can't tell you how awful I felt, Joe, about all that. How many times I lay awake at night, wishing I could take back those words, all those months you were gone—the way I treated you, anyway. I don't know. I can't explain it. I was terrified. I was obsessed with the war—I watched it nonstop. I was convinced you were going to get yourself killed, and I was so angry with you for putting yourself in that position." She slipped both hands beneath her thighs, pressing on them, then slipped them out again and set them awkwardly on her lap. "If it makes you feel any better, I was a mess the whole time you were gone. A total psycho. Ask any of my floormates. But I shouldn't have taken all that fear and anger out on you like that. It's the thing I most regret."

Joe ran his tongue over his teeth, looked toward the door of the yurt. "Okay. Well, that's easy enough to say. But why didn't you ever call me, then? Afterward? Or write me a letter, for Christ's sake? I mean it was like you just disappeared off the face of the planet, Rachel. Do you know what that felt like? You were my best friend, my greatest love, and you just went *poof*. Gone. Right when I really needed you, for the first time. Right when I really fucking *needed* you."

My greatest love, she heard. It echoed in her mind. *My greatest love*.

"I *did* call you," she insisted. "I called you back right away. Right after you hung up on me—which I completely deserved. I called you right back. I tried to apologize. But your mother answered and said you were resting."

"My mother . . ."

"I probably called you thirty times that week, trying to talk to you, and every time your mother said you were busy or resting or couldn't come to the phone. I wrote you dozens of letters, Joe. Oh, my *God*. I can't tell you how many letters I wrote, how many times I tried to call."

"And every time you got my mother?"

"Every single time. She was like this impermeable barrier. You mean she never once told you I'd called? She never showed you any of my letters?"

Joe was too shocked to respond. He just stared.

"I knew it. I knew she had to be standing in the way. I knew you wouldn't have held out on me that long."

"I can't believe it. I can't believe she kept you from me like that."

Rachel laughed. "Honestly, it's kind of a relief to know it was her and not you."

Joe shook his head slowly. "You know what she did? She took me at my word."

"What? What do you mean?"

"After you lost your shit at me and I hung up, I told her I never wanted to have anything more to do with you. I asked her to promise that I would never have to see you or talk to you again."

Rachel grimaced.

"I was angry."

"I don't blame you."

"But she knew I was angry. I was always saying stupid shit like that back then, being dramatic. And she *knew* that. But still, she took me at my word. For thirteen long years. Unbelievable."

"She didn't want you hurt, I guess. In a way, I can't blame her."

"Oh, I can. I'll happily blame her. I mean, sure, it hurt for you to lay into me like that. But at least you were talking to me, you know? At least we were connected. I mean, I knew on some level that all that anger was coming from a place of love. I knew that, even though it hurt, even though I thought you were totally out of line. But the thing that *really* hurt was being separated from you. Jesus Christ. What a mind-fuck."

Rachel stared at her cup of tea, which had stopped steaming.

"She's always doing this," Joe muttered, more to himself than to Rachel. "Trying to control my life. Thinking she knows better than I do what's good for me. But this one. This really takes the cake. Jesus Christ."

Rachel sipped at the cold tea, still hearing the melody of those words: *my greatest love.*

But Joe was staring at her again, holding her gaze. "I thought you'd just turned it off, Rachel. All those years, all that history together . . . all that phenomenal teenage sex."

She blushed furiously, a deep crimson all through her neck and cheeks.

"I thought you'd just put all of it in a box and set me up on a shelf to gather dust."

"No."

"And so then I started thinking that what we had must have been a lie, for you to be able to just switch it off like that. I thought the whole thing was a big put-on. That's what fucked with me for so long. I was so fucking *confused.*"

Rachel closed her eyes, swallowed. "God, no. It was never a lie."

Joe shook his head. "Unbelievable."

"Think how different things might have been."

Joe tore a little piece of cardboard off the box of tissues, his jaw working, and Rachel could see he was struggling to keep himself composed. "Honestly," he said finally. "I'd rather not."

At that moment, Sally, who was lying on the floor by Rachel's feet, lifted her head and cocked her ears. Joe looked at her. "What's up, girl?" he asked. She launched into a volley of barking and scrambled for the door flap. Deirdre, startled out of her sound sleep, began to cry.

"Shit," Rachel said, standing and moving to the bed.

Joe pushed the chair backward with his knees. "I'd better go see what she's about." And he followed Sally out into the afternoon.

Sally had already disappeared over the rise, but Joe could still hear her barking. Probably at some poor guy who'd come to fish off the causeway. Every time someone came out to fish, Sally ran out, barking, and Joe had to follow and call her off. Usually, he didn't mind: he was glad for the notice, and he'd spend a few minutes chatting with whoever it was about how they were biting lately. But this was particularly bad timing.

Or maybe it was good timing. Maybe he should take this as the universe's way of saving his ass. He breathed deep, allowed his hormone-addled brain to rebound a little, to take in the proper mix of nitrogen and oxygen, courtesy of the adjacent woods.

He followed Sal to the causeway, where, sure enough, the Davingers, a couple from downriver, had pulled up in their mini-van, and were unloading their poles and tackle boxes. They were a sweet elderly couple, the kind who'd grown to look just like each other—both of them short, a little hunched, kindly wrinkled faces, like the bark of good solid hemlocks—who'd retired to their cabin on the water, and did everything together. He called Sally off, exchanged a few words with them about the rain and the high water, and then took the opportunity to make one more check of the levels in the control house. Breathe deep, he kept telling himself every time he thought of Rachel waiting for him in the yurt, of the feel of her thumb on his skin, her face so very close to his own. Breathe deep. Breathe into your belly, like you do when you're just surfacing after a dive, gulping that fresh air. Breathe very, very fucking deep.

3

Diane stood in the open refrigerator, scanning the interior for the loaf of multi-grain bread she knew was in there somewhere, her mind still reeling. She felt awful about fighting with Rachel in front of Maddy. She had lost her composure, had spoken unprofessionally, and had embarrassed both herself and Maddy, whose good opinion she cared very much about.

Her eyes fell on the bag of bread tucked behind a pan of red Jell-O on the bottom shelf. She tossed the bread on the counter, then opened the cabinet above her head and palmed a can of tuna fish. There was no emotion she hated more than shame. Shame and its close cousin, guilt. Shame made her murderous. It made her want to impale the closest living creature on the end of a very sharp stick; it made her want to hurl plate after china plate against a wall.

She rolled the utensil drawer open, hard. Loose cutlery crashed against the back of the drawer. A can opener. Where was the can opener? She stared at the contents of the drawer for one, two, three minutes, seeing only the horror and grief on Maddy's face, those bulging wet blue eyes. She slammed the drawer shut. Lunch was going to have to wait.

Outside, the ground squished under her sneakers. The sky was beginning to clear, sunlight leaking through the cloud cover. She walked past the office window, where she stopped a moment, unseen on the other side of the rose bush, and listened for any sounds from Maddy, any intimations of need. Hearing nothing, she continued over the wet lawn to the path that led downhill through the woods, down to the lake.

When Diane was young, she used to visit the Farm in the winter, when the property was empty, the grounds covered with snow. She and her sisters and a pack of their friends would lash on their snowshoes and tramp across the frozen lake, dragging their sleds—dented metal saucers, a cracked wooden toboggan, pieces of broken-up cardboard boxes, plastic tarps. This path she was walking right now had been the best sledding slope around—clear all the way from the house to the lake, with a few bumps along the way to give you decent lift-off. They'd start at the top of the slope, just under the tallest pine, the one with the eagle's nest, and someone would stand at the bottom and shout "all clear!" and then, with a stiff push from behind, they'd be off, careening downhill, screaming in terror, snow-spray and frigid air scalding their faces. If they didn't spin off-course into the brush by the side of the path or tip over sideways into the snow, they might manage to reach the final jump: the little cliff at the end of the promontory. This was the apex of the ride: a heart-stopping flight from land to lake, where they'd shoot across the ice, still riding the momentum from their long, accelerating descent.

They used to sled for hours, finding new and ever-more life-threatening ways of arranging themselves—headfirst, backwards and upside down, two sleds tied together—but eventually they got tired of it, and their attention would turn to other things. Diane had been especially interested in the old graves that she knew were on the property somewhere, near the water. Her father had told stories about his grandfather, who had been buried there after he succumbed to tuberculosis, and his little one-year-old sister, who would have been Diane's aunt, had she lived. One winter, when Diane was thirteen or fourteen, she became obsessed with that little girl's grave. She fantasized about finding it and telling her father, and about the look of pride and delight that would appear on his face when she told him of her discovery. She imagined herself leading him there, through the snow-laden bracken, the two of them kneeling by the grave, heads bowed, their eyes on the frozen earth, and their minds in unison fixed on the singular sadness of that lost child.

Her father had described the grave to her, what he remembered of it. There'd been a spirit house over it—a little wooden house with a gabled roof—and inside a pair of tiny beaded moccasins that had belonged to his sister. But spirit houses fell down after a while, and the moccasins would have rotted after so many decades. Still, Diane and the gang of kids scoured the woods that winter, brushing snow off stones or pieces of sloughed-off birchbark, seeking something, anything, that might indicate a grave.

Eventually, her sisters and friends grew tired of the goal, but Diane kept looking. Half sunk in her own private fantasy, she searched the woods surrounding the Farm while the shadows of the trees lengthened across the snow and the air grew incrementally colder. In her teenage mind, she imagined she was traveling along the boundaries of the spirit world, that at any moment the veil between this world and the next might drop away, and she'd be face to face with an apparition—the ghost of her dead baby aunt, her arms extended in welcome. She found this possibility more exhilarating and terrifying than the steepest sledding slope, and so she kept at it, fueling her own fantasy with the sounds of the winter woods—the wind whispering through the trees, the thud of a patch of snow blown from a branch, a downed twig cracking under a browsing deer's foot. Sometimes she sat on a log or a stone and closed her eyes, listening hard to the deep winter silence, waiting in quiet ecstasy for some visitation—a touch on the arm, a word in the ear. One day, while she sat in this expectant meditation, a piece of bark hit her arm, followed by a suppressed titter: her sisters trying to spook her. Diane lobbed a hefty snowball in their direction. They ran, Diane in pursuit, tripping in the deep snow, up the slope toward the grand old farmhouse looming above them.

The house in winter seemed to exude loneliness as if it were a scent, something rank and rotting within: a forgotten bin of oozing onions, dank potatoes sprouting into infertile darkness. Houses were meant to be lived in, but here was this one, standing empty for nine months out of the year, growing lonelier, she imagined, with every passing day. As the sun set on the western shore of the lake that day, and darkness began to descend, Diane and her sisters peered in the windows, catching glimpses of the enormous bookshelves, the stone fireplace, the great dining room table.

They didn't know much about the Clayborne family back then. They'd never met Madeline or her husband Jacob, or either of the children. All she and her sisters knew were their father's stories about growing up on that land, back when it was a working farm, back when *his* father, Grandfather Tobias, was caretaker. The place he described seemed to be something entirely different from what lay before them. The old log caretaker's cabin had long since been demolished, the apple trees their father had picked from were wild and gnarled, and the barn where he'd milked the cows and hid from his own angry, whip-bearing father, had already, by the time Diane was a girl, been converted into a garage and a tool shed. But the farmhouse was the same. Diane's father hadn't been allowed in when he was a boy. His mother—Diane's Grandmother Mary—didn't want him tracking mud over the floors. So whenever he wanted her, he had to tap at the back door and wait until she had a free moment. When he was hungry, she'd feed him through that door, handing him a plate with scraps of food—chicken skin, a fried up liver, some crusts of bread—and he'd sit on the back stoop, the grease from the chicken fat mixing in his mouth with the dirt on his hands.

He never spoke bitterly about his childhood; to him, that was just the way things were. If anything, his memories were tinged with fondness. Grandmother Mary, he assured Diane, may have been hard and exacting, and maybe she'd made a bad decision when she sold her father's land, but she did the best she could with what she had—this was his attitude. And Diane respected that, up to a point. But the image of her father lapping up his dinner on the back stoop like a dog lodged in her mind, and lent the old farmhouse an oppressive, even malevolent aura.

She brooded on all of this now as she trudged down the muddy path, barely noticing her surroundings—the trembling leaves of the mayapple plants as they received a stray raindrop from the canopy above, the deep indigo wood violets—her mind consumed by her thoughts and the continuing slow burn of her shame. Eventually, she reached the bottom of the hill. The path opened onto a clearing, where a trio of paths converged, each of them leading to this place from different points on the property. The Claybornes had built a little bathhouse here—a flimsy structure with cedar shingles and a plywood roof. Inside, it smelled of mold and years of accumulated bat shit. A narrow boardwalk made a path from the bathhouse to a set of wooden steps, which led down to the swimming dock.

Diane took the stairs and stepped out onto the blue metal dock, which clanged under her feet. The water was high—almost licking the underside of the dock. She tried to remember the last time she'd come down to the lake. At least a week ago, maybe a month. Not since Rachel had come, anyway. She walked the length of it, avoiding the islands of duck poop, until she found a clean, dry spot to sit and look out over the great gray expanse of the lake. Out near the opposite shore, a fishing boat rocked on the low waves.

She thought again of Maddy's wet eyes, her anxious confusion. Maybe Rachel was right. Maybe she had influenced Maddy. But was there really anything wrong with influence, particularly if it brought about positive change? How else did people learn? How else did anyone get anything to *happen* in the world?

Diane sighed, watching a family of ducks bob along the shore. Why did she care so much about the Farm, anyway? Why couldn't she just let it go? Maybe it would release Maddy, make things easier for her. She could see the struggle on Maddy's face, the way she was being pulled in two directions: loyalty to family, loyalty to her, Diane, and to justice—and she could see that with Rachel in the picture, loyalty to family was winning out. Given the choice, Maddy would probably choose family every time.

The question was, was she really so different?

A speedboat passed, leaving a wake, its edges foaming white. The waves crested and fell, then swelled again into the next rise, and traveled this way, expanding outward and outward until, diminished, they rolled into the pebbles on the shore. That was the way of it, she thought. You spent your youth and most of your adult years climbing that upward rise, feeling the powerful momentum beneath you, carrying you up and up, believing that things will continue in just this way, despite any evidence to the contrary. And then one day, the momentum changed. You found that you were on the far side of the crest, and you were falling now, falling quickly, and everything you'd learned about how to live, how to be in the world, what to strive for—all of this was changed. You could feel the undercurrent pulling you downward, gravity asserting itself, claiming you, and you knew, moment to moment, that the rise had crested and you hadn't even known it. And that now you were headed toward shore, where you would thin into nothing, until all that would be left of you was a sheen of moisture on the face of the lake stones.

Diane lay on her stomach, the metal dock cold through her blouse. With one hand, she stirred a lazy circle in the lake. The disturbed water curled into itself. She made a figure eight, then a star, and each time the shape dissolved into a succession of ripples, bobbing and dancing away.

Of course she cared about the Farm. This was her great-grandfather's land. It was Indian land. *Anishinaabe* land. Her grandfather—tough bastard though he may have been, and white, okay, that much was true—but he was family, and he'd worked this land. She could feel it every time she walked across the lawn, weighed down with a load of wet laundry to hang. That lawn had once been woods, and her grandfather had cleared all those stumps, dynamited each one out and sprinted away from each hole, hands clamped over his ears, as the shards and splintered woods came whizzing past. He had sweated that house into existence, lifted each stone in that foundation, cemented each one into place. Her great-grandfather had died here. Her grandmother had buried a child here, had breathed life into that kitchen, had grown food in this soil. Her father had grown up on this land, this lake. And Joe had, too. Joe knew this land as well as Rachel. This place belonged to her family as much as to the Claybornes—more so, even. She knew that was true.

Ultimately, it was a foolish question, that why—why she cared about the Farm. She cared because she cared. It was who she was. She couldn't talk herself out of it. This, at least, was something she appreciated about aging: she knew who she was. She was no longer concerned—as she had been when she was young—with whether or not she was behaving properly, whether she was becoming the right sort of person. She was finished with becoming. She cared because she had been accustomed, her whole life, to caring, and to devoting herself wholly to whatever she cared about. Should she stop now, just because she was on the falling side of the crest?

But the problem, of course, was that Rachel cared, too. All of a sudden, out of the blue, she cared.

Diane sat a while longer, letting the water, the wind, and the open stretch of sky calm her until she felt able to head back up the path to the house. In the kitchen, she finished making lunch—tuna salad on toast and a Diet Coke for both her and Maddy—and took the trays in, one in each hand.

Maddy was sitting up against her pillows, staring out the window.

"Soup's on!" Diane chirped.

Maddy looked startled. Her glasses magnified her eyes into the wide stare of an owl. She blinked, cleared her throat. "I'm very busy right now. If you'll just set it down there," and she gestured vaguely to the center of the room.

"Busy watching the world go by?" Diane said. She laid the tray on the side table and briskly straightened the covers, pulling them tight around Maddy's outstretched legs. Then she unfolded the legs of the tray and slid it into place. "Tuna salad today."

"All right," Maddy sighed. She removed her glasses and folded them with shaky hands. Diane slid them into the embroidered cloth case. "Where's Rachel?" Maddy asked. "Isn't she going to eat with us?"

Diane sat at the end of the bed, beneath the extended reach of Maddy's legs, and propped her own plate on her lap. "She's gone for a while, I guess. Took the baby on an outing."

"Where did she go?"

"I don't know, hon. She didn't say."

"Oh, dear," Maddy said. "I hope I didn't say anything to upset her."

"You? What could you have said? If she's upset with anyone, it's me, not you. Now, don't worry about it, hon. Just eat your lunch now, and then you can have a rest. I'm sure she'll be back later."

"I'm afraid I'm not hungry," Maddy said, pushing her tray away. She turned her attention back to the window.

"You've got to eat, Madeline. It's not as if you've got a lot of fat reserves to draw on."

Maddy sighed. "I'm sorry, dear. I know you went to all that trouble. But it'll keep in the fridge, won't it? Maybe I'll have an appetite later on."

An unfamiliar ringtone—an electronic rendition of "Ode to Joy"—startled them both. It was coming from a phone perched on the windowsill.

"Well? Aren't you going to answer it?" Maddy asked, her voice full of irritation.

And to quiet the thing, Diane did. "Hello, Diane Bishop here."

"Oh," said a male voice. "I was trying to get Rachel."

"Rachel's out. Can I take a message? Or, better yet, I'll hang up and you can call back and leave a message on her voice mail."

"Wait. Diane? This is Michael, her husband."

Diane set her plate on the desk by the door and stepped out of the room, leaving Maddy—who'd apparently changed her mind about lunch—picking at her tuna salad with a tremulous fork. "Michael. Hello. How are things?"

"Things? Things are okay, thanks. Well, honestly, things have been better. How are things there? How's Grand feeling?" His voice was smooth, but underneath it buzzed a high-voltage current of anxiety.

"Fine, thank you, Michael. She's doing fine."

"Actually, I'm glad you picked up, Diane. I've called several times today. I was beginning to wonder if Rachel had misplaced her phone or something."

"Well, she left it behind. I wouldn't normally answer it, but the noise was bothering Mrs. Clayborne."

"Listen, Diane. Can I ask you something? I know you're a nurse, and, the truth is that I'm worried about Rachel. Would you mind filling me in on her behavior a little bit?"

"Her behavior?"

"Does she seem okay? Normal, that is? She seems fine over the phone and all, but I got this card in the mail from her today which kind of startled me—I mean, it was really sweet, but it just didn't seem like *her*. And before she left, she was having kind of a hard time—you know, very low energy and weepy." He sighed. "She won't like that I'm telling you this, but I think she may be suffering from postpartum depression. I was trying to keep a close eye on her at home. But now she's up there, and I have no way of really knowing what's going on . . . To be honest, Diane, I'm going a little nuts here—I'm not sleeping well—"

"Okay," Diane cut in. "Okay now. Take it easy. First of all, she's doing fine. She's taking good care of the baby."

"Well, that's good to hear."

"Has she seen anyone about this? Has there been a diagnosis?"

"No. She refuses to see anyone. She says she's not depressed, that she's just tired. But it's more than just that. She's not herself."

"Motherhood changes people, you know, hon. It's a big adjustment."

"Well, of course. But this seems like more than just an adjustment."

"All right," Diane said, wondering how seriously she should be taking this guy. If what he was saying was true, it could explain some of Rachel's behavior. But Diane had seen PPD moms before, serious cases of PPD, and Rachel didn't strike her as being seriously depressed. She was clearly exhausted, a little crazy, a little weepy, pissed at her husband, maybe, but—as much as Diane hated to admit this—the girl was trying hard, doing her best.

"Do you have any idea where she is right now? How I might be able to get in touch with her?"

Diane hesitated.

"Hello?" His voice was on the edge of panic. She sighed. She might as well tell him the truth.

"I do, actually. My guess is she went to visit my son Joe."

A pause. "Joe. Right. Okay. Would you mind giving me his number?"

"I can, but he rarely answers it. He doesn't have a land line at home, and he doesn't always get cell service where he lives. He's almost impossible to reach, actually."

"Well. Okay. What do you suggest I do, then, Diane? I'm kind of at a loss here."

Here it was again, this situation: someone explicitly asking for her opinion, for her influence. What was she supposed to do? Was there a crime in saying what she thought?

She cleared her throat. "Honestly, Michael, that's up to you. If you wanted to, you could come up here, talk to Rachel yourself. But I can tell you that physically, Rachel and the baby are doing fine."

Again, that heavy, anxious silence at the other end. "I don't have a car is the problem," he breathed finally. "Rachel's got it."

"You could rent one."

"True. I hadn't even considered that."

"I'm not saying you should, of course. You should do what you think is best."

"Of course." He thanked her and they hung up. Diane held the phone to her chest, wondering what she'd just set in motion. From the landing the grandfather clock *donged* once, and the single tone echoed through the house.

4

When Joe returned to the yurt, after inspecting, for the third time that day, the causeway and the dam gates and the control house and the office and the penstocks and the hydroplant, breathing deeply all the while, after hiking back over the slope, his shoes caking with mud, and using a stray stick to dig out the largest chunks from his treads before setting his shoes by the exit, he ducked through the canvas flap to find Rachel lying on his bed next to Deirdre, the two of them sleeping soundly. Sal, leaving muddy tracks on the floor, wagged her way in the direction of the bed, but Joe stage-whispered for her to heel, and then sent her back outside. He took a quiet step toward the bed. Rachel lay on her side, her back toward him, her long body stretched the length of the mattress, hips sloping over the curve of her waist. A sliver of skin peeked over the top of her cargo pants. Joe took a step closer. Her T-shirt was pulled up, barely exposing one breast—only a thin round of skin emerged from the purse of Deirdre's tiny mouth. The baby's eyes fluttered beneath the lids, and every so often the hushed hum of a swallow entered the quiet. As if quiet like this could only exist in the presence of periodic reminders of sound.

Joe stood there, a few feet from the mattress, forgetting to breathe.

From the bed, Rachel—who had woken up when he came in and was only pretending to sleep now—listened for his next move. As soon as Deirdre had fallen asleep, and she lay there, half-exposed, she had become aware of how she would appear to Joe when he entered the room, and had made a decision. It wasn't a calculated thing so much as a letting go, an interior *what the hell*, a surrender to the moment that was presenting itself—but now that he was here, watching her, her nerve seized up. Forcing herself to ignore her pounding heart, she shifted, turning her body as much as Deirdre's latch would allow.

"Are you spying on us, Joseph Bishop?"

"Sorry," he said huskily, and turned away, heading toward the door flap.

"Wait," she said. "Come back. Come here." And so he did, standing close enough to meet her eyes, but far away enough that he could no longer glimpse Deirdre's mouth encircling her breast. "Am I freaking you out?"

"A little," he admitted.

"Do you want to join us?"

He stared at her, not sure what she meant, exactly. She slid an arm under Deirdre and shifted both the baby and her own body toward the wall, making room for Joe on the edge of the bed, just behind her.

Awkwardly, he lowered himself onto the bed, lying first on his back, leaving a chaste zone of mattress between his body and hers. Then he turned on his side, and slowly closed the space between them until his chest met the upper curve of her back and his knees curled into hers. Her hair smelled of shampoo. He kissed the crown of her head.

"Mmm," she said.

He laid an arm over her waist, a hand on her hip and pulled her gently toward him. She hummed again. Deirdre swallowed. Together, they held each other on this cusp—both of them feeling as if they were stretched out along the thin edge of a high wall, and that with any movement forward or backward, even any excessively deep breath, the moment, this beautiful luxurious moment, would be lost. Even so, Joe couldn't keep himself from kissing the top of Rachel's head, smelling her hair, nosing the tip of her ear. And each time he touched her like this, she hummed, as if she were an instrument, the pipes of an organ in an empty church, vibrating in tune with each approaching footstep.

He lifted himself on an elbow again, his eye lingering on her collarbone, partly spanned by the thick strap of her bra. He felt completely devoid of will power. It was, he knew, entirely possible—in fact, even very likely—that this thing with Rachel, whatever it was, whatever they were doing, would come to a screeching, cataclysmic halt within the week. There were any number of ways in which this might happen. The husband might swoop in and whisk her away. Rachel might do a U-ey and run back into Michael's arms. Or, she might decide that he, Joe, was not her thing after all. Maybe she'd decide she needed to fly off to Alaska to protect the polar bears. Who knew? The fact was that she was the one with the ammunition. And in each and all of the possible scenarios, the likely outcome was that Joe would be left alone again, and hurting, for a long, long time. This was why his mother had stood between them—she'd wanted to keep him from hurting.

But hurting, as far as he was concerned, was a part of life. Rachel was here in his yurt right now. The future was a distant planet—was, quantumly-speaking, an infinite number of distant possible planets. It was, in a word, a dream. The only reality was now.

"I feel like I want us to catch up, you know?" she was saying. "I mean, I want to start from where we left off and just learn everything about you since then, everything I've missed. And I want to tell you everything about me. So it'll be like we were together during all that time, at least in our imaginations."

"You want to know about my ex-girlfriends."

She laughed. "Well, not *just* that."

"Women always want to know about your ex-girlfriends. You're like dogs that way—you've got to make sure you're the alpha."

"Hey, watch it, smart ass. That's not the kind of talk that's likely to get you laid."

Joe raised his eyebrows. The phrase *get you laid* crackled through the little yurt.

"Besides," she added, "I'm not a 'woman' to you. To you I'm Rachel."

"Granted. You're Rachel Clayborne, the one and only. But you also happen to be very much a woman."

She swatted him on the chest with the back of her hand. "Enough stalling."

"All right." He pretended to look at his watch. "How much time do you have?"

"Joe."

"You're persistent, you know that?"

"One of my better qualities."

"That's debatable. Okay. Let me think. After you, there's been—" here he stopped, and made a show of counting on his fingers, pretending to give each finger a great amount of consideration. He stopped at three.

"That's it?"

"Hey, be nice. I'm playing with a handicap, remember." And he patted his bad cheek.

"Sorry. All right. So who were they?"

"One was a one-night stand, just a drunk girl I picked up at the casino, long time ago."

"Lovely."

"She flipped out when she got a good look at my face the next morning. Ran screaming out the door. No joke."

"God."

"The next was more serious. An Indian girl I met at the gym. We were together a few years, actually."

"What was she like?"

"Oh, sexy. Very sexy. Voluptuous, shall we say."

"Big tits. I get it."

"But too Catholic for me. Wanted me to go to church with her. Save my soul. That whole bit."

"Yikes."

"Plus, she was boring. Basically, she liked watching TV and working out. That was about it."

"Did you guys ever talk about getting married?"

"All the time. After a while, it was the only thing we talked about. So I had to delicately remove myself from that situation."

"You don't believe in marriage?"

"I don't believe in marrying people you don't like spending time with."

"Ah. Smart of you." Then, out of nowhere, she was crying again. A tear slid down the side of her nose; another hung from her earlobe. He touched it with his thumb, letting it dissolve into his skin.

"Hey," he said in a hush. "What did I say?"

She closed her eyes and blinked out a few more tears. That was it, in a nutshell: he'd put words to it. She no longer liked spending time with Michael. Somewhere in the past few months, Michael had become a problem, something she had to manage—a stress, not a pleasure. The only time she could relax was when he was at work; as the end of the day neared and she knew he'd be coming home, she had to steel herself against his impending judgment. Everything, every word out of his mouth, was drenched in subtext. *How was your day?* meant *Did you do anything worthwhile today? Or did you fritter away yet another perfectly good eight-hour stretch?* And *What do you want for dinner?* meant *I guess it's my turn to cook again, seeing as how you haven't done it yet.* She could see how it was already translating into his relationship with Deirdre, this judgment, this continual evaluation of her—

their baby—as an achieving being, and this, this was what drove her crazy. A question as seemingly innocent as *What's Deirdre been up to today?* really meant *Has she accomplished whatever developmental milestone she's supposed to accomplish by now? And have you been doing whatever you can to help her accomplish it?* It was driving her mad.

But then there was the part of her that wondered if maybe it was *her* fault, if maybe she was misinterpreting all of this, reading into Michael's questions and statements, supplying the subtext herself when really he hadn't intended any at all. Maybe she was making the whole thing up. That was possible, too. Oh, it was a mess, an ugly, unholy mess. And though she knew, of course, that she shouldn't be here with Joe, shouldn't have come at all, that she might be making an enormous, self-destructive, life-changing mistake, she couldn't help herself: Joe was here, finally; after so many years of being inaccessible, he was right here.

"Rachel," he said. He kissed her eyes, one at a time, tasting her salt. "Oh, my Rachel." He kissed her again, this time on the tip of her nose, and then, finally, she turned her face toward his, her eyes still squeezed shut, and he kissed her mouth.

She shrank away.

"I'm sorry," he said quickly. "Am I pushing you?"

"No," she whispered. "It's just—it's different." But she moved toward him again, decorating his lips with tiny exploratory kisses, testing out the new boundaries of his mouth. She followed a trail from the corner of his lips, down the scar tissue to his chin and then along the jaw line, nibbling at the remnants of his wound. He submitted, closed his eyes and submitted.

"Where your scar is, the skin is so smooth," she whispered, tracing the edge of his jaw. "What does it feel like?"

He kept his eyes closed. "I had to get used to it after the surgeries. It's tighter, constricted, almost. But it's my face now. It's been long enough." He reached toward her again. They kissed more deeply now, relaxing into each other, into the strength of the other's hold. Then Joe felt a wetness bloom against his chest.

Rachel pressed her hands to her breasts. "Sorry," she said. "I'm basically a leaky dyke these days. No pun intended."

Gently, he lifted her top hand away and touched the wet cloth beneath, the cinched nipple under the bra. "May I?" he asked. She nodded, almost imperceptibly, holding her breath. He lifted the shirt over her head, gently pulling her arms through the sleeves as if he were undressing a child, and then stopped, beholding her in the afternoon light. Her arms were slender, the skin pale and luminescent. Her breasts, encased still in the complicated straps and hooks of her nursing bra, were blindingly, irresistibly plump. He closed his eyes again.

"What's wrong?" she asked.

"Nothing. Absolutely nothing is wrong."

"Want me to show you how this gizmo works?" In one deft sweep of a finger, she unclicked the top of one of the cups of her bra. The fabric still clung to the breast, but the top hung open, as if waiting to be peeled. "Easy access," she joked. "You don't even have to bother with the clasps."

Joe, silent and single-minded, took the top of the bra in between his fingers and gently tugged it down. The skin around her nipple glistened wet, then sprouted a constellation of white beads, which swelled into a single suspended drop. He bowed his head and touched his tongue to that drop, letting the sweet milk penetrate his taste buds, the base of his tongue, his throat. He felt as if his whole being, his entire sensing and thinking being, had collected in his tongue, all in single-pointed focus on the beading milk, the ridged landscape of her breast. He traveled that landscape, taking hours, days, maybe, ridge by valley by broad stretching plain.

Rachel closed her eyes and arched into his mouth, pressing the back of his head against her. She felt herself release everything she'd been holding onto, all the daily frustrations, the monotony, the irritations, the failures, the dashed hopes—all of it, having swollen within her to a threatening head, now rushed forth in a hot, fast, intoxicating flood. Her mind dissolved into her body, penetrated each cell with consciousness. She had no mind, she was only body, only sensation and reaction. She pulled Joe's head back by the hair and dive-bombed his mouth with her own, fumbling at his pants with her fingers. He grabbed her capris, wet at the crotch, and stripped them off, popping off the top button. Naked, she rolled on top and lowered her slickness onto him. Together, in synchronized wonder, they gasped.

Afterward, they lay together underneath the sheet Rachel had pulled over them. She wrapped her two arms around his one and slung a leg over his hip. Lazily, he stroked her thigh, the rounding flank, the dramatic dip of her waist, the scar on her belly, still there. Then, a squeak shattered the silence. Rachel groaned and rolled off of him to her other side, slipped a breast back into Deirdre's mouth. Joe raised himself on an elbow. Deirdre, sucking strongly, stared with wide eyes up at him, this strange man looming over her mother like a mountain that had appeared in the night where no mountain had been before. Joe chuckled.

"She's getting used to me," he said.

"I think so."

"We could do this all day, you know? All you have to do is just roll back and forth between us. You feed her, you feed me, you feed her." Joe clapped his hand playfully on Rachel's hip. She swatted him away.

"Shut up, you cretin. What about me? I might need to eat, too, you know. Who's going to feed me?"

"I will. I'll bring you apricots and grapes, and feed them to you, one by one."

"I might need to get up once in a while, you know. Go to the bathroom. Maybe, God forbid, read a book or something." Her tone came sharp, sharper than she'd intended.

"Hey, I'm just kidding around. Don't get angry."

"Sorry. I'm a little over-sensitive these days. Motherhood fucks with your brain."

They listened to Deirdre suck and swallow, suck and swallow. Then, with a pop, Deirdre released her grip on Rachel's breast and, a thin line of milk streaming from the corner of her mouth, she babbled a single syllable directly to Joe that sounded for all the world like "Da." Both Rachel and Joe laughed, and Deirdre cooed, looking pleased with herself.

"That's a first," Rachel said, raising herself up from the bed and snapping her bra back into place. "She's never said anything so word-like before."

"Right word, wrong guy," Joe replied, immediately regretting it. Michael's ghost-presence hovered in the silence that followed. But Rachel looked unfazed. She smoothed her hair back into a fresh ponytail with her hands, revealing two light brown furrings under her arms, then fastened it with the elastic around her wrist.

"You never told me about number three," Rachel said, to change the subject. She didn't want to think about Michael right now, not at all, not at all, not at all. Just the thought of him gave her that same queasiness in the pit of her stomach that she'd felt on the dam a few hours earlier.

"Right," Joe rolled onto his back once again, staring up at the canvas ceiling. "Number three. Number three is Susan, this woman I've been seeing lately. She lives down in Madison."

Rachel dropped her arms. "You didn't tell me you were dating someone."

"It didn't come up. Yet." He propped himself on an elbow again, studying her face. It was, he felt, the most beautiful face he knew: dewy skin, wide apart cow-eyes, smooth broad forehead, the faint tracings of lines at the corners of her eyes, pressing into arcs around her mouth.

"Well, what's she like?"

"She's cool. She's a vet, too—Air Force. She used to patrol the no-fly zone over Iraq back in the day. She's got two kids."

"Oh." Rachel lifted Deirdre up against her shoulder, and began to pat her on the back, a little harder than Joe would have thought a baby might like to be patted. "Is she divorced, then?"

"Yeah."

"How old are her kids?"

"Maybe seven and four or five or something? I'm not sure. I haven't met them yet."

"Oh." This seemed to relieve Rachel a bit. "So how long have you two been dating?"

"A few months."

"Are things going well? I mean, are you getting serious?"

Joe burst out laughing.

"What?" Rachel looked offended.

"I'm sorry," he said, chuckling. "You just look so—so earnest. Your expression."

"Well, I want to know," she retorted. "I mean, I just think it would be good information to have."

Deirdre let out a good belch, making Joe laugh even more, and loosening Rachel up a bit. "Good one, Dee," she said, then arranged herself crosslegged on the mattress, with Deirdre in between her legs, leaning against her belly. Deirdre, wide awake now, bobbed her head on her neck, her eyes traveling over Joe's face.

"Hi, baby," he said, moving a little closer to her. "You want to check me out?"

"So?"

"So, no. As of right now, we're not serious at all. Honestly. I mean, if we were serious, would I be here with you?"

"I don't know. Maybe."

"I wouldn't." Joe's tone was sober now, reassuring.

"Okay," Rachel said. Neither of them decided to pay much attention to the irony of this—that Rachel, the married one, the one with all the ammunition, was the one who needed reassuring.

"So now it's your turn."

"What do you mean?"

"Your history. After me."

"You know, on second thought, maybe we shouldn't do this. What's past is past, right?"

"Hey, now. That's not fair. I fessed up."

"Yeah, but you didn't have much to fess."

"Oh, I see. Well, now I really want to know. What did you do, sleep with the whole football team or something?"

Rachel considered a moment. "How many people are on a football team?"

"You're shitting me."

She grimaced. "I slept around a bunch in college after you. Punishing myself, maybe, for being such a shit to you. And then I met Michael, and I've been monogamous since." The memory of lying beneath Dr. Brian Speckel in his car flashed into her mind, but she pushed it away.

"How much is a bunch?"

"I don't know. Twelve? Fifteen? Something like that."

"More than a football team!"

"Shut up."

"So then Michael straightened you out, huh?"

"Yeah, actually. Michael was my spiritual filtration system. He was so good, such a good, conscientious person: good student, nice person, very kind, sensitive about other people's feelings. Mine, in particular. He was caring."

"Sounds like a good guy."

"He is a good guy. He's a very good guy."

Joe fell back against the mattress, his head hitting the pillow with a *flomp*. Above him, black silhouettes of insects—some corpses, some still alive—speckled the yurt's canvas roof. He'd known it would be this way. It's the way it always was, with drugs, liquor, unwise sexual encounters. The pain came on the heels of the pleasure. He just hadn't thought this particular high would be quite so short.

Rachel looked down at Deirdre's head, at the swirl of hair on her crown, and absentmindedly ran her fingers along the smooth hair there. "Too good, maybe," she added. "For me anyway."

"What do you mean, too good for you? Why shouldn't you deserve someone good?"

She smiled sadly. "Thanks. That's nice to hear."

Joe sat up and started putting on his clothes, slowly—T-shirt first, then his jeans. Rachel watched him. "What are you doing?"

He walked over to the window and looked out, checking the sky. The sun had disappeared behind the clouds once more, and it was threatening rain again. But for now, the surface of the lake was smooth, untroubled by drops. He rubbed his fingers across his forehead, as if trying to rub something off. "So if he's so great, why exactly are you here with me?"

"I don't know, Joe. I really don't know. I shouldn't be."

He waited.

"Things changed, I guess. With Michael, I mean. Somewhere along the line. Before Deirdre was born, even. I don't know when it happened, exactly. It was a gradual thing. I went to grad school, we stopped coming to the Farm, we moved to Illinois, and bit by bit I just got more and more unhappy. Then, once Deirdre was born, it was like I woke up. Here I was, in this weird college town, studying for a PhD I never wanted to have, far away from my family, and now a mother. Years ago, I thought I'd never have kids. All the married parents I knew seemed so tedious and miserable. I swore to myself that I'd never do all that. After you refused me, that is."

"Refused you?"

"That night on the beach in Maine."

"I didn't *refuse* you."

"That's how it felt. I was serious that night, Joe. I would have run away with you to anywhere."

Joe smiled ruefully. "I remember."

"Anyway, here I am now, married and with a kid. Living the life I swore I'd never lead."

Joe stared impenetrably at her.

"Sorry," Rachel said. "I shouldn't be laying all of this on you. Especially right after—"

He interrupted angrily. "Things were going pretty well for me, you know. Before you showed up."

She gazed at him, speechless.

"I was happy with my life, with my daily routine. Proud, even. This job, this place, this yurt. It's modest, but it's mine, and I like it that way. But then you came up here, and started talking to me and hanging out with me and telling me all this shit about your marriage . . ." He punched the yurt's canvas wall, sending the window bouncing. "What is it you *want*, anyway, Rachel? What the fuck do you want from me?"

Rachel, eyes welling again, buried her face in Deirdre's head, in the familiar freshness of her scalp, the down against her nose and cheeks. Deirdre swatted the zipper of the sleeping bag that had crept up over her thigh. "I don't know, Joe. That's my problem right now. I don't know what I want." She spoke the words into Deirdre's head, so that they came out muffled and barely audible.

"So in the meantime, you're going to run a battering ram through everyone else's life while you try to figure it out. Did it ever occur to you that you can't always *get* what you want? Even if you know what that is?"

"To quote Prophet Jagger," she joked bitterly.

Joe snorted. His eye fell once again on the black silhouette of a fly, this one clinging to the side of the yurt's outer canvas. He flicked the canvas with a cocked finger, knocking off the fly.

Deirdre was starting to squirm a little, so Rachel lifted her out from her nest between her legs, and laid her on her tummy in the center of the mattress. She raked Deirdre's back with the tips of her fingers, smoothing the cotton of her onesie taut. "I guess I wanted the Farm. I know it's out of the blue and impractical and politically incorrect and all of that. But I don't know, Joe, coming up here again, seeing Grand and you . . . I started dreaming big. I started thinking maybe I could start over, in a way. Do things right this time."

"Well, that's where you went wrong," he blurted out. "Never dream. It's bad for your mental health."

She studied him. "You used to dream."

"I used to fantasize. There's a difference."

"What's the difference?"

He shrugged. "Fantasizing involves concocting crazy unattainable goals in your mind, just for the hell of it. Mental masturbation. Dreaming is more—I don't know. For the privileged few. It's something people do when they have the means to make their dreams come true."

"That sounds like bullshit to me."

"All I know is that any dreams I ever had only led to disappointment. One day at a time seems to work better in the long run."

"Yeah, but what if your day just sucks, over and over again? And you can't see your way out of that? What if it just seems like the rest of your life is going to be as shitty as that one day?"

"I don't know, Rachel. Maybe you need to lower your expectations."

He looked out the window again. The sky was still mostly overcast, the lake becoming choppy, but not yet dimpled. A wind blew, a cloud moved, and a ray of light illuminated a patch of water across the flowage, near Old Bend Island. The island was barely visible from here—it just looked like a little clump of forest rising up out of the water. But it gave him an idea. He turned back to Rachel. "Let's get some air. I want to show you something."

❧

After Rachel changed Deirdre's diaper and got herself dressed, she settled Deirdre in the front pack and they set out, following the shoreline upriver, away from the dam. The path was narrow, tramped into existence by roaming deer, so they walked in single file, their way bounded by the woods on their left, and the open flowage on their right. The afternoon was wearing on—the sun had emerged from the cloud cover, and was casting intermittent rays slantwise across the water, giving shape to the vapor that still hung in the air. Occasionally, when the tree cover opened, they'd receive a dart of sunlight in their eyes; Rachel, having forgotten hats, wielded her hand as a sunshield in front of Deirdre's face. But for most of the way, the thick woods shaded them, exhaling a dampness that cooled their skin as they walked. Deirdre, oblivious to the new tension between Rachel and Joe, squealed happily, enjoying the fresh-washed air, the light dappling through the leaves. Joe walked heavily ahead, caught up in his own brooding. Rachel could feel his wounded mood emanating from his back like heat off a summer road, so she kept her distance, walking several paces behind.

Finally, after they'd walked at least a half an hour in silence, the path descended a shallow slope, forking to the left, while to the right it gave onto a small promontory decorated by a few saplings. Joe walked directly out to the tip and stood looking out at the lake. Rachel, unsure whether he meant for her to follow, found a spot on the ledge a few feet away. She looked to the southeast, back the way they had come. Neither the dam nor Joe's yurt were visible. Only the reservoir itself, choppy with white-capped waves.

"See that island?" asked Joe, his voice sounding strange and foreign, after they'd gone so long without speaking. He was pointing toward the northeast, where a small partially-wooded island rose out of the water.

"Yeah." Rachel moved an inch closer to him.

"See those two ruts in the ground? That kind of lead up from the water?"

"No."

"Look closely. See how the grass is a little taller at the top of the slope, and how it then kind of dips down?"

As he spoke, the grass took on dimension and shadow, and Rachel saw two furrows emerge from the green homogeneity that had existed a moment before. "Yeah. Okay. I've got it now."

"Those are old wagon wheel ruts. A road—a main thoroughfare—used to run right through there. That island used to be a hill. Before they put the dam in."

Rachel stared a long while, trying to envision what Joe was describing. For a moment, she could—the water disappeared, the island, denuded of trees, rose above a flat stretch of land, and the road cut through, rising up the slope of the hill, and back down the other side. Then the image slipped away, and once again she saw only an island in the middle of a lake, nothing more.

"Wow. That kind of blows my mind," she said finally.

"That hill was at the center of the village of Bend. That road led out to Clinton from the old trading post, which was just at the base of the hill. And then down the road from that was the jailhouse. Over there in that direction was the government day school. You can still see some of the foundation underwater there. And then if you swim out that way about a quarter of a mile, that's where my great-grandparents used to live. The ones that used to own the Farm."

Rachel stared at the island and the obliterating blue of the water, letting Joe's last words reverberate. *The ones that used to own the Farm.* She looked back at the island, trying unsuccessfully to picture a village hidden beneath. It felt to her like one of those optical illusions that was printed in kids' books with the purpose of both freaking kids out and illustrating the mechanism of the eye: a woman's face turns into a vase and then back again, if you kept staring at it. One minute it was an island, and the next a hill.

"It gets easier to imagine," Joe said, as if he'd read her thoughts. "Especially once you've dived here. You start to see the water differently. Not as the opposite of the land, but as—I don't know. Its clothing or something."

"Scuba diving, you're talking about? I didn't know you dove."

"One of the things that helped me recover after my accident."

She nodded, allowing a respectful silence at the mention of the thing that still loomed so large between them. "So what do you see under there, then?"

"Not much, usually. Algae and fish. The occasional kettle. A few fallen gravestones."

They watched the surface of the water a while. "I've heard about places like this," Rachel said. "Sunken villages. There's one in Scotland, I think, where you can still see a steeple rising out of the water." She paused. "It must be eerie, swimming amid all those remnants."

"That's not how I'd describe it," he said.

"How would you describe it?"

He thought a long moment. "I actually find it comforting. It's peaceful. Like walking through an old cemetery."

Rachel nodded thoughtfully. "I can see that."

"There's a Buddhist practice where you meditate on your own moldering corpse."

She raised her eyebrows at him in mock horror.

"It's good for you. Keeps you humble. Maybe it's like that for me."

"Wow, Joe," she said. "You're getting way deep on me."

He smiled.

She studied the island again, and then something occurred to her. "So they didn't live on the Farm then? Your great-grandparents? They lived in town?"

"My great-great-grandfather lived on that land, where the Farm is now, for a long time, until he got sick. Then he moved in with his daughter, my great-grandmother Mary. She's the one who tricked him into selling the Farm to your family."

"So they sold their land to my great-grandfather and then the dam went in and flooded out their house?"

"Pretty much."

"And they had nowhere to live, so they went to the Farm."

"Yup. They were caretakers of the Farm for years. My great-grandfather basically ran the operation. My great-grandma Mary, she was the cook and the housekeeper. They lived in the cottage on the edge of the property, before it collapsed back when we were kids. Remember that place? We used to go over there and wander around inside it, pretend we lived there."

And as he said it, she remembered what she hadn't before: the interior smelling of mold and sodden carpet, an old sideboard that still held moth-eaten napkins, a few stray utensils, an ancient box of rat poison. The broom by the back door. "I guess I always thought of that house as just a creepy, abandoned place. I never really thought much about who had lived there."

She looked once more at the island, at the wagon wheel ruts on the once-upon-a-time road. An image flashed across her mind of a man bouncing along over the old road in an antiquated automobile, one of those early open-air models, one hand pressing a pork-pie hat to his head, the other gripping the steering wheel. And horses. Horses would have traveled it before the cars. People probably walked it, too, for miles. Gone. All that life, all those stories, all those people, gone. She thought of Grand, lying on her hospital bed, lapsing in and out of consciousness, in and out of the dream-world of memory and illusion. Alone. God, but it was sad, this life. God, but it was unbearably sad.

Joe followed Rachel's gaze out to the island once more, and when he spoke, it was in a tone to match her quietness. "Even though you can try to imagine it, it's impossible to really get what this place once was. I mean, this was all river valley here—wetlands, floodplains, tributaries, and the longer winding river through all of it. There were lakes, too, but they were generally small, lakes you could circumnavigate on foot, if you wanted, not this mega, supersized lake. And the Farm, that whole piece of land? That used to be a hill that rose up out of the valley.

"That's the place your great-grandfather probably saw when he came here for the first time. An old cabin on a hill, plopped in the middle of nowhere. And no offense or anything, but I would bet money that he knew that once the dam was put in, that cabin was going to be prime real estate, lakefront property. He probably didn't mention that little fact to my great-grandma when he made her an offer."

Rachel walked away from Joe, over to a young birch with curling bark, and began to peel off a thin strip. The parchment-like band broke into chips between her fingers.

"Your family probably doesn't tell that part of the story," Joe added, watching her from his post by the water.

"No," she said. "They don't."

They were quiet again. Joe turned back to the lake, feeling satisfied at having said his piece, but also drawn out, exhausted. He hadn't meant to preach a sermon, and yet he had the distinct feeling that that was what he had done. He watched the water, waiting to see how Rachel would react.

Rachel, realizing mid-tear what she was doing—effectively killing the birch, which would die if its bark was stripped—stopped, dropped her hands to her side and leaned the side of her head against the smooth trunk. Deirdre reached out and grabbed a piece of bark herself, and brought it to her mouth. Rachel fished it out with her pinky. She could protest, if she felt like it. She could reflexively defend her family name, insist on Granddaddy's honesty and uprightness, if she had the heart. But she didn't. Joe was probably right. It wouldn't surprise her. Her great-grandfather may have been a proper and upstanding man—churchgoer, gentleman farmer, baseball aficionado—but he was also a born and bred capitalist, the type of man who wouldn't shrug at a chance to push for a deal, even if it meant telling a half-truth. She could easily manufacture the rationalizations herself—*there's no guarantee the water will come up this far, it's only a guess; what they don't know won't hurt them; they're just subsisting, they're not interested in a lake-front property; they're only Indians.*

"Okay, Joe. Point taken. Rich white people suck. I get it."

"No, you don't, Rachel. That's not why I'm showing you this. I'm not blaming you, or even Great-Grandpa Benjamin Turner, for that matter. I mean, he did what he was trained to do. He probably even believed in it, thought he was doing the right thing, building the dam. For the common good and all that."

"So why are you showing it to me, then? I mean, it's not helping me feel any better, I can tell you that."

"I'm showing it to you because it's a reality, Rachel. The village has *sunk*. There's no bringing it back. I've tried; I've been down there. There's nothing left."

She turned back to Joe, who was looking pointedly at her, his lopsided face serene, his eyes kind. "You can't go back," he said gently. "*We* can't go back."

She looked out to the island once more, the island that once was a hill. The water was dark at the shoreline, the shadows of trees stretching long over the lake.

"Listen," Rachel said. "I'm going to go for a walk."

He studied her face. "Okay."

"I just need some time alone for a while. Just to think."

"Okay, sure."

"I'll meet you back at the yurt later."

He nodded, then looked toward the western horizon. The sun was round above it, a pale sphere. "If you're gone too long, I might have to start worrying about you."

She smiled sadly. "Don't worry. We'll be back before dark."

He closed the space between them then, took her by the shoulders and planted a kiss in the center of her forehead. "Just stay by the water. You can't get lost if you stay by the water."

"All right," she said. And she stepped back off the promontory and started walking north, down the path, away from the yurt, her eyes on the lake beside her.

Joe watched her go a while, and then turned and headed in the opposite direction. Halfway back, he heard the cracking of a stick in the woods and whipped around, hoping it might be Rachel, having changed her mind. But there was no one there.

5

And so an hour passed, and then another. The pale sphere of the sun swelled and grew orange as it descended to the horizon and then past it, casting emanations of rainbow-spectrum colors into the humid sky. In the water beneath, the bluegills and trout and sunfish and northern pikes and muskies trawled their favorite feeding grounds, nibbling on minnows or hanging vegetation, snapping at promising flicks of movement in the darkening lake. Duck families waddled ashore, preening their feathers with their black beaks before folding themselves into their nests. Otters in their shore-side holts cleaned their whiskered muzzles with wet paws. The mother eagle snatched her last catch from the lake, and soared through the dusking air to her young, who waited in the Eliza tree. Inland, deer canvassed the woods for good leafy beds, relatively dry, and curled themselves into warm rings. Owls began to rouse, and as day bled into night, the woods came alive with sound: toad trills, bullfrog *jug-o-rums*, owl hoots, cricket chirps, bat squeaks, mosquito drones, and among them, the occasional squawk and hum of a single human baby, jostling in a pack as her mother walked, deeper and deeper into the night woods.

In the distance, thunder rolled.

6

Rachel's absence at dinner worried Maddy, despite Diane's attempts to reassure her. Diane had tried calling Joe several times, but had gotten no answer. Maddy went to bed anxious, and when, late that night, thunder shook the house, she woke disoriented and frightened. The night was very dark, she was in a strange bed, and it seemed the room had changed around her.

Shapes grew out of the dark, taking nebulous forms—blocky, pouched, angular, cylindrical. She tried to identify them, but her mind was empty of words or phrases that would mark this shape as a cabinet, that one as a wardrobe, that a trash bin. She stared at the objects, seeing them as conglomerations of shadow against the basic darkness of the room. She felt she was confronting a verge—an edge, definite, but shifting, like the reach of a rising lake. She felt herself before it, like a beachcomber on wet sand, knowing it was approaching, that eventually it would eclipse her position, overtake the sand on which she stood, wet her toes, her feet, her ankles—and she was somehow powerless to stop it. All she could do was stand as tall as she could while the water rose and rose.

The window beside her was cracked, letting in a cool, wet breeze. Outside, the rain pummeled the ground.

A memory surfaced: she was standing by the water, her toes wiggling in soft wet mud. The seedheads of long grasses tickled her elbows, her forearms, even her earlobes. She pressed her toes into the mud, felt the cool wet squelching ooze around and between her toes, then stepped back to see the prints her feet had made: small, a child's prints, the toes no bigger than marbles. But as soon as she stepped away, they filled again with mud, the impression of each foot swelling back into smoothness. The process fascinated her, and she repeated it again and again: stomping into the mud, feeling the ooze encroach, and then stepping off and watching the water-taut mud erase all evidence of her.

There was a smell to this memory, too—it stank of swamp, of wet grasses, of river-silt drying in the sun. She pressed and released, pressed and released. She was thirsty, but she couldn't drink the water—she'd been forbidden, strongly, from drinking the water. Nor could she stay very long. She'd been warned. They would be leaving shortly. They'd come for some express purpose, and once her father had accomplished that purpose, they would be on their way.

Her sisters were not there, nor was her mother. It was a special privilege, being here with her father, driving out with him in the car. He had not wanted her to go, but she'd cried and looked pitiful, and so he'd let her climb up onto the slippery leather seat next to him and hold tightly to his elbow while they bounced along the dirt roads. Stray grains of dirt had flown in her eyes and her mouth. She'd crunched her teeth against one, tasting the bitter dust. Her father was displeased about something; he was driving too fast, and she was afraid. And then he'd dropped her at the side of the water, where he left the car, and told her to stand there, not to move, and that he'd be right back, and in a few minutes they'd be leaving.

So she waited and squelched in the mud. And he did not return. She waited longer, and longer, and then, finally, she grew tired of waiting, and climbed back up into the car, forgetting her shoes by the water's edge (she would be spanked for that later by her mother). Sitting in the car, she examined the soles of her feet: they were caked with mud, the dirt turning the natural lines in her skin into dark sinuous things, a network of streams and rivers. She studied her feet, using her fingernail to scrape off what mud she could, feeling a creeping sense of foreboding. Her father would not like all this mud. On the floor of the car she'd made a print, and again on the footboard. She wiped these off as best she could with the flat of her hand. Still, the prints were there, and he would see it was she who had made them. He would punish her.

Where was her father?

From the perch of the car's seat, she sat herself a little taller, and looked out over the road ahead. The road, like a river itself, was bordered by tall grasses, which bent a little in the breeze. To her left, the river swelled at its banks, overtaking the grasses, widening itself into them, slurping at their base as it had slurped at her own feet. It was a wide, wide river.

There was no sign of her father, and the foreboding she had been feeling began to transform itself into genuine fear. What if something had happened to him? How would she get home? She thought about sitting herself in the driver's seat, to see if she would be able to reach the pedals. But she might get mud on them. Instead, she dismounted, reversing her steps and trying her best to place her feet in the prints she'd made when she got in, and stood a moment, listening. Nothing. Nothing but river-sounds—the wind disturbing the grasses, the water sucking at the shore. She walked a few paces down the road, ready at any moment to bolt back to the car should she see her father. He had forbidden her from going anywhere. But she saw no one. She walked a few more paces, treading silently on her little girl feet, the pebbles and hard dirt of the road poking into her skin.

She walked until she got to the place where the road curved right, then backed herself into the grasses, watching. There was her father, just down the road, close by the whole time. He stood in front of a house with another man—a round-bellied man in a checked vest and a bowler hat, and in front of them, sitting in a rocking chair on her porch, was an old Indian woman. The woman had her face turned away from the two men, as if they weren't there, her hands gripped in her lap. And the strange thing was that the house seemed to have grown up out of the river, the wide, wide river. All around its foundation there was water, as if the house were floating. Her father and the round man stood off a little ways, just at the edge of the water, and her father listened while the round man talked, moving his hands animatedly in the woman's direction. The woman ignored them, looking off over the river, and rocked in her chair.

The girl-Maddy, the Maddy of memory, felt a rush of relief, which turned quickly to affection and pride. Her father, tall, slender, his hands in his pockets, standing amid those strangers with the little stoop he always had, as if apologizing for his height. Her pride in his person, her desire to claim him, to show the strangers that he belonged to her, overcame the injunction he'd given her against moving from the car, and she ran toward him, not caring how he might scold her. But halfway down the road, a deafening report echoed through the air, stopping her in her tracks. Her father turned, his face a grimace of horror. In one motion, it seemed, he arrived, swept her into his arms, and ran with her to the car. She clung to him, her arms around his neck, her chin jostling against his shoulder. The round-bellied man followed them, his face a panic. And behind him, standing on the porch next to the old woman, was an Indian man holding a hunting rifle, a thin trail of smoke winding skyward from its muzzle. The Indian's eyes met Maddy's and she held his gaze until they rounded the bend.

At the car, her father deposited her onto the seat beside him and then fumbled with the ignition. Finally the motor caught, and they drove off, careening over the roads, away from the awful noise, away from the Indian man with the gun and the old Indian woman and the house growing up out of the water, away from the wide, wide river. Her father held her to him, steering with one hand, the other clutching her head to his chest, harder than was comfortable. His heartbeat galloped in her ear. His jacket scratched her cheek. She couldn't see. She squirmed away. Her eye fell on a smudge of mud she'd made on the seat. Quickly, surreptitiously, she tried to brush it away with the back of her hand, and then, when it wouldn't budge, she sat on it, looking up at her father's face to see whether he'd noticed. But he was not looking at her or the mud. He was focused on the road in front of him, his expression unfamiliar—tense, worried, far away.

A guttural roll of thunder sounded outside the office window, startling Maddy into the present: the dark, unfamiliar room, her own sand-dry mouth, full bladder, aching backside. The grief, as if afresh, at the sudden loss of her father. He was not here, was long dead. She was alone and anxious, her pulse racing, blood heating her face and neck. Something, she felt, was wrong.

"Hello?" she called out, her voice shattering the darkness. Emboldened by the sound of her own voice, she called again, "Jacob?" Even as she called his name, she knew it was not right—Jacob was not here. Jacob, too, was dead. Her children were gone away. Who would hear her?

The rain splattered on the brick walkway outside the open window; the leaves of the rosebush trembled and shook in the downfall. The air was damp and cool. This couldn't be death, Maddy thought. With rain like this, with such delicious air. And then there was the dryness of her mouth, the pressing need to pee. Surely one didn't have to pee in death. She called out again, "Hello? Can anyone hear me?" and then the door opened and a woman in a quilted robe stood in the doorway.

"Mother?" Maddy said. "Is that you?"

The woman came closer, and though she knew it wasn't her mother—this woman was shorter, with darker skin and a strange black helmet of hair—still, Maddy found herself speaking as if she were, knowing as she did, that it wasn't right, that something wasn't right. "It wasn't Father's fault, Mother. Please don't be angry. He didn't know. He didn't know what would happen."

"Shh, Maddy. Madeline. It's all right. It's me, Diane Bishop. Your nurse." Diane took Maddy's hand and held it tight. "Don't worry, hon. It was just a dream. You were just having a bad dream."

Maddy was silent a moment, feeling the pressure of this strange woman's hand on her own, wondering still where exactly she was, and what could be filling her with such anxiety. "Nurse. Nurse Bishop. Forgive me, I'm not myself. But tell me, please. What is this place? Is this a home you've taken me to of some kind? I'd like to see my children."

"You're at the Farm, hon. This is your home. We've just moved your bedroom to the downstairs office, so you wouldn't have to climb so many stairs. Everything's all right."

Maddy looked around the room once more. The mention of the Farm calmed her a bit—she knew the Farm, it was the place her father loved, the place she went in the summers, where there were cows and chickens and fresh apples from the trees and warm milk straight from the bucket. But still, there was something. "Nurse," she said. "Nurse. Listen: do you hear the rain outside? The water is rising. Where will we go?"

Diane placed a hand on Maddy's forehead, feeling for fever. "You're burning up, Maddy. I'm going to get you some Tylenol. I'll be right back."

"No!" Maddy grabbed at her hand, pulling. "No, please don't leave me here alone."

"Hon, you've got a fever, and you're delirious. I'm going to get you a couple of Tylenol. It'll help you to sleep. I promise, I'll be right back. Nothing's going to harm you while I'm gone. It's just rain outside, just nice, peaceful rain. Okay?"

Maddy, feeling that it would be useless to contradict this woman, just nodded her head, holding tight to the covers, gripping them in her fists and kneading them, waiting for her to return. This was not a nice, peaceful rain. This was a bad rain. She could feel it. This was a bad, bad rain.

7

After leaving Joe, Rachel followed the trail downhill a ways, keeping an eye on the water. Usually walking helped her think, but she found her mind drifting, unable to settle on any logical progression of thoughts. She watched a dragonfly alight on a blade of grass, resting its wings, and then buzz forward again into the air, humming over the water's surface. A wind kicked up off the lake's surface and blew Deirdre's hair across her forehead. The baby sucked in a squeal of air.

Rachel kept walking, watching for poison ivy, ignoring the sun's steady descent, the clouds encroaching from the north. It was good to be on a trail, good to be away from everything and everyone, good to just be a creature, walking a path. She wanted to walk and keep walking, to follow the path wherever it might lead. She stepped over fallen branches, negotiated low swampy spots and picked her way over stones that threatened to turn her ankle. She walked.

The first drops of rain took her by surprise. One fell on the bridge of her nose, another on her forearm, another on her throat. Deirdre turned her face to the sky to see where the water was coming from and received a drop in her eye. She gasped and blinked. Rachel stopped, knowing she should turn back: it was almost dark, and now the rain. But up ahead she noticed a trail that branched off into the woods. It was narrow and overgrown, but well-covered by trees, which would help keep them dry.

She turned once more to the lake, trying to fix in her mind what she saw, so that she would recognize this spot later and know which way to turn. There was that island with the wagon wheel tracks, the island that was really a hill, off to the right, its narrow pebbly beach pouching a little into the water. And then here, at the intersection of the trails, stood a wide birch, its white bark gleaming a ghostly glow against the dark of the woods behind it. This new trail, she noted, headed west, into the source of the shadows. She searched the ground and found a hefty stone, half-covered in mud, which she placed just in front of the birch, to mark the spot. Then she headed up the new trail, into the night woods.

The trees did keep them dry, and the trail, though narrow, was mostly straight. Rachel's eyes adjusted quickly to the darker woods. Deirdre bounced gently in the pack while the shifting cloudbanks eclipsed the last of the blue twilight as if a heavy curtain had been thrown across the sky. The rain fell more steadily, saturating the leafy cover, which would, from time to time, collapse under the water's weight in a sudden torrent. More than once, the torrent fell on Rachel and Deirdre. And it seemed as if the duff on the forest floor were exhaling a cold air.

Still, she continued through the wet dark, feeling unable to turn back. The deeper she got into the woods, the sicker she felt. Whereas before, with Joe, she'd wanted only to push Michael out of her mind, now she could do nothing but think of him. She'd betrayed him, faster than she could even fathom. In the moment, with Joe, it had seemed the thing to do. It had felt good—really fucking good—to do what her body wanted. And it had seemed somehow precious, a thing that concerned only them, that was separate, somehow, from Michael. But now, it appeared she'd invented that story out of convenience. Michael was not separate from her. Michael had been there in the yurt with them the whole time. And what she'd done would wound him deeply, would hurt their marriage, even destroy it. She kicked a stone that lay in the middle of the path, watched it roll head over heels down the trail, and then careen into the brush. It seemed she was an expert at wounding the people she loved.

Thunder rolled, close now.

She trudged on, immersed in her own disgust and confusion, Deirdre's whines and squeaks growing more extended and serious, both of them growing steadily wetter. Finally, she stopped, knowing she needed to get Deirdre out of the rain. She didn't want to see Joe right now, but she had no choice. Reluctantly, she turned around, and, moving in the direction from which she'd come, walked right into the low-hanging branches of a tree. Deirdre yelled. Rachel felt forward like a blind person: there was a tree directly in front of her, where no tree had been before. She stepped aside and bumped into another tree. She'd lost the trail.

Then, a stroke of lightning lit up the woods like a floodlight, and in the moment of its flashing, a shack appeared a short distance away, made of logs and branches and tossed off pieces of plywood.

A cabin. In the woods.

It went dark again, but the hut remained shimmering in her mind. She knew exactly where it was; it would take only a few steps to reach it, and it would be shelter for them until the storm passed. Still, she froze in place, her mind caught on the image of the cabin in the West Virginia woods, where the missing mother on the news had abandoned her baby. Her pulse began to race. What was happening? Had she stepped through some strange wormhole into the darkest places of her own gothic imagination? Was this some kind of sign, some kind of unsubtle suggestion from the universe? *Here's your cabin, Mother Rachel. The perfect place to lay your burden down.*

The rain fell harder still, sheeting down, the thunder cracking right overhead. She ducked instinctively; a tree limb crashed through the canopy, close by. Deirdre began to wail. Then lightning flashed once more, and she saw it again: a rude hut growing like a mushroom out of the forest floor. Arms outstretched to block Deirdre's face from branches, she moved toward the hut, felt for the opening of the door, and ducked inside.

8

When the rain started, Joe decided he'd give her an hour. He knew Rachel wouldn't like it if he went hunting for her at the first drop of rain, during the first minutes of nightfall; she'd feel checked up on, fussed over.

But he kept looking at the clock every five minutes, and finally, after forty minutes had passed, he couldn't wait any longer. It was dark, the rain was coming down hard, and he felt like a jerk sitting in his dry, cozy yurt while Rachel and the baby were out there getting drenched. He grabbed a flashlight, donned his heavy duty rain jacket and work boots, and tramped down the trail she had taken, waving the flashlight back and forth in the hopes she might see it through the rain.

But the storm was loud, the rain pounding the ground, the thunder coming strong and fast, the intermittent lightning flashes washing out his flashlight beam. The lake was lapping high on the bank, and though it was difficult to tell in the dark and the rain, it seemed to him higher than it had been when he set out.

After an hour or so of searching up and down the trail, calling Rachel's name until he was hoarse, Joe gave up. He couldn't even hear himself over the storm; there was no way Rachel could hear him. And he was growing increasingly anxious about the dam. He had to at least check the levels, see whether the gates needed raising.

He turned around and began to follow his own tracks back to the yurt. Sally ran ahead, wagging hopefully at the door flap. Joe pulled it back, hoping to see Rachel inside. But the place was empty, and so he continued on, up the slope toward the dam. Rachel was a big girl, he told himself. She knew the outdoors. She'd be all right.

He knocked his boots against the door of the control house before he entered, and a few tread-chunks of mud fell onto the concrete. Sally ran into the room first, leaving muddy prints on the carpet. Joe shucked his raincoat, sending a miniature cascade to the floor, and went directly to the water level gauge.

It was a foot and a half higher than it had been that afternoon.

Joe stared at it in disbelief. It was impossible—there hadn't been anywhere near that much rain. George at the upstream dam must have raised his gates again. He shouldered on his coat once more and ran to the office, but there was no message light blinking red. So he called George, who pleaded ignorance. "We're holding steady up here. You better call the company."

Which Joe did. Frank agreed to an immediate raise of the gates of four whole feet—not a normal interval, because it could send water rushing out too quickly and overwhelm the banks, but the situation was desperate. And he told Joe to trip off the emergency sirens before he did anything else. He would call the cops. This was a Level One emergency: the dam was in imminent danger of failing.

So Joe flipped the switch that set off the sirens, and then turned the dial and pressed the button to raise the gates, all the while wracking his brain for what could have happened. He listened beneath the sirens' wail for the familiar creaking and groaning of the great mechanical behemoth turning the winches and pulling the cables to raise the gates—but when it came, something was different. There was a strange grinding, muted by the sirens and the storm, but loud enough to turn his stomach. He checked the gate gauge: two of the gates were now at the proper height, but one of them—the one closest to the control house—had not budged an inch.

He ran back outside to the wheelhouse, where he pulled the wet pin from the lock and took the slick manual gatewheel in his hands, forcing it clockwise. The thing turned, incrementally, but then stopped and would turn no more, even with Joe's full weight behind it. He couldn't hear the grinding out here—all he heard were the sirens, cycling from a deafening wail when they were pointed in his direction to a more mournful call when they turned downstream, and then behind that, the wind and torrenting rain—but he could feel the vibration in the wheel, and he knew: metal was straining against metal, but the gate was not giving. Something was wrong.

He ran down the pier to see if he could get a view of the defective gate. A single security light beamed over the control house, illuminating a fifty-foot section of the causeway and the lake. Joe leaned out over the edge of the railing, searching the surface of the water for any clues, any hint of what might be the problem. And that's when he saw it: the jagged end of a tree trunk just above the water's surface a few feet away from the dam gate, obscured now and then by the waves.

Joe ran back up the staircase to the office, where he put in another call to Frank, who picked up on the first ring.

"The first gate's jammed," he panted. "That's the problem. A tree fell in the storm and got itself wedged in there, and the thing won't move."

"Jesus," Frank said. "All right, hang tight, Joe. I'm on the other line with the county. But we'll send someone over there as fast as we can."

Joe went back outside and paced the causeway in the sheeting rain, trying to stare down the rising water. Sally cowered in the office doorjamb, watching him. He knew he should get out of there, that walking on the dam in conditions like these was the singularly most stupid thing he could do. There was nothing in his contract that said he had to go down with the ship. But somehow, he felt that his presence there was the only thing keeping the dam together, and that if he should leave the dam would surely fail. And he didn't want that to happen. More than anything, he did not want this dam to fail. The failure of this dam, he felt, would be his and his alone; it would be the ultimate failure, a failure he wouldn't be able to recover from. Not to mention the danger it posed to the people downstream, to the whole area, and possibly to Rachel and Deirdre, wherever the hell they were. No, it was clear: this dam could not fail.

He thought, then, of his canoe, lying upside down on the shore. If he paddled out to the offending log with a chain, he might be able to loop it around the log and then hook the other end to a winch on shore. And then maybe, maybe he'd be able to work it loose. It depended how tightly it was wedged. And how strong the current was. Most likely, the current would catch the canoe, and he and the boat would get swept under the dam. And that would be goodbye Joe. But at least he'd have done all he could. This was his job, right? This was the sort of thing he'd trained for. As long as there was a chance, he felt he had to try.

9

And out on the causeway of the Old Bend Dam, the river filmed: a sheen of water slickening the asphalt, then narrowing into a trickle, which snaked toward the lip of the dam.

10

Inside the cabin, Rachel knelt on the dry earth. Deirdre's wails were desperate now, in between her shuddering hiccupy breaths. Rachel unclasped the front pack, removed it, and then undid her bra and set Deirdre to her breast. Immediately, she quieted.

Rachel tentatively leaned her head back against the wood wall of the cabin, testing its sturdiness. Nothing shifted or creaked, so she scooted along the ground until her whole back was resting against the wall. She wondered whose cabin it was—a hunter's, maybe, or fisherman's? Some vagabond's temporary shelter? A group of local kids who'd built a hideaway? Rain pounded the ground. Once again a flash lit up the woods—she saw the rain percussing the leaf litter just outside the cabin door. An occasional drop splashed onto her leg, but mostly, they were warm and dry. Rachel put a grateful hand against the inner branch-built wall and stroked it a minute, as if petting a dog. Whoever built this, she thought, thanks.

She understood how it might happen. How overwhelmed and grief-stricken the young mother must have been at having lost her whole life, at seeing it vanish, being consumed by the new creature, the ravenous, insatiable being that would not stop, just *would not stop* devouring her. How tempting it must have been, when faced with the opportunity, to simply lay the baby by, to set it down, just for a moment, and then, once free, to chase after that freedom, to run toward it with all her might, like a moth dancing toward the light. How easy it would be to convince herself that she could just start over again, forget the mistake she'd made, pretend it never even happened. That she could go back to the way things were only a few short months before, to the person she'd been and the life she'd had before everything had changed so drastically, before everything had been lost. How easy it would be to run toward that beautiful, tantalizing lie.

Rachel looked at Deirdre, her small body cupped in the shallow bowl made by Rachel's crossed legs. Her little hand was warm in Rachel's own, her chest rising and falling in steady rhythm. Outside, another clap of thunder shook the woods, and all around the trees the rain fell harder, each drop making its little explosion on the leaf litter, the pine needles, the fern fronds, the mud. It was a warm night and a warm rain, and the interior of the cabin kept them warmer still, and dry. The ground was soft, the rain steady, accompanied by the steady soughing of Deirdre's breath. They were okay. They were dry and snug and warm and just profoundly okay.

What had she done? What, exactly, had she done? Just like that missing teenage mother, she'd run away, away from Michael, away from her soul-sucking PhD program, away from the incessant demands of her daily life—her new, mind-numbing, slow-motion mommy life. She'd run to Grand. And Grand and the Farm both, with their magical healing powers, had helped her. But Grand was dying, was halfway in another world already. And the Farm was no longer hers, had never been hers. And so she'd turned to Joe, as if he had just lain dormant all these intervening years, waiting for her. As if he hadn't grown, too, from both of their mistakes. As if he hadn't learned to make a good life without her.

You can't go back, he'd said. It was one of those things people said, those truisms that seemed so obvious when you were looking at someone else's life, but that were so painful when you experienced them from inside your own. She could not go back to the way things used to be. Grand was dying, the Farm was changing hands, both she and Joe were changed—by the war, by the loss of each other, by time. She had chosen a different man years ago, a good man, a steady, kind, thoughtful, intelligent man, who loved her. They'd had a child; she was a mother now. Life had narrowed, had grown more limited and specific, tinier and more intense. It was as if she'd squeezed herself into a tunnel and, *Alice in Wonderland* style, the entrance had knitted itself up behind her. She could only move forward through the tunnel, until she discovered—or maybe created—another exit.

Which, in turn, would become an entrance. If she could only look at it that way.

"Fuck you, universe," she said aloud. Her voice was small against the storm, but still firm and strong. "Fuck you if you think I'd leave my baby like that. You want to take this baby from me, you'll have to pry her from my cold, dead boobs."

Only the perpetual drumbeat of rain answered.

She thought of the flowage, how the water would surely be rising with this new storm, and how close the levels already were to full. But Joe would know what to do. She would sit here in this quiet cabin with Deirdre in her lap and pretend she was a mama rabbit in her den, waiting for daylight. She would sit here, holding her daughter, and breathe in the clean scent of rain and decomposing wood. She would sit here and not want for anything. She would sit here.

Deirdre squeaked a little and squirmed, and then squeaked again, so Rachel lifted her to her chest once more and stretched her legs, then set the front pack on the ground for a cushion, laid Deirdre on top of it, and finally curled herself around Deirdre. Deirdre adjusted easily to the new arrangement, taking Rachel's offered breast in her mouth and almost immediately falling back into a contented, suckling slumber. Rachel rested her head against her upper arm and stretched her top leg out, letting her body relax into the ground beneath her. The newness of the position gave her aching joints some relief, and she closed her eyes once more and drifted off, the scent of wet wood in her nostrils.

Some time later, she woke with a start to the wail of a siren.

11

In the kitchen, Diane rummaged in the medicine drawer. The green numbers on the microwave read 2:24 a.m. She found the Tylenol—a little white bottle with a red cap—put it on the countertop, and retrieved a glass from the cabinet. This was not a promising development, Maddy's fever. This was moving into new territory, closer to death. These were the signs: the fluctuating body temperature, the confusion, the agitation. It was coming. One week, probably two at the most. She would have to call Christopher and Linda in the morning, tell them to start making their plans.

She filled the glass with cool water from the tap and grabbed the bottle of Tylenol. Then, on second thought, opened the drawer again and pulled out a second bottle, this one a brown translucent prescription bottle with a white pop-top: Ativan, for use as needed. This would relieve Maddy's anxiety, help her sleep.

She made her way back through the darkened dining room and living room, her mind on the day ahead. She would have to bring up the subject of Maddy's will with the Claybornes herself. Rachel was obviously going to be no help. But Ramsay was right: they'd take the news better while Maddy was still alive. Maybe they could come to some agreement after she'd gone. She had to face the music. Tomorrow, tomorrow she'd get it figured out.

As she crossed the threshold into Maddy's room, a light flashed intermittently through the window, like a signal from a ship. She stared at it, momentarily confused: was it some kind of extended bolt of lightning, some weather phenomenon? And then she realized: headlights. Rachel, coming home.

"Here we are, hon," she said briskly. "Medicine time. This'll help you feel a whole lot better, let you sleep."

Maddy, who had released her bladder into the diaper she'd forgotten she was wearing, was staring intently out the window, her hands gripping and releasing the bedclothes. "There's a light out there. I see a light. Someone's out there." Her voice was high-pitched, quavering.

"Shh, Madeline. It's just your granddaughter Rachel, coming home. Remember? You were worried about her earlier tonight, before you went to sleep. And here she is. No more need to worry. Now sit back. That's it. Open your mouth, please. Wide. Here's your first pill." She placed the Ativan at the back of Maddy's tongue and handed her the glass of water. "Swallow it down, now. There's a good girl."

Maddy closed her eyes and gulped. The mention of Rachel seemed to snap open a shade in her mind. "Rachel," she said. "Of course." She let out a little delighted laugh.

"I'm glad you're happy at that news. All right, pill number two. Open wide."

"Send her in, would you please? I want to see her."

"She's probably beat, Madeline. It's the middle of the night, you know."

"Just for a moment. Just so I can kiss her good night."

"All right. I'll tell her. Open up now." And Maddy, happy and compliant now, swallowed the second pill.

Diane brought the mostly empty water glass and the pill bottles back to the dark kitchen and looked out the window. The car parked there was not Rachel's Prius. Rain glistened on its roof. The driver's seat was empty.

The back porch door wheezed open, and a man's heavy footsteps sounded on the floor. Diane, her heart beating wildly, grabbed a cleaver from the knife rack, and pressed herself up against the refrigerator. A moment later, the man—trim build, goatee, round wire glasses—appeared on the kitchen threshold.

"Oh, good God," Diane breathed, lowering the cleaver to the counter beside her. Her pulse thundered in her head. "You had me about ready to slice you open."

Michael jumped and grabbed the edge of the refrigerator. His eyes went to her face, then to the knife on the counter, and back to her face again. "Diane?" he said. "Oh, wow. I'm so sorry I startled you. I wasn't expecting anyone to be up." Behind his glasses, his eyes looked bleary, and he blinked them over and over again. He carried a backpack slung over one shoulder, and his sheepish, ragged look gave him the appearance of a college student trying to sneak in past the dorm curfew.

"Sorry to appear so late," he said again. "I don't usually do this sort of thing. Our conversation earlier got me worried, and I started thinking you were right, that I should just come up, and then suddenly I couldn't wait around anymore . . ."

"Well, it's all right. I was up anyway."

He nodded, glancing toward the door on the opposite side of the room, then at the cabinets, then the braided rug on the floor. He reminded Diane of a jumpy animal—a chipmunk or a squirrel, ready to scurry away at the least provocation. Not exactly the type to battle it out over his girl with another man.

"I figured I could crash in a different room tonight, just so I don't disturb Rachel or Deirdre. I can see them in the morning."

Diane gripped her lips into a thin line. She was going to have to put it to him straight. She slipped the knife back into its proper slot before turning back to Michael. "Listen, hon. I hate to have to tell you this, but Rachel's not back yet."

"She's not?"

Diane shook her head.

"Oh, Jesus. Have you called the police?"

"That would be an overreaction. I'm pretty sure she's spending the night at Joe's." And, grimly, she told him about the past week, about the renewed friendship between Joe and Rachel, the long hours they'd been spending together.

As she spoke, Michael kept blinking. With each blink, he seemed to be willing the conversation to end, willing her to stop talking, to stop saying such unbearable things. She kept it brief. When she'd finished, he nodded and then, weakly, said, "Okay. Well. It could be worse. I mean, Joe probably lives a ways away, too far to drive back and forth."

"It takes twenty minutes."

He nodded again.

"I'm sorry to break it to you like this. But I don't really see the point in beating around the bush."

Michael dropped his bag on the floor and released his weight into the counter behind him. He stared at the braided rug with such concentration that he appeared to be counting each of the strands. "Goddammit. I wish she'd just talk to her therapist," he said finally. "She can be so stubborn."

Diane bit her tongue.

He sniffed. "The hardest thing about this has been trying to see the depression for what it is. I mean, I know intellectually that it's not Rachel doing these things, it's this demon that's gotten hold of her. My brain knows that. But it doesn't feel that way. It still hurts."

"I'd be careful not to jump to conclusions. I mean, if you don't have a diagnosis—"

"Oh, it's obvious she's depressed. If you'd known her before . . ." He trailed off, evidently remembering that Diane *had* known her before, had known her, in fact, longer than Michael himself had.

"Well," she continued. "I'm sure it'll make all the difference, now that you're here. She'll snap out of it. Now, what you need is to get some sleep, and then in the morning, you'll be fresh in your mind, and able to face all of this."

He sighed. "I am pretty tired."

"You can pick any room. Rachel's been staying in the corner bedroom. The one with the crib. You could just take her bed if you like. It's already made."

He winced. "If you don't mind, I think I'll take a different room. In case she happens to come back tonight. I mean, I don't anticipate she will—" his eyes went to the green numbers on the microwave: 2:46 "—at this hour, and in this weather. But just in case. I wouldn't want to scare her."

"Whatever you say. It's none of my business. As long as you don't mind making the bed up yourself. The linens are in the dresser drawers."

"Of course."

Then, Maddy's voice came floating in through the screened-in back porch. "Diane? Where's Rachel?"

Michael turned and stepped back onto the porch, squinting into the darkness.

"That's Madeline," Diane offered, following him. "Her voice is coming through the open window." She pointed toward the office, where a dim light shone.

"I thought there was someone out there for a minute. I hope I didn't wake her up."

"Oh, no. She was up. We don't believe in sleep around here."

"Does she—" he swallowed, tried again "—did you tell her where Rachel was?"

"No. Just that she's not here. I didn't want to upset her."

"Rachel?" Maddy's voice keened through the screen again.

"Like I said, we thought your headlights might be Rachel coming home. So excuse me." She walked through the kitchen, then stopped at the opposite door and added, "Make yourself at home. You know the way upstairs."

She strode quickly over the dining room carpet, feeling as if she had to make her escape before she was sucked back into the vortex of Michael's anxiety. But his voice came from behind her. "Diane?"

She stopped, closed her eyes. She was so, so tired.

"Do you think I should go in with you to say hello? I mean, I know it's late, but—I don't want to be impolite."

She turned. He was standing hesitantly in the center of the dining room rug. "Sure," she said, feeling an internal ungripping, a letting go. "Whatever," she added, sounding, she was surprised to note, a little like Rachel.

At the threshold to Maddy's room, Diane stopped and said in a low voice, "Wait here a minute. Let me tell her you're here."

Michael took a step backward into the shadows.

Then, putting on her bright nurse-voice, Diane sailed into the room, saying, "Lord, Madeline, anyone would think it's high noon around here right now." She stood beside the bed, hands on her hips. "Guess what?"

"Where's Rachel? I thought you were going to send her in."

"As it turns out, hon, those lights belonged to Rachel's *husband's* car. Michael. He's just arrived."

"Michael? Who's Michael?"

"Rachel's husband. The baby's father." She stopped, took a breath, making an effort to regain her calm. It wasn't Maddy's fault, after all. None of this was her fault. When she spoke again, she pitched her voice in such a way as to make it seem as if this was all a jolly farce, knowing, even as she did, that Maddy was not likely to be fooled. "He drove all the way up here tonight! Can you believe it?"

"He's the one who doesn't like the Farm."

"He's right out in the hall, Maddy."

Maddy squinted toward the door. "I don't see anyone."

"Michael?" Diane called. "That's your cue."

Michael stepped into the doorway, his backpack slung over one shoulder. The balding college student. But he smiled graciously at Maddy, and when he spoke, his voice was kind and sincere. "Hello, Mrs. Clayborne. It's good to see you." He leaned over and brushed his lips across Maddy's cheek.

"Well," Maddy said, studying him. "Well, Michael. I'm afraid Rachel's not here right now."

"Yes, I know."

"We're a little concerned about her, to be perfectly honest."

"Yes. I am, too."

"You don't happen to know where she is, do you?"

Michael glanced at Diane. "No. No, I don't. I'm hoping I'll be able to find her in the morning."

"Yes," Diane cut in. "In the morning, it'll all get sorted out. But Michael's very tired now, Maddy. He drove—what? Five hours?"

"Six."

"Six hours to get here. And it's almost 3:00 a.m. So you can imagine, he probably wants to get some sleep."

"I'm so glad you've come, dear," Maddy said, as if Diane hadn't spoken at all. "It's been a long while since we've seen each other, hasn't it?"

"Yes, Mrs. Clayborne. Too long."

"I probably look a lot different to you now, don't I? All skin and bones."

Michael gave a nervous laugh. "Well," he said. "Time does things to a person."

"That it does," Diane said. "So, let's get you settled, Michael, and—"

But Maddy interrupted. "That is so true. And I will tell you: one of the great blessings of being my age, and in my current—" she hesitated, trying to think of the right word "—situation, is that there's no more wasting time. So much of life we spend waiting for the right time, it seems. But when you're my age, there's no other right time. The right time is always now, because you don't know, from minute to minute, whether there will be another now, whether you'll have another chance. Do you see? You simply can't afford to wait."

"I see," Michael said.

"You're a regular philosopher tonight, Maddy."

"Actually," Maddy continued, "I think this is the way everyone ought to live all the time. I mean, none of us know when our last day is going to be, do we? And yet, when we're young like you, dear, and like Rachel, we live as if we're immortal. We make plans, we imagine futures for ourselves. The possibility of an end to all that simply doesn't intrude. And so we put things off. I know—I did it myself. I suppose it's as it should be. I mean, we can't always live under a cloud of doom. Life is meant to be enjoyed."

"Maddy—" Diane tried.

"It's awful, you know, when you're like me. Things, words, ideas—they all keep slipping away. It's like trying to grab hold of a wet fish with your bare hands."

"Yes, well—"

"I know!" she shouted, hitting the bed with the flat of her hand. "I remember now. Tell me—" and here she gestured toward Michael with a shaky hand, as if trying to pull his name out of the air, to no avail, "Tell me, young man: what is it you don't like about the Farm?" The question finally out, she closed her eyes, satisfied.

"Uh—it's not that I don't like the Farm," Michael began, glancing over at Diane once again, as if for support.

"Hon, Michael never said that."

"But you've made a point of not coming all these years. And I've never understood why."

Michael looked yet again at Diane, who stared back at him and shrugged. This one was all his.

"I don't want to offend you, Maddy," he began.

"You can't offend me. I'm too old."

"Nor do I want to lecture you."

"Bosh."

He laughed uncertainly. "For me it comes down to the keeping of a promise. Years ago, the federal government promised this land to the Name River Ojibwe Tribe when they delineated the boundaries of the reservation. Then they went back on their word, through an act of Congress that was supposed to benefit Native people, but that in reality ended up robbing them of over half of their land, nationwide. I believe they should have kept their promise, that's all. And that in cases where it's in our power to restore that promise, we should." He smiled kindly at Maddy, as if that simple statement of a complicated subject might be an end to it.

But Maddy was furrowing her brow in studious thought. "Yes," she began. "I understand that. That's all very honorable and just. But what I don't understand, dear, is how your beliefs should have kept Rachel from something she loves so very much." She shook her head disapprovingly. "To keep a person from what they love . . . it's like keeping them from themselves."

Maddy's words seemed to diffuse the room with a subtle light, like the night sky going from black to a pre-dawn gray.

"Please don't misunderstand me, Maddy. I think the Farm is a beautiful place, a place your family has cared for very well over the years."

"So you *do* like it?"

"Yes. Sure. I like it."

"Wonderful! Well then, that's settled!"

"What's settled, hon?" Diane asked.

"You told me Michael didn't like the Farm, but he's just said that he does!"

"That's not what I told you, Maddy. But you know what? Never mind. It's all right. He likes the Farm. We all like the Farm. And now it's time to go to sleep." Diane straightened Maddy's covers, pulling them up to her chin, as if she might be able to force her to sleep by trapping her in her own bedspread.

"Yes," Michael said, with apparent relief. "All right. Well, goodnight, Mrs. Clayborne. I'll look forward to seeing you in the morning."

"One more thing, Michael, if you please. Diane, dear, could you please leave us alone a minute? I have something I'd like to ask Michael in private."

Diane's breath caught in her throat. She exchanged a look with Michael, whose eyes were pleading with her to do something or say something to get him out of this situation. And suddenly, finally, she didn't care. All her care and fear and clinging lifted away. She was too tired to care. She didn't care about Maddy getting enough sleep—soon enough, she'd be eternally asleep; why not stay up all she wanted now?—she didn't care about Joe getting involved with Rachel, and she didn't care—at last!—she had stopped caring about the Farm. It was as if an enormous bird that had been nesting on her breast, in the enclosure of her ribcage, had suddenly taken flight. "All right," she said, filled with reckless glee. "I give up. I'm going up to bed. Michael, please turn out the light when you two are finished. Good night!"

"Good night, dear."

"Wait, Diane—" Michael followed her into the hall. "One more thing, just making sure—Joe's place isn't on the floodplain, is it?"

"What?"

"There was a notice on the radio just now, as I pulled up. They're evacuating the floodplain below the dam. I just want to be sure they're not in danger—"

But Diane was at the closet, shoving her feet into a pair of rubber rain boots, shrugging on a yellow raincoat. She grabbed an oversized purse from its spot on the table by the closet door.

"Diane?"

She turned to him, her face gripped and gray. "I need you to stay here with Maddy. I just gave her some meds, so in a few minutes she should be out for the rest of the night. If you need anything, you can call hospice. The number's by the phone." And she strode down the hall toward the kitchen.

"Where are you going?" Michael asked, chasing her.

But the only answer he received was the final bang of the screen door after it wheezed shut, and the wet shushing of her boots against the grass.

12

The sirens served as a compass for Rachel, who followed their sound through the dark woods until she found the trail that hugged the lake. She ran faster, slipping here and there on the mud. Deirdre wailed in tandem with the siren, the rain stung their faces. The hulking shape of the yurt appeared, and Rachel called Joe's name as they neared it, hoping he might run out to meet her. She looked inside, knowing he wouldn't be there, and when her doubts were confirmed, she resumed her ragged pace along the path toward the dam, now following the beacon of the security light. The lake was frighteningly high.

She stepped to the edge of the causeway and scanned the road under the security light for any sign of Joe. Her breath caught in her throat: there, under the light, a stream of water was gushing over the lip of the dam.

A bark startled her and she turned to see Sally, rigid at the lakeside shore, her head raised to the sky. Then, just beyond Sally, something moved, a dark figure in the shadows. She took a few steps toward the dog, squinting. "Joe?!" she called, her voice weak under the crashing water and the rain.

The shadowy figure grew taller, running toward her, and she saw that it was Joe in a wetsuit, slick as an otter. Behind him, she glimpsed a flash of aluminum: his canoe, halfway into the water.

He rushed at her, taking her forcefully by the shoulders. "Where were you?! Jesus! I looked everywhere!" He was yelling, but his voice was still faint beneath the sirens, the rain, and the rushing water. "You've got to get out of here! Up to higher ground! The dam is about to go!"

"What are you doing?!"

"There's a log jamming one of the gates! Go on now, Rachel! Get up the hill!"

"You're not going into that water! You'll get sucked under!"

"Don't worry about me! Worry about Deirdre! You need to get her to safety! Go on!"

She backed toward the parking lot, her heart pounding in her ears, then stopped. "I won't let you, Joe! It's suicide!"

"I trained for this kind of thing in the Marines, Rachel! I know what I'm doing!"

"You told me just today that anyone who approaches the gates can get sucked under! Rule number one, remember?!" She was yelling at the top of her lungs, her face streaming with rain. She moved forward again, grabbed his arm and held. "I won't let you!"

He shook her off and pushed her away, up the shore toward the car. "Rachel! Goddammit! You don't get it! This is what I'm here for! It's either this, or the dam goes! Now get the fuck up the road and let me do my job!"

And then, beneath the still-wailing sirens, another sound came: a rapid crashing, as if a big animal—a bear or moose, or even a herd of moose—was lumbering through the woods in their direction. Joe looked toward the dam, then, in one swift motion, lifted Rachel—who held tight to Deirdre—in his arms and half-ran, half-stumbled up the bank to the road, then partway up the hill, until his strength gave out. Sal kept pace with them. He dropped Rachel onto the road and fell forward on top of her, blocking his fall with his hands. They both turned toward the sound.

Beneath the security light, the causeway had split, giving way to a channel, which was funneling through its center a new river—or, really, an old, old river, newly freed, glimmering here and there as if studded with indefinite dark jewels. This new river splattered against the rockfill below the dam, but the fill, already sodden by the weeks of incessant rain, could not absorb the new influx of water. The top layer of grass peeled away to reveal the black mud beneath, and soon the channel poured into the embankment, funneling the water down the slope. The water in this new streambed collected into itself the grains of sand and dirt, the chunks of grassy earth, so that it grew cloudy and silty as it flowed, moving alongside the splash wall, in tandem with the still-greater flow of water that crashed through the dam gates. The new river boiled darkly through the grass until it joined its mate, that other river, below the spillway. The new river brought with it the clods of earth and grass that had come loose beneath its force, clouds of roiling pebbles, as well as a few chunks of concrete that had melted away from the lip of the causeway—but it also brought with it the memory of what it had once been and the desire, paired with that memory, to be that thing again, that wild, creative force that had gushed freely through these woods for centuries, swelling and roaring with the spring thaw, consuming trees when it was hungry for them, cutting new paths in the earth when it wanted, and then slowing to a majestic flow in the summer months, regally bearing itself downstream, continually renewing its own identity as it gathered and accepted all flows: rain, snowmelt, animal urine, creek-water, tears, liquefied remains. The river flowed now as if it remembered its path: through woods, beside fields, over shallows and sandbars, it had coursed southward and westward, as forest transformed to prairie and prairie back to forest, until at last it would barrel into the mighty Mississippi, merging with the storied current there, dying, in effect, to be reborn as something greater than itself, to be an element of the greater current that flowed ever southward, and which would, in turn, willingly suicide in its inevitable plunge into the far greater, far vaster body of the Gulf of Mexico. Yes, this new—or old, old river—remembered all this, and remembering it, flowed with greater and wilder enthusiasm over the dam.

From high up on the access road, Joe and Rachel and Deirdre and Sal watched as the new river surged forward, carrying along an upright pine ripped from its roots, and sending up a new, swelling smell: wet and earthy and rank, like the woods when they woke from winter, except stronger and charged, electric. The water raged forth with a mythical roar, a voice from the age of giants and gods, a voice that shook their bones and teeth, that sent their brains buzzing with the voltage of a thousand rivers surging down a thousand mountainsides.

On it rushed, bearing down upon the land, crashing and seething and raging, while they clung to each other, four sorry animals amid the darkness and the water and the shadows of debris bobbing and tumbling in the current, the apocalyptic woods. It was as if all the trees around them had morphed into risen ghosts, as if all the long-buried graves up and down the river had opened and sent forth their residents, as if they had all merged into this new monster, this dark-jeweled leviathan of a river, which had been asleep these many years, drugged into quietude, and just now was beginning to awaken, to come alive.

BOOK FIVE

Restoration

June 2003

1

Back at the farm, Michael was feeling a little out of his mind. After Diane had stormed out—he'd gathered that Joe's place *was* on the floodplain—he'd listened to Maddy prattle on about Rachel and her love for the Farm. Then abruptly, she'd fallen dead asleep. He'd paced the living room, reflexively dialing Rachel's cell before he remembered she'd left it behind. He dialed the Clinton hospital and asked whether a Rachel Clayborne, Deirdre German, or even Joseph Bishop had been admitted. Negative. Finally, unable to do anything else, Michael trudged upstairs and lay on top of the covers, too bone-tired to make up the bed. But his brain could not rest. Even if Rachel was safe, their marriage wasn't. Their marriage was broken, in need of fixing. She'd spent the night with another man.

The only image he could call up of Joe was from a picture he'd seen in one of Rachel's parents' albums, and even then the kid had been barely visible, his face turned away from the lens as he ran to catch a ball. Michael had no concept of what he looked like as an adult—no image on which to hang his sadness and anger and hurt. And in the midst of the storm and his bleary state of mind, he imagined Rachel had somehow crawled through a portal into the past, back into the grainy, faded photos of her own childhood.

Michael fluffed the pillows, arranging them in a tower that collapsed as soon as he laid his head on it. He'd forgotten how soft these beds were, how he'd always had trouble sleeping up here. His limbs seemed to disappear into the insubstantial cottony nothingness of the mattress.

He decided to try the floor. He threw the pillows onto the dusty carpet, then stripped the covers off and carried them with him, arranging himself in a yogic corpse pose, his head supported with a single folded pillow.

He closed his eyes, breathed slowly and deeply, trying to quell his buzzing thoughts . . .

There came a blinding flash and then, a moment later, a deafening, heart-stopping *crack*, like a gunshot at close range. Michael rushed to the window, but the night was too dark to see anything clearly. Still, there was motion out there, and then another strange sound—this one a thud heavy enough to shake the house. Something falling to the ground.

Michael was not a believer in the supernatural. He had long ago dismissed the stories he'd grown up with in his Catholic upbringing—the apparitions of the Virgin in peanut butter sandwiches and in the post-shower steam on a bathroom mirror, the saints who helped a person recover lost things or who could communicate with animals, and, above all, stories of people who came back from the dead—but he still possessed a kind of residual lapsed-Catholic awe of such stories, and a partial admiration for people who still believed in them. He brought this attitude to his research, and it fueled his general awe for indigenous spirituality, and so what he thought of as he sat in the silent dark and watched this storm blowing outside was the story of the thunderbird. In Ojibwe culture, a thunderbird was one of the most powerful supernatural beings you could find. Thunderbirds were servants of the earth, keeping her clean and well-watered, giving her drink when she was thirsty. They lived in the mountains, and, in general, didn't care about human affairs. But if a person entered their domain, they became furious and violent; more often than not, that person would never return. Eagles were said to be relatives of the thunderbirds—or perhaps *were* thunderbirds themselves.

As the storm raged and the thunder rolled tympanically, Michael shook out the folds of an afghan draped over the foot of the bed and wrapped it around his shoulders. He paced. Outside, the rain fell hard and fast. Tree branches bent and whipped to and fro, and the thunder cracked with what seemed like a pointed insistence, as if it bore a message that Michael was intended and yet unequipped to hear. He thought of the thunderbirds and then of the eagles' nest in the big tree out back, and it occurred to him that maybe their presence—the Claybornes' presence and now his—here on the Farm, so close to their nest, had angered them. Maybe they were stirring up this storm as punishment. Maybe they were seeking to destroy him, to destroy all of them.

A well-buried part of him, a voice that surfaced only in his most fearful and desperate moments, whispered that maybe that was just what was needed. Destruction.

He pushed the voice away, pulled the afghan tighter around his shoulders, and set about trying to talk himself out of his irrational fear. Among the many valuable lessons that science taught, he told himself, was the eminently reasonable assumption that meteorological events were not affected by the desires of earth-bound creatures, eagles included. No matter how hurt and angry and completely *rocked* he might be feeling right now, no matter how much he wished he were the sort of man who packed a gun and had no compunction about waving it in the direction of other men who threatened his family, no matter how much he might feel a longing for divine retribution, the rational side of his brain knew that neither human beings nor animals had the power to call down destruction from the skies. He told himself that there was myth and there was reality, and that myth—while it had its purpose—was not a reliable indicator of what was actually going on in reality, and that when one was afraid or angry or in danger, it was better to rely on the sober, rational, precise calculations of reality, rather than to get sucked into the emotional world of stories. He reminded himself that though there weren't any eagle nests nearby at home, storms happened all the time, and that usually, he took no notice of them—unless they interrupted the power, in which case he would wait them out impatiently, lodging a call with the power company and keeping his fingers crossed that he hadn't lost any work on the computer. And these rational thoughts did help, they did calm him a bit. But still, the undercurrent of emotion pulled at his reasoning mind, and he found himself whispering a little prayer that the rain would stop and the storm would die down. That Joe would suffer some minor, non-life-threatening blow, preferably to the pelvic area. That Rachel and Deirdre would return to the Farm safe and in one piece. And glad to see him.

Michael's thoughts turned to the summer he'd first come up to the Farm, the summer they'd been married. He'd stayed in the little guesthouse—a tiny one-bedroom plumbing-free cabin on a bluff above the lake. A trim little thing, with flower boxes in the windowsills and cheerful green shutters. He'd stayed there alone until the day of their wedding. Rachel's parents were old-fashioned that way, insisting that the two of them sleep separately, even though they knew Rachel and Michael shared a bedroom in Cambridge.

They believed in keeping up appearances. So the guesthouse had earned the nickname "the stud pen." Rachel's brother Derek came up with the nickname, but everyone had taken it up, making joke after joke about it—*They let you out this morning, stud?* they'd say, or if Michael would approach Rachel to give her a chaste good morning kiss on the top of the head, they'd yell *warning, warning! The stud's on the loose! Call in the horse wrasslers!*

The jokes got old, but Michael didn't mind staying in the guesthouse. The interior consisted of a single room with a double bed, a dresser, a desk and a chamber pot, for middle of the night emergencies. It was cozy and peaceful and cool. The wind came up off the lake and blew through the windows, and as he lay in bed at night, he could hear the lake lapping at the shore. He remembered lying there the night before the wedding, listening to the sound of the lake on the stony shore below, thinking about how satisfied he was with how his life was proceeding, how things were really going pretty much according to plan: the PhD was almost finished, he'd landed himself a smart and attractive wife-to-be, and he'd already had some early nibbles from a couple different history departments who'd heard about the fellowship he'd won the previous year, and made it known that they were interested. And soon he'd be married and then, after that, when he'd gotten that first job, and when Rachel was ready of course, they'd have their first child. Life was good; all was as it should be. He'd been looking up at the bare unfinished ceiling, congratulating himself on his own good planning and decision-making, when he'd become aware of something hanging from one of the ceiling beams. A brown cocoon-like thing, except bigger than a cocoon. And, incredibly, as he watched, the thing unfolded itself and dropped, plummeting toward the floor before its wings caught the air. A bat. Michael let out a yelp and pulled the bedcovers over his head, his heart drumming in his chest. When he peeked out from under the covers, he saw that the bat was circling the light fixture, flying around and around, looking, presumably, for a way out. Michael leapt from the bed, dashed to the door, and ran outside in nothing but his briefs. There he stood, shivering in the night chill, while he waited for the bat to escape through the open door.

Then, to his horror, a voice called to him from the house. "Everything all right?" It was Maddy, sitting on the back porch, her little reading light burning through the dark.

Michael, pretending he wasn't mortally humiliated, explained the situation, and she went inside and then emerged with an old wooden tennis racquet, the head warped with age. "I keep this old thing around just for this purpose," she told him. "Only don't tell Rachel. She hates it when I do this. But it just stuns them, and then you can pick them up and put them outside." She'd followed him out to the guesthouse, armed and ready, but thankfully, by that point, the bat was gone. Michael sheepishly thanked her, and she gave him the racquet for the night, just in case. He'd slept with it, his hand wrapped around the grip.

The next morning, as he tramped blearily across the wet grass toward the house, he was greeted with Derek's booming voice, "Here he comes, the Batman himself!" and there'd been a general roar of laughter from the kitchen.

He'd learned, that visit, of how brutally Rachel's family teased each other, even to the point of humiliation. For Michael, who'd grown up the only child of two book-ensconced academics, this was physically painful, something he didn't understand and couldn't pick up on, no matter how hard he tried. There was an art to it, that much he could see, and Derek was pretty much the master of the form, though Rachel wasn't any slouch herself. But Michael was hopeless. Nor did he really care to learn. To him, their teasing seemed mean, occasionally vicious. But when he brought it up to Rachel, she waved it off. "Don't let it get to you," she said. "They don't mean any harm." As the years went by, this refrain had become stronger and more dismissive, more along the lines of, "Don't take yourself so goddamn seriously." And this, of course, was the message behind the teasing: Rachel, her brother, her father and—maybe to a lesser degree—her mother, even her unfailingly gracious grandmother, all believed fervently that to take oneself seriously was one of the more foolish and unforgivable things a person could do, despite the fact that each of them took themselves seriously enough to pursue worldly success in its various aspects: politics (Jacob), society (Maddy), public interest law (Christopher), corporate law (Derek), education (Lily, Rachel's mother), business consulting (Linda), medicine (Linda's husband), religious scholarship (Rachel's cousin Zachary), and of course, academia (Rachel). Her family was nothing if not a catalog of successes, accomplished by people who were deadly serious about themselves and each other. And yet to let on to that publicly was to open oneself up to humiliation. This Michael had learned the hard way, and it was one of the reasons—truth be told—that he hated the Farm. The moral issue, the land tenure issue was there, yes, and this was the reason he'd given Rachel, but he might not have gone to the trouble of researching the original boundaries of the reservation if he hadn't felt the way he did about her family when they were up here together. There was something about the Farm that brought out the worst in them, he felt—the tennis games were ultra competitive, the political discussions at the dinner table barbed and unrelenting, the banter cruel. It's as if they were all trying to outdo one another, while simultaneously pretending it was all a big joke, and if you couldn't take it, well, that was your problem.

That, and the fact that her first love belonged to this place—the boy she'd lost her virginity to, the man she might have ended up with if it hadn't been for the war, and (weirdly) Brian Speckel and the NRCM, and "real life," as Rachel had called it all those years ago, when he admitted to her his persistent insecurities about Joe. At the time, she'd insisted that her love for Joe had been teenage love, puppy love, I-want-to-have-sex-a-lot love, not the real, lasting, reliable kind of love she had for Michael.

Well. That was obviously a big old soup tureen of bullshit she'd ladled out for him.

Michael gave a weighty sigh, feeling as if his insides were being carved out with the dull edge of a spoon. Then he heard a strange sound that seemed to come through the floor. It was a kind of garbled gurgle, like words being spoken underwater, and then a heavy sickening thud. He froze, listening for more, for another clue that might indicate that what he'd heard was not what he feared it might be. Maddy's room, he knew, was just below him. But there was only silence now, silence inside and the quieting—finally!—the quieting storm outside.

He went downstairs, passing through the miniature library with its sagging leatherette sofa, its graceful writing desk and beautiful bay window that opened onto the surrounding woods and the impressive pines—and then he cracked the door to the old office, just barely, just to check if Maddy was all right. Maybe the sound had been something falling off a shelf. Maybe that was all.

He saw an empty hospital bed, the covers pulled back to reveal the bottom sheet. On the floor by the bed was a pile of discarded clothing, a rich green satin. He looked again, and only then did the picture come into complete focus: the cottony cloud of hair at one end, the leg twisted underneath, the arm outstretched toward the bed, the upturned hand. He rushed in and knelt beside Maddy's crumpled form, wondering in a panicked paralysis what to do, what to do. Should he lift her back onto the bed? But what if she'd broken her leg?—it certainly looked horribly wrong, the way it was lying beneath her. But how could she have broken her leg? She'd been fast asleep. And if he tried to move her, would he just make things worse? And was she breathing? Her face was turned toward the carpet. He was hesitant to move her at all, as if Maddy's body was a crime scene, and any adjustment by him might be construed as tainting the evidence. Finally he put a tentative two fingers on the transparent skin at her wrist and held his own breath: her pulse was there, faint, weak, but there.

He looked frantically around the room until his eyes fell on the telephone hanging on the wall. It was an old-fashioned rotary phone. He wondered if it still worked. He picked up the receiver and, to his relief, heard a dial tone. He dialed 911.

2

"But Sam, for God's sake. I'm his *mother*," Diane said, for the third time, to the jowly tribal cop who had pulled her over. He stood at her door in his browns, the rain collecting in the brim of his hat. Blue and white lights flashed in her rearview mirror.

"Sorry, Diane," he drawled. "It's too dangerous. This whole area is under an evacuation order. No exceptions." He dropped his head in a show of sympathy and sent a rivulet of rainwater cascading to the ground.

Diane pressed her forehead against the steering wheel. She was almost there. A little ways on, and she'd be at the access road. If she'd just driven a little faster, she could have disappeared down the road and goddamn Sam would never have intercepted her.

"Hey!" he yelled. Diane raised her head to see him jogging toward a silver Prius that had just pulled out from the access road. She jumped out of her own car, following Sam. The Prius stopped on the opposite side of the road. The window opened, unleashing a stream of infant wails.

"What are you doing out here? Don't you know there's an evacuation order?" Sam asked, panting, putting one hand on the roof of the car for support.

"Diane!" Rachel said, looking past him. "What are you—?"

"Where's Joe?" Diane scanned the car.

"He's all right. Don't worry. He's down there, keeping an eye on the water. The dam broke. But he's okay. Hey—!"

Diane was off, running down the access road, her feet gaining momentum as she hit the downward slope, her legs pumping air. The cop ran after her, his hat flying off his head, the rain coming wet on his bald scalp. Rachel craned her neck from the car to watch.

The cop's belly was big, which hampered his speed, and Diane might have made it if her heel hadn't caught in the mud. But it did, and she fell, hard, to the ground, knee twisting beneath her. Sam was on top of her immediately, grabbing her wrist with one hand. With the other, he reached behind him and slung out a pair of handcuffs.

Rachel, seeing her chance while the cop was busy with the cuffs, took off down the road as Diane had. She was faster and more nimble, and Sam, struggling with Diane, didn't notice until she was halfway down the access road, and by then, she was yelling for Joe to come quick, that his mother was in trouble, and then Joe was running uphill, his strong legs pushing the ground away, Sal, as always, not far behind. He passed Rachel and reached Diane, who was lying on the muddy road, weeping, her wrists bound together in the metal Sam had finally clicked in place. Sam stood over her, looking doubtfully triumphant, as if realizing he'd won a minor battle in a losing war.

"Ma, Ma, it's okay. Everything's all right, Ma." Joe knelt beside her and pressed her head against his chest, stroking her wet hair. "I'm all right," he repeated tenderly.

She wept so hard and fast, burying her face in Joe's chest, smelling his good Joe-smell: sweat and wood-smoke and fresh air. Calmed, finally, she looked up at him, into his precious scar-marred face. He was wearing his wetsuit. "Joe, honey. Please don't tell me you were diving in this weather."

Joe kissed her on the top of her head. "Can you get these things off of her now, Sam? Please?"

"She ran past me, Joe," Sam spluttered, as he bent once more to the cuffs, his key in hand. "I didn't have a choice but to restrain her. She wouldn't listen."

"Sounds about right," Joe quipped. Then, helping Diane to her feet, he said, "You can thank Rachel for my life, Ma. She kept me from going in. I would have been a goner if it wasn't for her."

"So you're not angry with me?" Rachel asked.

"I didn't say that," Joe replied. But his eyes were soft and forgiving.

Diane hugged Joe around the waist and looked to Rachel, her eyes glistening. "I don't think I even want to know what went on down there. But thank you, hon. For whatever you did."

"We saved each other," Rachel replied.

"Come on, Ma. Let's get you in the car." With his arm around her shoulders, Joe guided Diane, who leaned into him, limping. Sam and Rachel followed.

"Jesus, Sam," Joe scolded. "You really did a number on her."

"I'm sorry, Joe. I was just trying to keep her safe. You know what the evacuation order says."

"What's the status on that? Did everyone get out?"

"Everyone's out," Sam answered. "Or I thought they were, till these two came along. But yeah, we're good. You hit it right on time, big guy. No lives lost."

"That's good to hear."

"All right, I do want to know," Diane said. "What on earth happened?"

"Let's get you to a dry place, Ma. I'll tell you all about it." He opened the passenger door of her car and climbed in, water streaming down her neck. The seat was almost soaked before she even sat down.

Rachel stood aside, watching Diane ease herself into the car. Deirdre's wails still sounded from inside the Prius.

"You'd better help that baby, Rachel," Joe said as he strode around to the driver's side. "Sounds like she's about to cry her guts out."

"Oh," Diane leaned over to speak to Rachel through the driver's side window. "I almost forgot. Your husband's here, Rachel."

Rachel looked around, as if she expected to see Michael emerge from the woods.

"Not here here. I mean at the Farm. He's with Maddy."

Rachel and Joe exchanged a look, and then they each climbed into their respective cars and drove in opposite directions, away from the Old Bend Dam, leaving Sam scribbling in his log in the cruiser, blue and white lights flashing in the pre-dawn darkness.

3

When Rachel turned onto the lane that led to the Farm, the first sign of dawn was bleeding at the edges of the dark, casting everything in a ghostly gray light. Deirdre had fallen asleep on the way, and so it was in a dread-filled silence that she drove up the road toward the barn. She had no idea what was coming, how Michael would react, what she would say, what the end result would be—what she even wanted it to be. All she could do was step into the next moment and greet whatever it revealed.

As she eased the car around the barn, she saw a strange light flashing into the morning dim. An ambulance was parked at the flagpole.

She parked the Prius behind the unfamiliar red Hyundai beside the house, and ran to the open ambulance. It was empty, but a moment later, the screen door slammed, and out came two EMTs carrying a stretcher, a blanketed, unconscious Grand lying on it. Michael rushed on their heels, but stopped when he saw Rachel.

"You're back!" he announced.

She could only stare. He looked different somehow. Smaller, maybe, as if he'd lost weight.

"Maddy fell," he explained, his hands fluttering toward the stretcher. "I found her on the floor. They came quickly. Are you all right? Where's Deirdre?" He looked toward the car.

"She didn't want an ambulance, Michael," Rachel got out. "You called an ambulance. She said no more ambulances. No more hospitals." She turned to the EMT, who was sliding the stretcher into the rear. "She explicitly told us not to call the ambulance," Rachel tried. "Can't you just bring her back inside? Forget we called?"

"No, Ma'am. Sorry. Once the call is placed, we have to follow through." The stretcher clicked into place on its track.

Michael's eyes got wide. "I didn't know! She was on the floor. I found her on the floor, unconscious. No one was here. I didn't know what else to do."

She heard the blame in his words: *no one was here. You were gone. I was the responsible one.*

"What should I have done, Rachel?" Michael continued. "I did what I thought should be done."

She paused, hearing his defensiveness, noticing her own. "I know you did, Michael. It's not your fault. You did the best you could."

Then to the EMT, she said, "Wait. I want to ride with her. I'm her granddaughter."

He stepped aside to let Rachel climb in.

"Listen, Rachel," Michael said to her back, "I know where you were last night." His voice cracked.

"Diane told you?" She turned to look him in the eye.

He nodded, and she could see from his silence and the fierce look in his eyes how he was struggling to control his emotions.

Another pause. "I'm sorry you had to hear it from her, Michael. I would have told you myself. I'm sorry."

"Folks," said the EMT.

"We'll talk when I get back, okay? Just, please, stay with Deirdre."

And Michael backed away as the door closed between them.

4

The ambulance sped down the lane, sirens blaring, lights flashing. Inside, Maddy lay still on the gurney, Rachel beside her, stroking her hand and whispering. But Maddy couldn't hear, didn't feel. She was deep in the inner rooms of her mind, where a little house appeared, a little house on a hill overlooking a lake. The house was hidden away in the woods, half-covered in leaves and sticks, and it was old, she could tell, even at her age—for she was young, now, a little girl. It came only to her waist and was made of wood, with a sloping roof, and just beneath the peak of the roof was a little window through which Maddy, kneeling down and peering in, could see, lying on the ground, a pair of tiny moccasins, dirty and half-chewed by mice. There was some kind of sadness about the house, some special mood it seemed to give off, which drew Maddy close. With her child's hand, she pulled the moccasins out through the window one by one and brushed them off. They were soft and yellow and beaded on the top. One by one, she pulled them on her bare feet, wiggling her toes against the soft, pliable leather. They squeezed her feet, and one pinky toe stuck out of a hole, but she loved them. She pranced through the woods to the farmhouse, which still smelled of fresh-cut boards and paint, rising like an unnatural island beneath the pines. Standing there, at the edge of the woods, she called for her older sister Jennie, who was some yards away, neck-deep in raspberry canes.

And Jennie came, her cheeks flushed with the heat, a bucket half-full of berries tied around her waist, and when she saw the moccasins she exclaimed in delight. And Maddy, proud to have something to show her older sister, took Jennie by the hand and brought her to the little house. Jennie declared it to be their prayer place. She ran back to the farmhouse and returned with their middle sister Dorothea, a packet of larkspur seeds, and a bible. And the girls planted larkspur seeds in a circle around the little house and then sat and listened to Jennie read aloud passages of the ceremonious and incomprehensible words, and then, at Jennie's instruction, they all three bowed their heads and prayed. And Maddy, who was too young to know doubt or to be interested in prayer, closed her eyes and witnessed the ecstasies of light that spattered themselves across her eyelids. And when they had finished with their ritual, and said goodbye to the little house, and had made their way back to the farmhouse to their mother, Maddy displayed the moccasins, turning her feet this way and that, and her mother looked with astonishment at the feet of her littlest girl, clad in the soft leather of the dead.

5

The EMTs told Rachel to wait in the waiting room while they rushed Grand in through the double doors. Rachel sat on the edge of one of the orange plastic seats. Slumped in the corner opposite her was a fat woman with thinning sandy hair in a dingy green overcoat, picking at something in her hands—or maybe *at* her hands, Rachel couldn't be sure. Across from her, a cowboy and his lady—the man wore a ten-gallon hat and actual spurs on his black boots; the woman a leather vest and Farah Fawcett-style feathered hair—sat together. The cowgirl held her wrist gingerly with the other and wept softly while the man looked straight ahead, at nothing at all. Down the aisle from Rachel a twenty-something kid sat on the edge of his seat, bouncing his knee up and down so hard it rocked the row of chairs back and forth. He held a bandage to his side with a splayed palm. Beneath his fingers, the gauze was bright red and tacky-looking. Rachel looked away.

A TV screen hung from the ceiling, broadcasting the news with the sound turned way down. An anchorman stood in front of a strange, moon-like landscape—a flat stretch of rilled sand, strewn all over with debris: up-rooted trees, massive branches, slabs of rock sticking up from the sand at strange angles. As she watched, straining to hear, Rachel realized that the anchorman was standing right near the spot where she'd parked just yesterday, a few feet down the road from where she and Joe had watched the dam breach. Then the camera panned to the right, and she drew in a sharp breath. There were the remnants of the dam. The buildings were completely gone, as was the splashwall and the stairs they'd walked down just the day before—all of it vanished. What she saw now was a road to nowhere—a length of asphalt that dropped away into nothingness, into a hill of mud, a canyon wall of silt and scree.

The camera panned down, focusing in on the river that ran at the bottom of that canyon. River was almost too strong a word: it looked more like a healthy creek, a gentle, benign-looking run of water meandering innocently through the crevasse. You would never guess that this modest stream had supplied the monstrous current that had caused the break. The camera then followed the anchorman a little ways along the shore—or what had once been the shore—to take in the emptied reservoir. The lake was gone. In its place was a wide sandscape scattered with driftwood, incongruous boulders, washed-out strips of plastic and cardboard and other unidentifiable trash, and several fish carcasses, all of it strewn across the desert-like floodplain. And through the center of this apocalyptic terrain coursed the river, the old Name River, blithely wending its way downstream.

The camera didn't take in Old Bend Island, but Rachel could imagine what it might look like now: a smooth hill of silt rising above the floodplain, topped by a toupee of green. And those greened-over ruts, untouched by the floodwaters: the old story still present, still living amid the new.

Someone called her name and she turned toward the double doors to see a young blond woman in blue scrubs. Rachel went to her.

"Hi, I'm Dr. Stevenson. I understand you're Mrs. Clayborne's granddaughter." Rachel nodded and followed the woman through the doors. The woman spoke in a softer voice now. "I'm sorry to have to tell you this, Rachel, but your grandmother has passed."

Rachel swallowed, cleared her throat, swallowed again.

"We did all we could," the doctor continued.

"It's okay," Rachel said, feeling, absurdly, like it was necessary to comfort this doctor, who knew nothing of Grand at all. "She didn't want—" she stopped herself. "She was ready to go."

The doctor nodded, visibly relieved.

They moved quickly through the hallways, passing dark rooms with hulking machines, nurses whizzing patients on gurneys, abandoned IV racks, the whole place humming and beeping, a vast amalgam of mechanical parts. Suddenly, the doctor stopped before a blue curtain and whisked it back, with a sharp *ching* of metal. There, lying on the gurney, was a body that would fit a description of Grand—the same cloud of hair, the same twiggy arms and bagging soft skin. It was clearly *not* Grand. Grand was gone.

"I'll leave you alone for a few minutes to say your goodbyes," Dr. Stevenson said. And she pulled the blue curtain closed again, the metal rings once again singing against the metal bar. Rachel stood apart, gazing at the wax replica of her grandmother. Her still, still body. Her mouth was half-open, the lips—dry and cracking—pulled grotesquely back from the teeth. The blanket was folded neatly over her chest and beneath her arms—those skinny, papery arms. She slid a folding chair from the wall close to the bed and sat down. She took one of Grand's hands in her own.

It was cool, but not yet stony, the skin like well-worn denim. Rachel brought the hand to her mouth and kissed it, then set it gently back down on the blanket. She sat there for a long while, her eyes traveling the length of Grand's body, feeling as if she should do something, say something, mark the moment somehow. But anything she thought of saying seemed inadequate, too simple, a reduction of who Grand was to her, to the family, to the world. And so she simply kissed Grand's hand one more time and set it back down on the bed. "You're my hero, Grand," she whispered, and then she slipped out from behind the blue curtain, looking for the way out.

Dr. Stevenson, rushing by, stopped in surprise. "Did you need something?" she asked.

"No. Just—I'm finished."

"Oh! All right then."

"What will they do with her?"

"We have a place to keep her until your family has made your arrangements. I'll need you to sign some papers," she added, handing Rachel a green folder with the words "Information for the Bereaved" embossed in a cursive script on the cover. "They're in there, along with a packet of information for you. Please sign the top two forms and return them to the receptionist out front. Once you select a funeral home, they'll handle all the details, according to your family's desires."

"All right."

"I'm sorry for your loss," Dr. Stevenson added kindly. And she escorted Rachel back through the double doors into the waiting room.

Rachel opened the folder and flipped through the glossy pages inside. A list of funeral homes, a sheet on coping with grief, a list of counselors and another of area law firms. She closed the folder with a sigh and went to sit in one of the orange chairs, looking up at the TV, which was now showing a commercial for teeth whitener.

She sat in a daze, feeling gutted and raw, idly wondering what she should do now. Her car was at the Farm. She'd lost her phone somewhere—hadn't seen it since sometime the previous day—and while she was sure the receptionist would let her use the phone, she did not feel like calling Michael to come pick her up. She didn't want to go back just yet. Going back meant facing him, not to mention facing the Farm without Grand. There would be details to take care of, phone calls to make: her parents, her brother, the funeral home, etc., etc. And then what? After all of it was done? Would she really be going back home to Illinois, she and Michael and Deirdre, and picking up where things had left off? The thought made her feel as if she were cinching closed, as if someone were pulling a drawstring tight around her mind. She felt she would rather die than pick up where things had left off. She couldn't, no matter what, pick up where things had left off.

"Rachel!" a woman's voice called. Rachel turned to see Diane, leaning on an orthopedic cane, limp through the automatic doors of the emergency room.

Rachel stood up. "Diane! What are you doing here?"

"How is Maddy?"

Rachel smiled sadly, then shook her head. A lump swelled in her throat, and the tears came. Diane limped toward her and hugged her with one arm, squeezing her tight.

They stood there, the two of them, hugging each other in the middle of the emergency room entryway, while people passed and the automatic doors opened and shut, a warm outdoor breeze blowing in. Finally, Rachel pulled away, wiping her eyes.

"She looked—" She hesitated, unsure how to put it, what she wanted to say. "She looked like someone else."

"That wasn't her, what you saw," Diane said gently. "She's all around us now. She's free."

6

After Rachel signed the necessary forms, she and Diane walked together out of the building to Diane's car, which was parked close to the entrance. "The good news is that as long as I'm using this cane, I get to park in the handicapped spot. Which is nothing to sneeze at."

On the way back to the Farm, Diane tuned the dial to the local news. The morning talk show was on, and they were talking about the flood. The floodwaters, they said, had reached an approximate height of fifteen feet, scouring the woods along the floodplain and taking several homes and buildings along with them. But, incredibly, there were no casualties. "The emergency system was in place," one of the talk show hosts was saying, "and the thing *worked*. I mean, that's the amazing thing. The system worked. The sirens went off, the right people were called, the evacuation teams were on the ball—the whole thing went off basically without a hitch. Makes you grateful for our first responders, doesn't it, Steve?"

"Yes it does, Larry. Amen to that. They're heroes, every one of them. Clap a first responder on the back today, folks. Hell, give him a smooch—he could probably use it."

"How's Joe doing?" Rachel asked, when a commercial came on. Diane turned the volume down.

"He's just fine. He's helping the work crews clean up the debris. He's glad to be alive." She glanced at Rachel. "He told me what happened, hon. And I'm grateful to you, for stopping him like you did. We'd be mourning two deaths today if you hadn't."

Rachel shrugged. "Anyone would have done it. I mean, it was clearly a bad idea, trying to pull that tree out of there. He'd have thrown away his life."

Diane sighed. "When Joe loves something like he loved that dam, he just never lets go. He's always been that way." She put a hand on Rachel's and squeezed it gently.

And Rachel heard—finally—the sound of recognition in Diane's words.

She looked out the window as they sped along. The roads were deserted. Theirs was the only car around except for the occasional semi barreling by, its driver unaware of the cataclysmic night the community had just lived through. She watched the landmarks drop away one by one—the dairy farms, the wood lots, crops of white pines planted in pristine rows, the sagging motels and taverns with neon Leinenkugel's signs glowing weakly in the morning glare.

"I wonder what he'll do now. Now that the dam's down, I mean."

"I was wondering the same thing. But he doesn't seem worried. He seemed strangely cheerful, actually. Said he was about ready for a change anyway."

Rachel smiled. "Sounds like Joe."

"Rachel, listen," Diane began, and her voice sounded uncharacteristically shaky. "I owe you an apology."

"Me? For what?"

"For standing between you and Joe all those years. Not passing on your messages, destroying your letters. It was wrong of me. I'm sorry."

She glanced again at Rachel, who nodded thoughtfully. "Okay. Thanks." Then, "Joe's probably the one you need to apologize to more."

"We talked about it. I did. Not that it's any of your business."

Rachel snorted. That sounded more like Diane. "Fair enough."

The car slowed as Diane prepared to turn onto the county road. The bait shop on the corner looked as deserted as the roads. "I'm sorry, too, Diane," Rachel said, "for how I behaved the other day. I was out of line."

Diane flipped on her blinker. It clicked rhythmically in the silence.

"Yesterday," Rachel continued. "I guess it was only yesterday."

"Apology accepted." Diane made a wide left onto the county road. "At some point, we'll talk about all that, but not now. We're a little overwhelmed now."

"About the Farm, you mean?"

"Yes."

"I'm okay with it, with you having it. I mean, I think it's the right thing."

Diane looked at her with surprise.

"Really. I've been thinking about it a lot, and I agree with you, and with Grand. It's only right. And plus, it's what Grand wanted. She loved you a lot."

Diane smiled ruefully. "Thank you for that. The feeling was mutual."

"You're welcome."

"But the fact is, hon, that I've been doing a lot of thinking myself, and I'm not so sure it *was* what she wanted. She said it was, and assured me it was again and again, but . . . she had such a hard time keeping things straight at the end, it was hard to tell."

"I confused her. Laying all my feelings on her like I did. I muddied the water."

"The thing is, hon," Diane went on, "I don't really want to live on the Farm. I love my little house. I'm looking forward to going home, actually, getting settled back in my quiet life, living on my own again." She paused, breathed deeply. "I can't tell you how much I'm looking forward to that. And Joe isn't interested in the Farm either. Wants nothing to do with it, he tells me."

"He likes his yurt."

"He does, God knows why. Really, what I think is that it makes more sense for me to transfer the ownership of the land to the tribe, with the stipulation that you can live there as long as you like. I've spoken with my lawyer, and he thinks we could arrange it."

Rachel stared at Diane.

"I know your grandmother would have wanted for you to be able to enjoy the place and take care of it, if that really is what you want. So I guess that's the question you need to consider: if that's what you really want." Diane looked pointedly at her.

Rachel stared out the window. The cranberry bog appeared, its sprinklers sending arcs of water over the sunken fields. It was hard to believe the plants needed a watering after a storm like last night. But there was a lot she didn't know.

"It's very thoughtful of you, Diane," Rachel said finally. "But I'm not sure I could afford it."

"Maddy left a trust fund for maintenance. Which I would sign over to the tribe, but which you could access, as needed. You'd be something like a caretaker, really. Think of it that way."

"Just like your grandparents. Years ago."

"I suppose so." Diane took a curve to the right, past the cottage with the hand-painted craft shop sign outside. "You don't have to decide now, hon. Let all this blow over. Talk to a lawyer about it. Talk to your husband." Rachel heard a distinct emphasis on the word *husband*. "It would be a big thing, a big change. A big responsibility."

They drove past the stream where the heron fished and the turtles deposited their eggs. It was low now, sodden grasses drying in the sun. They crossed the little bridge, and passed the meadow full of wildflowers, the rusted-out pickup with the birch growing through its window. And up ahead a ways rose the big green and blue welcome sign that marked the border of the reservation. Which, she realized, would need to be moved if the Farm was restored to the tribe.

"Thanks, Diane," she said. "I will definitely think about it. It's very generous of you."

"I think your grandmother would like the idea. Both justice and love are served."

Diane slowed to approach the lane. Rachel followed her habit of looking for flashes of lake-blue between the trees, then sat forward in her seat, gripping the dashboard. "The lake is gone."

Diane stopped the car in the middle of the road. They both got out and stood gazing at the strange absence of blue. "My God," Diane whispered.

There was no blue because there was no lake. It had disappeared in the night.

An approaching car made them climb back into their seats. As Diane turned onto the lane, they strained to catch glimpses of the changed landscape. But the trees at the shoreline were too thick to see much of anything beyond the striking absence of glimmering blue. They took the drive, pebbles crunching beneath the tires. At the barn, Rachel asked Diane to stop and let her out there. She didn't want Michael to see she'd returned, not yet. She had to go down to the lake—or the *not*-lake first. She had to see what it looked like now.

"Thanks again, Diane," she said, as she slid out from the passenger seat.

"Sure thing, hon. We'll be in touch." And she backed the car up the drive and drove away.

Rachel strode quickly from the barn to the stairs that led to the bayside dock, taking care not to look at the house, in case Michael might see her and wave her down. When she reached the stairs, she took them at a jog. At the bottom, she passed the old boathouse and stepped out onto the grassy spit of land that used to open onto the bay.

It looked like beach, like ocean beach. Like a Maine beach at low tide, when the water had run off somewhere else. Sand—dark, silty sand—stretched out from the shore in little scalloped ridges. The dock was now a long metal bridge leading to nowhere, like the road over the dam: it spanned a stretch of sand, then dropped off into air. Off in the distance, maybe a hundred yards away, ran the river, winking in the mid-morning sun.

Rachel walked along what had been the shore, her feet sinking a little into the silt. A line of lake-smooth stones and pebbles marked the place where the water had once reached. She bent to pick up a flat one, good for skipping, then dropped it again. Stretching out from the point of land that used to jut into the lake was a long sandbar, extending away from the point toward the new river. Along the bar and on either side of it, lake-grasses lay plastered to the ground like wet strands of hair on a cheek.

Rachel took off her shoes and walked along the sandbar, away from the old shoreline, out toward the new. Sand slid beneath her feet, making her stumble. She thought of how her father used to fish off this bar years ago, at the drop-off. She'd gone with him sometimes, when she was young. He'd wake her early, before the sun, and she'd blearily pull on her clothes while he packed their breakfasts and readied the gear. Together they'd walk across the dew-wet lawn. He carried the tackle and the poles and she carried the bucket, which knocked against her calves. Down by the water, they pushed the old rowboat out, her father guiding from the prow, his jeans rolled up to his knees. She climbed in while he held the boat steady, then he got in, sending them both rocking. He took the oars and pulled them out beyond the dock, the water slapping against the hull, the oars creaking in the locks. The wind came up, cool on her bare arms.

They rarely said a word to each other those mornings. The quiet was too holy, somehow—the movement of the oars through the water, of their own bodies shifting in the boat, losing and regaining balance, the wind moving at their ears and in the tops of the trees on the shore, the gradual dawn rising with a symphonic silence. They rowed out to the drop-off—where Rachel stood now, her toes curling over the edge of the sand-ridge just at the place where it sloped precipitously down to what had once been deeper water—and dropped anchor there. Her father would get out the peanut-butter sandwiches and they'd eat them in silence while the edge of the sky grew pink and the day opened into itself in its inexorable way.

Rachel stepped forward, skidding down the slope on her heels, leaving little avalanches of silt in the wake of each foot. The river was just a few yards away now. She walked toward it, and when she reached its edge, she was surprised to see that it had already begun to carve a visible channel in the sand. Or maybe, she thought, it had been carving this channel all along, even beneath the lake, beneath the weight of all that water.

She waded into the river a little ways, feeling the cold current slide over her toes, tugging her gently. This new river was relatively narrow—only about twenty or so feet across. Barely swimmable. Rachel wondered if that would change. Maybe they'd decide to demolish the upstream dam, too, and let the river swell to more natural proportions. She hoped so. Still, even a modest river like this one had a strong current. She stepped back onto the sand.

A shadow fell across her vision, and she looked up to see a huge mottled-brown bird flying out over the open expanse of sand and water. This was the juvenile, she realized—the young eagle she'd heard squalling for its food so many mornings this past week. Flying now. It soared over the sand until it came to the river, swooped low and then careened clumsily back up into the sky. Still unsteady. It probably wouldn't make a successful catch for a while yet. She watched the bird glide toward the tree line, and thought of Grand, of her absent corpse on the hospital bed, how unlike her it was, and she felt a startling, incongruous rush of joy, the sort of joy she used to feel as a girl when she'd come up the drive to the Farm and Grand would be striding across the lawn toward the car, her arms open like wings. She watched until the eagle disappeared over the trees.

What did the eagles make of this new landscape, she wondered, of this sudden restoration? Who could tell? Whatever they made of it, they would adapt. That was what animals did. The earth shook and cracked open at the seams, centuries-old icebergs melted into the sea, hurricanes tore down swaths of forest, whipped up mountains of floodwaters—still, there were young to feed, flights to be made, nests to be built, miles to travel. They would adapt.

Rachel followed the path of the river with her eyes. Strange objects were strewn here and there on the sand: a greenish enamel bathtub lay on its side some distance away; a huge log sat, parallel to the river, as if it had been placed there by the county parks and recreation department, a perfect bench on which to sit and watch the water roll by. In the distance, something metallic glinted in the sun—a long-sunk boat, maybe, having languished for decades at the bottom of the lake. She thought of Joe, how he might be walking this new landscape now, miles downriver from where she stood, looking for remnants of Old Bend, now newly exposed to the sun, the air, the curious.

And then she thought of Michael waiting—anxiously, no doubt—for her up at the house. And of Deirdre, who she missed suddenly with an all-body ache. She gave one last look at the river before turning and walking back along the sandbar toward the old shore.

7

Rachel found Michael behind the house, picking up fallen branches. A neat pile of them sat by the back steps. He straightened from a bend, branch in hand. She stood off a little ways, waiting. He dropped the branch on the pile, then made his way over to her.

"Where's Dee?" she asked.

He nodded in the direction of the house. "Asleep. I left the window open so I could hear. She was a mess when she woke up—screaming non-stop. She finally settled down enough to take a bottle and then fell right back to sleep after she sucked the whole thing dry." He paused, then added, in a wounded voice, "I guess she didn't sleep much last night, huh?"

"No." That was her opening, but she wasn't ready to take it yet. "Grand is gone," she said.

"Oh, no. Really? When did she—?"

"She died at the hospital, as soon as we got there. Or maybe on the way. I don't actually know."

He put a tentative hand on her elbow. "I'm sorry, Rachel."

"It's okay. It was her time, I guess. Her quality of life was pretty compromised. She was ready."

He turned away from her toward the pile of sticks by the door of the house. "I thought I might as well make myself useful. Lots of branches came down in the storm." He rubbed his forehead, leaving a streak of mud above his eyebrow. "Something else, too," he added. "Come here—I'll show you."

He led her over the damp duff to a massive tangle of branches on the ground, several feet away from the base of the Eliza tree. "I heard it come down in the night," he said. "It made this massive crashing sound."

Rachel looked again: the branches, she saw, were not tangled but woven—a rougher weave on the outside, then denser, the branches thinner as the arrangement grew toward the middle. At the very center was a soft grass bowl, sticky with matted down, scattered here and there with tiny bones, all of it glued to the nest with a white paste: eagle shit.

"Oh *no*," she said with genuine grief, as if this loss was the worst, the most tragic, of the day.

"I know," Michael commiserated. "I thought you'd be upset. I wonder what the juvenile will do."

She stood staring at the nest. "It'll be okay," she said finally. "It's flying now. It'll find another place to nest."

The flag-line beat a melancholy rhythm against the pole. A warm wind blew up from the valley, from the place the lake had been.

"We should probably call someone to come pick it up," Rachel said. "The natural history museum down in Rice Lake or something."

"Or the tribe," Michael said. "They might want it, eagle feathers being sacred and all."

"Right," Rachel replied. "Or the tribe."

She walked toward the edge of the hill, looking down once more toward the changed lake. The thick woods blocked most of the view, but she could see glimpses of dark silt and snatches of river-water, glinting sharp and bright as it coursed in the sun.

She felt Michael standing beside her. "It's breathtaking, isn't it?" she said. "How fast it happened? Overnight, the whole place is totally transformed."

"Yeah."

"We should go down when Dee wakes up," Rachel offered. "Check it out." But the invitation sounded hollow, insincere.

"Rachel. Did you sleep with him?"

She took a deep breath. "Yes."

"Fuck," he whispered.

"I'm sorry, Michael. I don't know what happened. I kind of . . . I lost my head. I lost sight of things."

He nodded, looking off into the trees.

"I'm so sorry."

"Are you in love with him?" His face was pained, the streak of mud on his forehead an accusation.

"I don't know, Michael. I'm not sure I know what that means, really, 'in love.' I mean, he's a part of me. I don't think I ever stopped loving him."

He was nodding again, staring at his hands.

"But that doesn't mean I don't love you, too." She stared at the mud on his brow, thinking how a few months earlier—maybe even a week ago—she would have wiped it away automatically. Now it seemed too far a distance to bridge.

He closed his eyes. "Don't say that."

"What?"

"Don't say what you don't mean."

She started to protest, then silenced herself.

"I've known that, you know. All these years. I've always felt like I've been living in his shadow. Like he was some phantom, lurking at the corners of our marriage, just waiting for the right moment to leap out and steal you away."

She stared at him. "Really? But I haven't felt that way. I mean, it's been years since I've really thought about him like that. I never talk about him—"

"No, but it's been there. It's not the sort of thing you can hide, Rachel. I mean, when you love someone that way, it's there always. In all the words you say and don't say about him. I guess I was just hoping that time and distance would keep you apart."

"But listen, Michael. My feelings for Joe . . . They're different. I love him, yes, but it's a different kind of love than my love for you. They're two different loves."

Michael stiffened. "But you married *me*, Rachel. I'm your husband. We have a daughter together. A life."

"I know."

"You can't just throw all that away so easily."

Silence.

"Rachel."

"I didn't say I wanted to throw it away."

"Well, what do you want? You can't have us both. You have to choose."

She bristled. "I don't like how that sounds. What if I don't want to choose?"

"If you think I'm going to just hang around while you and Joe—"

"No, listen. That's not what I mean. What I mean is, what if what I want to choose is a *life*, not a person? What if it's *my life* I'm choosing?"

"I don't know what you mean, Rachel. We have a life. Together."

"Okay, but our life is mostly *your* life, Michael. That's what I'm trying to say, that's what I've realized up here. Our life has been about your priorities: we moved for *your* job, we stopped coming to the Farm for *your* ideals, we had a child when *you* felt it was the right time. Somewhere along the line my priorities kind of fell away." She stopped, her face and neck hot, her heart beating fast in her throat.

He stared at her, taken aback. "I never knew you felt that way."

A breeze blew through the woods, cooling her skin. "I know you didn't. Neither did I, really. Not consciously, anyway."

"Well, God. I'm sorry. If I'd known—"

"I know, Michael. I know it's not anything you did intentionally, and I'm not saying this to blame you or shame you or anything. God knows I'm the one who deserves the blame in this situation. It's just that I want you to understand that I can't go back to the way I was living. That life, that PhD, that oppressive little college town . . ."

Michael was squinting at her, as if she were a distant object he was trying to bring into focus. "You've really been unhappy."

"I have." Tears sprang to her eyes at this simple truth, finally stated plainly. "And you keep trying to label it, to explain it away. But it's not just some aberrant hormonal fluctuation. It's *me*."

"But it's not you, Rachel. You've been acting so—so different."

Rachel opened her mouth to object, but Michael held up a hand. "I know, I know," he went on, "We've had a kid. We've been under a lot of stress. It changes people. I know. But I guess—I don't want you to make any rash decisions. I mean, you're upset, Grand has just died, Deirdre's still so young—"

"Michael. This is what I'm talking about. You keep trying to explain all this away, as if it's all temporary, as if in a few months everything will settle back down and we'll be just as we used to be. But what I'm telling you is I don't want to go back to that. I *can't* go back to that."

"Why not?" He was gazing at her with so much pain and bewilderment in his eyes that she had to turn away. She looked out into the trees. She didn't know how to answer him. She didn't know why. All she knew was how she felt.

"Goddammit, Rachel." He took off his glasses and wiped his eyes. "What do you want me to do? I don't know what to do."

"Nothing! There's nothing you can do, Michael, that's what I mean. It's not up to you. *I* need to do it, to figure out . . . I don't know . . . who I am now, now that I'm a mother. I just need you to *let* me do it, without trying to *fix* me."

He eyed her warily, his eyes naked and wet. "Okay. But what does that mean, exactly, Rachel? Because if letting you figure it out means letting you go off with Joe until you 'find yourself,' then I don't have the stomach for it."

She shook her head, unable to speak. He waited. Finally, she said, "What happened last night was a mistake. We both realized that, afterward. It was like we were trying to go back to the way things were so many years ago, like we were trying out a version of what might have been."

Michael pressed his fingers in the divots beneath his eyebrows.

"I'm so sorry, Michael. I'm so sorry I hurt you like that." She stepped toward him and reached to wipe the streak of mud from his forehead, but he backed away.

"It does hurt," he spat. He put his glasses back on his face. "All of this. You slept with another man, for fuck's sake. And now you're telling me you aren't happy in our life? I mean, Jesus. I thought we were doing pretty well."

"I know. We were. Or at least you were. I was trying. I was trying to be the person I thought I should be, the person you wanted me to be. I was really trying. And then, after Deirdre was born, it was like I just couldn't try anymore. Like I'd built a sand castle out of trying, and it finally just collapsed."

A woodpecker hammered at a nearby tree, startling them both. The *ratatatat* echoed through the quiet woods.

Michael waited until the sound died away before speaking again. "Grand said something to me last night. She said that keeping someone from the thing they love is like keeping them from themselves." He studied Rachel. "She was talking about you and the Farm."

Rachel nodded.

"Is that how you feel? Is that how you've felt all these years? That I've somehow kept you from yourself?"

"Maybe. Maybe so."

"I never meant to do that to you."

"I know you didn't. I'm to blame as well. I shouldn't have let it happen."

They listened to the breeze rustle the leaves of the beeches, feather the tops of the pines. The sun was high overhead. Already, the drenched land and woods were beginning to dry, stretching and expanding in the warmth.

Soon, the deer would venture out to explore the new boundaries of their feeding grounds; the heron would fly down to fish a narrower rush; the otters would pad out across the sand and dig new holts, new slides. Eventually, the dropped acorns and pine cones and beechnuts would lodge themselves in the silty new soil of the river's floodplain and flush and crack and grow, sending out sprouts to meet the sunlight. In no time, things would fill in the gaps, find the fertile ground, plant themselves where they might take root and thrive. It would happen, sure as anything. It was already happening, all around them, all the time.

"I noticed something while you and Dee were gone," Michael said. "I realized how much *easier* it is to be alone. To only have to answer to myself, eat when I want, come home when I want. I didn't mind it at first. I kind of liked it. And that scared me. Because I know what would happen. I'd just kind of slide into solipsism, doing my work, eating, sleeping, going back to work. I'd become one of those crazy old professors who keeps a bedroll in his office and a toothbrush in the pencil jar. I don't want to live like that. You know? I don't, Rachel. I want you and Dee around."

Rachel looked into his familiar eyes, dilated with anxiety and hurt. Tentatively, she took his hand, and when he didn't pull away, she stroked the back of it with her thumb.

"I've been trying so hard these last few months," he continued, sniffling. "Trying to make it easier on you. But whatever I do to help, you take it as a criticism. And that's not how I intend it. I truly want to help, I want to be useful."

"Michael, I know. I know how hard you've been working. You've been amazing, actually. The perfect husband and father. Honestly. It's me that's the problem."

"But it's not, Rachel. That's not true. You're the *solution*. I mean, you're the essential ingredient. I'm marginal. Deirdre doesn't need me like she needs you. And I don't know how to make her need me. I don't know what to do when I'm holding her. You somehow know instinctively how to jiggle her and soothe her, how to talk to her, all of that. For me it's like a foreign language. A whole new alphabet. Mothering comes so naturally to you."

She stared at him, astonished.

"I mean, I know you're not exactly Florence Henderson—"

"More like Mrs. Munster."

"No. No, actually. No. What I mean is that despite everything, despite your own . . . sadness and frustration lately, whatever it is, you actually haven't been a bad mother. You haven't been happy, but you've been caring for Deirdre from day one, despite that. That's what I mean. You haven't let your own sadness get in the way of her well-being."

Rachel considered these words, let them sink in. She had provided for Deirdre's needs, that much was true. And maybe that was the point, maybe that was enough. A parent did the job no matter what, even when it sucked, even when you were painfully bored or keeling over with exhaustion or grief. Even then, you did the job. And maybe it was the doing of it that saved you.

"Thank you," Rachel murmured. "That means a lot, to hear you say that."

"So," Michael said, giving her hand a tug. "What happens now?"

Rachel regarded him sadly. He was so good, all the time. So well-meaning, so considerate and good. She took her hand from his and reached up once again to wipe the mud away. He closed his eyes and let her. "I don't know," she said. "I have to call Dad, first of all. I haven't even talked to him yet." But she knew that was not what he meant.

"Yeah. But what I mean is, are you coming back home?" He was trying to keep the want from his voice, she could tell. But at the end, he failed—his voice cracked and split, and he fell into a sudden wracking sob. "I've been so scared Rachel, the whole time you've been gone. So scared that you and Deirdre wouldn't ever come back."

She put her arms around him and held him, shushing him, as she did with Deirdre when she tried to get her down to sleep. He cried and she rocked him gently back and forth, trying to absorb his pain, to take it into her own skin, to lift it away. After a while, he gathered himself, pulling away from her, wiping a finger beneath his nose. "Sorry," he said. "I didn't intend to fall apart like that."

"Don't apologize, Michael. I'm the one who screwed everything up."

"Not everything. It's been a hard time. It's been rough for both of us, for all of us. But, you know. Families go through these things."

She flicked a few flakes of dried mud from her thumb. The word family seemed to swing in the air between them like a noose. "I don't know anything, Michael. All I know is that I'm not coming home right away. I want to be here a while, as long as I can anyway. My parents will probably come up as soon as they hear. They'll need some help going through all Grand's things, all of that."

"Of course," Michael said. "That goes without saying. But what about after that? When everything's over. Will you be coming home then?"

"I'm not sure, Michael. I'm not sure I know where home is anymore."

The words hung in the air, quiet but monumental, like the silence after the felling of a great tree. Rachel turned back toward the breezy woods, the hill that led down to the torn-open valley and the sparkling Name River below, the river that was even now winding its way past the ancient graves, traveling old paths and new, coursing downstream with a current as wise as it was silent, following the reach of its own momentum, hugging, always, close to the skin of the earth. This was home. These woods, this air, this river, this land. Home was right about here.

A cry broke through the quiet. They turned and, in separate unison, made their ways over the wet ground toward the house.

ACKNOWLEDGMENTS

This book has been several years in the making, and I have relied on help from so many people, start to finish. I'm almost afraid to name names, for fear of leaving someone out. If that someone is you, please know I'm grateful, despite the lapse. Unwise though it may be, here I go . . .

For loving and reliable childcare in the early years of this book (and of my son's life), I'm indebted to Chris Wilson, Jen Brown, and Amy Freund. For reading draft after draft and always giving me wise and valuable feedback, I thank the members of my writing group over the years: Gale Walden, Audrey Petty, John Rubins, Umeeta Sadarangani, and Carol Spindel. Also, for reading or listening to drafts-in-progress, my writers' group at large: Patricia Henley, Karen Shoemaker, Teri Grimm, Allen Gee, Trish Lear, Steve Langan, Richard Duggin, my aunt Susan Thomas and uncle Frank Thomas, my dear parents Kathy and Rich Hassinger, and all of my compatriots at the University of Nebraska MFA in Writing Program. My book club was willing to read a draft when I thought it was finished (and before it really was)—thank you Stephanie Nevins, Amy Freund, Emily Laugesen, Gail Hug, Julie Zilles, Astrid Ferrer, Sonya Darter, Ellen DeWaard, Cheryl Silver, Tara Larrison, and Petra Jelinek.

There was a great deal I had to learn to write this book, first and foremost about the experience of being Native in this country. For generously and patiently educating me, I thank James Treat, LeAnne Howe, and Alison Adele Hedge Coke, and for teaching me specifically about Ojibwe culture and history—also with patience and generosity—I thank Anne Marie Penzkover, Jill Doerfler, Phyllis Wolf, Paul DeMain, Rusty Barber, Jerry Smith, Caryl Pfaff at the Lac Courte Oreilles Ojibwa Community College Library, and Lori Taguma at WOJB. I spent a lot of time with Charlie Rasmussen's book *Where the River Is Wide*.

Also, dams! I knew nothing about dams. Timm Severud and Blake Landry taught me everything I know as well as much I've since forgotten. Brad Knop at the Midwest Scuba Center guided me through the murky world of scuba diving. For giving me access to other various bodies of information and experience, I'm grateful to Molly O'Dell, Sally Babbitt, Gail Schiesser, Ron Kreisman, John Epiphanio, Jan Christensen, Wendy Robertson, Beth Gollan, Barbara Mann, and my aunt Holly Bean.

Editor Amy Cherry gave me several hours of her very valuable time when she didn't have to, and changed the course of the book profoundly. Stéphanie Abou, my loyal, trusted, brilliant bulldog of an agent read about seventy drafts with astounding patience and good humor. And then worked her ass off selling it. Literary goddess and whip-smart editor Kate Gale helped knock the final draft into place and welcomed me into the Red Hen family.

Finally, I would be nowhere at all without my sainted husband, Adam Davis, and my beautiful and amazing children, Hannah and Gabe. Good lord, I love you three.

Biographical Note

Amy Hassinger is the author of two previous novels: *Nina: Adolescence* and *The Priest's Madonna*. Her writing has been translated into five languages and has won awards from *Creative Nonfiction*, *Publisher's Weekly*, and the Illinois Arts Council. Her work has appeared in numerous venues, including *The New York Times*, *Creative Nonfiction*, *The Writers' Chronicle*, and *The Los Angeles Review of Books*. She is a graduate of the Iowa Writers' Workshop and teaches in the University of Nebraska's MFA in Writing Program. You can find out more about her at www.amyhassinger.com.

CPSIA information can be obtained
at www.ICGtesting.com
Printed in the USA
FFOW03n2118040118
44368748-44069FF